Fire of the Frost

A Midwinter Holiday Fantasy Romance Anthology

With Novellas by

Darynda Jones

Amanda Bouchet

Grace Draven

Jeffe Kennedy

Thank you for reading!

Credits
Cover: Daqri Bernardo

Contents

A Wynter Fyre

by

Darynda Jones

In a world where vampyres have been hunted to near extinction, the daughter of a demon is sent to save their race. Wynter ends the Blood Wars, but a single drop of vampyre blood accidentally crosses her lips. As punishment, she's encased in stone for a hundred years. When she awakens, she vows revenge. Even if it means her demise. Her quest leads her to the vampyre prince who supposedly started the wars. He comes to her aid after she's attacked, and Gareth's deadly prowess may be exactly what Wynter needs to defeat the woman who created her. Or exactly what she needs to thaw her frozen heart.

~ 1 ~

Cold hands, warm heart.

S NOW FELL FROM a starless sky, a silent symphony of
movement in the crisp night air. Of all the snowflakes that
drifted from the heavens, those that landed on the statue were
the most blessed. Each delicate crystal quivered when it
touched down, seemed to hesitate, to think twice, before
settling upon her like a single stitch in a shimmering quilt of
ice. The stone woman stood erect, proud yet resigned to her
fate as she gazed from underneath layers of a billowing
alabaster robe. One small hand gathered the skirts of her cloak
into a fist. The other clutched the hood, holding it back as she
fought an eternal wind.

As stunning as the robes were, it was the woman's face, a
face that had been sculpted by gods, that drew crowds of
stargazers to the convent every year. Alabaster eyes, large and
alert, kept careful vigil on the village below. A full mouth,
shapely and sure, rested beneath an elegant nose. A neck as
graceful as a swan's disappeared beneath the smooth folds of
the cloak.

From her lofty position above the gates, the woman observed the comings and goings of the inhabitants, her stone irises never moving. Never wavering.

Then she blinked.

Life began to seep into her, beginning at her heart and spreading throughout her chest. Its warmth turned stone to flesh, the stirrings of life startling her. Disoriented, she wondered momentarily why she had been awakened. As though in reply, the paralyzing terror of a child taken in the night cinched the cage around her lungs tighter. At that exact moment, a rush of blood forced her heart to beat for the first time in decades, the initial thrust excruciating. The second less so. Nerves sparked to life and shot through her body like the pinpricks of a thousand needles. Her knees buckled, but she held firm, even as the wind caught her cloak and tried to dislodge her.

"Gabriella," she whispered onto the night air, but the eminent being below her answered.

"Yes, Gabriella. And the triplets."

She looked down. Sara, her lady's maid and most trusted confidante for over two centuries, smiled up at her, heavy-hearted yet welcoming.

The cloaked woman jumped from her perch above the huge rustic gates to land as softly as the falling snow at Sara's feet.

"My Lady Wynter," Sara said as she reached up and pushed Wynter's hood back, revealing long silvery locks. Sara's eyes were at once filled with a heartbreaking sadness and an all-consuming joy. "I have missed you terribly."

Wynter pulled the woman into a fierce hug. "I have missed you as well." She stood the maid at arm's length to study her. Same blue eyes, same button nose, but, "You cut your hair."

"Yes," Sara said, self-consciously tucking a recalcitrant lock behind her ear. "Over thirty years ago."

Wynter frowned. "Have I been gone so long?"

Sara dropped her gaze. "Seventy-two years, my lady."

Wynter gasped as softly as the snow fell. "Sixty-two longer than last, but twenty-eight too early."

Though sent by her mother to protect the occupants of the village—vampyres one and all—from being hunted to extinction, a feat Wynter had accomplished decades ago, her mother had given her one rule and one rule only. Wynter was never to know the pleasure of vampyre blood. If it were to pass her lips, even the smallest drop, Wynter would be punished in a tomb of stone for ten years. That was the first time, when a droplet of blood from an enemy's axe flew onto her tongue. She was frozen before she realized what was happening.

A second offense brought about a 100-year sentence, but again, Wynter played no part in the transgression. She remembered standing on a practice field then nothing.

"We prayed to your mother," Sara said, glancing nervously over her shoulder, "begged her to release you so you could go after the princess."

"And in return?" The ice demon Skadeesh did nothing out of the kindness of her heart.

"She wants double the blood for the solstice celebration tomorrow night."

Wynter scoffed. "She'll drain you all dry if you let her."

Sara nodded, unwilling to argue the point. Skadeesh had saved them all from extinction. Wynter understood the loyalty the people of Ellery had for her.

"But why was I imprisoned?" Wynter asked, scanning the area for any eavesdroppers. Unfortunately, nobody had more spies than a village full of suspicious vampyres. "I didn't drink blood."

"Someone spiked your wine, my lady." When Wynter only stared at her, Sara added, "The alchemist tested the liquid. There was hardly a drop, but—"

"It was enough. Someone wanted me gone."

"Yes. And we have paid the price ever since."

"What do you mean?" Wynter asked, playing her part. Thanks to Sara, she knew full well what had been happening under her mother's nose.

"Our children are being taken one at a time. Princess Gabriella was simply the latest. Eighteen in the years you've been gone."

"And my mother is just now doing something about it?" Wynter wondered once again why her mother didn't bring her back sooner. Why allow this to happen?

"If I had to guess, I would say she only agreed to your release because this time it's the king's daughter." A vampyre king, but a king no less.

"I'm sure that had something to do with it." Wynter now wore a blanket of snow, not that she felt the cold over much. Nor did Sara, but Wynter flung part of her robe over the woman's shoulders regardless and motioned her toward a well-lit tavern.

Sara shook it off. "I'm fine, my lady. You must hurry."

She was right, of course. She had to go, no matter how loathe she was to do so. It had been so long since a good ale had crossed her lips. Or a fine stew had filled her belly. "I love your hair. You look splendid."

"Well, you look a fright," Sara said, waving off the compliment.

Wynter grinned. It would seem her mandatory scolding for everything from the sun setting too late to the lack of gold at the ends of rainbows was not to be overlooked after all. "You stayed away too long. The village is a mess. The council is in an uproar. And now this. Another of our children taken."

"Were it my choice, Sara, I would not have gone." Dawn began to sneak past the bonds of night. A soft glow illuminated the huge snowflakes as they drifted onto Sara's dark hair. "Go," Wynter said, "before the light catches you astray."

"But Gabriella and the boys…"

"Yes, I can feel them. The triplets went after their little cousin. They aren't far. They'll sleep soon, and I can catch up to them then."

"Will they… interfere with your rescue?" Meaning, would the triplets interfere with their well-thought-out, years-in-the-making plan.

"Possibly. I'll send them back."

Sara nodded. "And Gabriella?"

Wynter bent her head in thought, searching the world for emotion. Her brows furrowed as she felt the sickening dread of a child lost. "She's scared."

Sara's fingers curled into fists reflexively.

"Ravagers took her. Three. Perhaps four." With a powerful burst of concentration, she tried to reach Gabriella, to let her know the ravagers meant her no harm. She would come for her. But fear blocked her entrance. A sickly warmth trickled between the girl's legs as she urinated over her thigh. Wynter clenched the muscles between her own legs to keep from doing the same. She could taste the dirty cloth shoved into Gabriella's mouth, smell the oil that permeated it. She could feel the brutal bite of rope cutting into the child's wrists.

A palpable but necessary terror washed over Wynter as she tried to absorb some of its sting. It was like releasing a dam in the child. Fear pushed Wynter back like a bitter gust of wind. Her knees gave beneath her, sending her to the frozen earth, gasping for air.

"My lady!" Sara said, dropping to her knees beside her.

After a moment, Wynter shook herself and glanced at Sara to reassure her. "They've not harmed her. She is well. For now."

Sara eyed her doubtfully. "Judging by your reaction—"

"No, she's just scared. Fear is a very powerful emotion. I simply need to catch my breath."

"After more than seventy years as stone, it's no wonder. I'll tell the king and queen she is unharmed. It will bring them at least some comfort."

"Please do."

They stood as a stable hand brought out a horse, a huge dappled gray with a silvery sheen. Wynter sucked in a soft breath. She couldn't help but admire such a beautiful creature. It was only when the mare shook her head that Wynter realized what she was. The beast's head shook first, her long mane cascading over her elegant neck like water. A split second later, her spirit followed, separating into two beings before fusing into one once again. Two separate entities in a single animal. A dyaus, said to be kissed by the gods, able to travel outside of its body and take its rider's spirit with it.

Wynter had never seen one. Her lips parted in awe as she sent one hand over the beast's smooth coat.

"A gift from the king," Sara said. "May your journey bear fruit."

"What's her name?"

"Silver Snow."

Wynter smiled. "Fitting."

"I thought so. Her coat matches your eyes."

She rubbed its chin. "I suppose it does."

Sara risked a glance over her shoulder to make sure the stable hand was gone. Satisfied, she pressed a cloth into Wynter's hands and whispered, "A gift from the queen. May your journey bear fruit."

Wynter offered her the barest nod of acknowledgment then used her cloak to conceal the fact that she was stuffing a dagger into the back of her leathers.

"Do you know why they took her? Princess Gabriella?" Sara asked, skirting her true question, the only one that would concern her: Do the ravagers know what they have? A vampyre's blood, even a young one, was worth a fortune on the black market.

"No, but I'll find out. Are all my things here?" She already knew they were but she opened the saddle bags anyway, hoping to sway Sara from questioning her further. She hadn't the time and the more they chatted, the more they risked discovery.

"Yes. Please be careful, my lady."

Wynter nodded and turned toward the horizon. The approaching sun filtered light through the tops of the trees. Pointing toward the heavens, she raised her brows at Sara in warning.

"All right, I'm going. Godspeed."

"Thank you." She started to lift herself into the immaculate saddle when a disturbance shuddered through her. "Sara."

The woman turned back.

"Something is wrong."

Sara rushed to her side. She glanced around wildly then refocused on her. "What is it, my lady?"

"I don't know. Not yet." She shook her head to clear the rift. "Someone is near. Someone who shouldn't be. Just be careful." Then she looked at Sara's snow-covered head. "And get inside before you burst into flames."

Sara giggled at the joke. "You jest, but silly superstitions have helped keep us alive for centuries." She placed a quick kiss on Wynter's cheek and rushed back to the tavern.

Wynter glanced around the abandoned convent-turned-innocuous rural village, knowing the real city, miles of glistening streets, lay far below her feet. But the convent was beautiful in its own right. Built in the age of iron, it served as a façade, a hidden entrance to a veritable fortress underneath. A fortress once again living in fear.

~ 2 ~

A girl walks into a barn...

Vampyre blood once gave kings eternal youth. Queens eternal beauty. Soothsayers uncanny accuracy. But the creatures were too strong and too cunning for the royals to risk keeping them alive and draining them slowly. With their powers of compulsion, vampyres would inevitably escape. And they did not forgive easily. Entire villages had been massacred with the escape of a single, angry immortal. It took only one unfortunate incident to tip the scales forever.

A young queen had grown enamored with the beauty of a certain vampyre boy. So enamored, she captured him. Not knowing the boy was a beloved vampyre prince, she tried to keep him imprisoned in her chambers. But the prince compelled her to loosen his chains—moments before he ripped out her throat and escaped.

Infuriated, the king declared all vampyres a blight and vowed to slaughter every last one—draining them of their blood first, naturally. A king who brought the vampyre scourge to extinction would be heralded by his people and feared by his enemies, for his armies could be healed over and over to fight again and again.

The king sent out soldiers disguised as hunters, seeking the immortals' total annihilation. But he wanted the young vampyre prince above all others.

With their numbers dwindling and their future king in hiding, the old vampyres summoned the ice demon, Skadeesh, asking for protection. Her aid would not come without conditions. For their allegiance—and their blood—she gave them her only daughter to end the Blood Wars once and for all.

There was a time when Wynter obeyed her mother without question. She was a warrior, after all. A champion. But she grew to love the vampyre people. After the Blood Wars ended, she refused her mother's summons and stayed on to help train new generations so they would never be hunted to such dismal numbers again.

In all that time, she saw the boy—the future king—only once, and that was from a great distance. Whispers abounded that his father had kept him in hiding for so long, he had grown used to being alone and preferred the company of tree sprites and wolves to that of his own people.

Wynter had a better explanation. He simply did not want to be king, and she could not blame him for avoiding his calling. She had eschewed her mother's summons to return to her side countless times. Either way, the villagers started calling him the vagabond prince, and Wynter felt the epithet appropriate.

Her thoughts traveled back to him as she rode the dyaus.

The one time she did catch a glimpse of the raven-haired child rumored to be the most beautiful vampyre any clan had ever seen, she felt something else. His energy. The power radiating out of him. It was said his compulsion was the strongest ever witnessed and Wynter didn't doubt it. Even from afar, she felt the potency seep into her.

And that was what she'd felt tonight with Sara. That same energy. That same power. She felt it still. Even in daylight, he was nearby. Every molecule in her body sensed it.

Sunlight wouldn't kill a vampyre, but after mere moments of exposure, they'd wish it did. Sara said the pain was excruciating, so how was the prince following her in broad daylight? And why?

Before she could find out, she came upon the decrepit outbuilding she'd seen in her vision. The one that held the triplets, the three rascals she'd trained—or tried to train—decades ago. They were the king's nephews and they'd known too well what they could and could not get away with. Combined with their constant antics and their inability to pay attention, that made the task of training them impossible, but she'd had fun trying.

They'd been on the right trail. She'd give them that. Maybe they had grown up despite her reservations that they ever would. But she could hardly have them discover their niece before Wynter was ready for her to be found.

Her breath fogged on the air as she slid off Snow. She tied the dyaus to a post and raised her face to the early morning sun, absorbing its warmth. It had been so long since the sun touched her flesh. After a moment, she walked around to the side of the building. Praying it wouldn't crumble when she entered, she pried open a door and stepped inside. The moment she did, she could see why they chose it.

Her eyes adjusted instantly, as would theirs, but she was met with total blackness.

"Your Graces," she said into the void, though they would likely be slumbering. "I am Wynter of Skadeesh, awakened to help find your niece. Show yourselves."

She heard movement and closed the door behind her to let her eyes adjust completely.

A voice sounded from somewhere high. "You show yourself, demon."

Wynter could finally make out the general fixtures of a barn. The voice came from a hayloft. She stepped farther inside just as one of them brushed past her, spinning her around.

"If it isn't our keeper come to keep us in check."

"Keeper?" she said, growing more wary. "That was never my purpose."

"Wasn't it?" another said as he rushed past, slamming into her before scurrying off.

She fell back against the door. When she straightened, she drew her short sword. Though her eyes had adjusted, the vampyres were simply too fast and the room too dark for her to get a handle on their positions.

The third one made his attempt but she was ready that time. The moment he rushed past her, she stuck out her foot and tripped him.

He lost his balance, barreled forward, and slammed his shoulder into a beam with a whoosh. The wood splintered and he cursed.

"You are no better than a king's slayer."

"Perhaps she is one."

"If I were a slayer, you'd be dead." She squinted, trying to see into the veil of darkness only to realize it was too dark. It was a spell. *"Finio,"* she said, ordering it done. The spell vanished and small tendrils of light filtered in through the cracks of the barn walls.

Before her were three beautiful blond vampyres. They'd grown up. Though they were well into their nineties, they barely looked old enough to consume liquor. One stood in front of her, feet apart, head down, hands behind his back as he watched her from underneath long, moth-wing lashes. The sneer he wore would suggest he saw her as his enemy, and Wynter wondered when that came about.

Another sat on a mountain of hay, the bales stacked high against a wall, one knee drawn up with his elbow resting on it. He wore a grin instead of a smirk, so there was that.

The third one sat even higher, on the floor of the hayloft, looking down at her, his legs dangling over the side.

Their names were Arlo, Alto, and Arro, and they were dressed exactly alike—black on black—not that she could've told them apart either way, so there was no use trying to remember which was which.

"If you were a slayer," the one standing before her said, "we would have taken you the moment you walked through that door."

Wynter started to respond, but the world tilted slightly before snapping back into place. She frowned and studied the floor at her feet, wondering why it was moving.

"Is something wrong, demon?"

"Yes, tell us."

Wynter looked at her hands and realized she'd been bitten. Three times. Blood dripped from each wrist and she felt a trickle on her neck. They'd been so fast and she had yet to get her bearings. She sank onto one knee but before she could blink she was on her back.

They swarmed around her, biting her again and again, sinking their teeth into her flesh, their venom soaking into every cell in her body. And what sweet venom it was.

"You must stop," she said breathily. "I must go after your niece, and you need to go back to the village."

One of them lifted his head, blood dripping down his chin, and said, "You would presume to tell us what to do?"

"We are nothing more than prisoners to you," the one on her right said as he bent to spread her cloak and untie her tunic. "To be contained like chattel."

"No," she said, but the ecstasy that pulsed through her body was bringing her closer and closer to a climax. Heat pooled between her legs, a delicious pressure forming there.

She felt a hand on her breasts and threw back her head even as she tried to push it away. Her skin tightened around her body, her nipples hard against the vampyre's palm. It sent strands of delight coiling through her nether region.

"We could ravish you."

"You could grow up," she parried, mustering her last ounce of bravado.

In all of her years fighting alongside the immortals, not one of them had ever sunk their teeth into her flesh. Not one of them would dare. But the triplets were both entitled and ignorant. They'd clearly never met her mother as the old ones had.

One of them sank his teeth into her neck and that bite took her to new heights. She parted her legs and sent a hand down her leathers, begging for release. Before she could accomplish it, she felt cool air against skin as her breeches were peeled off. The vampyre took her wet fingers into his mouth and moaned.

"Stop." Her plea was weak; no matter what her head said, she wanted nothing more than for them to continue. They seemed to swim around her, to kiss every inch of exposed skin, to bite and rip even her tenderest parts. The pressure in her abdomen that started so far away rushed toward her. She felt a climax build. Giving in, she grabbed the closest one to her and kissed him, knowing that even one drop of his blood would imprison her in stone for a thousand years. At the moment, she couldn't bring herself to care.

But just as their venom sent her reeling, her blood sent them into an erotic frenzy of their own.

The one she kissed lifted his head to revel in the taste of her blood. In the sensations it was causing. "I can see sound," he said, gazing down at her, his beautiful blue eyes shimmering in the low light. "Your scent rushes over my skin like cool water. Every beat of your heart sends vibrations over my cock."

"If only we had known sooner," the one at her crotch said.

She grabbed a handful of his hair and pushed him back down to the task at hand. He parted her folds with his tongue, and she bucked off the ground. But he wrapped his arms around her legs and held her down as his tongue tasted and his mouth suckled.

She spiraled deeper and deeper, the hunger, hot and raw, her undoing.

"We have waited so long, demon."

"You are the forbidden nectar we have craved all our lives."

"We have looked upon your image…"

"…kissed your marble lips…"

"…touched your cold body for decades…"

"…waiting for you to wake."

One of them turned her face to his and made eye contact before admitting, "We have come on that face a hundred times."

"A thousand," another whispered in her ear.

"And watched the rain wash our efforts away."

"You are heaven and hell and everything in between."

"We will spend every waking moment pleasing you until you beg us for reprieve."

"Or until you die."

One of them got onto his knees beside her and slid down his leather breeches. His cock, slender and long, sprang to life. He bent over her. "We know our blood in your mouth will turn you to stone, but what of our seed?"

She took him into her mouth, swallowing him whole. He groaned and grabbed her hair to guide himself deeper down her throat.

Then, without warning, all three vampyres stopped. The

one in her mouth pulled away. The other two followed.

"No," she protested, writhing when the cold air hit her skin once again. "What are you doing?"

A man's voice, deeper than any of the triplets', sounded from overhead.

"When you three are finished, I'd like a word."

They looked up and the shock on their faces barely registered in Wynter's brain. They started redressing, adjusting their pants, tucking in undershirts quickly like kids caught in an illicit act.

"Why?" Wynter asked in utter disappointment.

One of the triplets, the one she had taken into her mouth, climaxed unexpectedly, spilling his seed on the ground. She could hear his grunts. He turned away, humiliated, and secured himself inside his leathers.

"Go back to the village," the voice ordered, his tone sharp and unyielding.

"What? No," Wynter whispered, still in the throes of ecstasy.

"But our niece."

The owner of the voice loomed over at Wynter as she lay half naked and panting, her head thrown back. But in those fleeting moments when she could focus, she recognized him. Though she hadn't seen him since he was a boy, there was no mistaking Gareth of Abilene, the vagabond prince. Straight shoulder-length hair, so black it looked like wet ink. The same blue eyes that all vampyres had, but his seemed bluer somehow. Clearer. Like the ocean on a summer day. The same full mouth and strong jaw, only now it was covered in several days' worth of growth.

"We'll find her," he told them. "You would be of no help."

The one who'd kissed her intimate parts so expertly looked up at the prince and argued while continuing to dress. But he did so cautiously, as though afraid of him. "She is ours, Your Highness. You have no right to her."

The man's silvery-blue gaze hardened to glistening steel. "Don't make me come down there, Arro."

He could tell them apart? How in the Three Kingdoms did he manage that?

"We want her when you are done."

"She is ours."

"She has always been ours."

"I have a feeling she'll have something to say about that once your venom leaves her system. You might want to steer clear of her for the next decade or so."

"You don't understand. Her blood—"

"Is not yours to take."

Another wave of ecstasy rose inside her like the evening tide, a rush of heat washing over her in quivering, pulsating bursts. She rode it out, waiting for the feeling to ebb. When she looked back at the prince, he stood over her and the triplets were gone.

"No," she whispered, needing to come more than she needed air. And right in front of her was the most beautiful creature she'd ever seen, also all grown up and looking much more worldly than her previous companions.

In a move so quick she surprised even herself, she pinned him to the barn wall. She braced her palms on the wood on either side of his head and pressed her naked torso into him as he studied her through thick dark lashes. Remarkably, she still wore her cloak.

"Bite me," she said, wanting more of the drug the triplets had offered her so generously.

"I am well aware of what your blood will do to me, demon."

"Exactly. Bite me." She ran a hand down his torso and over his crotch, raking her nails along the hard length of his cock. "Clearly you're interested."

"And taking you now would be tantamount to rape."

"Not at all. I give consent freely."

"Says the drunkard."

The wave rose again and the muscles between her legs clenched as her head warred with her body. On some level she knew what was happening. She knew she was practically assaulting the poor man. She leaned in to kiss him nevertheless.

He turned his head away, wrapped both arms around her and pulled her close to speak in her ear. "I can't risk my blood entering your mouth, demon. We have much to do."

She whispered in his ear, almost helplessly. "I need to come."

"I know." He sent his hand between her legs, stoking the embers already there. "I'll make you come, but we cannot kiss."

She grabbed his wrist, pulling his fingers deeper, and circled her other arm around his neck, practically clawing at him.

He sank to his knees, lay her on her cloak, and reclined

beside her.

"Please," she said as the pulsating wave grew, built momentum, crackled with energy every time her heart beat.

"Shhhh," he said softly. "Hold still." He parted her folds with his fingers and sought out her clit, his ministrations painstakingly slow as he feathered his fingertips across it.

She writhed beneath his expert touch but he locked his other arm around her, holding her like a vise as he rubbed her. Dipped. Rubbed again. Slicker that time. Smoother.

She threw back her head, reveling in the exquisite release inching toward her.

He put a knee between hers and locked her leg to him. "Listen to my heart," he said once he'd immobilized her. "By the third beat, you'll come."

Many believed vampyres lacked a pulse. They did not. Their hearts just beat very, very slowly. Approximately one beat per breathtakingly long minute.

She buried her face in the curve of his neck, his scent mingling with her desire, lifting her to new heights.

One.

A flare of primitive energy swelled inside her, thickening the air in her lungs, flooding her sex with need.

Two.

She knew he was compelling her to climax and she couldn't have cared less. She parted her legs farther, begging him to go deeper, to release the sensuality coiling tighter and tighter inside her.

Three.

The sweet sting of orgasm burst inside her, crashing into

her bones and drowning her in a pleasure like she'd never known before. It pulsed through her far longer than any climax she'd ever had, her muscles pulled taut, her head thrown back, her jaw clenched until the world slowly faded into oblivion.

~ 3 ~

More than one way to appease a cat...

S HE AWOKE FROM a dead sleep, unsure of how long she'd slumbered. Gareth lounged beside her, his head resting on a folded arm. And she was nigh naked. She rushed to cover herself with her cloak, humiliation burning through her.

Her movements stirred him and she cursed under her breath. He raised onto an elbow and pulled back the cloak. "You're already healing, but it will take some time for the venom to leave your body." He reached over and grabbed a bladder of water. Handing it to her, he said, "The more you drink, the faster it will leave, demon."

She took it from him, having had enough of the demon game. "I'm not a demon. I'm human."

He lifted a single brow in surprise, then grinned. "You're no more human than I am."

But she was. Her mother once told her she'd created her from a human girl. She often wondered who she was in the before time. Did she die? The girl before her? Or did her mother simply steal her away from her family? Wynter stood and started to pull on her discarded leathers.

"You may as well leave them off," he said, his sensual gaze travelling languidly over her.

"Why?"

"We're not finished."

She bristled. "Thank you for what you did, but I don't think risking my turning to stone again with an afternoon of debauchery will benefit anyone."

"Debauchery? Is that what it was?" He rolled onto his back and put his hands behind his head. "I do feel a little debauched."

She bit down, but fair was fair. "Would you like an orgasm then? It's the least I could do."

His gaze sought hers out. Almost sadly, he replied. "I'll survive. What I meant was, *you're* not finished."

"I don't understa—" The words had barely left her mouth when a sharp pang of pleasure spiked in her lower abdomen. It almost sent her to her knees. She looked back at him in shock.

He patted the ground beside him. "It's going to be a while."

"I am going to kill those three little fucks."

"Few would blame you. In the meantime..."

She gasped as another spasm rocketed through her. She started pacing, sure she could wait it out.

"You're only causing yourself more grief."

She braced herself against a heavy wood beam. "If you would be so kind as to leave, I can see to myself."

"Then I definitely won't be going anywhere."

She glared at him, but the grin he gave her—one part mischief, two parts challenge—was her undoing. She kicked off her leathers and straddled his head, sinking onto her knees until her sex was at his mouth. He licked his lips and watched her from beneath hooded lids, his own arousal apparent from his dilated pupils and the soft moan he emitted when she lowered herself onto him.

He wrapped his arms around her hips so he could reach between her legs and part her with his fingers. Once there, he saw to her needs using both his fingertips and his tongue, whipping her into a frenzy with an expert touch.

She fell forward onto one palm and grabbed a handful of his hair with her other hand, groaning with every feathery flick of his tongue. Molten lava once again flooded her abdomen as he worked, the venom and her desire pulsing through her like the waves of a relentless ocean. When his fingers pushed inside her and stroked her core, milking her to another climax, her body seized around him, the pleasure so sharp she spilled her essence onto his fingers.

He moaned, finding his own kind of pleasure in seeing to her needs, and kissed her softly as the last remnants of the orgasm shuddered through her.

She fell onto her cloak again to catch her breath, then asked him, "How long will this go on?"

"Like I said. It's going to be a while."

The reprieve after that orgasm lasted a little longer than the first, but she was begging for his help again in less than half an hour. This time he focused on her breasts, sucking and nipping at the peaks while pinning her wrists over her head. She writhed beneath him. Begged him to enter her. Wrapped her legs around his hips and pushed her clit against the outline of his erection. Honestly, she'd seen cats in heat with more control. But he brought her to climax, like an invisible string connected her nipples to her clit and he knew exactly how to strum it. Was he compelling her to come or was she really that desperate?

Just when she thought she would rather die than have another orgasm, the desire would wash over her again. And again. And again. Each time she swore more earnestly that the triplets would breathe their last breaths sooner than they'd ever imagined.

WYNTER AWOKE TO feel Gareth at her back. Her head rested on his outstretched arm. With as much stealth as she could muster, she rose to her feet and gathered her clothes.

It was dark out. An entire day. She'd wasted an entire day. She was going to kill the triplets if it was the last thing she did. She only partly assembled herself, saving the rest for when she was out of earshot, lest she risk waking the sleeping vampyre. But when she opened the door, wincing as it creaked, she realized he wasn't asleep at all.

"Your plan will fail without my help."

She turned back to him and frowned. "I don't know what you're talking about."

He released a long breath and raised to a sitting position, settling his back against a wooden beam. "You sent the ravagers."

She stilled so completely, she worried she'd turned to stone again.

"It's a good plan," he added. "Don't get me wrong."

She raised her chin a visible notch. "What plan might this be?"

He smiled patiently. "Your timing is perfect. A day too soon and you risk finding my baby sister early. You risk being turned back to stone before the celebration even begins. A day too late, and the celebration would be over. The one time of year your mother takes physical form would slip past and all would be lost for another year. Probably more, because getting her to set you free took a heartless kind of cunning. And guts. I cannot risk you squandering this opportunity. I cannot have your mother imprison you again. This ploy will likely only work once and you are the only one who can get close enough to kill her."

She stared at him, wondering if she should decapitate him with her short sword or gut him with the dagger. Perhaps both. He knew everything. Every aspect of the plan she'd constructed with Sara. How? Sara would never have told him.

"Like I said, a good plan. It just won't work without my help."

Making her decision—decapitation by short sword—she'd barely tensed a single muscle when he held up a hand.

"Don't kill me yet, demon. You haven't heard my part of the plan."

She drew her short sword anyway. Now that she had her faculties, he would not get the jump on her like the triplets had. She'd still been shaking off the aftereffects of such a long slumber when they attacked. Those aftereffects were now shaken off completely. Though she had yet to eat, her strength did not come from food alone, no matter how much she liked it. "What you are suggesting is treason."

"At the very least, but I understand." He lifted a shoulder. "You can hardly confess openly to a plan of such magnitude. Killing a demon, after all, especially one who is part goddess, would be difficult on your best day. A single mistake and she'll turn you to stone before you even reach for that fancy dagger you have stuffed in your boot."

She gasped and checked her right boot. The dagger was still there, hidden in a sheath sewn into the leather.

"I can get you close to your mother without her turning you to stone, but we have another problem."

"And that is?"

"You're either forgetting something or you never got the whole story. The dagger must be dipped in the blood of an ogre before it can penetrate the skin of a demon. Surely you know that."

Wynter shivered. Ogres. Disgusting creatures. "You're lying."

"Why would I?" He stood and lifted his tunic over his head. The shadows played havoc with the hills and valleys of his muscles, sliding hither and to with each movement, mesmerizing her more than she desired to admit. He was slim but well defined, his shoulders wide, his skin like baked porcelain fired to a shimmering sheen. He stepped to a bucket of water and splashed a few handfuls over his face, slicking back his hair before returning his attention. "You must understand, demon, I want this to work as much as you do."

"Why?" She sank onto the balls of her feet, crouching, ready to pounce if need be, ignoring the spasm of pleasure she felt at seeing his body and knowing it had nothing to do with the venom that had been rushing through her blood. "She saved your race from extinction."

"Ah, yes. How could I forget?" He wiped his face on a blanket that almost assuredly smelled like horse. "Of course, it was her fault we were hunted so relentlessly in the first place."

"That is not possible."

He turned back to her, growing the teensiest bit frustrated. "Is my word not enough, demon? Even after the day we've had?"

"No," she answered, matter-of-fact.

"It was your mother who sold me to the young queen."

Wynter eyed him like he'd lost his mind. "Why would she do that?"

"I've wondered that many times myself. The money, perhaps? To gain favor with the crown?"

"My mother is an ice demon. She hardly needs favor with the crown."

"I don't know what to tell you, then."

"And why would a queen buy you?"

"For the escape."

"Escape?"

"Yes, the queen was dying. She'd seen me from afar and knew by the color of my eyes I was vampyre, so she asked Skadeesh to deliver me to her for one night of unbridled bliss."

Wynter stood and took a step closer to him. "But... you were just a child."

"So was she," he said, sadly. "And let's just say I was older than I looked. Unfortunately, her request brought me to your mother's attention and she decided she wanted me for herself."

From everything she'd learned about her mother over the years, that did not surprise her.

"It was not the king who wanted my head. It was your demon mother. My father hid me so thoroughly, even she could not find me."

"I'm certain that didn't sit well."

"It infuriated her. So she sent armies to hunt me down and kill anyone who stood in their way. It was only when our numbers dwindled to double digits that my father had no choice but to make a deal with her. He would still not give me up, but he promised my blood would be delivered to her every year during the solstice festival. Mine along with many others, but she wanted mine most. She agreed, reluctantly, and sent you to kill the very people she'd sent to find me." He scoffed and shook his head. "Your mother is as twisted as her spine."

"So you want me to kill her to end her decades-long search?"

"No. I don't care about that. I can stay hidden forever. I want her head on a platter to end the abduction and exploitation of our children."

"Your children?" she asked in surprise, though she hardly knew why at this point. "Then you know she is the one taking them?"

He nodded. "I do. I just don't know why and I'm not sure I want to."

Wynter sank onto a bale of hay. "Sara and I heard about

the dagger through the most discreet channels. To be honest, however, we didn't know if it was real. Still, we had to do something. We've never heard the ogre thing."

"Why would you? If word got out, any Tom, Dick, or Shadrack would be clamoring for your mother's head. If there is only one way to kill you, wouldn't you keep it a secret, too?"

"Of course, but where are we going to find an ogre and how are we going to get his blood? I doubt one will just hand it over to us."

He smiled. "You let me worry about that."

"Let me guess. You just happen to know where one is."

"I do, demon. Nothing to worry about just yet."

"Stop calling me demon. If I were truly demon, the triplets' teeth would never have penetrated my skin."

"Agreed. And if you were truly demon, your blood would have poisoned them, not driven them into a feeding frenzy."

She cast him a sideways glance. "Then I'm human?"

He laughed. "Not in the least."

"Fine, what am I?"

She didn't miss the sadness that came over his face before he looked away. "Does it matter?"

Well, it damned sure did now. But that was a fight for another day. Horrified by the fact that her heritage was enough to sadden him, she stood. "We must go if we're going to make the celebration."

He tipped an invisible hat. "After you."

~ 4 ~

Don't throw the plan out with the bathwater.

THEY RODE ALL night. According to the vagabond, the beautiful black stallion grazing a short distance away owned him. Not the other way around. Named Fosse for reasons Gareth refused to disclose, they matched in both color and personality. Coincidence? Wynter thought not.

Their breakneck speed made conversation impossible, which suited her just fine. She was still healing from all the bites. And the humiliation. Thankfully both Gareth and Snow could see in the dark, probably better than she could, making their journey all the faster.

"We'll stop here for a couple of hours," Gareth said as they rode up to an inn. The sun had just crested the horizon and ribbons of pastels stretched across the sky, setting it aflame.

Wynter slid off the dyaus, marveling at her ability to move her physical form then wait while her spirit caught up. "If we stay here today, we can still make the city by tonight," she offered. Surely, he could not ride in the broad light of day. As long as they made it to the city by midnight, they would be okay.

Once a year, Wynter's mother took physical form to celebrate the winter solstice with her most loyal followers. It would be Wynter's one, and probably only, chance to send her to hell once and for all. From what Wynter understood, her mother enjoyed the festivities until dawn, at which time she slithered back to her own realm. They could take the day and still make it.

"I'll be fine. My longcoat is... special."

She handed the reins to a stable hand, grateful that mortals couldn't see into the spirit realm. To the boy, Snow was simply a beautiful horse. "Special how?"

"It's made with a fiber known to reflect the sun."

She eyed it in doubt. "It's black. Would it not absorb it?"

A humorous grin stole across his face. "That's why it's special."

"Ah." As loathe as Wynter was to admit it, she had watched the vagabond prince ride quite often throughout the night. His patience, his confident maneuvering of the beast between his legs... He rode with the skill of a master horseman, yet vampyres and horses rarely got along. Most vampyres in Ellery who owned horses also owned carriages. Sitting atop a horse when one's very scent made them skittish was not ideal, and because vampyres were so fleet of foot, they rarely needed livestock. Only the royals rode in carriages and it was more for show than anything.

This was yet another side of the vampyre prince so at odds with everything Wynter knew about the creatures. She'd lived with them for decades and he was nothing like most of them.

They walked into the tiny inn, the only one for miles, and stopped at the innkeeper's desk. When the man turned around, his shoulders almost too wide to be standing behind the cramped area, Gareth said, "A room and food brought up for two."

The innkeeper scowled at him far longer than was socially acceptable before turning to retrieve a key.

With his back to them, Wynter whispered, "I thought you said we were only going to eat."

"And rest. Also, you need to bathe."

Her eyes rounded with shock and more humiliation. "I didn't realize," she said, feigning nonchalance as she lift her cloak to sniff.

He laughed softly. "You smell divine as always."

As always?

Before she could question him on his word choice, the innkeeper turned back around and Wynter couldn't help but wonder if he were part ogre. Cumbrously large with a face only a mother could love, he glared once again at her companion.

"You'll be paying up front, I'm thinking."

Gareth pulled out two coins and slammed them onto the tall desk. "Will that cover it?"

"Aye, this time, but what about the last? Or the one before that?"

"I paid fair, old man."

The innkeeper reached out, grabbed Gareth by the collar, and practically dragged him onto the desk. "You have a lot of nerve, vampyre."

Gareth grinned. "That's because I've watched your children on several occasions. I now have nerves of steel. I could take on a kraken and be at ease."

Wynter had placed a hand onto the hilt of her short sword, but she dropped it the moment she realized these men were probably the best of friends.

"Are you calling my children—"

"I'm calling them monsters. It's not like you can deny it." Gareth looked to the man's side, a grin widening across his handsome face when a little girl popped up from behind the desk.

"You knew I was there the whole time," she said, pouting.

"Not at all." He turned back to the innkeeper who still held him over the desk. "Are you planning on letting go any time soon, or are you going to kiss me as heartily as your wife does?"

The man laughed and pulled Gareth into a hug—the kind of hug that would crush a lesser man. He dropped him and picked up the tiny being beside him, handing her over to Gareth. A vampyre. A vampyre who could kill her before the man could blink.

"How are you, smidgeon?" Gareth asked.

The girl threw her arms around his neck as an even smaller boy ran up and wrapped his body around Gareth's leg. "Oh, no!" he said, pretending to fall. He sank back onto a bench, taking the children with him.

"Children," a woman said sharply, clapping her hands. "Leave that poor man alone."

Completely unmoved, the girl said, "But he started it,

mama."

The boy agreed with a nod.

"Let him up so I can hug him, too."

Gareth stood easily and pulled the woman, who was as tiny as her husband was gigantic, into his arms.

"That's enough there, lover boy," the innkeeper said. "Ye scoundrel."

Gareth started to reply, but then he stopped and tilted his head. He turned to Wynter, his expression resigned. He gestured toward the interior of the inn with a nod, and said, "Prepare yourself."

"There's more?"

In the next second, a trio of massive hunting dogs ran through the establishment, barking, wagging their tales, and upending more than one table. They took a running leap onto Gareth and he fell back once again, protesting loudly about the amount of drool he had to endure every time he visited.

"And that's why I need a bath as well. Innkeep!" he yelled as though the man weren't standing right there. "A bath, if you will."

"You know what that does to my back," the man said, but the moment he turned around, a grin stole across his face.

After a round of introductions, Gareth showed Wynter to their room then went to help Whistler—as she'd suspected, an old friend of his—with the bath water.

Though hunger had finally begun to gnaw at the lining of her stomach, she craved the bath even more. She disrobed behind a screen, marveling at the quickly-healing scars that covered her body. There must've been a hundred bite marks and she recommitted to killing the triplets first chance she got.

She heard heavy boots coming up the stairs and stiffened. Part of her worried Gareth would want his kindness reciprocated. Part of her worried he wouldn't. But it turned out it was the food.

Wynter slipped on her cloak and went to sample the fare the cook had brought up. He simply had to be related to Whistler. Same build. Same wiry hair. Same square face. She dipped a piece of bread into the stew and tasted it, trying not to moan.

"This is delicious," she said to him.

He beamed at her and bowed all the way out the door.

It was incredible, the little things she'd missed. She'd been living vicariously through her lady's maid, though it had taken her over forty years to figure out how to communicate with her. Once she did, once the lines of communication were open, they talked incessantly night and day. Wynter had been isolated a long time.

"You first," Gareth said as he carried in the last bucket of hot water and poured it into a copper tub.

"Are you sure?" she asked, reluctant to leave the food. When he only lifted a brow, she gave in.

He crossed his arms over his chest to watch her, but she pulled the screen around before dipping her toes in the tub. "I've seen it all and then some, demon."

"Yes, under duress." She stifled a moan when her body sank beneath the water. "Are we free to talk here?"

"Completely," he said, his mouth now obviously full.

It always amazed her how some vampyres thrived on human food and some never touched it. He was clearly the former.

"Your friends are adorable."

"Agreed."

"Are you going to tell me this plan of yours?"

"I told you. We have to get you close enough to your mother for you to plunge the dagger into her heart."

"What's so special about the dagger?" She'd heard rumors it held the power to kill a demon, but she'd never learned why. Sara and Queen Anne of Abilene—Gareth's mother—had risked their lives to steal it from a troll named Rooter. Not an actual troll, mind. A nasty cur who lived in the hills outside of Ellery and collected everything from faery-spun lace to dragon's breath. How he stumbled upon a dagger that could kill a demon, Wynter didn't know, but Sara swore the queen had it authenticated. And yet, how does one go about doing such a thing?

It was all very secretive. Wynter had overheard the king and queen talking in the courtyard one day, and she realized they were allies. She told Sara she could trust them, so she went to them and confessed to having the ability to communicate with Wynter. Together they came up with the plan to kill Skadeesh, once they realized it was her stealing their children. That and the fact that Skadeesh still sought their son, Gareth, made convincing the royal couple to join their cause effortless.

It crushed the queen to have her own daughter taken by ravagers, but Skadeesh had to feel the girl's terror lest she never be convinced to release Wynter from her imprisonment long enough to help with the search. Perhaps Gareth had been in on the plan all along.

"From what I understand," he said, taking another bite of something, "it was forged in the fires of hell."

"And how does one go about forging a dagger in the fires of—"

"This cheese is spectacular."

"How do you know so much about killing demons?" she asked, not giving up her quest.

"I could tell you, but then I'd have to kill you."

"I'm just supposed to trust you, then? You could be walking me into a trap."

"My Lady Wynter," he said, suddenly in front of her, lounging against the wall, his arms crossed over the expanse of his chest. She gasped and tried for a modicum of decency by covering her breasts. "Why would I go to all the trouble of walking you into a trap when I could easily have turned you to stone in the barn?"

"Easy. To earn favor with my mother."

"The last thing I want from your mother is favor," he said, letting his gaze linger a little too long on her mouth.

Fair enough. "Then tell me how you know. It certainly isn't common knowledge. Especially the bit about the ogre blood."

He drew in a deep breath before answering, clearly reluctant to explain. "The queen."

"Your mother, Queen Anne?"

"No." He straightened abruptly and strode out of sight once again. She heard a chair scrape against the floor and creak as he sat back down at the table. "The queen who bought me when I was a boy."

Wynter rose up out of the water. It cascaded around her as she leaned over the side of the tub, trying to peer at him between the slats of the screen. "I don't understand. How could she know such a thing?"

"Because your mother was in love with the young queen. When I said she was dying, I meant that metaphorically. Your mother had a death grip on her and she could no longer live under her constant eye. She chose to end her life. Slowly with belladonna."

"Hold on." Wynter submerged her head in the water to rinse and then grabbed a sheet off a nearby stool. She wrapped herself up so she could face him. Wanting to catch every word he tossed her way, she sat across from him, put her elbows on the rickety table, and plopped her chin in her cupped hands. "All right. She was slowly killing herself. How old was she? Was she human? Did she love you?"

His gaze slid past her to the fire on her right as he thought back. "She was human. And she was fifteen."

Wynter sucked in a soft breath of disbelief.

"Your mother began visiting her every night in different forms. If Queen Evelyn did anything your mother didn't like, the ice demon let her know. She... was not kind."

"I'm sorry, Gareth," Wynter said, as he was clearly pained by the memory.

"One night, the queen was ready to end it, to take a lethal dose of belladonna. She poured the beads into some wine, but your mother appeared and drank the wine before she could." He refocused on Wynter. "And the oddest thing happened.

Your mother started disclosing all manner of cruelties. She confessed atrocities the likes of which you would never believe."

"I would, actually. She is a demon, after all. Those who seek her favor often get what they deserve."

"Often," he said softly, studying the indention at the base of her throat. "Not always."

She nodded in agreement.

"That night," he continued, "while she had your mother drunk on belladonna, the queen asked the demon to find a vampyre boy she once saw. She promised your mother she would give her anything in return. Money. Gold. Even her love. I was delivered to the queen within the hour."

"I'm sorry."

"It's of no consequence. The admiration was mutual."

Startled by a pang of jealousy that spiked within her, Wynter shifted in her chair, feeling ridiculous. She'd heard rumors about how beautiful the young queen had been. How adored. Naturally, Gareth would adore her as well.

"That was when the queen told me some of the things your mother had done. She asked for release from her bonds, for during the evening she'd realized your mother had cursed her. The belladonna was not working. It would not kill her no matter how much she ingested, thus her fervor to have her throat ripped out by a vampyre. But before the ripping commenced, she told me how to kill the demon. How to kill any demon. Apparently, your mother had confessed that as well."

Wynter sank back in the chair, astonished. There was no

love lost where her mother was concerned. Her impending death was a necessary evil. But for her to divulge such sensitive information, even under the influence of belladonna... "Gareth, could my mother have tricked the young queen? What if this information is false?"

He frowned, thinking back. "I don't think so. Your mother was completely enamored with the queen. Even the faintest prospect of winning the queen's love had her euphoric. Love," he added, bequeathing Wynter the barest hint of a glower, "is after all, the weakest of all emotion."

"Or the strongest," she countered, curious to learn what had jaded him so. "What happened next?"

"When your mother came to and saw that I'd killed her beloved queen, she exploded with rage. I was mist by that point, but I saw the fearsome creature she became. That is neither here nor there, I suppose. And the rest is history."

"I'm sorry, can we perhaps go back to the part where you can *turn to mist*?" Only the strongest vampyres could turn to mist, and they were always—*always*—the oldest in the clan. Wynter had never heard of a vampyre younger than three hundred acquiring the ability.

"Did I not mention that?"

"No," she said, suddenly annoyed. "But it explains how you were able to eavesdrop so effortlessly on my conversation with Sara. And then again in the barn. How long were you there before you intervened?"

He lifted a salacious brow. "As much as I might've enjoyed the show, I wouldn't have stood by while those whelps assaulted you. I was sorry I got there too late to stop them from biting you in the first place."

"Wait." Wynter's mind raced as the new information sparked revelation after revelation. "That is why she was never able to find you. You could easily elude her huntsmen."

He nodded and ate another grape.

"But, if you could turn to mist, how was she able to take you to the queen in the first place?"

"With my permission, of course. Call it professional courtesy."

Her expression flattened. "Or morbid curiosity."

"There is that." He stood and started to disrobe.

Suddenly the consummate virgin, Wynter averted her gaze, ignoring the heat spreading over her face. And other body parts. "You said you could get me close to my mother without her turning me to stone. How exactly do you plan on doing that?"

"Oh, yes, that's the part of the plan I'd rather not explain. Not yet."

"Why?" she asked, alarmed. She turned back to him, less sure of him and anything he had to say, and was met with wide shoulders and muscles shifting along his back like the tides. Unable to resist, she let her gaze journey to his lower extremities. To steely buttocks. Strong thighs. Muscular calves.

"Finished?" he asked, watching her from over a wide shoulder.

She blinked and studied her sheet. "Quite. Why can't you explain a plan that may or may not involve my death?"

He chuckled and she heard him walk around the screen and sink into the water. He released a soft breath, then said,

"Because if I tell you, you'll never in a thousand years go along with it."

"I don't believe you. Is it because it's dangerous? Or because you don't trust me?"

"Yes."

~ 5 ~

If I had a coin for every time someone bit me...

WYNTER DRESSED WHILE His Highness scrubbed his nails or his toes or whatever it was princes scrubbed and went downstairs to ponder the meaning of life. She ended up playing with two ogre children and three hellhounds instead, having the most fun she'd had in... well, in seventy-two years.

By the time Gareth emerged from their room, he was clothed in formal attire. While the fresh longcoat was the same cut as his previous one, this coat was newer and made with a much finer material. He was freshly shaven and wore gloves and a scarf as well, as though ready to attend a royal function.

He said goodbye to the adorable family and slid a pair of dark, round glasses onto his perfect nose before wrapping the scarf around the lower half of his face and lifting the hood over his head.

When Wynter covered her staggeringly savage interest with a raised brow, he said, "We're going to a party, are we not?"

Her stomach clenched with the reminder. "I suppose we

are."

They rode the rest of the day, stopping sparingly and only to let the horses rest. The closer they got to the city of Santa Alaina, the more aggressive the butterflies in Wynter's stomach became. She had waited decades for this day. For this opportunity. The closer the hour drew, the more her body quivered, the response seemingly out of her control.

Gareth noticed. When they stopped in a snowy glen to give the horses a brief respite, he sat upon a boulder and asked, "Are you having second thoughts?"

It would be so easy to say yes. To go back. To retrieve the princess and return to stone to finish out her hundred-year sentence. And then what? She could run. She could put as much distance between her and the vampyres as humanly possible. That was the only rule she had to adhere to. No vampyre blood in her mouth. How difficult could it be?

But, just as quickly, she realized the futility of it all. She'd slowly been going mad in her stone fortress. In the never-ending blackness of eternity. She thought she'd arrived at irreversible crazy until one day, by happenstance, she heard the voice of her beloved lady's maid in her head, the lilting tones more familiar than her own. Sara had saved her from complete and irreversible madness. But to expect that of her for the next twenty-eight years was asking too much. Sara had things to do, after all. A family of her own now.

"I must ask a favor, Your Highness."

He'd been watching her from beneath his lashes, but he raised his head in surprise. "It's *Your Highness* now, is it?"

She barreled forward, not bothering to explain. "If anything happens, if I... if I become stone again, will you destroy me?"

He'd schooled his features as she'd noted him doing any time she brought up a difficult subject. A subject he'd rather not discuss.

"I mean, if you broke me into pieces, that would kill me, yes? That would set me free?"

He still didn't answer.

She dropped her gaze, suddenly self-conscious. "I'll beg if need be. I cannot... I cannot face that darkness again."

Without speaking a word, he slid off the boulder, grabbed Fosse's reins, and mounted the stallion in one fluid motion. Then he clicked his tongue and led him out of the glen. She followed suit, lifting herself onto Snow and trailing in his wake.

Perhaps he just needed time to think about it. She'd give him that before insisting upon an answer. Because if the answer was no, she had another plan in place. If she'd learned nothing else over the years, it was to always have a fail-safe.

They rode the rest of the distance without stopping. Or talking. Even when Wynter caught up to him and asked him about this mysterious plan of his once again, he said nothing to her.

Fine. He was being taciturn. She could be taciturn. One does not live over seventy years as a rock without learning to be taciturn. Had she said something wrong? He'd killed before. Why should it bother him now? And yet the mere thought seemed to.

She steered Snow into his tracks as they came upon a particularly narrow part of the woods. It was a nice place to be.

She watched his wide shoulders move as though one with his stallion. Both startingly beautiful. Both alarmingly powerful, full of grace and stealth.

They crested the last hill before the city just as the sun settled below the mountains in the west. Thousands of lanterns lit the streets with a warm glow as citizens prepared for the festivities. This was Santa Alaina, capital of the First Kingdom, and Skadeesh's favorite city. The one in which she took physical form one night a year to grant favor to her most loyal subjects.

It was also the city she would die in if Wynter had any say in the matter. It was Skadeesh's time. She'd committed more than enough atrocities to warrant such action, only one involving the abduction of vampyre children. Who knew how many human children she'd taken over the years? How many people were buried under mountains of dirt? How many people lay frozen in her coffins of ice? She'd once frozen an entire family because their young daughter had mispronounced the ice demon's name in her prayers. And still they prayed as though she were a deity. She may have an ounce of god blood rushing through her veins, but she was hardly a deity. She didn't deserve their loyalty or their respect.

Gareth pulled Fosse to a stop and waited for her to come alongside him.

Snow picked her way through the brush until Wynter reined her in. "Have you decided?" she asked him.

He bit down, his jaw working hard under the pressure as he studied the glowing city.

When he didn't answer, she continued. "I would like an

answer either way, Gareth. I need to know where to put my energies should it come to that."

"Meaning?" he asked, breaking his silence at last.

"Meaning, if you won't do it, I have another plan."

He gestured a greeting to a family traveling on the road into the city as they waved at him, the children's faces bright and full of excitement. He removed the dark glasses, folded them, and slid them into an inside pocket in his longcoat. "So, you have another way to kill yourself."

"If it comes to that. In the meantime, I would like to know if you will honor my request. If you agree, it might give me an extra second or two to carry out our plan. And since you won't tell me yours, I have no way of knowing if it will work. I cannot risk it. If you refuse, I will have to spend those two seconds taking my own life before that witch turns me." He still did not answer and Wynter thought she would explode with frustration. "Fine." She took out the dart she'd had Sara stow in her saddle bag. The one dipped in a poison so deadly, one prick and her heart would stop before she hit the floor.

Her hands shook as she took the dart, uncapped it, and slid it carefully into her pocket. She need only a finger prick to ensure her demise.

"That's your backup plan?"

"If you won't honor my request—"

"I won't."

"—then yes," she said, disappointment stinging the backs of her eyes. "May I ask why?"

He finally met her gaze, his face so impossibly handsome, it hurt to look at. But his eyes glittered with anger, so much so it stole the breath from her lungs. He leaned forward, grabbed a handful of her cloak, and whispered, "I killed you once upon your request, demon. I'll not do it again." Then he released her with a solid shove, as though the very sight of her disgusted him.

She blinked in confusion, but he wasn't finished.

"Did you think you were the only one in love? Do you honestly believe I would have let that demon bitch lay a hand on me if her intentions had been anything other than to take me to see you? Her Royal Majesty. The most beloved queen ever to rule the First Kingdom?"

"Gareth—"

"But you are right," he interrupted. "We need a backup plan. Preferably one better than a poisonous stick." Wynter was still processing his words, still trying to catch her breath when he leaned over her horse and ran a gloved hand over the mare's neck. "Snow, girl," he said into her ear, "are you ready?"

Snow lifted her head in affirmation and pawed at the ground with a huff. Her spirit followed, a split second out of sync with her physical body.

Wynter shook off the shock she felt, mostly because she was suddenly more offended than she'd ever been in her life. "So, she's in on the plan, but I'm not?"

"Something like that." He ran his hand over Snow's neck again, the act so intimate, so beautiful. "Did you ever wonder why your mother will not allow a vampyre's blood to cross your lips?"

"No. Well, a bit, I suppose."

"Did you know that vampyres can be made?"

"Made? Do you mean created?"

"From a human, yes."

Wynter gaped at him. Surely, he jested. "How is that possible?"

"First, you must be bitten."

"And… and second?"

"You must drink the blood of the vampyre that bit you."

He waited as she absorbed that nugget of gold. How did she not know this? "And then a human can become a vampyre?"

"It's not quite that easy. There is a final step."

"Which is?" She waited for him to answer, but as he sat on top of Fosse, he blurred for the barest of moments.

"It's what I should have done to you when I first met you."

"In the barn?" she asked, still in a rather pathetic state of denial when she noticed a droplet of blood on his lower lip.

"But it's forbidden and I was young. Too young to know how to break the rules and get away with it."

She glanced down at a warmth spreading in her hand and saw a smear of blood there. "Did you bite me?"

He began rolling up the left sleeve of his longcoat. Then the cuff of his tunic. "If this doesn't work, your mare's spirit will separate and leap forward out of her physical body."

Confused, she frowned at him. "I'm not sure how that's a plan. Mine is still better… in the grand scheme of things."

He leveled a steady gaze on her. "And she'll take your spirit with her."

Alarm rushed through her, but she forced her expression to

remain neutral. When she had regained her inner composure—somewhat—and slowed her pulse—somewhat—she asked, "Why would she do that?"

"Because," he said, lifting the inside of his wrist to his mouth, "I don't know if I'm fast enough."

Before his words even registered, before anything he'd said in the last five minutes registered, he sank his teeth into the flesh at his left wrist, grabbed the back of her head with his right, and forced his blood into her mouth.

She gasped and bucked, fighting him off even as the cold sensation of stone crept into her body. Her hand reached reflexively for the dart in her pocket, but he subdued her wrist until she could not move. In the next instant, the world spun, she heard a sharp snap, and everything went dark. Her last thought before she lost consciousness completely was the realization that he'd honored her wish after all. By breaking her neck.

MOVEMENT, A GENTLE swaying actually, nudged her awake. She fought the bonds of slumber tooth and nail, trying to claw her way to the surface. Had she dreamed the last two days? The last seventy-two years?

She lay cradled in powerful arms, her head lolling against a wide chest. She smelled a thousand scents at once, but his reigned, part musk, part leather. He pushed back a lock of her hair and tucked it under her ear.

"Is she okay, then?" a man called out to the rider.

"She recently discovered hard cider," the rider said.

The man laughed, a boisterous thing that had Wynter smiling inside. "It's that time of year," he said. "Good fortune to you, brother."

"Good fortune to you."

They rode a bit farther, the sound of the rider's slow heartbeat lulling her back to oblivion. "If you sleep all night," the rider said to her, "we'll miss our opportunity entirely. Then where will we be?"

"Our opportunity?" she asked, her voice more of a croak than an articulation.

He leaned closer and whispered in her ear and she wanted nothing more than to eat him, he smelled so delicious. But when he uttered the words, "To kill your mother," she sprang up in the saddle and almost fell off for her efforts.

He tightened his hold on her and she turned to gape at him only to realize the sun had risen. "It's daylight out," she said, looking around at the colors, so vibrant they hurt her eyes.

"No. That's your vision. It's almost midnight and you've been out for hours."

"Hold up," she said with a squirm, trying to slide off the horse, but he held her fast.

"We need to get to the castle. There isn't much time left."

"The castle? This is…" She looked around again. "This is real. This is happening."

"It is. How do you feel?"

Her gaze flitted from one thing to another. A drunk couple stumbled out of a tavern, both men falling face first into an icy puddle. But when their faces hit the water, Wynter watched as everything slowed. The one nearest her hit first, his face displacing the frigid water. It rippled out, then burst up around his head, and she could account for each droplet as it rained in an arc around him. The second man did the same and the droplets crashed and merged into one another.

"I hate to interrupt, but you need to learn to control your movements quickly."

"Am I... Am I..."

"A vampyre? Yes. You are a little bit of everything at this point in your life, like it or not."

"Everything?"

"You were human first. Then a demon warrior with a little god sprinkled in, thanks to Skadeesh's demon blood. And now you're vampyre and... a little of this. A little of that. But we can discuss it more later. For now, you need to control your movements."

"What do you mean?"

"When Skadeesh allows us entry into her party, she needs to believe you are still susceptible to her power. You'll still bend to her will."

"She needs to believe she can still turn me to stone."

"Yes."

"Are you sure she can't?"

He smiled and pulled her close again. "Yes. You're free, Wynter. But you must learn quickly or all is lost."

"Perhaps you should have done that sooner? Given me time to adjust. Just a thought, vagabond."

"I couldn't. Your eyes are the most incredible silver now, but they'll soon turn blue and the game will be up."

"Oh." She hadn't thought of that.

"I can't wait to see which shade they take. I think, because of your demon blood, they'll retain much of the silver."

She turned from him, everything he said before the transformation coming back to her. "I don't remember being her," she said, saddened with the knowledge that she was the famed queen who'd had her throat ripped out by a beautiful vampyre prince. "I don't remember that life at all."

"With your new status, it may come back to you eventually. But I hope it doesn't."

"Why?"

"You were tortured then. By your mother. By a tyrant king. Even by your human mother, from my understanding. You were simply a pawn in a game over which you had no control."

She nodded. "I would still like to remember."

"Why?"

"I'd like to remember our one night together."

It was his turn to be shocked. He lifted a hand to her face. It was the wrong thing to do. The smell of the blood on the cuff of his tunic filled her nostrils. Before she knew what she was doing, she grabbed his wrist and sank her teeth. He pulled her into his longcoat to conceal her as she fed.

"This is good," he said, his voice smooth. Soothing. "This will give you strength."

His blood splashing onto her tongue saturated every cell in her body. It sparked to life and ignited causing a bloodlust to take hold.

Gareth stopped Fosse and pulled her tighter with his free arm.

She looked up, saw the pulse in his neck, and went for his throat, wanting more. But he held her fast, refusing to let her budge as he waited for her to get control.

"I'm sorry," she said when she realized what she'd done.

"No, you're stronger now," he said. "You'll need it."

"You'll finally let me in on your plan then?"

He reached behind him to his saddle bag and brought out a set of irons. "First, you chain me up."

She brightened instantly. "And then?"

"And then, you hand me over to your mother."

~ 6 ~

Nothing burns like ice.

ONCE WYNTER ANNOUNCED she had caught the vagabond prince, she and Gareth were allowed entrance immediately. They were led down hall after opulent hall, the castle like a village unto itself. And according to Gareth, she used to live here. She was the young queen. After she died, Skadeesh grieved for days and threw a tantrum the size of the Three Kingdoms. She preserved the queen's body and performed a ritual on her during the next full moon, creating a daughter she could control in her twisted game of one-upmanship. She simply wanted to own Wynter. Or Evelyn, as she used to be called. The thought of losing her, of Evelyn rejecting her, was unacceptable.

What would she think now?

The chains rattled as they walked. The chains that could no more hold Gareth than the air she breathed could. He could turn to mist any time he wanted to, but few knew he had that capability and he would never tip his hand to Skadeesh if he didn't have to. As of this moment, she had no idea how he'd evaded her efforts for so long, and he planned on keeping it that way.

Wynter concentrated on her movements. She was fast before, her speed envied even by vampyres. Well, most. She had nothing on Gareth, a fact she wanted to know more about. But whatever magic flowed through his veins had seeped into hers, and now she was so fast, her slightest shift was akin to teleportation. Thus, she had to concentrate on slowing each and every movement. On fooling her mother.

No, not her mother. That creature was as much of a mother to her as an ogre was. It might take some time, however, for Wynter to relinquish that title when thinking of her.

But as they drew closer and closer to the festivities, to Skadeesh in physical form, Wynter's nerves began to get the better of her. She thought she quivered before. Now she practically vibrated.

"Easy," Gareth whispered under his breath. "You'll give us away, love."

It was his use of the word *love* that calmed her. She replayed his statement in her head, letting the warmth of it cascade over her, as the herald opened the massive doors to announce them.

His shocked expression would suggest Wynter had surprised him when she gave him her name. He stepped across the threshold, the festivities so far in swing they were beginning to wind down, and said loudly, "Queen Evelyn of Armitage and her prisoner, Prince Gareth of Abilene."

Wynter sought and found her mother the moment the doors opened. The creature lay on a divan, her gaudy dress unable to hide the demon curvature of her spine, the greenish hue to her skin. Wynter had never noticed the hue before, her vampyre eyes clearly picking up shades she'd never seen.

The woman's head jerked up at the mention of Wynter's previous name. But when she heard Gareth's name, Wynter thought her mother might seize right then and there. She shot upright on the divan and gazed up at them, her jaw going slack. They descended the stairs, Wynter holding the chains in both hands and concentrating on moving slowly.

Nothing surprised her about the festivities. Partygoers dressed in the finest fabrics lined the room, some of them swaying and half-naked, some of them passed out and fully-naked. Even the new king, a middle-aged man who'd inherited the crown when his cousin was suspiciously torn apart by wild boars during a hunting expedition, sat in a wingback near the fireplace, guiding his cock into a young maid's mouth.

He pushed the girl off him with the mention of Evelyn's name, for she was the true heir to the throne. He would have to think fast if he was going to rid the kingdom of her once and for all.

But none of that mattered at the moment. The one thing that did surprise Wynter was the fact that the triplets had been invited to the party. Perhaps they delivered the coveted blood from the vampyre village of Ellery.

Wynter paused when she saw them, worried their plan would be foiled, but how could the triplets know she and Gareth were working together? They simply didn't strike her as being that smart. It would seem fortune would smile down on them once again when they bent to whisper in Skadeesh's ear. No matter how soft, Wynter heard every word.

"She is ours," they whispered into the ice demon's ear.

"Please let us have her."

"Please, my queen."

She held up a hand and they quieted instantly. One of them slithered to the side, probably afraid he would get hit. Or worse.

"Evelyn?" Skadeesh asked, addressing her but she had yet to take her eyes off Gareth. She was clearly just as enamored with him as she had once been enamored with Evelyn. "You remembered your heritage?"

"Not exactly." She shoved Gareth to the ground at the demon's feet. "He has been trying to bargain with me for two days. He told me I was Evelyn and he tore out my throat at my behest. And then he wondered why I did not set him free after that."

"Those chains—" Skadeesh said, questioning their hold on him.

"Have been dipped in faery blood. Can't you smell it?"

She sniffed the air. "Yes. Of course. You have done well, daughter."

"Thank you, mother. I still have to find Princess Gabriella, but thanks to the vagabond, I know where she's being held. I just thought you would like this," she wrinkled her nose at him, "creature to keep you company in the meantime." She bowed to her. "I'll leave you to it."

"Wait, daughter!" While still wary, Skadeesh couldn't help but get excited. "How did you catch him? I have been trying for decades."

She was just about to answer when a scent hit her, bringing a memory crashing into her fragile façade. She recognized the smell of their blood. The triplets'. It didn't smell like Gareth's, coppery and sweet. Theirs smelled putrid and she remembered the subtle taste of it in her wine. "You spiked the wine with your blood."

"What?" the one closest to her asked, pressing a hand to his chest, his performance a bit melodramatic.

"Decades ago. On the practice field."

The one next to Skadeesh bowed his head and twisted his neck like a snake's. "We just wanted to know if it was true."

"If you would turn to stone."

"We regretted it."

"A thousand times over."

"If we could take it back…"

"Why?" she asked, stepping closer. "Did you tire of coming on my face?"

Their eyes rounded and they all three glanced at Skadeesh, afraid of what she would do.

But she simply smiled. "Don't be too hard on them, daughter, but they're yours. Do with them what you will. You have brought the only thing I've wanted for decades."

"My queen," one of them said.

"Please spare us."

"Please, my queen."

She ignored them, another smile sliding across her rancid flesh as she gazed adoringly at the man on his knees before her, his chin held high. "You will be rewarded, daughter. Beyond your wildest imaginations."

"Thank you, mother. Oh," she said, as though just remembering, "he had this on him." She pulled the dagger out of her waistband and held it out to Skadeesh.

Skadeesh lunged back with a hiss. "How?" She glared at Gareth. "How did you find that? How do you know?"

Wynter went to hand it to her, but she shrank back, something Wynter had never seen the woman do. "It's all right, mother. He said it won't work unless it's been dipped in ogre blood."

She relaxed, though just barely, and glanced around to see who was listening, probably already plotting the deaths of anyone within earshot. After all, she could not allow something so sensitive to get out. "That is true." She went to reach for it, but Gareth lunged at her, causing her to rear back again, her teeth glistening yellow in the lanternlight.

"Be still, vampyre scourge," Wynter said, holding the dagger at his throat. It was the best insult she could come up with on such short notice.

He glared up at her and the world stilled around her as he shot her a conspiratorial wink a heartbeat before he grabbed the dagger from her and lunged at the demon. He pounced on Skadeesh so fast, she didn't have time to react. He brought the knife down into her heart. At least he tried to.

As legend told, it could not penetrate her skin. She gasped, her eyes round with fear, but the moment she realized it wouldn't go in, she burst into a tinny laughter.

Several of the guests laughed too, as though obligated to laugh every time she did. As though it were a job.

Wynter stood in horror, not knowing what to do next, as

her mother took the blade out of Gareth's hands and plunged it into his heart.

"No!" she screamed. She caught him as he fell back, the dagger protruding from his chest. She eased him onto her lap and cradled him much like he'd cradled her. "Gareth, no."

"It would seem," her mother said, coming to her full height, "there is a traitor among us."

"May we have her?" one of the triplets said.

"Please, my queen."

"She is everything."

"You little bitch," Skadeesh said, both stunned and impressed. "I didn't think you had it in you, to fight against me. Too bad you'll live the rest of eternity as a rock."

Wynter brushed back Gareth's hair, his pained expression more than she could bear. He looked up at her just as Skadeesh started reciting the spell that would once again imprison her. She waited, no longer caring. "I'm sorry, Gareth. I failed."

"Why didn't that work?"

Wynter looked up in surprise as the demon studied her with a quizzical brow.

"Why aren't you stone?"

It worked. Gareth's plan worked. He'd been right. She gazed at him just as Skadeesh bent toward her.

She grabbed Wynter's chin and looked deeply into her eyes. "Impossible." She leaned closer. "It's impossible!" she screeched.

But underneath her mother's ranting and raving, another word drifted toward her. Oh so softly, Gareth whispered, "Now."

Without thought, Wynter pulled the blade from his chest and plunged it into the ice demon's heart.

She blinked at Wynter, her mouth lightly ajar as her gaze drifted to her chest in disbelief. She glanced back at Wynter then at Gareth as her skin began to crack. Her screams filled the stunned silence, the fractures in her skin splitting and widening. Molten lava oozed underneath and rushed to the surface, catching her entire body on fire. She burned to ash as her screams echoed off the walls around them.

Everyone stood in shock, but not Wynter. Wynter crouched in shock, still holding onto the man she'd apparently been in love with since she was human.

She looked down at him. "I can't believe that worked."

He grinned and rolled onto his feet.

She followed suit.

"See here," the king said, stalking up to her. He had guts, she'd give him that. Unfortunately, he was a horrible person and an even worse king. And this land had seen enough of horrible kings.

Without taking her eyes off Gareth, she drew her short sword and slashed the man's throat where he stood. His younger brother would make a much kinder monarch. "How did that work? I thought the dagger needed ogre blood."

In a rare moment of uncertainty, Gareth clenched his teeth and sat on the divan Skadeesh had just vacated. The king made a show of dying all over the place as partygoers scuttled away from him. Many ran out of the room, but a few stayed behind, possibly to find out what came next.

"I was sickly as a child," he said, examining his ruined tunic.

She leaned in and ran her fingertips over the wound that had already healed. Much faster than any vampyre's she'd ever seen.

"My parents worried I wouldn't make it, so they sought counsel in all manner of beast." He ducked his head as though ashamed. "I have the heart of an ogre, Wynter. And the blood of a faery king."

Wynter only gazed at him, even more in awe. "That's why you're so powerful. Why you can turn to mist at such a young age. Why you can compel anyone to do your bidding."

"As are you," he said. "As can you."

She'd knelt before him. Now she sank back onto her heels. "I have your blood running through my veins. I have vampyre blood and faery blood and ogre blood."

"And, not to dampen the mood, but demon blood with a touch of god as well. You are even more powerful than I, Your Majesty."

She frowned. "I have no desire to take the throne."

"You could be great. The First Kingdom could do with a suitable monarch."

"True. But I think I'll give that one's little brother a chance before I do anything drastic." She gestured toward the finally dead king.

"My queen," one of the triplets said, "we are here to serve."

She turned toward them, her face stone. Metaphorically. "Your father will hear of this. Everything."

"No." They dropped to their knees and clasped their hands.

"Please, my queen."

"We will do anything."

"We are yours to command."

Their groveling was making her seasick. "Leave."

They didn't hesitate. They scurried off like rats. Really pretty rats, but rats nonetheless.

"You know I can't let them live," Gareth said. "Not after what they did to you."

"I have a feeling their father will punish them accordingly, if yours doesn't get to them first. You have some of the strangest relatives. Speaking of which," she added with a gasp, "we must get Gabriella back."

"Already done. I dispatched a courier while you were transitioning. My parents will bring her home and word of Skadeesh's demise will spread fast."

"It will." Her brows slid together in thought. "It will leave the realm open to attack."

"Then we have just found our calling, don't you think?"

Wynter brightened at the thought, unleashing a smile she was certain took up half her face. She glanced at her hands, noticing every line. Every vein. Every rush of blood. "I can't believe this. I can't believe I am one of you."

"Took you long enough."

She laughed. "What shall we do now, Your Highness?"

He shrugged. "Well, Your Majesty, look at all this food. I'd hate for it to go to waste."

Her mouth watered instantly. "I still crave human food."

"Good. It would be a shame to lose that."

She began planning her assault on the buffet immediately.

"The real question is," he said, watching her assess the fare, "what shall we do after?"

"Depends," she said with a mischievous grin. "Do you bite?"

He leaned forward and whispered, "Every chance I get."

With something akin to a schoolgirl giggle, she climbed onto the divan with him. Stradling his hips, she sank onto the outline of his already hardening cock. "I think we should start there."

Thank you for reading **A WYNTER FYRE**. We hope you enjoyed it! If you liked this book – or any of Darynda's other releases – please consider rating the book at the online retailer of your choice. Your ratings and reviews help other readers find new favorites, and of course there is no better or more appreciated support for an author than word of mouth recommendations from happy readers. Thanks again for your interest in Darynda's books!

Darynda Jones

www.daryndajones.com

Never Miss a New Book from Darynda Jones!

Sign up for Darynda's newsletter!
darynda.com/contact/mailing-list

Be the first to get notified of new releases and be eligible for special subscribers-only exclusive content and giveaways. Sign up today!

Also from DARYNDA JONES

PARANORMAL

BETWIXT & BETWEEN
Betwixt

Bewitched

Beguiled

Moonlight and Magic

Midnight and Magic

Masquerade and Magic

Love Spells

Love Charms

Love Potions

Samuel

CHARLEY DAVIDSON SERIES
First Grave on the Right

For I have Sinned: A Charley Short Story

Second Grave on the Left

Third Grave Dead Ahead

Fourth Grave Beneath my Feet

Fifth Grave Past the Light

Sixth Grave on the Edge

Seventh Grave and No Body

Eight Grave After Dark

Brighter than the Sun: A Reyes Novella

The Dirt on Ninth Grave

The Curse of Tenth Grave

Eleventh Grave in Moonlight

The Trouble with Twelfth Grave

Summoned to Thirteenth Grave

The Graveyard Shift: A Charley Novella

The Gravedigger's Son

THE NEVERNEATH
A Lovely Drop

The Monster

Dust Devils: A Short Story of The NeverNeath

MYSTERY

SUNSHINE VICRAM SERIES
A Bad Day for Sunshine

A Good Day for Chardonnay

A Hard Day for a Hangover

YOUNG ADULT

DARKLIGHT SERIES

Death and the Girl Next Door

Death, Doom, and Detention

Death and the Girl he Loves

SHORT STORIES

Nancy: Dark Screams Volume Three

Sentry: Heroes of Phenomena: audiomachine

Apprentice

More Short Stories!

About Darynda Jones

New York Times and *USA Today* Bestselling Author Darynda Jones has won numerous awards for her work, including a prestigious RITA®, a Golden Heart®, and a Daphne du Maurier, and her books have been translated into17 languages. As a born storyteller, she grew up spinning tales of dashing damsels and heroes in distress for any unfortunate soul who happened by. Darynda lives in the Land of Enchantment, also known as New Mexico, with her husband and two beautiful sons, the Mighty, Mighty Jones Boys.

Connect with Darynda online:

www.DaryndaJones.com
Facebook: facebook.com/darynda.jones.author
Instragram: instagram.com/daryndajonesofficial
Goodreads:
goodreads.com/author/show/4175419.Darynda_Jones
Twitter: @Darynda

Of Fate and Fire

by

Amanda Bouchet

The Kingmaker Chronicles meets modern-day New York City! Piers, an exiled warrior from Thalyria, finds himself in the Big Apple just before the holidays. The world and everything in it might be utterly foreign to him, but that won't stop Piers from helping to complete a vital mission for Athena and protect Sophie, a French teacher from Connecticut who's suddenly knee-deep in inexplicable phenomena, danger, and henchmen after an Olympian treasure that should never have ended up in her hands—or remained on Earth after the Greek gods abandoned it.

For Sébastien,

Thank you for brainstorming with me. You know how much you helped!

This is a novella in The Kingmaker Chronicles world

December in northwestern Connecticut—or what Sophronia Iraklidis affectionately called "The Boonies"

S NOW BEGAN FALLING as Sophie swept the crumbs from the last *Bûches de Noël* off the desks in her classroom. Decorating and eating a Yule log was her special treat for her French students as the semester wound down, and the kids who already knew her started talking about it from day one of the school year. They cared more about the sugar rush and being allowed to make a huge mess than about the Christmas dessert's origins, but if they could read her recipe in French and understand the directions and ingredients by the end of the lesson, she was happy.

Her mom and sister had come over to the saltbox house Sophie had plunged herself into debt for two years ago—in her defense, the little red colonial was irresistible—and helped her with the baking, filling, and rolling. She could make four cakes by herself in a weekend, maybe five, but ten was pushing it. Mom, Xanthe, and she had pulled up their sleeves and listened to old-timey Christmas music as they worked, sang along, and chatted. When Sophie started teaching, it became a holiday tradition for the three of them to "bake the boosh," as they called it, for Sophie's high-school French students, and she liked the idea of creating new traditions with her family just as much as she liked creating them in her classroom.

Of course, Mom and Xanthe tried to grill her about her love life. Since it was nonexistent, Sophie tossed the ball back at Xanthe, which her younger sister had appreciated about as much as stepping in dog poop with clean sneakers. Xanthe, at home for the weekend before college finals, might've had something juicy and exciting to share, but nope... As usual, her romance prospects were just as abysmal as Sophie's. For two women who couldn't deny being lucky in the looks department—they'd somehow inherited all the best parts of their striking, statuesque parents—they sure had trouble finding good boyfriends.

Sophie knew she was too tall, too blonde, too blue-eyed, too athletic, too traditional, too attached to her huge, overbearing family, too...everything. Xanthe was the same. The sisters were convinced they intimidated the hell out of men, which seemed to have one result: the normal ones ran away from them, and the sleazy ones hit on them. As far as Sophie could tell, there was nothing in between, which left her home alone most nights either with a novel in her hands, binge watching something on TV, or grading homework. Usually, a lot of all three.

During the weekend cake-making fest, Mom started talking about "baking the boosh" with grandchildren soon, and Sophie nearly spit out the icing she'd been tasting. The men of Pinebury, Connecticut were going to have to seriously up their game before she got anywhere close to having children.

And she doubted her four brothers, all older than she, got

the grandchildren comments from Mom, even though they were always popping in and out of Mom and Dad's house for something. Like dinner.

But her mother's half-joking comment had stuck with Sophie into her workweek, and for the first time since finishing her degrees and starting teaching, she almost wished settling down and having a family of her own didn't seem quite so far off or unrealistic.

Maybe it was her Greek roots—something genetically ingrained in her to crave a big, raucous, affectionate, opinionated family. Her grandparents on both sides had left a lot of their Greekness at the border when they immigrated to the United States, but the family had held on to tons of traditional recipes, a few bizarre superstitions, and unusual first names that had plagued both sisters since childhood. Her brothers got lucky. Alec, Seth, Jason, and Hector. Well, maybe Hector wasn't so lucky. Poor Xanthe. She had the worst of it. No one ever knew to pronounce the *e* at the end, like in Persephone.

At school, everyone just called Sophie *Mademoiselle*, including most of the other faculty. Sophronia earned her strange looks, and Ms. Iraklidis rolled off the tongue about as easily as cold peanut butter.

Humming "Jingle Bell Rock"—which had been stuck in her head since the weekend—Sophie gave the desks a squirt with the cleaning spray she kept in her desk and wiped them down before sweeping the floor of her classroom. Janitor Charlie already had enough work cleaning up after the students without her adding chocolaty fingerprints and powdered sugar to it.

When the kids decorated cakes, it was…an event. They'd had two Yule logs per class and free artistic license. Eating them was somehow even messier. But the *Bûches de Noël* had looked so pretty with the dark-chocolate shavings, red-and-green gumdrops, and little sugar-dusted marzipan pinecones. Sophie had taken pictures throughout the day and would add them to her *Album de l'année*, a scrapbook she made every year and kept in her classroom. She had six lined up now and planned on adding a career's-worth of them.

Finished at school, Sophie snagged her purse along with the two slices of cake she'd saved for her helper elves, Mom and Xanthe. She arrived home at the same time as a delivery person and signed for a package from her friend Aaron in California. He used to live in Michigan, but a big science technology company snapped him up right out of college— Aaron was a total genius—and he'd been there ever since, working for one of those *I'll-rule-the-world-someday-mwahahaha* types who scared the shit out of Sophie. They never cared about actual people.

Aaron wasn't like that, and she had no idea why he'd let himself get swept into an evil machine like Novalight Enterprises.

Sophie set everything on the hallway table and hung her bright-pink parka on the coatrack beside the door before making a quick detour to the kitchen to stick the cake in the fridge and put on the kettle. Curious as heck, she came straight back to the hallway and the package from Aaron, picking up the small, tightly taped-up box with her name on it.

She turned it over in her hands. Aaron and she had started

out as pen pals through a middle school writing project and kept in touch over the years. He'd always liked hearing about her odd Greek stuff, like pretend spitting on people to ward off the evil eye and protect loved ones. Their contact had whittled down to holiday cards lately, and even that was pushing it. They definitely didn't send each other Christmas presents. Or Hanukkah presents—Aaron was Jewish. Or any presents at all. They'd never even met in person.

Sophie split the tape with a letter opener. She dug through some wadded-up yellow notepad paper and found another box, this one about the size of a matchbox, plain but pretty, and made from olive wood. She picked it up and opened it.

Her eyes widened. Inside, a glacial-blue crystal glowed. Brightly. No, it *pulsed*. And it was *cold*. Its icy sting blasted over her like a winter wind. Goose bumps rose on her arms, and she shivered.

Confused and a little scared, Sophie set the wooden box on the table and backed away from it. The crystal seemed to shine from within. Was it poisonous? Radioactive? "What the heck, Aaron?" A weird vibration thrummed inside her, keeping her hair on end.

Grabbing the cardboard box the crystal arrived in, she looked through it for a card or note or something. Nothing.

No, wait. She frowned. Was that writing on the yellow notepad paper?

Sophie smoothed out one of the balls of paper and found half a word on it. Leaving the glowing crystal where it was, she took all the yellow papers into her living room and spread them out on the big Oriental rug her parents had given her as a housewarming present. The papers were a puzzle. Aaron had always liked puzzles. Sometimes, mostly during high school, he'd sent her letters in code, and it had taken her weeks to figure them out. This didn't look nearly as complicated, which meant he'd done it in a hurry.

In the end, heart racing and hands shaking, Sophie pieced together Aaron's message on the dozens of torn and crumpled pieces of paper. The scribbled writing only made sense to her in one order, and even then, she didn't understand much of anything.

Don't let Novalight get the Shard of Olympus. Too much power. Unstoppable. If it glows for you, you're Heracleidae. *I KNOW you are. The Greek gods are REAL. Contact Athena and GIVE THE SHARD BACK TO THE GODS OF OLYMPUS.*

Sophie swallowed hard, not wanting to believe a word she was seeing or how much danger Aaron must be in if he *stole* this precious, priceless, powerful object from his ambitious and frankly terrifying employer. How much danger *she* might be in.

Why would he do this to her? Because she had Greek origins? So did millions of people. Even Aaron, somewhere way back when on his mother's side. They'd thought it was cool they could both trace ancestors back to the Peloponnesus.

So then why...

She glanced toward the entryway for the millionth time in the past hour. The shard still glowed across the hallway from her, even brighter in the twilight of a December afternoon in New England. She felt the shard's cold, primordial power deep in her bones and knew that things weren't at all as they seemed. That maybe *she* wasn't.

Sophronia Iraklidis. Her first name meant sensible or wise. Her last name meant *son of Heracles.* Sure, she was a daughter, but whatever. The name was her father's. Most people knew the Roman version now—Hercules. The *Heracleidae* could be any of the ancient Greek hero's children and other descendants. And according to legend, he'd had plenty. Sophie's father had always insisted it was true, that they descended from *gods*, and she'd always thought he was full of it and kind of funny.

She wasn't laughing now.

In fact, she was terrified.

~ 1 ~

WHERE AM I? *Why am I here?*

Two questions Piers didn't like asking.

At least he still knew his name, although even that felt a little hazy at the moment.

Standing perfectly still, he looked from side to side, his eyes narrowing on the unfamiliar surroundings. *No*, not just unfamiliar. Totally and completely foreign.

Tension gripped him. His hands curled into fists. He couldn't process what he was seeing. He had no words for this.

All he knew was that he'd gone through a long dark tunnel before popping out into a bright, blaring, incomprehensible metropolis.

This must be why babies entered the world wailing. If he weren't a grown man and a warrior, he'd want to wail, too. This place was awful.

Thank the gods, infants didn't remember. Life was traumatic enough already, especially when you had no idea what was happening. Or why. Something Piers could attest to right now—and then some.

Words magically flashed on the side of a tall building. The

letters weren't familiar to him, but for some reason, he could still read and understand them instantly. *Welcome to the Big Apple.*

Piers frowned. That made about as much sense as the rest of this.

Sudden movement kicked up around him, in front and behind. He stayed where he was—apparently in the center of a wide, two-way thoroughfare. Strange, box-like units of transportation zoomed past without any horses or oxen to pull them. Many of them were yellow.

His heart galloping faster than a centaur, he turned in a slow circle. On all sides, buildings rose higher than any he'd ever seen in his full thirty-one Thalyrian year cycles. Endless windows climbed them, but instead of being deep-set, open arches, the windows contained reflecting glasses.

Suspicion stirred inside him. Windows like that were for people who hid things.

As he gazed skyward, an enormous, winged beast roared overhead, discharging a trail of smoke behind it. Another shiny sky dragon crossed the first one's path, leaving writing above him. Piers stared at the two intersecting tracks of cloud fire. Did that X mean something?

Surrounded by objects and sights he'd never encountered let alone imagined, he knew with absolute certainty he was no longer in Thalyria—or at least, not on the known continent.

Was he dead? Could this be the Underworld?

That didn't make sense. The Underworld followed a pattern. You arrived on the Plain of Asphodel. If you had your obol—he checked his pocket, feeling the hard little nugget of the coin there—you handed it to Charon for passage across the River Styx. On the far side of the Styx, you either walked into a normal, everyday afterlife, or you followed the golden path to a glorious one in Elysium.

This definitely wasn't Elysium. And Piers didn't think it was the Underworld. Surely, he'd remember *dying*?

So, what was this Big Apple? And how did he end up here?

And *gods,* the noise. The place stank, too. Like everything else here, it was a smell he didn't recognize.

Jaw tight, eyes sharp, and hands ready for battle, Piers stayed where he was on the little island in the middle of the loud, zooming boxes. Buildings loomed over him like giants upon giants. More dragons soared overhead, their skywriting unrecognizable to him.

Worry thumped in his chest. If he knew what qualified as a threat here, his assessment of the situation would be far easier.

The last thing he remembered was traveling toward Castle Tarva to try—*again*—to talk to his brother Griffin and Griffin's hot-headed harpy of a wife, Cat. They'd been holed up behind castle guards and high walls for days after successfully conquering a second realm and bringing Cat two thirds of the way to ruling all of Thalyria.

Fury stabbed Piers in the sternum. Cat's warmongering and lust for power had nearly gotten most of his family and friends killed. One friend didn't make it.

The knife in his chest twisted, and Piers growled, the sound covered by the terrible roar of the colossal city. Cat's fault. All of it.

Piecing his jumbled memories together made other things

fall into place. Everything until... Was it mere minutes ago? Hours?

Uncertain, he shook his head. His youngest sister Kaia had been with him on the road to Tarva City. They'd seen Griffin and Cat in the distance, riding out to meet them. He'd been so angry. So worried and angry. His family in danger.

What else happened?

He pressed his lips together. He had no idea. Where had that hot, dusty day gone? Where had *he* gone, for that matter?

There was no dust in Apple. Only stone, glass, and metal. Barely a tree. And no sun beating down, either. He shivered. It wasn't *I'm-going-to-die-within-minutes-without-shelter* weather, but it sure as Hades wasn't hot. Everyone wore odd, puffy garments that covered them from hips to shoulders.

And earlier today... He'd had a plan in mind. Something important. What was it?

Hating his lack of clarity, Piers tensed as the horseless wagons stopped and other people joined him in the center of the thoroughfare. They didn't remain where he was, though. They kept walking toward the far side to where a small brightly lit striding man glowed pure white in a black box. More strange magic. He studied it, trying to understand the utility. The pedestrians gave him a wide berth as they passed, the kind you gave an unsavory ruffian or a drunkard covered in his own vomit and urine.

Scowling, Piers sniffed himself. Not fresh, but no vomit and urine. It could be worse.

At least the people of Apple looked more or less the same as Thalyrians, except strangely dressed and all seeming to be late for something. They raced by, heads down, many of them holding little rectangles that might've been glued to their fingers. No one carried any weapons that he could see, which made Piers itch to hide the sword strapped to his back and the knives in his belt. Were they why people avoided him?

He glanced down at himself. Belted tunic, boots, dust. His forearms were all scratched up for some reason. He worked his mouth from side to side, his jaw sore and aching. Most of him hurt in one way or another. He touched a hand to his throbbing nose. Blood came away on his fingers.

Wondering who he'd fought and why, Piers licked blood off his teeth and spat it in the street. A woman looked up from her rectangle and cringed away from him. She hurried to cross with the others.

Piers watched her go with a prickle of annoyance. He didn't attract females like his brothers seemed to, but he knew he wasn't repellant, either. Well, he might be a little repellant at the moment. He'd definitely been in a brawl, and most women didn't like that.

Wait. Maybe she could answer some questions for him, such as how far this Big Apple extended, and where he could find the person in charge of it.

He leaped after her just as a gigantic four-wheeled wagon charged forward. It swerved to avoid him, screeching. Piers reared back toward the middle where he'd been standing, but another metal cart blared a horrible noise, squealing to a stop just in front of him.

His pulse pounding, he scrambled back to the center island, wondering who'd come up with this aberration of a system.

How did children survive here? He glanced at the small striding man. He was gone. A commanding red hand had overtaken the box he was in.

Ah. Got it.

White magic held the horseless wagons back so that people could hurry across this deathtrap. Red magic propelled the wagons forward.

The red sorcery swept the big yellow wagon that almost hit him away, but not before the man inside it made what Piers could only assume was a rude gesture out a half-open window, yelling at him in a language he somehow understood as if he'd been born to it. *Get out of the road, asshole!*

Piers stared after him. No one had spoken to him like that in enough time for him to forget how infuriating it was. Not only was he a prince now—because his family had gods damn conquered a realm—but he led *armies*.

His brow furrowed. That didn't matter here, though. In Apple.

Information flashed everywhere, magically appearing and disappearing from building walls and huge freestanding panels. Some of it glowed, as though lit from within by different colored fires. The Magoi here must be very powerful, more favored by the gods than even the magic-wielders in Thalyria.

Been in an accident? Call Mo. Mo's your man. He's got your back, especially if yours is broken.

All you can eat fried chicken! Every Friday night at Cluck Cluck's!

Reading and comprehending another language instantly would've been exciting if Piers had any idea what was happening. As it was, the strange ease just worried him.

Could this be Atlantis? Or Attica?

No, Attica lost its magic ages ago when the people there stopped worshipping the Olympians. Their lack of devotion caused their magic to dry up and the gods to abandon them. Only Athena supposedly still cared what went on in what she'd once considered *her* world.

Piers sent off a silent but heartfelt prayer to Athena, the deity his family worshipped above all others. He wasn't too proud to ask for guidance, especially since he was incredibly lost right now.

He turned and scanned the magic signage behind him.

Broadway is back and better than ever! Go to heartbeat-ofnewyorkdiscounttickets.com for the best prices the internet has to offer!

New and Used Cars! Delany's Dealership has what you want at the prices you need! Special deals for veterans!

That last gigantic parchment on the wall had incredibly realistic drawings of the horseless wagons. *Cars.*

Piers grunted, internalizing the information. They had a name now. So did other things as he looked around. Reading the magic panels somehow helped him tame some of the unknown. Not enough, though. He still felt more lost than found.

A woman ran into the street while cars still moved forward, darting in and out of them like a cricket between hooves. One made a gods-awful noise. Someone yelled an insult, but she didn't even glance over her shoulder. Piers narrowed his eyes. Did she not know about the glowing-man, red-hand magic? She'd get herself killed.

She raced onto the central island and came to a screeching halt not far from him. The cars on the opposite side from where she'd started didn't provide an opening, whizzing by too fast for this cricket to risk launching herself into them. She sucked down air, her face red from cold and exertion. Piers swiftly took inventory. Tall. Blonde. A good runner—although he wasn't sure how in those little boots that hugged her ankles. Her puffy pink upper body apparel rose and fell on quick breaths as she frantically looked behind her.

Something in the woman's wide, frightened eyes made Piers's chest tighten. He followed her gaze, seeing two men step into the street, risking the oncoming cars to narrow the gap to the target they were obviously chasing.

"Shit." She spun in a half circle, feverishly looking for a way off the central island that didn't involve certain death—or at the very least, broken bones. Grimacing, she gathered herself to run.

Piers's protective instincts roared to life, and he reached for the woman just as she decided to throw all caution to the wind. His hand closed around her upper arm, stopping her from rushing headlong into traffic. She whirled on him with a gasp.

Bright blue eyes shot even wider than before. So blue. They punched into him like twin lightning bolts and stole the breath from his lungs.

"Don't cross yet." He sounded just like the people all around him. Since that went far beyond luck, he knew it was sorcery. "You have to wait for the striding man to hold back the metal wagons."

She gaped at him. "What? Let go of me!" She started twisting.

Piers turned his grip to stone, even though he didn't want to hurt her. "You'll get yourself killed."

"*They'll* kill me!" She glanced sideways at the oncoming men.

"Why?"

"*Why?*" Her jaw dropped farther. "Because they're hired thugs, and someone paid them to!"

Piers nodded. That was good enough for him to defend her. She could be lying, but he didn't think so. Something about her bright, inflated attire and tight little head covering with the multicolored zigzags running across it told him she was trustworthy, while the burly men in dark clothing hunting down a lone woman probably weren't the good guys.

"Stay here. Stay behind me," Piers said.

Her delicate brows snapped together. "Why?" She glanced toward the two big warriors. "I have to get out of here."

Piers followed her frightened gaze again. He had to admit, the two men looked formidable. Large. Muscular. One was blond. The other had brown hair. Beyond that, they looked interchangeable. Same size, shape, and posture. He wouldn't have minded having his brothers with him right now, but since he was alone, he'd handle it.

"Stay," he repeated, letting her arm go with a little squeeze to help convince her.

She wrenched away from him. "I'm not a dog!" Her frosty indignation hit him at the same time as the cold wind barreling down the thoroughfare. She looked him up and down, probably seeing his goose bumps. "Just because you escaped from…I don't know…the set of *Gladiator* doesn't mean you get to order me around like some Roman general!"

While her words themselves made sense to him, Piers had no idea what she meant by any of that except for *general*— which was true. But right now, he didn't have time to deal with his questions. The warriors arrived on the central island, barely sparing him a glance as they focused on the woman.

"Nowhere left to run," the fair-haired one said with a satisfied chuckle.

Her breath shuddered. She backed toward the cars racing behind her, her golden hair flying on the wind, her eyes wide with terror.

"Stay!" Piers growled.

Her eyes snapped to his. She swallowed and stopped moving.

"Hand it over." The second man's flinty stare was as dark as his hair and clothing. "Give up the crystal, and you can stop running. Don't you want to go home to your family for Christmas? Or maybe we should pay *them* a little visit?"

Behind Piers, she sucked in a sharp breath. Anger sparked inside him, and he placed himself even more squarely in front of her.

"I think you should leave now," Piers ground out. The

hired ruffians could go back the same way they'd come, cars and all. The magic would change soon anyway. It alternated.

The blond jerked his chin at Piers. "This isn't your problem, Zorba. Go back to the Theater District."

The other man moved closer, holding out his hand and beckoning for this crystal the woman must have in her possession. "There's no reason for the same thing to happen to you as to your friend in California. He took something that wasn't his and sent it to you. He should never have put you in the middle of this. All my employer wants is the crystal. He doesn't give a shit about a French teacher from Connecticut. And you"—his eyes flicked to Piers—"get out of the way, asshole."

This insult was obviously in fashion. Piers was going to have to start using it. "No. Leave her alone and back away unless you want to lose that hand…asshole."

Piers didn't check over his shoulder for confirmation. If the woman wanted to hand over the crystal, she would. Instead, she'd led two ruffians on a difficult chase they were obviously sick of. Good for her. He smiled.

Both men's demeanors shifted. Half a step back, shoulders stiffer, necks shorter, brows lowered. Had they only just now noticed the broken nose and blood on his teeth? People weren't very observant in Apple.

Traffic stopped, and the woman bolted. *Zeus's bollocks!* Piers grabbed the blond who leaped after her, hauling him back with a snarl. The dark-haired one darted wide, jumped a barrier, and chased her.

The ruffian he'd caught had some combat training. It was

enough to break free and land a blow to Piers's ribs. The son of a Cyclops must've thought that was it, because he tried to sprint away again. Piers yanked him back and punched him in the jaw. The man stood there like an idiot, his mouth ajar. Since he was pressed for time, Piers shifted his weight and cracked his elbow into the man's nose. Not the most sporting of moves, but effective. The big thug squealed like a piglet. He clearly didn't know how to fight someone who could fight him back, which was probably why he was preying on a weapon-less and fleeing woman.

Pink's frightened stare and panicked little breaths struck him anew, right in the gut this time. Piers spun into a kick, slamming the man in the head with zero remorse and probably harder than he needed to. The lout crumpled.

"Asshole." Piers turned without a backward glance and ran after the dark-haired man and the woman.

He barely beat the magic and made it across the road before the glowing red hand propelled the traffic forward. He pumped his arms, pushing for as much speed as he dared with frost slicking parts of the hard ground. Cold air filled his lungs, biting his chest from the inside out. He grimaced. What a time to have an aching everything.

Just when he feared he'd lost her, Piers caught a flash of bright color. He followed, slipping once and nearly falling. People jumped out of his way. That was helpful, but not knowing the lay of the land infuriated him. In the blink of an eye, the blue-eyed beauty could disappear, and he'd have no idea where to go, or how to find her.

Or if she was still in danger.

Pink skidded around a sharp corner. Piers followed, sliding but somehow keeping his balance and coming out running. The woman moved fast, with nimble surefootedness even on the sometimes-icy surfaces. Piers barely gained on her. He didn't see the second warrior. *Warrior* might not be the term merited, but he wasn't about to underestimate the second ruffian-for-hire just because the first had been incompetent.

Pink ran as though Zeus's thunderbolts dogged her heels, and Piers chased her down another narrow street between high buildings. The times he lost sight of that bright, puffy garment and bouncing yellow mane made his pulse race even faster. She turned a corner up ahead, and he pushed himself to his limit, his lungs working like bellows. He turned the same corner just in time to see the dark-haired man pounce out at her from a side alley. The thug slammed into her, sending her sprawling across the pavement.

Piers didn't know where the word *pavement* came from and didn't care. His heart exploded with her scream. He drove into the man like a battering ram, shoulder first, head lowered. They scraped across the pavement. *Holy gods!* He exhaled sharply.

Piers blocked out the pain of several fresh, raw abrasions and jumped to his feet. So did the ruffian. The man drew a knife. Piers drew his sword.

The other man's eyes narrowed. "That's not real."

"Try it," Piers growled.

The coward tossed his knife aside and pulled out a smallish black thing Piers could only assume was a better weapon. But what kind? He didn't see a blade. Was this magic?

"Get down!" Pink screamed.

Piers ducked as she darted in and slammed a wooden plank into the thug's hand. The man dropped the weapon.

Piers kicked it aside. The black thing slid under a big refuse receptacle that smelled even worse than the rest of Apple. The hired thug leaped for his discarded knife. Faster by two steps, Piers swept it up first, finding himself in the pleasant position of being double-bladed while his enemy had nothing.

"Who the hell are you?" The man's eyes darted to the alley he'd just popped out of. If he thought Piers was going to let him run back down it, he had another guess coming. "Fucking lunatic."

"I like that name better than Zorba," Piers said.

Pink laughed. The sudden burst sounded a bit hysterical, but she still laughed, and Piers's chest swelled with it.

He glanced at her. "Does he live or die?" Piers figured he should give her the choice, since he didn't know much about this. He kept his blades pointed in the right direction.

Her frantic laughter abruptly wilted. "Wait? You're serious?"

Piers didn't kill for sport or enjoy it, but when it came down to eliminating threats that could come back to haunt him—or her—he was dead serious. He nodded.

"You can't just *kill* people," she whisper-hissed, moving closer to him. She gripped his arm, trying to move him away from the ruffian. *Warrior* was definitely a stretch, and Piers wouldn't credit the man with the moniker. Either of his younger sisters could've kicked this man's arse from here to Olympus. As for his brothers... Griffin would've snapped his neck, no questions asked. Carver would've gutted him.

Something deep inside Piers shifted uncomfortably at the idea of Griffin. But why? He'd been riding toward Griffin and Cat, and then… Nothing. He didn't remember what happened.

Pink tugged again, but Piers didn't budge. "Come on," she said, pulling harder.

"He was going to kill you." Piers wasn't the bloodthirsty sort, but he was tempted to make an exception if it meant keeping the woman safe. "He'll try again."

"No! I wasn't! I won't!" The man shook his head, raising his hands in surrender. "I just want the crystal. That's it. Then it's over."

"Can you give him the crystal?" Piers asked.

She shook her head, her blue eyes wide again.

"Then he has to die." The ruffian-for-hire had threatened her. Her family. What if she had a large family like he did? He would do anything to protect them.

Pink gaped at him. She did that a lot. "I don't know what circus decided to spit you out, or what wardrobe from Narnia, but life has *value* here. And murder has consequences. *You can't just kill people*," she insisted.

"Fine." Annoyed, Piers flipped his sword around and brought the hilt down on the man's temple. Thug Two slumped to the side, unconscious near the refuse pile along with the rest of the garbage. With any luck, he'd have forgotten this coveted crystal when he woke up as well as the blonde woman. He might also have forgotten his own name, but Piers didn't consider that his problem.

~ 2 ~

SOPHIE'S LIFE HAD gone from normal, if a little boring, to utterly insane. How could a handful of days make such a difference? She kept wondering if she'd blinked and woken up in an alternate reality—one where she had to flee her house in the middle of the night when she heard people breaking into it, where hopping from hotel room to hotel room in the city under false names didn't throw off the people chasing her, where she ran for her life—*repeatedly*, where incredibly hot—if really strange—men jumped in to help her for no apparent reason, where Greek gods were real, where...

She started breathing so fast her vision turned spotty.

Where she was about to have a breakdown.

"Breathe. Slowly." The man put his hand between her shoulder blades. He didn't press, or rub, or do anything, really, but the heat from his hand gave her something to concentrate on other than the ice-cold panic beating through her system.

Or maybe that was the freezing-cold crystal in her pocket. The Shard of Olympus. The darn thing wasn't a rock. It was an icicle. And it *never* melted.

Sophie drew her shoulders back and took a deep breath.

She shook herself out a little. The man let his hand fall away from her, and oddly, she missed it. But her pulse was getting back to normal, and they had to get the hell out of here. Novalight's lackey could wake up any second. Or more could come. He seemed to have an endless supply of minions.

"We need to go." She glanced from side to side at the miraculously still people-free alley, at a loss for what to do next after days of exhausting herself and her resources. She was a French teacher, not a millionaire expert at subterfuge.

Nerves made that odd, low buzzing hum in her veins again. It was almost electric. Her fingers tingled with it, heating. She shoved her hands in her pockets.

"Do you, um, have a place in the city?" Her latest hotel room had been compromised—hence today's run-for-your-life episode. She'd lost a toothbrush and her pajamas, but everything else was in her car, which she'd parked in a whole different neighborhood.

The man shook his head.

Darn. Maybe he was from New Jersey.

At least these two hired guns from Novalight Enterprises would think twice about chasing her down again. She'd given everyone who'd come after her the slip so far, but she'd never left anyone unconscious. She giggled.

"Are you well?" Her rescuer's gray eyes filled with concern for her. A cowlick lifted his black hair away from his forehead, even though parts of it were long enough to brush his cheekbones. He had a strong brow. A strong jaw. A strong—and swollen—nose. A strong everything, really. *Wow,* those arms were like tree trunks. And he didn't even look cold when he was wearing…a toga?

Sophie swallowed more inappropriate laughter. "No. I don't think I'm well. Are you?" He looked as if he'd been hit by a bus on the way to a costume party.

"I'm…not entirely certain," he answered.

Well, that made two of them.

He offered his arm as though they were headed to the dance floor for a waltz. Sophie automatically slipped her hand through the crook at his elbow, and they strolled out of the alley to the music of a police siren in the distance. Hopefully, the cops were after someone else.

When they'd put a block between themselves and the Novalight security agent, Sophie steered them east toward where she'd left her car the night before. She didn't know New York that well and had figured her car was safest in a central neighborhood. Hopefully, it was still there.

"Do you have a name?" she asked the man beside her. She was glad he'd stuck around so far and kind of dreaded the moment he'd leave her.

He shrugged.

"Does that mean no?"

"Everyone has a name," he answered.

"Well, can I have yours?" Sophie let a teasing note creep into her voice. This guy was taking being an enigma to a whole new level.

He pursed his lips. Full lips. Extremely kissable. A little tinged with blue now that he was cooling down from the fight. Poor guy. He wasn't dressed for December.

Sophie couldn't believe she was noticing her companion's

physical attributes when her life was in danger and stopping
Novalight from taking over the world was apparently at stake,
but it was too hard not to. Her rescuer was glaringly handsome, even all scratched and bruised, with a somewhat freshly
broken nose, and in his bizarre Caesar outfit. All that was
missing was the laurel wreath crown.

Her brows flew up. She stopped and pulled him to a halt.
"Do you not remember? Do you have amnesia or something?"
Judging by the state of him, she was pretty sure he'd been
knocked in the head a few times.

He tugged, moving them along. "Or something."

Sophie took a quick step to keep up with his long-legged
stride. "I'll give you a name, then. A temporary one—just till
you remember your own."

"Why?" he asked.

Why? "So I can stop calling you *The Man* in my head. Or
Caesar."

"Caesar's not bad." He'd never heard it before, but he liked
it.

She grimaced. "Please, no. Even dressed like that."

He glanced down at himself. "The people of Apple don't
like strong names?"

Sophie did her best fish-out-of-water impression. When her
throat stung from the cold, dry air, she snapped her mouth
shut. This was getting weirder by the second, and her current
life was already weird enough. "Okay. I'll call you Bob."

"*Bob?*" He couldn't have looked more incredulous if she'd
suggested Yoda or Spock.

"Bob's a good name," she defended. She had an uncle on

her mom's side who'd escaped the Greekness and ended up with Robert for a first name. Bob for short. Half her family couldn't pronounce it and called him Boob instead.

"Bob sounds like something you'd name a goat."

"Okaaaay. How 'bout Bill?" she suggested.

"Now I'm to be called the mouth of a duck?" His jaw visibly tightened. "Fine. I have a name. You might've heard of me, in which case, maybe you can point me in the direction of home." He took a deep breath. "Piers. Piers of Sinta. Gamma of the realm and third in line for the throne."

Sophie mashed her lips together, quelling a chuckle. Was he a performer? She appreciated a person so devoted to their craft that they stayed in character despite near-freezing weather and a very-real fight with a power-drunk megalomaniac's henchmen, but it was time to drop the act. "Yeah, I don't think I can point you in the direction of *The Realm*. Sorry. Got any other information, Piers of Sinta?"

His eyes narrowed. "Are you mocking me?" It didn't look like anyone mocked him often, or easily.

"Maybe." She squeezed his arm to ease the sting. "Sorry. I come from a big family. Teasing is second nature."

Something in his eyes both brightened and darkened. It was pure devotion. Worry. Sophie bit her lip, shocked by how hard that pained look made her heart flip over. "So, I guess you don't have amnesia?"

His reply was a low grunt. So helpful.

A moment later, he asked, "Do *you* have a name?"

"Why?" she teased. She couldn't help it.

His—*Piers's*—lips twitched. "So I can stop calling you Pink in my head. Or *The Woman*."

Sophie laughed. Considering how scared she'd just been, this whole conversation seemed surreal to her—as surreal as being helped by a gladiator named Piers of Sinta.

"It's Sophie. Sophronia Iraklidis."

"Now, *that's* a normal name," he said with a firm nod of his head.

Oddly, he was dead serious. "You're the only one who thinks so."

"The prudent and wise descendant of Heracles." He cocked his head, his coal-dark hair catching the first snowflakes as they fell. "If you're Magoi, why not defend yourself?"

Magoi? Sophie was so confused right now, it wasn't even funny. She was also getting really cold after the adrenaline rush and flat-out sprinting. She shivered. "Are you a classics professor? Were you at a reenactment or something?"

His nose wrinkled. "Or something."

They continued toward Midtown. Piers obviously liked his secrets. She decided not to push. She had a thumb-sized secret of her own icing a hole in her pocket right now. Her teeth started chattering, the cold attacking her from inside and out.

"We should get you to shelter." He made a beeline for the nearest shop. It was a frilly underwear boutique. Sophie nudged him one door farther down the avenue. As luck would have it, it was a men's clothing store.

"Do you have anything to change into?" she asked. Somehow, she knew he didn't. If it weren't complete insanity, she'd think this was a bit of a Thor situation, but instead of finding a mouthwatering Norse god with a magic hammer, she'd found a tall, dark, fine-as-hell swordsman who seemed to have gotten lost on his way to the Trojan War. The whole thing was starting to feel less strange by the second—which was strange in itself. Sophie supposed people were adaptable. Humans could get used to anything, good or bad.

Letting go of Piers's arm, she headed through the automatic revolving door. Piers stayed on the other side, eyeing the transparent glass with suspicion. His hand twitched toward his sword.

Sophie did the full circle and went back for him, the damp cold outside hitting her like a snowball to the face. She grabbed his arm, drew him into the little moving wedge, and they shuffled sideways together, nearly chest to chest, until she stepped out and pulled him into the blissfully warm shop. The heater was going full blast, especially near the entrance.

Piers held out his hand and moved his fingers, as though trying to catch the heat circulating around them. He glanced back at the doorway, his eyes narrowing. If the revolving door were a dragon, he would draw his sword and slay it. Forthwith. She grinned at him.

He frowned. "Are you from the Ice Plains? Is that where we are?"

It was certainly cold enough to ice things over, but Sophie shook her head. "I'm from Connecticut."

"Cunnetakit." His frown deepened. "This place is new to me."

"I'll bet." Her lips twitched. She didn't want Piers to think she was mocking him, but it was hard not to get a kick out of his mistrust of a revolving door and obvious fascination with central heating. "Do you have any other clothes?" she asked again.

He shook his head. "I wouldn't mind one of these puffy things everyone is wearing." He glanced at her pink parka. Hesitantly, he reached out and poked the zipper with a really tanned finger for New York in December. "Do you have another one of these?"

"Uh...not on me. But I'm pretty sure we can find something here."

"Do they accept coins?" he asked, glancing around the store.

She rolled her lips in to keep from smiling. "Well, you'd definitely need a lot of them."

His color rose. "I'm a little lost here...Sophronia. I might not have the means to pay." Piers started for the exit.

"Hold on." Sophie grabbed his arm and steered him toward the jackets. "You just saved my life. Literally. I have money in the bank, and the least I can do is buy you some proper winter clothing."

"You don't need to buy me anything." He looked as if she'd tried to call him Bob again.

"I know I don't *need* to, but I want to. Don't people repay debts in Sinta?" Wherever the hell that was.

A muscle ticked near his eye. "They don't pay a prince back for helping a lady in distress."

"Oh, you're a prince, now?" Sophie laughed. "That's right—third in line for the throne."

He glared.

"Sorry." She cleared her throat. "I'm sure you can pay me

back from the…eh…royal coffers. But let's just get what you need for now."

He finally agreed, but it was like pulling teeth from a rhinoceros. Sophie had never met a more stubborn man in her life.

Or one more sinfully handsome. They finished with Piers in a cream-colored V-neck sweater that hugged his strong torso (she could see his six pack—possibly eight—practically waving at her from under the material), dark cargo pants (he really liked all the pockets), solid leather boots (he did *not* enjoy laces instead of buckles), and a navy-blue winter jacket they'd had to get in XL because nothing else fit Piers's tall, muscular frame. Those arms and shoulders… Sophie had snuck so many looks her eyeballs were tired from all the bouncing back and forth.

She had to admit, Piers looked pretty darn amazing in the clothes they'd picked out for him, even though he definitely needed a shower. And probably a doctor. At the very least, some disinfectant. She'd dig a painkiller out of her purse when she could stop staring, although he'd probably refuse her "sorcery" and just look around for the next enemy to wallop.

Sophie hid her smile, especially because Piers didn't seem all that comfortable in his new outfit. He kept plucking at his sweater and muttering about how formfitting it was. She wasn't the only one gawking. The salesman was just as impressed with Piers's physique as she was. The salesman wanted to *be* him, even with all the cuts and bruises. It was cute and funny. They got ten percent off, which was even better.

When they'd finished, Sophie paid, although Piers didn't

look at ease with that, and he really didn't understand the idea of a credit card. She wasn't sure she should be using her card with an evil genius like Novalight tracking her for the shard, but what choice did she have? It wasn't as if she had oodles of cash stuffed down her bra. Besides, New York was huge. She'd stop at the nearest ATM to get money for a new hotel room and food, not use her card again for a while, and leave the neighborhood. Rinse and repeat, as necessary—or until her funds ran out. At least now, she had a bodyguard.

With Piers just outside in the now heavily falling snow— and discovering what *waterproof* meant for his new boots and jacket—Sophie pretended to have left something at the register and zipped back into the shop for another full change of clothing and some men's underwear in what she hoped was the right size. Piers had saved her *life*. He could at least get two outfits and some boxers out of it. While she did that, he went through the revolving door three times.

"Mastered the door now, have you?" she asked with a smile as she joined him on the icy sidewalk.

Piers gave the storefront a last long look. "There are some very interesting things here in Apple. The Magoi must be extremely powerful, and you don't even see them. I'm impressed."

She wasn't sure about the whole Magoi thing, but... "Apple? As in, the Big Apple?"

Nodding, he asked, "Is Apple just one city or the whole continent?"

Eh... "Actually, it's New York City. The Big Apple is just a nickname. And it's only a tiny part of the continent."

He stopped, his brow knitting. "This continent must be huge."

"North America?" She shrugged and tugged him along. Her car wasn't far now. "It's pretty big. And there are six more continents around the world."

"Seven whole continents?" He shook his head in apparent wonder. "And nothing is God Touched?"

"God Touched? What does that mean?"

"Beyond the known continent—where you can't go. No one goes there."

"Why not?"

Piers looked at her as though *she* were the crazy one saying crazy things every two seconds. "Because you don't come back."

She frowned in confusion. "Like...the Bermuda Triangle?"

"Like *everywhere* beyond the established borders."

It was Sophie's turn to stop and stare. Was he saying he came from a finite place hemmed in on all sides by some sort of deity or power? It sounded more like Asgard by the second—or at least how she imagined it after watching *Thor* for the she-wasn't-sure-how-manyth time. A woman had to entertain herself on weekend nights at home.

She took a steadying breath, trying to understand what Piers was saying. Acceptance had been growing all morning, but now, she started truly believing he really wasn't from here. Here, as in, Earth. He looked human enough, but what if the hot guy she'd apparently picked up between bouts of running for her life was an alien? What if this gorgeous façade was some kind of glamour, and he was actually slimy and covered in scales?

No. She refused to believe that. Or she didn't want to, which was different, but at this point, she didn't care. Besides, if Piers was an alien, he probably needed her help right now just as much as she needed his. "Okay. So, if you're not from Earth, where *are* you from? Where's this Sinta?"

"Thalyria," he answered.

Zero hesitation. Zero thought. Not that Sophie was an expert lie detector, but he seemed like he was telling the truth.

"I've never heard of it." She doubted anyone had.

He shrugged. "I'd never heard of Apple, either. Or...New York City." The words sounded foreign on his tongue.

Sophie slowly nodded, trying to hide the tremor in her hands as she readjusted her reality. Wasn't her reality already off-kilter enough these days?

But Piers wasn't making this up. She knew it somehow, just as she knew the ice shard's cold, hard power pulsing too close to her skin for comfort was no joke. None of this was.

"Yeah, you're definitely not from Earth. *Everyone* knows New York. It's just...one of those facts of life." She started walking again, deciding to embrace the weirdness rather than try to fight it. She needed to conserve her energy for the next time Novalight's goons came knocking, because she had no doubt they would. At least she and Piers fit in better now that his Caesar outfit was out of sight.

She almost missed the belted robe. Piers pulled that look off like a champ. He'd kept his sword, stuffing it and the whole harness contraption under his jacket. The hilt poked up over his shoulder now. That was still a bit conspicuous, but hey, this was New York. Tons of weird stuff happened here.

The knot in Sophie's stomach unraveled for the first time in days. Peace settled over her. Maybe it was wrong of her—she always figured she'd be more the *I-am-woman-hear-me-roar* type—but she was just happy not to be alone anymore. Piers seemed willing to help and didn't appear to have anything else to do. She'd called in sick for the last week of school and run away from Pinebury to try to keep her family out of danger, but Sophie wasn't used to being on her own, and she didn't like it. Sure, she lived by herself, but that wasn't the same as being *alone*. Especially at Christmas. It was almost as if Piers had been sent by the Powers That Be just when she needed him most.

The Greek gods are REAL.

Sophie shivered, a chill racing down her neck and spine. Suddenly, Aaron didn't seem so crazy with his whole *you're-Heracleidae, contact-Athena* message, and Piers might be the only thing that made sense. She had the glowing, ice-cold, apparently *magical* Shard of Olympus in her pocket. And by her side, she had a man who looked and acted as if he'd just popped straight out of antiquity, protecting her. What were the chances of that?

Don't let Novalight get the Shard of Olympus. Too much power. Unstoppable.

Worry shuddered through her again. In Greek mythology, the gods were always watching, manipulating, and interfering. They were violent, remorseless, jealous, horrible, and hella-messed-up for the most part, but sometimes, they did surprisingly good things. Like Prometheus. He defied the gods, stealing fire from Olympus and giving it to humans so that they could cook and keep warm with it. Sure, that brought down Pandora and her Box on humanity and got poor Prometheus chained to a rock in Tartarus, but his intentions were good.

Supposedly, Sophie's ancestor Heracles freed Prometheus from his punishment, but she had a hard time believing it—and everything else. She thought the Titan was still there—if *he* and *there* even existed—chained up and getting his immortal liver pecked out by a giant eagle every day.

And if he could take that, then she could take this.

Sophie pulled her shoulders back, finding courage from the myth her father used to tell her at bedtime. She'd take her current weirdness over Prometheus's fate any day, along with a bowl of soup, a hotel room that didn't have cockroaches, and a plan. Assuming she didn't need to check herself into a psychiatric unit, she had to figure out how to contact Athena, and she was pretty sure *Google* didn't have a workable answer to: *How do you call a Greek god.*

~ 3 ~

MORE SORCERY. THIS time, it was called a shower.

Piers stood under the hot stream of water, groaning. Sophronia probably thought he was dying in here, but he couldn't help himself. It was incredible. The whole room was. Human waste flushed away at the press of a button. Water turned on and off with a flick of the wrist. Bright lights that required neither oil nor wick. Soap that smelled just like something you could eat. He wanted to lick it off his arm and see what it tasted like. He didn't, but he was tempted. The bubbles were hard to resist.

The only thing intruding on Piers's bathroom bliss was wishing he could tell his family about the wonders of this place. His sisters, especially, would love it. Egeria would explore every nook and cranny, discovering how things worked. Jocasta would quietly observe until she produced a pearl of insight that would transform everyone's vision of things. And Kaia. His heart pinched. Her boundless excitement would be contagious.

Piers squeezed his eyes shut. Would he ever see his family again? Not only his three sisters, but Griffin and Carver, too?

His parents? He'd always lived in the middle of a constant throng of people, activity, and projects, and suddenly finding himself lost and alone—well, not quite alone—made it hard to breathe sometimes. The truth was, he didn't know how to get back to them—if he even *could* get back to them. And it was hard to make a plan when he didn't know where he was or why he'd ended up here.

The one thing he did know was that humans didn't travel between the gods' worlds. Gods could. Magical creatures could. But not regular people. Which meant something had gone colossally wrong.

Knowing where he was would help. "Earth" meant nothing to him, but maybe what Sophronia called her home world was just a different name for something he *did* know. It was too big for Atlantis, too pleasant—despite the ruffians chasing an innocent woman—for Tartarus, and he'd already ruled out the Underworld. It definitely wasn't Thalyria, even if he took into consideration the places he wasn't familiar with, such as the nearly inaccessible Ice Plains. The northern reaches of Thalyria weren't quite God Touched, but they were almost dangerous enough to be so, especially with Mount Olympus looming in the distance.

Which brought him back to Attica. Athena's favored world.

But that didn't add up, either. There was magic here. Wasn't there? Sophronia called it technology, but to him, it seemed synonymous so far.

"Are you okay in there?" she called through the door.

Piers reluctantly turned off the water. "Your turn in just a moment," he called back.

He'd been hesitant to go up into this hired chamber with her, but she'd insisted, and in the end, he didn't appear to have the correct currency to pay for his own space. He'd pulled out several gold coins, but Sophronia had just closed his hand back around them, her eyes wide, telling him they'd look into that later, when they had time.

"There's no hurry. I took a shower this morning." She paused, laughing a little. The sound made Piers's skin tighten. "Although, that was *before* I got tackled in a filthy New York alley."

It was suddenly hard not to picture her in this very shower. Warm water, soap and suds, hands gliding all over her wet, heated body. A low groan escaped him as he pushed at the sliding doors, opening them and stepping out of the box, the perfectly transparent glass now clouded with steam and moisture.

"Are you sure you're all right? You're pretty beat up. That nose…"

Cool air swirled over him, and Piers reached for the fluffy white drying cloth the hotel provided. His nose ached somewhat. The rest of him seemed fine. He didn't *look* exactly fine—the miraculously clear mirror in the bathroom told him so—but he'd been more broken and battered than this. War wasn't fun, which was why he'd wanted to avoid more of it.

He cinched the big cloth around his waist, frustrated. What wasn't he remembering?

Meet Griffin and Cat.

Avoid more bloodshed.

Protect his family.

Griffin and his ferocious wife had already conquered two realms. Did they really need a third? Cat's ambition would get his family killed. He needed to stop it—stop *her*—before it was too late.

He could've sworn he'd found a solution. What was it? And how had it landed him here?

He looked around the steam-clouded bathroom, but no clues jumped out at him. Since there were extra drying cloths, he used a second one to scrub his hair. "*That nose* is fine," he finally answered. "I fixed it."

"What? Like, yourself?"

He scoffed. "I hardly need a healer for that."

"Okaaaay." Pause. "Do you like the other outfit?"

Piers winced. Sophronia had purchased more clothing for him when he hadn't been looking. He blamed the wonder of waterproof and that fascinating zipper contraption. It wasn't that he was ungrateful. Sophronia was kind and thoughtful. He just didn't want her spending her money on him, and especially on useless items, such as those thin, tiny pants. What was a man supposed to do with those things?

"Everything's perfect," he called back. "Thank you."

He donned the same cargo pants and sweater he'd worn before. They were still fresh enough. Finished in the bathroom, he hung up the drying cloths, finger combed his hair, and pulled open the door. Sophronia was right on the other side of it.

He stopped short, warmth surging through him.

She sucked in a breath. "Sorry." She backed up a step. "It

was just... We were talking."

Desire stirred, a thudding pulse low in his abdomen. Piers hadn't stood this close to a woman who aroused him in what felt like years. Maybe it *was* years. He spent all his time between the knowledge temples and the battlefield. Women seemed to like a warrior better than a scholar, at least in his world, but he'd always leaned more toward scrolls than swords. And if he wasn't battling, he wasn't sure he looked up from ink and parchment often enough to even notice who might be around.

"Please." He sounded as if he'd swallowed a handful of rocks. "This is your room. Stand where you like."

"It's *our* room," she corrected. "At least, until we figure things out."

Piers nodded, tension sizzling inside him. There was only one bed, but he'd sleep on the floor. Or maybe he just wouldn't sleep. He'd keep watch. He'd watch her.

Well, he'd try not to stare, but he was pretty sure he'd fail.

"Shower time," Sophronia said brightly, gathering a little pink bag from the bedside table. "I'm going to wash that trash-filled alley out of my hair while you settle in, and then we'll... I don't know." She shrugged. "Make a plan? Too bad *Run-For-Your-Life 101* wasn't a class in college. In retrospect, it would've been way more useful than French literature."

Piers stared at her, fascinated and confused. "You say the strangest things. I don't know what they mean half the time."

"Oh. Well, men like a mysterious woman." She grinned and shut the door to the bathroom, leaving him on the other side, alone, and thinking only one thing: *he* liked Sophronia

Iraklidis. Probably more than he should.

THEY SAT IN what Sophronia told him was a *café*, drinking something called *coffee*, and eating something called *croissants*. It was good but not very filling. Piers wanted lamb, hearty vegetables, and thick brown bread. But since he was dependent on her little pieces of green paper to pay for their fare, he kept his mouth shut. He'd eat mutton the next time he came across it. Until then, he'd starve.

Snow still fell outside. He'd only seen snow once in his life before, on a scouting trip to the very north of Sinta during the rainy season. It had gotten cold enough for the rain to turn to snow. It hadn't stuck to the ground, as it did here, coating everything in a dull white blanket that seemed to suck all the sounds from the world. Inside the eating establishment, it was noisy in comparison, which made their low conversation seem even more intimate. He liked being ensconced in a private *tête-à-tête* with Sophronia. She'd said a few words in French to the waiter and filled Piers's mind with another complete language. If that wasn't magic, he didn't know what was.

Still, Sophronia denied being Magoi. Or knowing anything about magic.

"You can eat it, you know." She pushed her plate toward him. "Half was enough for me. I'm too stressed to be hungry."

Piers took what was left of her croissant and downed it in one bite. It was basically butter and air. How did a whole people survive on this?

Finished chewing, he wiped his fingers on a red-and-white

checkered napkin that matched the tablecloth. A little candle burned in a glass bowl on the table, brightening the afternoon gloom. It reassured him. At least not all the light and heat came from unknown sources.

"Thank you, Sophronia." He could eat ten more, along with a leg of lamb, but he didn't mention that.

"*Please*, call me Sophie. Sophronia is what my mother calls me when she wants to guilt me into something I'd rather carve out my left eyeball than do."

Piers chuckled. He didn't know how he could laugh when his life had been turned inside out, and Sophronia—*Sophie*—was in danger, but she made him smile. He liked that. "I'm comforted in the knowledge that mothers are the same the cosmos over."

She quirked a brow. "The cosmos, eh? I guess you really are an alien."

"If that means I'm not from here, then yes."

She leaned forward, whispering, "Are you human?"

Piers pretended to think about it. "The last time I checked, yes."

Her lips twitched. "Not Thor's long-lost brother, then?"

"I don't know this Thor. Where's he from?"

"Asgard."

Dismayed, Piers shook his head. Yet another world he didn't know about? He was starting to think his time in the knowledge temples wasn't well-spent. "I'm afraid I don't know Thor. Is he your friend?"

Sophie laughed. "I don't know him personally. I think you two would get along great, though, if you ever met."

Piers nodded. He was always interested in meeting new people, especially if they weren't out for blood.

"I can't help thinking I'm in Attica," he said. "Nothing else makes sense. Though...that doesn't make sense, either. We all know Attica lost its magic. Unless the tales aren't true."

Sophie blanched. "Did you say Attica?"

The word obviously struck a chord with her. Piers could tell by the way she stopped. "Why? What is it?"

"You don't mean the prison in Upstate New York, do you? The one where they had that horrible riot?"

He shook his head. "Attica isn't a prison. It's a world. Athena's favored world—or that's what we're taught."

She visibly swallowed. "Attica is the region around Athens. It's a big city named after Athena."

Hope jumped in Piers's chest. "Is she there? Is that her main residence? I mean, other than Mount Olympus."

Sophie couldn't have looked more shocked if Hades had just come knocking from the Underworld. "It's halfway around the world," she whispered, "and the Greek gods aren't...real." She trailed off, squeezing her eyes shut. They popped open again, blue fire in a pale face. "Or I *thought* they weren't real until a few days ago. All that's just stories and myths. Ancient history—here." She added *here* as though she couldn't quite believe there was anything *other*. Piers knew better.

"Athena is as real as you and I. It's the people of Attica that forgot her, not the other way around. When Atticans still worshiped the Olympians, the gods remained. And there was magic, not this *technology* you talk about."

Her brows drew together. "Is there a way to contact Athena?"

Wariness stirred inside him. "Why would you want to do that?"

Sophie sat back, failing to look casual when, clearly, that was her misguided aim. She had no reason to pretend with him, and Piers would have to make sure she knew that. "Just say...hypothetically. Is it possible?" she asked.

He didn't know where she was going with this, but he hated to disappoint her, especially with her thunderbolt-to-the-heart gaze so intense on him and her breath trapped in her lungs. "I've prayed to Athena all my life and never received an answer. But that doesn't mean she isn't listening. She answers those she chooses to."

Sophie grimaced. That caged exhalation gusted out in a rush. "So how do you make yourself heard?"

From out of nowhere, a surge of dread rose inside Piers. It came with the echo of a chant, indistinct in his mind, but gut-wrenching and awful. Somehow, he knew down to the very marrow of his bones that finding the words and saying them aloud led to heartbreak and loss.

"You pray. The gods come if and when they want." The words scraped past the stranglehold some memory had on his throat. Days of studying... Weeks of searching... But for what?

Whatever he'd discovered could only be bad, considering his visceral reaction to it. His body must remember something his brain didn't. Piers hated that.

He cleared his throat. "Only those they choose to favor ever see or hear from them. Men aren't meant to have a say in it."

Sophie cocked her head. "What about women?"

"*Humans* aren't meant to have a say in it." Piers wasn't sure how, but he knew bending those laws would be bad.

His last, indistinct moments in Thalyria tried to take shape in his mind. They stayed vague and just out of reach, slipping and sliding until he lost them again. He nearly growled in frustration. Why couldn't he remember? What had Cat done to him? Because he had no doubt his brother's hot-headed wife was the one who'd broken his nose and left him bruised and aching. But why? Cat was a self-centered brute, but she'd never attacked him before. So...

What had *he* done?

The question churned like spoiled meat in Piers's stomach. He set it aside for now. From the look on Sophie's face, her troubles were just as bewildering and pressing as his.

"What's going on, Sophie?" He reached for her hand across the table. If he couldn't solve his own problems, maybe he could help Sophronia with hers. "Why this sudden interest in gods you think are pure mythology? They're not, by the way." He had to add it. The urge was too strong. "Tell me what's wrong, so I can try to help." He was beginning to think he was here for that—for her—because nothing else made sense.

Sophie chewed her bottom lip, which Piers tried hard not to find distracting. "It's why those men were chasing me. A friend of mine sent me this ice shard. He works"—she gulped down a quick breath—"*worked* for a completely unhinged billionaire scientist who must've dug it up from somewhere. Maybe Mount Olympus." A distraught laugh tangled in her throat, and she lowered her voice. "My friend said it's super powerful. Or else, it *makes* people powerful. I'm not really sure. He sent it to me because I'm supposedly vaguely related to Heracles, and he somehow thought that meant *I* could give the Shard of Olympus back to Athena. But I can't. I don't know how."

"The Shard of Olympus?" Piers's interest exploded, and he was already interested enough.

"Right?" A harder laugh burst from Sophie. She shook her head. "A few days ago, Athena and the rest of the Olympians were just stories to me, and even if they're real, you don't just dial up a goddess and say, 'Hey girl, come get your shard back.'"

Piers wondered if *dialing up* was the equivalent of praying here. "Can you show it to me?" he asked.

Sophie sliced her head back and forth. "Not here. *It glows.* Those hired guns were calling it a crystal, but I think it's ice that never melts. It's so freaking cold." She shivered from head to toe.

Piers tightened his hold on her hand, instinctively trying to warm her. "I've seen something like this before. My brother Griffin's wife Cat has a necklace made from the same type of ice shard from Mount Olympus. It shores up her already considerable power when it's depleted and amplifies it when it's not."

"Power...as in...magic?" Sophie wrinkled her nose. She didn't *want* to believe. Piers could tell her skepticism wasn't stopping her from starting to accept the truth, though.

He nodded. "I don't think even Cat knows this about her necklace, but I've done some research. Those rare chunks of

Olympian glacier that never melt? It seems they've been struck by Zeus's thunderbolt. The intensity of the magic hardens them to rock—crystalizes them, in a way—and infuses them with a small portion of the primordial power the Elder Cyclopes used to forge Zeus's lightning bolt. But magic only works where magic exists. It's strong in Thalyria. Here, it's supposed to be long gone."

"Then what does it mean if there's magic in the ice shard?" Just from her low, trembling question, Piers knew there was—and that Sophie had felt it.

Unfortunately, he wasn't sure. "It must mean it's very powerful. Maybe from Zeus's first lightning strike. Or..." His nostrils flared. *Could it be?*

"What?" Sophie asked.

"What if your shard goes all the way back to powerful, new magic created not for just one god but for *three*? The Titan War happened here, on Attica. Zeus and his brothers were instrumental in toppling the Titans—Zeus with his lightning bolt, Hades with his invisibility helmet, and—"

"Poseidon with his trident," Sophie finished for him. "What if the shard contains magic from all three gifts from the first Cyclopes?"

Piers was thinking the same thing. And it was a frightening concoction of power. "Then it would truly be *the* Shard of Olympus—one of a kind and made when the brothers stood back-to-back, conquered the Titans, and forged a new kingdom."

"Holy shit." Sophie gaped at him.

"That might explain how it still holds magic after thousands of years in a place with none," Piers said, starting to worry about the lack of color in Sophie's cheeks. "Power like that doesn't fade," he added. "It's just too strong."

"I knew this was bad." Her fingers curled around his, gripping hard. "In the wrong hands, it could be a weapon. A terrible weapon."

Piers squeezed her back. "But yours aren't the wrong hands." He'd seen enough to know that. "The instructions were to give it to Athena?"

She nodded. Her eyes ate up half her face, and a visible swallow tracked down her throat.

"Then that's what we'll do," Piers said.

Sophie nodded again, less hesitant this time. Her expression blared fear, but something else, too. Strength. Determination. A woman who didn't give up without a fight—who maybe didn't give up at all.

Pride welled in him. His Sophronia was a warrior. And suddenly, this world didn't seem so foreign to him. "What do you feel when you touch it?" he asked.

"Cold." She shuddered.

"What else?"

Reluctantly, Sophie added, "A vibration. A kind of constant buzzing, deep down."

Magoi. He knew it. Maybe once she understood her magic, and with the help of the Shard of Olympus, she could send him home.

The thought twisted inside him as though wrapped in thorns, and Piers drew her hand closer across the checkered tablecloth, keeping it tucked in his. "We'll figure this out. If

Athena wants that shard off this world, she'll come for it. We just have to make it easy for her."

"You really think so?" Hopeful now, a little breathless, her cheeks gaining some color again, Sophie outshined everything in the room.

Piers could safely say she blinded him, and he was used to the dazzlingly bright Thalyrian sun.

He nodded, his fascination growing by the second. The urge to touch her, comfort her, *protect* her, intensified, and he reached for her other hand as well. Holding them both felt right—righter than the idea of letting them go. "The shard doesn't belong here. Not anymore. It must've been buried. Or forgotten and left behind. If it made its way to *you*, there's a reason the Fates wove it into your life." *Into mine...* "You must be able to connect with it somehow. Or connect to the gods."

"The Fates..." Sophie's brow furrowed, but then she nodded. Something about the idea of destiny seemed to calm her down. "Thank you, Piers of Sinta. Gamma of the realm and third in line for the throne."

Piers wasn't extraordinarily fond of being teased, but if it put a glimmer back in Sophie's blue eyes, he could get used to it. Gruffly, he muttered, "You're welcome."

She grinned. "It seems crazy, but I'm starting to think Athena put you in my path. Or maybe the Fates did."

Piers thought it was likely some combination of both. Athena could just as easily have knocked on Sophie's door and asked for the shard, but the gods didn't work like that. They watched events unfold and set possibilities into motion. Then they saw what came of things, good or bad. There was destiny, and there was free will. It was the sticky, confusing, interlocking mix of both that fascinated the Olympians as they observed, sometimes neglecting, and sometimes nudging, from their mountaintop.

"I'm really glad you're here." Sophie's thumbs swept over his knuckles and back again, her skin silky-soft and warm.

Piers's flesh tingled, his blood heating to her touch. Their eyes met, and his pulse sped up. He couldn't remember the last time he wanted to throw all caution to the wind, wrap his arms around a woman, and kiss her.

Emotion expanded in his chest. He wanted to be the man Sophie turned to for more than just the Shard of Olympus, and the thought simultaneously elated and terrified him. It pierced his heart and stuck there like a barbed arrow from Eros. She'd become precious to him too quickly for anything other than the Fates to be steering this strange and unexpected course. Then, what happened when he found his way back to Thalyria and his family? What happened if he *didn't*? In both scenarios, he lost.

His gut churned again, tight with worries. Piers was sure of one thing, so he focused on it.

"I want to help you, Sophie." He wouldn't fail her, no matter the cost. "If there's a way to contact Athena, we'll find it. I promise." He might have a sword strapped to his back—and gaining him odd looks from the other restaurant patrons—but he was a researcher and a scholar above all else. He'd investigate; he'd find a solution; he'd do whatever needed to be done. Then Sophie would be safe.

"As insane as all this sounds, I believe you. And I'm not half as scared anymore. Two is stronger than one, and together is way better than alone." Sophie's smile punched Piers right in the chest and left him short of breath.

Sophronia's was a thousand-ship smile, the kind nothing was off-limits to protect. His heart drummed. His world shifted.

So, this was how lightning struck.

"Then consider me your other half," he rasped.

Her smile gained a playfulness he hoped she'd never lose. "I might not be great at math, but don't two halves usually make one?"

Exactly.

Sophie finished her coffee, her spirits brighter than before, and Piers kept watch with new vigilance. The Olympian treasure she had in her possession was no laughing matter, and whoever wanted it would send more soldiers. He'd be ready when they did.

Not long after, Sophie caught the waiter's attention and asked for the bill—apparently, a multipurpose word.

Piers narrowed his eyes. Luckily, he hadn't let her call him *that*. It was almost as bad as Bob.

~ 4 ~

"IT'S JUST A small detour," Sophie insisted, linking her arm through Piers's and tugging him in the direction of Rockefeller Center.

Man, this guy was stubborn. When he set his mind to something, he was like a donkey with a carrot. Only way hotter. He smelled good now, too. Too good. She kept trying to sniff him, and she wasn't usually a sniffer. Was anyone? She'd have to read up on pheromones. There was definitely something like that at work here. She'd seen a book back home in the window of her local bookshop: *Alchemy and Opposite Sexes, The Mystery of Attraction*. That was what she needed—information. Maybe it would explain why she couldn't stop staring.

"Don't you think we have more important things to do?" Piers grumbled.

Yes, in fact, she did. But she'd been on the run for days, scared out of her mind, and totally alone. Right now, she had company, felt almost safe for the first time since Aaron's package turned her life upside down, and was actually starting to believe there might even be a way out of this mess that didn't involve someone from Novalight Enterprises prying the Shard of Olympus from her cold, dead hand. Sophie needed a break, so she was taking one.

"You'll love it. I swear." Who didn't like a little holiday sparkle? "Christmas is in two days. You've gotta see the tree all lit up."

"Fine. Shiny tree. *Then* the ice shard." Piers gave in, letting Sophie drag him beyond their hotel. He glanced back at the revolving door as if he wanted to give it a whirl. Earlier, he'd gone through one at a department store just for the hell of it. She'd tried really hard not to laugh, especially when he did the whole circle a second time to get a better look at the cheery window displays. That was when she knew they had to do the most touristy thing in New York City in December.

"Good. You won't regret it. I'm not letting you get sucked back to wherever you came from without seeing Rockefeller Center at Christmas." A stab of apprehension tried to dim Sophie's smile. She didn't like the idea of Piers suddenly getting plucked from her life by some unknown force. In half a day, she'd come to rely on him for safety, appreciate his insight, and crave his company. Talk about quick work. Her rational mind had whiplash.

She wasn't sure how—possibly all those paranormal romance novels and fantasy TV shows—but she'd adjusted surprisingly quickly to the idea of Piers being from a different world where they worshipped the gods of Olympus. Aaron's whole *the-Greek-gods-are-REAL* thing probably helped. And the glacial-blue shard *glowed* for her. She'd inspected it from top to bottom, her fingers turning numb, and there was no reason for the chunk of ice to shine, let alone not melt into a puddle. Piers said it was magic, and she believed him.

As to why it glowed for *her*... Apparently, that had something to do with her being *Heracleidae*. It really wasn't such a stretch to accept that she truly descended from Heracles. Herakles to Greeks. Hercules to the modern world. Sophie didn't believe—or rather, *hadn't* believed—a lot of that stuff about him completing his twelve herculean labors and becoming immortal, but she'd always thought he was a real person who'd become famous thanks to a certain number of monumental exploits. Heracles supposedly had sex with the fifty daughters of King Thespius in one night and impregnated every single one of them. They gave him fifty sons, and that was on top of his other children, so it wasn't crazy to think there were Iraklidis all over the place. Maybe they didn't all have the name, like she did, but they were out there. She knew that. Besides, as insane as everything sounded, she didn't feel unhinged. Piers, for all his weirdness, didn't seem unhinged, either. And if they didn't mutually require a psychiatric hospital, then they needed to figure out how to contact Athena and give her the Shard of Olympus.

Okay, that sounded a little crazy. But she was going with it.

Sophie savored the smell of roasting chestnuts and smiled to herself as they walked, light snow falling around them. She wasn't alone in this anymore. The Olympian gods had sent her a guardian angel. She didn't care that she was tragically mixing her religions. It felt right to her. *Piers* felt right. Like destiny.

"Do you think I'll get *sucked back?*" he suddenly asked her. "To Thalyria?"

"I don't know." It was on the tip of Sophie's tongue to say she hoped not, but that would be incredibly selfish. She had no idea what Piers wanted, but it probably wasn't to be stuck on a foreign planet helping a woman he'd only met a few hours ago. She was honest, though, so she added, "If you do, I hope we figure out how to get the ice shard to Athena first. I don't think I can do this on my own." She didn't have the first clue where to start. A trip to the Acropolis? Manhattan was expensive enough. Last-minute tickets to Athens would break her bank account.

The helplessness she'd been feeling for the last several days flared up again, though not quite as bad. At least her family was safe in Pinebury, but she couldn't go back until Novalight knew she didn't have the shard. She couldn't risk her family being used against her. She'd hand that magic icicle over in a New York minute, global consequences be damned. Unfortunately, there was nothing stopping Novalight's hired guns from going to Pinebury anyway and using her family as leverage. Just because they hadn't done it yet, didn't mean they wouldn't. Which meant she and Piers had to resolve this fast.

Sophie shivered. Piers stopped and pulled up her hood even though she had a hat on. Her heart tumbled. She murmured a thank-you as he gazed down at her, his gray eyes dipping to her mouth. Warmth coiled through her, and her pulse sped up. Sophie's lips parted. She hadn't been kissed since a not-too-tragic date ages ago. The kiss had been utterly uninspiring, and she'd felt so much *nothing* she'd started to wonder if her girl parts were broken. But lack of use apparently hadn't damaged anything. All Piers had to do was look at her like he was thinking about kissing her and a hot thump sprang to life between her legs.

"Sophie." The soft, low rumble of his voice caressed something deep inside her. He brushed a wisp of hair off her face.

Heat shivered down her spine. She swallowed. "Yes."

"Your nose is very red."

She blinked and burst out laughing. "Like Rudolf?"

Piers frowned. "I don't know this Rudolf."

"Well, he has a very red nose. He's also a reindeer, which—before you ask—is an animal with four legs and antlers."

"What makes this animal special? Does it breathe fire? Spit poison saliva? Shoot venomous darts from its tail?"

Her eyebrows crept up. "Wow. Thalyria sounds like fun."

Piers cracked a smile and started walking again. "Well?"

"Okay, I'll give you the scoop on Rudolf." Sophie slipped her arm back through Piers's. She liked it there. "He brings holiday cheer and helps deliver presents to children around the world. He's also totally made up—a myth. And our version of magical, I guess, because he flies and has a glowing red nose. Regular reindeer—feet on the ground, no lightbulb noses—are real, though. They're super cute, but I think they're kind of smelly."

"Have you encountered one?" he asked.

"I've never been up close and personal with a reindeer. I hit a regular deer with my car once, though." It got up and ran away, but she'd been so shaken she'd driven well under the speed limit for days.

Piers's brow drew low. "Were you all right?"

"I was sad. I was scared I hurt it."

"More worried about the animal than yourself..." He seemed thoughtful all of a sudden. "Life *does* have more value here. Killing is so common where I come from. People war, and people die. That's just the way of it."

"It sounds..." *Awful.* "Harsh."

"Maybe it's because the Olympians abandoned this world. You seem to have done better without them."

Sophie winced. "You wouldn't think that if you watched the six o'clock news."

He frowned. "The what?"

"I'll explain later." She squeezed his arm. They'd almost reached the most spectacular winter sight in the city. "Look." She pointed as the massive ice-skating rink and huge Christmas tree came into view. Snow swirled in the air, bells jingled somewhere, and all the bright, colorful lights looked festive and wonderful.

Sophie sighed in happiness. Not *everything* was a mess. This was just as it should be.

"Good gods." Piers stopped and stared. "That's...impressive."

"Right?" Excited, she tugged him closer. Rockefeller Center at Christmas took her breath away, and she'd seen it before, both in person and on television. "It's not magic, like you have where you're from, but I think it's pretty magical."

Nodding, Piers wrapped his arm around her shoulders while he took in the plaza. As one, they inched closer together, eliminating the gap between them. Sophie's heart beat faster. Excitement thrummed inside her. She couldn't imagine so easily touching anyone else, but she looped her arm around Piers's waist and leaned her head against him. She loved how towering he was, how broad, and how freaking warm on a winter afternoon. He was the very definition of tall, dark, and handsome.

She relegated her worries about the shard and everything else to the back burner and just let herself enjoy the closeness, her body a riot of sensations she hadn't felt in forever. And never this strongly. Sophie was starting to think she was going to try to have her wicked, wild way with Piers back at the hotel room, which would probably shock his old-fashionedness into the next world over.

And what would that be? Atlantis? She would've laughed at the thought if she hadn't been so breathless.

It took a huge effort not to turn and jump on Piers, lips first. She'd never trusted someone so completely this quickly. Add to that trust a blood-sizzling attraction, and her girl parts hadn't only woken up; they were clamoring for action.

"It's beautiful. Stunning. Special." Piers hugged her tighter, his jaw pressing against her forehead. Somehow, Sophie knew he meant her just as much as Rockefeller Center. Her heart clenched, and the idea of Piers being torn from her life just as quickly and surprisingly as he'd entered it suddenly made her want to hold on to him with all her strength and in any way possible.

Maybe it was the harrowing circumstances. Or maybe that stray thought she'd had about destiny hadn't been just a stray thought. If the Olympian pantheon Piers worshipped had a hand in this, the Fates probably weren't far behind. In fact, they were probably well ahead of everyone.

Sophie breathed Piers in, along with the crisp scents of pine boughs and winter. Mulled cider. Rink ice. Snow and a hint of exhaust. It was New York, after all. Piers's big hand squeezed her shoulder, half comforting and half an erotic zap she felt deep in her belly. She wanted his hands on her. She wanted them everywhere. Her whole body tightened. Luckily, she was good at multitasking, because she'd just added *Seduce Piers* to her immediate agenda.

A red light flashed, distracting her. She glanced down. The little dot stopped on her chest, right over her heart. Her pulse exploded. "Oh my God," Sophie breathed out, her muscles freezing solid.

"What is that?" With his free hand, Piers swiped at the little red spot on her parka. He tried again, scowling.

"Someone's aiming a gun at me." Fear shattered her voice down to a broken whisper. "They're hidden somewhere. A rooftop. A window." Only her eyes moved as she scanned the buildings in front of them, seeing nothing. "They can kill me from a distance."

"Like with an arrow?" Piers's sharp gaze followed hers to the rooftops. His arm tightened around her shoulders.

"A bullet. More powerful than an arrow. Faster." She'd be dead before they even heard the shot go off. A tremor went through her. And here, she'd been feeling almost safe. *Stupid.* She should've stayed out of sight. She should've run to a new city. *Stupid. Stupid.* Panic surged, turning her heart into a sledgehammer.

Something sharp pressed into the small of Sophie's back.

Her eyes shot wide, and she sucked in a breath.

"You're almost making this too easy," a rough voice said behind her. "Give me the crystal, and you walk away from here. No mess. No questions. That's what we all want, isn't it?"

Piers dropped his arm from around her shoulders with such a hard downward strike that Sophie heard the knife clatter to the pavement. He yanked her hard at the same time, whirling her away. She dove behind the barrier overlooking the skating rink.

"Piers! Get down!" she shouted. A shot could go off any second. Why didn't it? Too many people? Too conspicuous? If a shooting in the heart of New York City at Christmas ever got traced back to Novalight Enterprises, it would ruin a man already disliked by millions.

She glanced anxiously around the plaza. Maybe the gun was just to scare her into cooperating, and the man with the knife was supposed to retrieve the ice shard.

Piers stood between her and Novalight's agent, the laser dot still there and trained on the back of his head now. The sight of it made her stomach flip over. Piers gripped the knife wielder's forearm. He squeezed so hard the man grimaced. A second later, Sophie heard a crack.

The hired gun gasped. "Holy... Fuck!"

"Come after her again, and I'll break your neck instead," Piers growled. He threw her assailant six feet using nothing but one hand and the man's mangled forearm.

Sophie's jaw dropped. People all around them screamed and scattered. She didn't know whether to be impressed or horrified. She decided on impressed. Who needed Thor? She had a freaking gladiator protecting her.

Piers turned to her just as the dreaded shot finally rang out. He winced and grabbed his shoulder.

She lunged for him and pulled him down beside her. "Are you hurt?"

"Not much." He shoved her in front of him and propelled her along the barrier, both of them keeping low as they ran away from the ice rink and melted into the crowd as soon as possible.

"I'm looking at that *not much* back at the room." Her breath came hard and fast, the cold air stinging her lungs as they fled Rockefeller Center.

They should never have left the hotel. First, it was to eat, but she could've ordered room service, even at the exorbitant prices. Holiday sparkle definitely wasn't required for the body to function. Neither were croissants. She'd just wanted one.

Sophie hated herself and her choices as they sped back to their room. She'd decided to play tour guide in the middle of a crisis, and Piers got shot for it. *Shot!* This wasn't a game. And this wasn't her life. Her life was teaching French to semi-motivated high-school students, cooking moussaka with her mother who lived practically next door, and too much Netflix.

"This isn't my life," she said aloud. "It can't be."

Piers slowed at the revolving door to their hotel, pulled her through with him, and dragged her into the lobby. His new jacket had a hole in it. She touched the dark material, finding it hot and wet. *Blood.* Spots swam in Sophie's vision.

"Easy now." Piers swept her into his arms. He kicked the button for the elevator. *Kicked it!* Still holding her, he strode into the first box that opened, elbowed the knob for the twelfth floor, and waited, hardly even breathing hard while she hyperventilated.

"You've been shot," she panted.

"Hmmm."

"*Hmmm?*" Sophie tried to slip out of Piers's arms, but his grip tightened. "We need to go to a hospital!"

"If this hospital is an eating establishment with meat, then I agree. Otherwise, we're going back to the room to look at the Shard of Olympus."

Sophie gaped at him. She'd gaped so much today she feared the expression would freeze on her face, and she'd be gaping forever. "Hospital food sucks," she said as the elevator doors opened.

Piers strode toward their room at the end of the hallway. "Then we'll avoid it. Croissants aren't bad, but I'd need about fifty more of them."

Sophie stared at his strong profile, starting to feel a little less woozy and a little more focused. The man needed protein. She should've known that just from ogling his fit, hard-as-a-rock body. "I'll order room service."

"Will there be cheese?" he asked. "Bread? Lamb?"

"I don't know." She'd been living off coffee and soup—and half a croissant—for days now. "I'll show you the menu."

He nodded. "Choices. Excellent."

"How can you look so normal when you have a bullet in you?" The men she knew would've been squealing in agony. Even her brothers, and they were big and strong—*Heracleidae*, like she was.

But then, she also didn't know anyone who could casually break a man's arm and throw him across the sidewalk. *One handed.*

"It's not in me," Piers said. "It went straight through. I saw it hit the pavement."

"Oh." Sophie swallowed, woozy again. She'd fainted twice in her life, both times at the sight of blood. It was a good thing she wouldn't have to operate.

~ 5 ~

PIERS WANTED TO look at the Shard of Olympus. Sophie wanted to clean his wound. Since he was apparently incapable of saying *no* to her, he found himself seated on a stool in the brightly lit bathroom getting something called saline solution spewed all over him. It didn't feel good.

"It's nothing," he mumbled. This wasn't the first time something had gone in one side of him and come out the other. It happened. That was war.

As if to echo his thoughts, Sophie murmured, "Jesus, you're covered in scars."

"Piers," he corrected, stung she'd somehow forgotten his name. That hurt more than this ridiculous little bullet wound.

She paused, then laughed. "I know—Piers. It's like saying *holy shit* or *oh my God*. Honestly, I was taught not to say any of those things, but I slip sometimes. Maybe you have an equivalent from Thalyria I can use. It'll be totally guilt free, which I would *love*."

He thought about it, trying not to get distracted by Sophie's light, delicate touch as she patted his torso dry with a clean towel. "Well, there's *oh my gods*—plural. Everyone uses that, and there's no guilt involved. A friend of mine—Flynn—he likes *Hades, Hera, and Hestia!*"

"That's catchy." Sophie set aside the towel and picked up another bottle from the counter. "Maybe it's the alliteration."

Piers shrugged, immediately regretting it. His wound wasn't terrible, but it was still there and aching.

"Don't move," she scolded. "Now, brace yourself. This might sting." She squirted his shoulder with an ice-cold liquid that nearly sent him flying from the room.

"Zeus's bollocks!" Piers roared. He clenched his teeth. It was all he could do to keep his backside on the stool while the fires of Hades consumed his skin. "What in the Underworld is that?"

"Ooh, I like those. *Zeus's bollocks! What in the Underworld?*" She squirted him again, this time from the back, pushing his hand away when he tried to probe his shoulder. "No touching!"

"What. Is. That?" Piers ground out, breathing hard.

"Antiseptic," she said brightly. "It sterilizes the wound."

"Humph." As much as it hurt—and it did—*now*—Piers couldn't argue with that. His mother and sister—both accomplished healers—were always talking about cleaning open injuries to prevent infection. Besides, anyone with half a brain knew from simple life experience that keeping clean prevented a variety of unsavory conditions. "You could've warned me."

"I did. I said *brace yourself.*" She snorted. "Then you started screaming like a baby."

Piers glared at her. "I did no such thing."

"Oh, sorry..." She wasn't sorry at all, the little witch. He narrowed his eyes at her. "You started swearing like a sailor."

"That's better," he said stiffly. "And there's more where that came from."

"I'll bet, Mr. Macho Man."

"*Piers*," he said, exasperated. "It's not that hard."

Grinning, Sophie knelt and patted his torso dry with another clean towel. "Okay, *Piers*. We'll let the bullet wound airdry, but let's wipe off the rest of this. At least it's not bleeding anymore."

Piers glanced at his shoulder. It looked fine. Sure, there was a hole, but it was very small. "I'm sorry I ruined the clothing you gave me."

Sophie scoffed. "Are you kidding? You saved the day. You saved *me*," she added quietly.

Piers saw goose bumps wash down her arms, and the urge to comfort her swelled inside him with the force of a lightning storm. He almost moved but then remembered he was still half dripping with antiseptic.

In a low rasp, he said, "I hope I'm there whenever you need me."

Dipping her head, Sophie finished patting him dry. "I hope you're there even when I don't."

Her soft confession made the muscles in Piers's chest go bowstring tight. A hot twist of longing wrung a hard beat from his heart. Sophie's hair slid forward, brushing his skin. He barely suppressed a groan. He wanted to sink his hands into that thick golden mane and pull her mouth to his.

Gods, she smelled so good. Like wild roses and that soap

he'd wanted to lick. Sweet almond and honey—that was it. Two foods he never could resist.

He turned, bringing his nose to the top of Sophie's head. He inhaled deeply, his pulse thudding. His fingers twitched on his thighs, his senses clamoring for more than just sight and smell. He wanted to touch. Taste. He inhaled again, and Sophie went absolutely still. There wasn't a sound in the room except for her breathing. It quickened.

Still kneeling next to him, she tipped her head back. Their gazes met and held. Slowly, Piers reached out and traced the line of her jaw. Sophie leaned into his touch. Then she stretched up and pressed her mouth to his.

The groan he'd been holding back came out like an avalanche. He slid both hands into her hair and pulled her closer, molding his lips to hers. Every time they moved, breathed, Piers deepened the kiss. Sophie opened for him, and his tongue touched hers. She licked him back, a needy little sound purring in her throat. Arousal sizzled down his spine. She was soft, delicious, *on fire*. She blazed to life, and he burned to the ground.

Piers stood, bringing Sophie with him. Her fingers sank into his sides. Her mouth welcomed his. In two steps, he backed her against the wall. Lips fused, hands in her hair, he tilted her head back and kissed her like he'd never kissed anyone in his life—from the very depths of his soul.

A siren shrieked outside, jarring them apart. The sound continued down the avenue, fading quickly, but it broke the spell. Beyond the bathroom, the Shard of Olympus glowed as brightly as an oil lamp in the otherwise dim room, reminding

Piers that he needed to protect Sophie, not devour her whole.

She dropped her head back against the wall. "Oh my gods."

He grinned, his blood pumping fast. He couldn't resist another quick kiss and then took her hand, leading her into the larger room.

"No, wait." Sophie pulled him to a stop. "We're not done." She carefully placed two large beige squares over the bullet wound, front and back. They stuck to his skin all by themselves.

Piers contemplated the odd bandages in fascination. They'd gone back out after taking a moment to regroup and obtained their healing supplies at the interestingly named drug store, again using Sophie's little green papers to pay. He could've stayed there for hours exploring the wares and reading the boxes on the shelves, but he'd still been bleeding on and off then, and Sophie had been worried about taking care of him.

He moved his shoulder, finding the ache bearable. Sophie had done a good job, and he told her so.

She shrugged, her already flushed cheeks deepening in color. "I wasn't sure how to explain you at a hospital anyway. I did the best I could."

That was fine by him. If it didn't even serve good food, this hospital was a place to avoid.

"Come," he said. "Let's look at the shard together."

"*Come*," she teased in a deep voice. "You sound very imperious sometimes."

"Is that a bad thing?" Piers was used to giving orders and being obeyed, but he hadn't meant to treat Sophie like one of his soldiers.

She looped her arm through his and moved toward the ice shard. It radiated cold blue light from where it sat on the desk across the room. "It'll be an acquired taste." She glanced up at him with a glitter in her eyes and a smile on her lips. "I might call you Caesar here and there after all."

Piers's heart gave a tight, hard bounce. Did that mean she meant to keep him around and get used to him? Even when all this was over, and she was safe?

He gazed down at the top of her head, feeling something shift in his chest. If he couldn't go home, he'd like that.

What if he *could* go home?

The question hit him like a Cyclops's fist, leaving his head ringing with doubts. Home was home, *family*, and everything he'd ever known and worked for. But lose Sophie? He'd only just met her, but somehow...

Fear sent a hot-cold rush of panic through his veins. His nostrils flared.

Somehow, now that they'd found each other, he knew they weren't meant to be apart.

SOPHIE GAPED AT him. Piers liked it.

"I'm supposed to believe that people can do powerful and crazy *magic* with this thing?" She turned a skeptical look on the Shard of Olympus.

Piers nodded. "If you're Magoi, then yes. It'll amplify your natural abilities. Otherwise, it's useless."

"Magoi—a person with magic?"

He nodded again.

"As opposed to Hoi Polloi—the many." Her blue eyes owlishly wide, Sophie reiterated what he'd said earlier. *Hoi Polloi* was a term she'd known anyway. Apparently, people used it the same way here, to describe the general populace.

"In Thalyria, there are many more people without magic than with."

"More Hoi Polloi than Magoi. Got it." She used both hands to sweep her hair back. "But Earth is what you've been calling Attica all this time. No one has magic here. Not *real* magic."

"Are you so sure?" Piers glanced at the Shard of Olympus, which illuminated Sophie's face with an eerie luminescence. "That doesn't glow for everyone. It didn't glow for me." They'd proved it. Sophie went down the hallway and back to test their theory that the ice shard only shined for her. The moment she'd shut the heavy hotel-room door behind her, the shard went dark. The moment she came back, it lit up again. Being out of the room, she hadn't seen it for herself and didn't want to believe, so they'd documented the experiment on her phone. Piers now knew about a fantastical thing called *videos*, but she still insisted there wasn't magic here. It was absurd.

"You're not only *Heracleidae*; you're Magoi." He was sure.

"Pfffft." She waved her hand in the air.

Piers caught her hand and held on to it. "Think about it. Who was the father of Heracles?"

"Zeus," she said slowly.

"Heracles, the man, died. His immortal side went to Mount Olympus, joining Zeus and the other Olympians. Your lineage isn't only powerful, it's the *most* powerful. You're a direct descendant of Zeus." Just like Griffin's wife, Cat. But while Cat already used her incredible power to conquer realms, Sophie was only just becoming aware of hers. "Any magic that remains in Attica would definitely be trapped inside a person like you."

Her eyes grew rounder. "A person like me?"

Blink. Breathe, Sophie. Piers squeezed the hand he held. "I mean you're special. You're *more.*"

Her troubled gaze darted to the glowing blue shard. "But if Novalight can't use the shard for anything, what does it matter if I just give it to him? Then I'll be safe. My family will be safe. I can go home."

"We don't know his origins. Maybe he can."

Sophie chewed her bottom lip, thinking. "I don't think so, which means he's going to eventually figure out that he needs *me* along with the shard."

Piers wanted to crush that possibility under his boot heel and kick it all the way to the Underworld. "Or someone else with a direct ancestral line to a powerful Olympian."

Her face fell. "*That's* what Aaron figured out. That's why he sent me the shard. He knew I could make it work, but Novalight couldn't. But why send it? All that did was put me and everyone else in danger. If it was useless in Novalight's hands, it could've just stayed that way."

"Your friend trusted you to do the right thing with it." Piers pulled Sophie into an embrace he hoped was comforting. She wrapped her arms around his waist and laid her head on his chest, making his heart thud in satisfaction. "If Novalight's as smart and powerful as you say, he'd eventually have discovered how to use the shard to his advantage. You're definitely special, but you can't be the only person in all of Attica with dormant magic. There must be other Magoi. There was just nothing to wake their power like the shard woke yours."

She sighed, her arms tightening around him. "Maybe you're right. I just wish I knew more about it."

"I know one thing. We're lucky the shard ended up in your hands and not in the hands of someone who'd use it for their own gain rather than try to give it back to the gods of Olympus."

"Which we have no idea how to do." She sighed.

"Understanding your magic might bring us closer."

She sighed again. "Whatever it is just feels like the occasional baby earthquake in my bones."

An image of Cat slid into Piers's mind again. Griffin's wife had never struck him as inherently *bad*, just unbelievably reckless and sometimes selfish. Right now, he'd be willing to humble himself and ask for her help. He was Hoi Polloi to the core and didn't know what magic felt like, let alone how to draw it forth and use it. Cat could teach Sophie everything she needed to know. She could probably even make enough noise to get an Olympian to take notice.

Except she was a world away, and Piers had a feeling he'd done something terribly wrong.

Was Cat all right? Griffin?

Unease ignited under his skin, burning through him like a house on fire. He let go of Sophie and turned away, spearing a hand through his hair. *Gods damn it!* Why was he here? What happened?

The ghost of a word flitted through his mind. *Exile...*

"Piers?" Sophie laid her hand on his uninjured shoulder. "Are you okay?"

He made a gruff sound, shaking his head in frustration. He *hated* being confused. He'd been confused enough for one day. "I can't remember something. Whatever it is will help us. It's important. It's about why I'm here—or how I got here. I think it's all connected—to you, to the ice shard—but there's this...wall between myself and *knowing*. The information's there. I just can't get to it." He hit both fists against his head, trying to jar the knowledge out.

"Stop." Reaching up, she took his hands. "That won't help either of us."

"I think I did something." Voice turning bleak, Piers leaned his forehead against Sophie's. He squeezed his eyes shut. "Something awful."

He could still see them. Griffin and Cat. Kaia. And three shadowy figures he couldn't quite bring into focus. Who were they? Griffin's expression was so damning. If anything, Cat's face showed more sympathy. And Kaia... The fear in his little sister's eyes, the heartache. *His* fault. Piers knew it.

"I must've done something unforgiveable. Something that hurt my family." His throat thickened. "I don't understand. I would *never* hurt my family."

"Maybe you didn't," she whispered.

"No, I did." He was sure of it.

"Okay. Even if you did, that's the past now. Another life. Another *world*." Sophie tipped her head up, bringing her lips so close to Piers's that he could feel them calling to his mouth. Calling to *him*. "You're here now. With me."

"With you?" He swallowed. Maybe he hadn't lost everything. Or maybe he had, but he could start over.

Her eyes flicked up, locking with his. She nodded. Her warm breath swirled against his lips, and Piers's abdomen tightened.

Unable to resist, he anchored one hand on her hip and slid the other around the back of her head. After only a day together, he already couldn't imagine a day apart. "Sophie." Her name sounded so right on his lips.

She gripped his shirt and tugged. That was all the encouragement he needed to claim her mouth for a kiss that turned into a fiery mating dance so fast it incinerated his senses.

Piers clasped her tighter, the heat of her body scorching him through their clothes. Pressure built inside him. His shaft grew heavy and hard. Sophie slid her hands under his shirt, sweeping her fingers over his bare skin. He shuddered in pleasure. He'd never been so aroused.

She broke away, breathing hard. "I can't believe I'm saying this to a man I met this morning, but I want you."

Piers groaned. "Gods, I want you, too." The gift he had in his arms left him reeling, especially when he was sure he didn't deserve such a reward. "You're incredible. Brave and beautiful." He kissed her jaw, her neck, her mouth again. "But there's no rush. I could kiss you for days." He barely knew himself right now. There was no way Sophie could know him. He didn't want her to regret anything, no matter how perfectly their bodies melded together, or how desperately they ached to join.

Wide eyed and beautifully flushed, Sophie huffed a laugh. "No rush? We have Novalight's henchmen after us and a magical ice shard to get rid of. I'm not getting killed tomorrow and missing out on this. On *you*."

"I won't let you get killed." Piers took offense she'd even thought it.

"What if *you* die?" she challenged.

He scoffed. "I've lived this long. I don't plan on dying to-morrow." Besides, the ruffians here were pathetic. They only stood a chance because of guns.

"That's man-reasoning if I ever heard it." Slowly, she backed toward the enormous bed with pillows for four. "Besides, we're safe for now, alone, and I'm feeling"—she cast about for the right word—"hot." Defiance flared in her eyes, and she dragged her shirt up over her head and tossed it to the floor.

Piers's mouth went dry. Sophie's hair flew in every direction. She smoothed it down as she stood there in her jeans and a bright-pink breast-catching contraption that made his blood roar in his ears. He stared. He could barely breathe, was afraid to move.

She shucked off her socks and jeans, leaving only a tiny pink garment that matched the upper part of her underclothes. He swallowed hard.

Sophie bit her lip, waiting. Piers devoured the sight of her, catching fire from the inside out. He'd never seen anything more erotic in his life than those little pink scraps of clothing—and the magnificent woman underneath.

~ 6 ~

SOPHIE'S HEART BEAT so fiercely, it pounded her ribs.

Piers stepped closer. "Are you sure?" he rasped in that low, sexy voice of his.

Her belly clenched. That rough hitch… She could *hear* how much he wanted her, and it made putting herself out there in a totally uncharacteristic way surprisingly easy.

"Very." She nodded.

Why wait until tomorrow? A week from now? This strong, capable, selfless, and frankly hot-as-hell man dropped straight into her life today like a penny into a wishing well. She'd needed him, and here he was. The rest was inevitable. Destiny, maybe. All Sophie knew was that she wanted him. And not just for tonight. For as long as possible.

Their kiss still scorched her lips, and the way Piers looked at her sent heat tumbling through her middle. Want pulsed low inside. "You're not going to make me beg, are you?"

He moved so fast he startled her. He lifted her and brought her to the bed, laying her down and settling over her. She brought her knees up. He cradled her head and took her mouth for the most sinfully delicious kiss of Sophie's life. She melted. She wrapped her arms around him and devoured him back, because he was the most delectable thing in the world.

With a ragged sound, Piers broke away and tore his shirt over his head. Sophie saw his bandage and nearly had a heart attack.

"Oh my God, your shoulder!" A big spot of blood stained the bandage.

Ignoring that, Piers pulled off the rest of his clothing. He was totally naked underneath, tanned to perfection, and utterly magnificent. Sophie's mouth almost watered at the sight of him. She'd never seen a flesh-and-blood man who was as perfectly honed and sharply chiseled as a classical Greek sculpture. And wow—that was one hell of an erection.

Her eyes widened. "You didn't figure out the boxers, did you?"

Piers ignored that, too, and leaned back over her, kissing her from jaw to collarbone to the top of her lacey bra. Sophie's breath shuddered. Nuzzling her chest, he dipped his finger under the material, exploring deeper with every stroke. He finally brushed her nipple, and she gasped, heat simmering between her legs.

Piers seemed fascinated by the little details of her lingerie, but Sophie grew impatient when he didn't finish undressing her. She unhooked her bra and tugged off her panties herself. She'd never been so bold or wanton in her life, but with Piers, going full steam ahead not only felt natural; it felt *necessary*.

"I need you," she whispered, arching into his touch.

Roughly, Piers said something in a language that resembled Greek as he smoothed his hand down her body. He stroked and explored as if he had all the time in the world when Sophie had never been so desperate to move faster. She pressed against him, twisting and straining. She needed contact. She needed friction. After breath-stealing minutes of driving her to the brink of insanity, he finally slid his fingers toward her throbbing center.

"Yes." She nearly sobbed in relief at his first light stroke through her hot, aching slickness. "More. There."

Her senses exploded as he touched her. They were just getting started, and this was already the most aroused she'd ever been. Sensation raced like liquid fire beneath her skin. Piers pressed on just the right spot, and it was like hitting a reset button. She moaned in pleasure. Her sex life started now, she decided—with Piers. She grinned at the idea.

"Is my lovemaking funny?" he growled against her neck. His deep voice resonated inside her. "Do they do it differently in Attica?"

"Are you kidding?" she panted. Piers was acing this. "I think they do it wrong here. Don't stop. I love it."

He paused, maybe surprised by her candor. Then he started working the little bead of her clitoris that even *she* had trouble finding. Sophie nearly flew off the bed, which might've been funny if she hadn't been so intensely absorbed in chasing what was sure to be the best orgasm of her life. Piers slid his mouth over her breast and sucked on her nipple. His tongue lashed the tip, and she let out a sharp breath, tension peaking inside her.

She gripped his head, sinking her fingers into his hair and holding on as if her life depended on it. Maybe it did. If Piers didn't make love to her right now, she would implode. She was sure of it.

"Wait," she gasped.

He drew back without question. Voice thick with desire, he asked, "What is it?" He scanned the room for danger.

"Nothing bad," Sophie said. "I've got protection." She always carried a few condoms in her purse and made sure they weren't expired. It had seemed like a pretty useless precaution until several incredibly hot minutes ago. "I'm sure you have ways of preventing pregnancy in Thalyria. This is our method." She leaned over the side of the bed and fished around in her handbag for a little foil package. She finally found one, tore it open, and reached for him.

Piers sucked in a breath when she touched him. His big shaft pulsed in her hand. An answering throb thumped deep in Sophie's belly. She stroked him, the condom in her other hand, watching his gray eyes drift closed and his jaw tighten. She smiled, feeling sexy and powerful as his throat moved on a hard swallow. Piers made her feel like a goddess in the bedroom. It changed everything.

She stroked him harder and licked his lower lip, coaxing him to open his mouth for her. The moment he did, she kissed him fiercely. Possessively. She'd never felt anything but awkward and bored during intimacy. This was so far from awkward and boring that she knew she could never go back. It was this man or nothing.

Piers's breathing turned sharp and uneven. "*Sophronia mou.*" That, she understood. *My Sophronia.* Oh, yes—she was his and then some.

She fumbled with the condom.

Piers took it from her unsteady hands. He covered himself, understanding everything that needed understanding, including that she was no expert at putting it on him. "A sheath but different. Like a second skin."

"That's the idea," she murmured.

He gave himself a long, slow stroke, his arm and shoulder muscles rippling. Heat washed through her, and the raw, needy sound that poured from her throat could've come from a porn star.

Piers clasped the back of her head and drew her in for a kiss that branded her soul. Desperate to feel him inside her, Sophie nudged him onto his back and straddled him. She didn't want any weight on his shoulder. She kissed his rock-solid chest and worked her way up to his mouth again. His sounds of desire came hard against her lips. He gripped her hips and kissed her back, sometimes gently and sometimes like he wanted to eat her alive. It was incredible.

Slowly, she rose up and then sank down on him. Fully joined, she could feel every inch of him inside her, and for one breathless second, they both went still, savoring the sensation. Then she started moving.

Piers slowly exhaled. His eyes grew heavy-lidded. He watched her from under a gleaming, pleasure-hooded gaze, touching her breasts as she slid on him. He tugged on her nipples, lightly at first and then with a hint of roughness that brought Sophie to the brink of orgasm. She held off, keeping the hot pulse from exploding inside her too quickly. Piers took over rocking her. He threw his head back, eyes closed, lips parted, chest rising and falling. The fire-bright pressure mounted. His grip tightened, and he pulled her hard against him. Sophie gasped. She clenched all over, and release pounded through her. Piers joined her with a groan, his hard throbbing adding to her pleasure.

"Wow," she murmured. Breathing as if she'd just run a marathon, Sophie sank down against his chest and nestled her forehead into his neck, careful of his shoulder. She kept making little noises she couldn't seem to control and didn't want to. She couldn't stop kissing him. Chest. Neck. Jaw. Mouth. Piers wrapped his arms around her.

"*Sophronia mou.*" He sighed her name this time, a low, satisfied rumble.

She smiled. She didn't mind when Piers used her full name, and the way he rolled the *r* made her shiver.

They stayed all tangled up in each other for a long time, the room dark except for the city light streaming in through the window and the eerie blue glow of the Shard of Olympus. Piers's stomach eventually growled.

"I'll order room service." Sophie tried to motivate her muscles to move. They felt like jelly.

"Meat," Piers said.

She grinned, reaching for the menu. "You got it."

~ 7 ~

PIERS HAD TWO words to describe Sophie. Incredible. Terrifying. Her idea to visit a museum filled with works from what she called "Classical Antiquity" and find sculptures of ancient Greek gods, especially Athena, seemed solid. A good place to start, anyway. If nothing about the ice shard's behavior or any of the statues gave them a hint as to how to return the shard to an Olympian, they'd try a museum with more modern interpretations of Greek mythology.

He shook his head. What he called reality, she called mythology. What he called every-day life, she called ancient civilization. It was enough to make a man feel old and senile.

And what manner of idiot had decided to call important houses of knowledge Met and MoMA? They sounded like names you'd give pets, not places.

At least Sophie had a plan, which was more than Piers had. But the idea of her being exposed and vulnerable on city streets and in public places made him feel as if he were trying to breathe underwater. It was funny—no, *frightening*—how a single day could change his entire existence. And he wasn't even talking about the inexplicable world-hopping. He meant

Sophie.

Piers got it now. Why Griffin would choose Cat over anything. Why Carver lost himself when he lost Konstantina. He was just like his brothers. The right woman hit them like a lightning bolt and scorched herself down to their very essence. Sophie was his lightning strike. He had no doubt the Fates had thrust them together to keep the Shard of Olympus out of the wrong hands. And now that their life threads were weaving the same tapestry, he was going to make damn sure they didn't get cut short or unravel.

Which made Sophie's reckless running around New York City almost unbearable. He grumbled about it again, scanning the surprisingly vast wilderness in the heart of the city for signs of danger.

Sophie sipped coffee from a cup made of paper, his protests rolling right off her. "I haven't been to the Met since I was a kid. I can't wait to see the Greek sculptures again."

"Why Greek instead of Attican?" Piers asked. "Isn't that where they're from?"

She shrugged. "Back then—and now—Attica was just one region around Athens. Ancient Greek civilization spread all over the Mediterranean. It was made up of independent city states that shared a similar culture and language."

"And gods."

"And gods." She nodded.

Piers understood and could even picture what she meant, just as he understood more about this world by the minute. He now knew that Sophie could show him a detailed map of ancient Greece with a few taps of her finger. At the time, it seemed the people there had called their land Hellas.

Why stories of the Hellenes and their ancient kingdoms came to Thalyria as tales from Attica, he could only guess. Perhaps Athena had liked her glorious role as the patron goddess of the area and spread to Thalyria only the information she liked best.

Sophie's phone fascinated him. He could understand why the little rectangles were glued to everyone's fingertips. They'd used hers several times today already. They could buy entrance tickets to this Met. They could check the incoming weather. They could listen to music—if one could call the odd *thump thumping* and endless *la la laing* music. She could even contact her family, her thumbs flying over little letters, to say she'd try to be home soon and not to open the door to any strangers.

Piers wished he had a magic rectangle. But there was no contacting *his* family with Sophie's phone, no matter how powerful the tool seemed to him.

A horse and carriage rolled by. At least that was something familiar, although he preferred a fast two-wheeled chariot if he wasn't riding. Bells jingled from the harness, and the horse's breath steamed the air. The driver had dressed himself as one of these jolly, red-robed men with big white beards Piers kept seeing everywhere. Sophie said they were Santa and related to the upcoming holiday, although he still hadn't grasped why they were *all* Santa or why one city needed so many of them.

The horse and carriage trundled away, and Piers rubbed his hands together, feeling nostalgic for his home, his horse, and his warm weather. *Good gods*, it was cold here.

"The Met." Sophie pointed to a huge columned building. It looked a lot like Castle Sinta.

Piers stared at it. It was far bigger than any knowledge temple he'd ever been to. "Do they only have these buildings in New York City?" he asked.

She arched her brows. "Well, there's nothing quite this grand in Connecticut."

Ah. Her homeland. "Could I maybe…visit this *Cunnetakit* with you?" It was a bold question, and worry tightened his lungs. What if Sophie said no? What if for her, this, *they*, were only temporary?

A frown slid over her expression. "I would never just abandon you in the city."

Piers nodded, but there was a difference between abandoning someone and bringing a man into your life as a partner. A lover. He decided not to press. It was good enough for now that Sophie planned on keeping him by her side. He'd convince her of *forever* later.

She flashed her phone to gain them entrance to the Met, and they went through a security scan. She'd warned him to leave his weapons at the room, which Piers had wholeheartedly resisted. He understood better now. He'd have been forced to give them up anyway, and Sophie had been worried his sword and daggers looked so "authentic" that the museum might ask questions they couldn't answer.

As they strode through the classical rooms, Piers had to admit, if only to himself, that he hated it. Here was absolute proof that his gods had been abandoned. Left to rot, fall apart, and be scattered throughout museums for people to gawk at without even an inkling of the power the Olympians still wielded across the cosmos. At least the marblework was appealing when it wasn't disintegrating. These statues were the first things to truly remind him of home—but only to prove just how very far away he was.

"Any difference in the shard?" he asked as they stared at yet another rendition of Athena. This one had a hand missing. And half a nose.

Sophie discreetly pulled up her sleeve. She'd fashioned a bracelet to hold the shard out of some thin wire she'd had in her car—leftovers from a school project to build a model of the Eiffel Tower, whatever that was. She shook her head. "It feels the same. Glows the same. Pulses the same. It's still really cold."

"And inside you? Is there a vibration? A call?"

She let her sleeve drop back over the bracelet. "Nothing— or nothing *new*. It's the same as before. Just a weird buzzing in my bones. I know it sounds ridiculous."

"That's the magic inside you, ready to use."

She scoffed. "Use *how*?"

"To defend yourself." Piers glanced back and forth between Sophie and the statue of Athena. "To contact her?"

"Yeah, that's not really working out so far."

No. They'd both tried talking to Athena and the other Olympians as they gazed upon their marble likenesses. They'd muttered prayers, internally and aloud, and even discreetly touched the ice shard to the statues, even though ropes were meant to keep them away. They'd been shushed and scolded by museumgoers several times, and frankly, Piers was losing hope that this would help them. He thought they needed to pray in a temple specifically dedicated to Athena, but Sophie said the most important one was half the world away, in ruins, impossible to actually stand in, and too expensive to get to anyway.

His hands fell to his hips. He pursed his lips. "Should we try your MoMA?" They'd covered the Met's classical sections twice now—Greek and Roman. Apparently, these Romans had come along and adopted his gods but given them different names. Didn't that just confuse people?

"I guess so." Sophie rubbed her fingers over the Shard of Olympus through her clothing. "I'm not sure we're on the right track, though."

Piers leaned in and kissed the top of her head, her sweet-smelling shampoo making his mouth water. "It's all right, *kardoula mou*. We'll figure it out."

"Sweetheart?" She smiled. "That's nice."

"You understand?" he asked in surprise.

She nodded. "We still use some of the same terms of endearment in my family. I guess that somehow trickled down from our common heritage."

Emotion pushed at Piers's ribs. He liked the idea of them having something in common. It made him feel less lost.

"Come." He squeezed Sophie's hand, holding on to it. "To MoMA."

"To MoMA," she echoed in a soldier's voice.

THEY WERE OUTSIDE and in a quiet, tree-covered section of the park when Novalight himself stepped into their path. Piers recognized him from seeing pictures on Sophie's phone. Self-importance rolled off him like the stench of dung. Several of his hired ruffians flanked him.

"I'd like my crystal now." Voice flat, eyes flatter, Novalight clearly thought he'd get what he wanted now that he'd deigned to show up himself.

"What crystal?" Sophie asked. "Who are you?" She was a surprisingly good actress. Piers doubted anyone but he heard the slight reediness in her voice or noticed how her eyes dilated.

"*My* crystal." Novalight held up a hand to keep his guards in place when they started forward. "Don't play stupid, Ms. Iraklidis. We both know you're not."

"Fine." Sophie's chin notched up. "How did you find me?"

"I have endless resources, and you're not exactly the queen of stealth." Tall and easily in his fourth decade, Novalight looked as if he might put up a decent fight. Thick jowls gave him a heavy-set appearance, but Piers wasn't fooled. There was at least some muscle beneath that bulk.

Sophie stared Novalight down. A small tremor jumped from her fingers to Piers's, and he tightened his grip on her hand. "It's not yours," she said.

"It *is* mine. I found it. I own an archeological site on a Mediterranean island that's coming closer and closer to being declared the lost city of Atlantis."

Piers scoffed. Atlantis wasn't lost. It was another world—like this one.

Novalight swung an annoyed look on him. "Do you have

something to add?"

"More of a question," Piers said. "What do you plan to do with it?"

"Study it. Reveal its potential. Use it." It was impossible to miss the power-hungry gleam in Novalight's eyes. He obviously knew the shard was important, but Piers doubted the man would know magic if it kicked him in the forehead. He must believe the shard could unlock some other prize.

"For what?" Sophie demanded.

"For whatever I deem necessary."

"Spoken like a true psychopath," she muttered.

"I've had just about enough of you, young woman." Novalight's expression hardened. Piers figured the man had been trying to seem non-threatening up until then, but Novalight dropped the act faster than Icarus fell from the sky. "I thought you'd get scared and give up, but then this guy showed up and put me in a difficult position. I'm not a bad person. I don't *want* to hurt you."

"So don't." Sophie hid it well, but Piers felt her shudder.

Rage ignited inside him. How dare this asshole threaten Sophie?

He released her hand, preparing for battle. Novalight might not be the type to get his own hands dirty, but Piers had no problem with bloody knuckles, especially if the blood was Novalight's.

"Then *give me* what's *mine*." The scientist was done playing. That was clear to everyone.

"You killed my friend." Sophie sucked in a breath. Tears gleamed in her eyes.

Piers curled his hands into fists. Did Novalight think several-to-one odds intimidated him? Because they didn't.

"Your friend stole from me and put you in danger. That's no friend." The scientist extended his hand. "Now, give it to me."

"I threw it in the East River. I don't have it," Sophie said.

Novalight huffed. "I trailed you through the museum. I saw it, and I want to know why it glows now." Understanding happened fast. Sophie was right; the man was intelligent, and the calculating look Novalight swept over Sophie turned Piers's blood cold. "It glows for *you*, doesn't it? Your friend must've known something about you that I don't. Or something about the crystal." His voice turned silky, eager. "I guess we'll find out together, won't we?"

Sophie made a quiet sound of distress. Piers let out a growl. He took a menacing step.

Two of Novalight's guards pushed back their jackets and flashed their guns. Piers stopped. Guns didn't make for a fair fight, and Sophie could get caught in the crossfire.

His nostrils flared. No sword. No knives. A wounded shoulder. He tipped his head toward Sophie, whispering under his breath, "Now would be a good time to figure out your magic."

Her frightened gaze flicked to his. "What?"

"Call it up. See what happens."

Her eyes widened. Piers usually enjoyed her shocked and bewildered expression, but right now, she just looked scared. Scared wasn't cute, and he flat-out despised this Novalight for scaring Sophie.

"Come quietly," Novalight said, "and I'll have no reason to go back to Pinebury."

Sophie froze solid. "What?"

"Such a lovely woman, your mother. Makes a mean baklava. And your father, the renowned architect, is overseeing one of the biggest projects in Connecticut. I hope the ceiling is solid on that new building he's working on. It would be a shame for a freak accident to sully his illustrious career so close to retirement. Or worse, kill someone."

Sophie's voice turned low and seismic. "Leave my family alone."

Novalight's menacing smirk intensified. "Now, Xanthe... She's a treat. Enjoying college for now, her whole life ahead of her. So much potential. Don't you think? But campuses—they can be dangerous. Drunken frat boys... Pathways covered in ice... Rogue delivery trucks..."

Terror twisted Sophie's face. She scuffed back a step, a near-silent "No" leaking from her lips.

Shielding her with his body, Piers bared his teeth at the scientist. "Back. Away," he ground out.

"And you'll make me do that how?" Novalight asked scathingly.

Piers moved fast enough to surprise everyone. He jumped on Novalight like an animal and showed him exactly how savage he could be when his mate was in danger.

Novalight went down hard on his back. Piers followed, pinning him in the cold grass beside the sidewalk. He got in three skin-splitting punches before Novalight's men yanked him backward and threw him down. Their mistake was letting go. Piers surged to his feet and charged the guards, yelling at Sophie to run.

He smashed two heads together. The men crumpled. Someone hit him in the back of the skull with something hard. Piers dropped to one knee, his vision darkening. He spun on instinct with one leg out and knocked over the person behind him. He blinked hard, his head ringing. Lurching up, he punched the blond he recognized from the day before. The blond staggered. Novalight started to stand. Piers grabbed a midsized female before she could free her gun from its holster and tossed her into Novalight, toppling him again.

"Piers!"

He whirled. They had Sophie. Fear tore through his chest.

One man gripped her from behind while another tried to rip the shard from her wrist. Sophie twisted, kicking out, and a third darted in and punched her in the face. She blanched.

"Soph!" Dread gripped his throat.

She sagged, but her eyes lifted, meeting his. Then she lit up like a torch. Lightning cracked from her body and sent the three men flying off. She reeled in shock. The last two ruffians charged, including the blond. She held up her hands to ward them off and twin thunderbolts shot from her palms.

She gasped. So did Piers. She'd laid out five men. They smoldered on the sidewalk.

Sophie looked at her hands in horror. "Oh my God."

Novalight shoved the female soldier aside and crouched. The woman scrambled to her feet and ran. With his power-fevered eyes avidly trained on Sophie, the scientist didn't even see Piers's boot coming for his head. Piers knocked him unconscious and raced to Sophie's side.

He grabbed her still-hot hand and pulled her from the scene of the fight. A family out for a walk had just stumbled upon their secluded pathway, and the mother lifted her phone just as he and Sophie ducked into the woods.

They ran until their lungs burned. They ran until they left the park. They ran all the way back to their hotel room. They ran until Sophie collapsed on their bed.

"I killed people. I killed people. I'm going to jail." She turned and sobbed into his chest. The lightning in her blood—the most incredible and rare of all magic—had long since sunk back inward, leaving her cold to the touch.

Piers gathered her close, trying to warm away her shock. He rocked her as she cried, telling her again and again that she hadn't killed anyone. He'd looked, and he was sure. Novalight and his henchmen were all alive—which meant they weren't done yet.

~ 8 ~

SOPHIE THOUGHT SHE was scared before? This was worse. Her hands had lit up and *electrocuted* people. Her entire body had become a high-voltage *weapon*. She'd thrown a bunch of men off her with only the *intention* of defending herself. She'd made *lightning*.

She kept trying to wrap her head around the idea, but apparently, her mind wasn't that bendy. Nothing made sense to her. Except for fear. There was plenty of that.

According to Piers, lightning wielders only came from Zeus's bloodline. And the magic only manifested in the most powerful and unique of people. His brother's wife, Cat, was apparently one of these mega-special Magoi, and she was practically a demigoddess on her way to ruling an entire continent!

What a special snowflake.

Evidently, so was Sophie. A special snowflake. Alone on Earth. Able to zap people.

"Oh my God," she murmured for the five hundredth time in an hour.

"*Gods.*" Piers squeezed her shoulder with strong, reassuring fingers, stopping her manic pacing. "I think it's time to start believing."

Oh, she believed, all right. She believed she needed to get the hell away from that ice shard and go back to Connecticut. She loved Pinebury. She loved teaching. She loved her family. She did *not* love the Shard of Olympus. "We have to get rid of that thing."

"You might lose your magic. The shard might be the only thing giving you access to it here in Att...on Earth," he said.

"Good." Sophie glared at the shard on the desk, backing away from it. "I want it gone forever."

"Are you sure?" Piers frowned in thought. "You—and the Shard of Olympus—could be the key to bringing magic back to this world."

Possibly the most inelegant sound she'd ever made shot from Sophie's mouth. "That's the last thing this world needs. People are already destructive enough without adding unstoppable superhero powers to the mix." She huffed, shaking her head. "You can't tell me everyone in Thalyria uses their magic for good. Even your sister-in-law, Cat. You keep saying she's a reckless, power-hungry warmonger. And she's your *family!*"

Piers's lip curled. "She's Griffin's wife. Not my family."

That sounded like the same thing to Sophie. "You don't always get to choose, Piers. Sometimes, it's someone else's choice, and if you love that person, you just have to accept it."

A shadow flitted through his eyes. He pinched his forehead. He looked guilty as hell, but Sophie didn't have the emotional capacity right now to deal with whatever troubled him. She had her own epic freak-out going on. "And besides—"

"What's that?" Piers pointed at the television.

Sophie glanced over. They'd turned on a local news station to try to see if there was, you know, a *manhunt* going on for them. She half expected to see Novalight hopping up and down and proclaiming himself a victim, but it was only an advertisement for tours to the Statue of Liberty and Ellis Island.

"The Statue of Liberty." She waved a hand toward the screen, distractedly explaining, "It's a symbol of freedom and hope to anyone seeking a new home or refuge in this country. Kind of like you, I guess."

"It's Eleutheria. It's a colossus of Eleutheria. She personifies Liberty."

"You mean Libertas? Oh, wait..." Sophie watched the images scroll by on the muted television. "Eleutheria must be the Greek equivalent. Libertas is the Roman goddess they used as a model."

Piers stared at the screen as if he didn't even hear her. "*Zeus Eleutherios,*" he murmured. "Protector of freedom."

Sophie's heart started to pound. "Is that where we need to go? Should we bring the shard to the Statue of Liberty?"

Aaron's cryptic message had been burned into her mind since the second she put all those torn-up pieces of paper together. She saw it again.

The Greek gods are REAL. Contact Athena and GIVE THE SHARD BACK TO THE GODS OF OLYMPUS.

Sophie glanced at the glowing ice shard. She swallowed. At first, she'd just wanted to avoid getting caught and losing the shard to a murderous megalomaniac like Novalight. Then Piers showed up, and the whole *Contact Athena* thing went from pure fantasy to possible reality. Same with *magic*. Now, he was staring at the screen in utter shock, as though the Statue of Liberty were just the temple they needed to finally contact the gods.

Or maybe it was something else?

"Piers?" He had a really weird look on his face.

The news channel switched to an advertisement for car insurance, Lady Liberty disappeared, and Piers lost it. No, he didn't just lose it. He lost it like a boss, grabbing his head, curling in on himself, and *howling*.

Sophie froze in shock. Her own massive freak-out took a backseat to Piers's sudden breakdown. She watched, her jaw sliding loose as he wrapped his arms around his head and rocked, groaning and muttering names she knew from hearing him talk about his family. Griffin. Kaia. Cat.

Fear jackknifed through her. She reached for him. "Piers? What is it?"

He abruptly stood and brushed her off. Pale as snow before it hit the New York sidewalk, he turned away from her. Sophie's heart clenched. Something was seriously wrong with him. She tried again, reaching out, and he strode to the bathroom and closed the door. A second later, she heard a huge crash.

She flew to the door, knocking. "Piers? What happened?"

A second huge crash and a bellow.

Jesus. Her pulse throbbed in her ears. "I'm coming in there." She turned the handle. It didn't budge. "If you break it, you pay for it, so *stop* before I can't afford clothes for either of us."

Total silence, then the door flew open. He stood there, his hair in disarray, his chest heaving. Sophie glanced behind him. He'd shattered both big glass panels to the shower. There wasn't any blood on him, so maybe he'd kicked them. The chrome towel rack caught her eye amid the wreckage. He'd ripped the bar from the wall and bent it. How freaking strong was he?

"Holy shit." Sophie snapped her mouth shut. She wanted to be angry at Piers for going all caveman on the hotel bathroom, but he looked so devastated. Beyond devasted—*wrecked*. His eyes glistened, and her heart broke for him without even knowing what happened. She stepped closer and wrapped her arms around him.

Piers stood there for the longest time, stiff and unmoving. Finally, he gripped her back and ducked his head into her neck, holding on as though she were his lifeline. "It's all my fault," he whispered.

She tried to comfort him, smoothing her hands through his hair. She kissed his temple, his forehead. "Whatever it is, we'll figure it out. Just tell me what happened."

"There's nothing to figure out. I made a huge mistake, and now I'm paying for it. I'm here forever. In exile."

The dull monotone of his voice scared her. His will to live seemed to have blinked off faster than a bum string of Christmas lights. At the same time, *here forever* didn't sound that awful to her. It was too selfish to say aloud, but she didn't want to lose him, even if it meant he couldn't go back to his family.

"And you suddenly remembered?" She pulled back enough to look at him. "What just happened?"

"It was your colossus of Eleutheria. Libertas." The Roman equivalent didn't roll off his tongue as easily. "It all came roaring back. Athena said I wouldn't remember at first—that something would trigger my memory when the time was right." His voice turned rough. "That time is now, I guess."

"*Athena* said?" Sophie was getting good at suspending disbelief, but...*Athena?* "Well, that's good, right? We need her."

Piers speared a hand through his hair and started pacing. "No, it's not good at all. I tried to get Cat exiled from Thalyria to keep her from bringing more danger to my family. I didn't want her dead, just gone—*permanently* gone—and she's always picking fights and getting into battles, so I stupidly thought I'd give her a taste of her own medicine and turn her over to Ares, the god of war. I managed to get his attention, which was a colossal error. He would definitely take someone away with him, just not Cat. I didn't count on how strongly the gods favor her, the plans they have. Three Olympians showed up and debated who to seize in Cat's place. Ares threatened to take Kaia—to take my little sister away forever and throw her into endless wars—so I did the only thing I could think of to fix the mess I'd made. I offered myself instead."

Sophie swallowed hard. Of course, he did. She wasn't surprised at all.

"And Cat... She forgave me. Griffin didn't. He won't." Piers's voice rasped hard. He cleared his throat. "Ares could've taken any of us—whoever he wanted. I could've doomed my brother or my little sister to eternal war, but Athena stepped in and argued that I could be useful here, in her world."

"You've been useful to me," Sophie whispered.

Piers prowled back to her, his gray eyes two pain-filled thunderclouds. She'd almost stopped noticing his slightly swollen nose and scraped chin, the scratches on his arms…

"Did you fight with Griffin?" she asked, gently touching his jaw.

"With Cat. She could've killed me. She didn't."

"Maybe she's not so awful, then?"

"*I'm* the awful one," Piers bit out. "I tried to control forces I didn't know enough about and nearly ripped my family apart. As it is"—he laughed harshly—"I'm the only one who got torn from everything. From everyone."

"Does your family know what happened to you?"

"They know Athena took me to Attica. She said she had scientists 'running amok with sensitive information,' and that I might be of help."

"So, they know you're gone? Forever? They must be devastated." Tears burned her eyes. She'd only known Piers for two days and already knew his family was everything to him. She imagined the devotion went both ways. How could it not? Terrible families didn't make a person like him—loyal, kind, caring. Everything she'd always wanted in a man.

He shrugged, then shook his head. "I'm dead to Griffin. I know that. Cat's pregnant." He swallowed. "I didn't know *that*, but my actions could've taken his wife and child from him in the blink of an eye. *I* did that. I just did."

Sophie reached for him again, but Piers avoided her. The

look on his face said he was toxic, and she'd better stay away or get contaminated. She wasn't having it. She planted herself in front of him and stopped him with both hands on his chest. His torso shuddered. "Tell me. What happened."

His face twisted. But instead of shrugging her off, he stayed where he was and put his hands over hers, holding them. "I never liked Cat. She's hot-headed, a know-it-all, and always needs to be the center of attention. I could deal with all that. I mean, she wasn't *my* fated woman, so I was just going to grin and bear it for Griffin's sake, but then she started dragging my family—my friends, too—into extraordinarily dangerous situations. Quests nearly to Mount Olympus. Arena games to the *death*. Trying to overthrow enemy royals in their own throne room." His mouth went flat. "My sister Jocasta ended up in the middle of it. My brother Carver almost died. Griffin was in constant danger..."

"So, you thought if Cat was out of the picture, all that would stop?"

He nodded. "But it wasn't her. It was Griffin. Cat was the weapon—and the emblem. But he was the driving force. That was the partnership the gods decided for them. *Griffin* pushed Cat toward her destiny. I didn't see it until that last moment. Never truly saw *her*... or her worth."

Softly, Sophie asked, "Do you regret what you did?"

He squeezed his eyes shut. "More than you can imagine."

She tried not to let his words cut like a knife. This wasn't about her. Piers could never say he was sorry to his brother. Never make amends with Cat. Never see his little niece or nephew. Never see his family again. "I'm so sorry." She leaned into him, offering her arms as comfort.

"You're not to blame. I am."

Throat thick, she said, "That doesn't mean my heart can't ache for you."

Piers wrapped his arms around her, holding her tight. His voice dropped to a whisper. "Thank you."

As they stood there, Sophie wondered if Piers really believed in fated mates, and if things like that really happened. Because that would explain how she'd fallen in love with him so quickly. A lightning-bolt attraction—no pun intended—and the unusual situation probably made everything more intense, but somehow, she *knew*. Piers was it for her.

"There is some good news," he murmured. "What I did to get exiled? It was a summoning chant. I know how to call an Olympian. I can compel Athena to us here, right now. That must be why she pushed us together."

Sophie's eyes shot wide. She tilted her head back, looking at him. "Really? That's amazing! That's perfect!" Her gaze darted to the shard. She could get rid of that glowing bit of Olympian ice and get back to her safe, *sane* life just in time for Christmas!

So why did Piers's expression say it was anything but amazing? He looked as though he'd swallowed a razor blade, and it was cutting him in two.

"Piers?" A terrible feeling sank through her.

"Call a god, lose a soul. You see, I figured out just enough to know that summoning an Olympian could be a means to exile. I didn't understand that the summoner doesn't get to choose who goes. Someone's permanent exile is the *result* of calling on a god for a favor. It's not supposed to be the favor itself." His eyes darkened and locked with hers. "Athena will come when I call, but she'll rip us apart. That's the price we'll pay for using magic that's supposed to be long lost. That's the price to pay for summoning a god."

~ 9 ~

SOPHIE STUMBLED BACK, and Piers's lungs tightened. His punishment was just beginning, wasn't it? He knew he'd been an asshole to Cat and deserved to suffer, but if the gods' goal was to finish him off, they were on the right track. He'd already lost his home and family. He didn't think he'd survive losing Sophie.

"Rip us apart?" She scraped her hair back with shaking fingers. "You mean…take one of us away? Exile?"

"Those are the rules." Piers barely recognized his voice. His words hitched on the lump in his throat. "And we don't get to choose who goes, although I'll offer myself and hope she takes me."

"No!" Then Sophie winced, her face washing of color.

Piers shook his head. "Not you, *Sophronia mou*. You have everything here. I have nothing."

"You have me." The tremor in her voice nearly undid him. Piers's heart folded in on itself.

Having Sophie was precisely the problem. She was *all* he had. And the summoning chant meant losing a soul close to him. Piers hadn't understood that part of the old texts until it was too late, and Kaia, especially, ended up in grave danger. He'd offered himself instead, and the gods had accepted. They might not accept again.

"You should be far away from me when I summon her. Distance might help, although I'm not certain. I'll give the shard back."

"Why wouldn't distance help?" Sophie's blue eyes ate up half her face. So scared. So beautiful. So *his*.

A chasm cracked down his chest. *Why?* Punishing him shouldn't mean punishing Sophie. Later, he would rail against the Fates, but right now, he could sacrifice without question as long as she was safe.

"The price is a soul close to me." That likely meant someone he cared about, but it could maybe simply mean a person in the room.

Her breath shuddered out. Piers would give anything to comfort her. He even thought there might be a small chance at a way for them to stay together, but he refused to get her hopes up. And maybe his own.

He glanced at her phone. He'd have to make a call before he started chanting. He'd have to time it well.

"Why would this happen? Any of it?" Sophie abruptly sat on the edge of the bed. Her fingers curled into the blanket. "If the gods are all-powerful and everywhere, why not just pluck the shard from Novalight's people in the Mediterranean? Or from Aaron? Athena could've just knocked on my door in Pinebury and asked for her shard back. What was the point of letting any of this happen? Of letting us..." She choked back a sob.

Piers sat beside her. He took her hand. *"Kardoula mou."* He brushed his lips over her knuckles. "The gods don't work that way. There's nothing straightforward about their machinations. They arrange, nudge, influence, sometimes shove. But it's all with a *potential* outcome in mind. After, it's up to us, their players and pawns, to make our choices and move our pieces around the board. If it all comes together the way the gods desire, then it's done, and they move on to something else. If it doesn't, they begin again with a new set of players who make their own moves, just as we did."

Tears shimmered in her eyes as she looked at him. "I never thought of there being a balance between fate and free will. I never even believed in destiny, but now..."

Piers gently kissed her. "I don't know if there's a balance, but it's not all or nothing. It's both."

She nodded. It was unsteady and forced. "So, this is it? I should call my parents. Say goodbye. Just in case." Her voice broke, and Piers's heart crumbled to dust.

"No, my love. You get in your car and go home." He glanced at Sophie's phone again. "You said it takes about three hours? That's how long I'll wait. Then I'll summon Athena and give her the shard."

Sophie sniffled, straightening. "But I have to check us out of the hotel. No." She shook her head. "No, Piers. None of this works."

"I have at least thirty gold coins. Surely, the hotel can find a way to exchange them for little green papers and settle this debt. I'll leave the money in the bathroom." He grimaced, regretting his fit of temper. He could've left that gold with

Sophie instead.

Piers unbuckled his belt and slipped the leather pouch from it. Rising, he strode to the bathroom and set the coin purse on the counter, hoping there would be steaming-hot showers wherever he ended up next. After Sophie, they were what he liked best about this place.

Returning to the main room, he sat beside her again. "The gold just needs to be turned into a useable currency. You can leave without worry."

"Leave without worry?" She frowned at him. "What if you *don't* get taken? What will you do then?"

He reached for her phone. "Call you. Show me how."

Her lips thinned. Then she took the phone from him. "Assuming *I* don't get taken, either, you'll have to dial my home number if I leave my cell phone with you." She opened *Contacts*, scrolled to *House*, and showed him how to launch the communication. "If I don't answer, leave a message. I'll come back and get you. I can be back tonight."

"Tonight is Christmas Eve. It seems special to you. You'll spend it with your family." He hoped.

"I don't care if it's the freaking apocalypse. I'll come back for you."

Piers's heart swooped in his chest. "We'll meet again, *Sophronia mou*. In this life, or in the next."

She shivered at his words. "Maybe the gods will be merciful," she whispered, her voice thick with tears.

Piers drank in the sight of her, memorizing every detail of her face. His soul recognized her as his, but what that really meant was that he was *hers*.

"Maybe." It was his deepest wish. More so than even to return home. Sophie was his home now.

They reached for each other, and there were no more words. There were long kisses and tender touches. There was breath-stealing passion that might have to last them a lifetime, until they met again in the Underworld.

PIERS WATCHED THE snow fall outside and waited for the call that would change everything. It wasn't the one he'd made earlier. That had taken some trial and error, but he'd finally reached Novalight Enterprises and then the all-powerful man himself—after a long time spent persuading person after person that *Mr.* Novalight *really* wanted to talk to him.

Sophie had left nearly three hours ago, and Piers still felt as though a Cyclops sat on his chest, the crushing weight keeping his lungs from expanding. His heart seemed to beat out her name, and he couldn't stop thinking about how she'd stopped him from using one of her little sheaths when they made love. She hadn't wanted it. Maybe they both hoped he'd left a part of himself with her. Although the idea of his child growing up without him made Piers's stomach plummet. But Sophie... She could handle anything. The week she'd just endured would've broken a lesser woman. She would persevere. She would *thrive.*

The hotel phone rang, and Piers nearly jumped out of his skin. His pulse pounding, he picked up the handle and put it to his ear. "Yes?"

"There's a man here to see you. Mr. Smith."

Mr. *Novalight* Smith. Piers picked up his sword. "Thank you. You can send him to the room."

If the next few minutes didn't go as Piers hoped, the last thing he would do on this world would be to run Novalight through. The billionaire scientist wouldn't bother Sophie again—because Piers had no doubt the man would try to study and use her abilities, with or without the Shard of Olympus to make them work.

Earlier, he'd made sure people in the lobby had seen Sophie leave, her luggage in hand. He'd spoken to the concierge about the Christmas tree in Rockefeller Center, just so the man would remember seeing her go. He'd even gone back to the desk and told them he was staying one more night on his own and would take care of checkout in the morning. Piers had watched enough of this *news channel* during the afternoon to know that killing people, even dangerous ones, carried a different weight here than it did in Thalyria. Systems in this place kept people accountable in ways he'd never seen in his life, and he wanted to make damn sure no one could blame Sophie for the dead man in their room.

Between the slow elevators and long corridors, it would take Novalight several minutes to get here. Hopefully, just on time.

Piers started chanting.

Call a god, lose a soul. He couldn't believe he was doing this again. He knew it brought misery. But he also believed it would keep Sophie safe. And put the shard back where it belonged.

Power gathered in the air around him. The chant required

several repetitions. He spoke faster, louder. The windows frosted over, filtering out the day's last light and the gently falling snow.

Piers started the final repetition. Would he even remember his time on Earth after Athena took him? Would he remember Sophie?

Yes, by gods. She'd burned herself into his soul.

He ended the chant and spoke the name of the goddess who put him here to begin with. "Athena!"

Golden light swirled in the room. It heated the air and melted the frost on the windows. Athena slipped out of the sunlit glow and regarded him with interest. She was a good foot taller than Piers even with her head cocked to one side. She wore a flowing white gown as opposed to the armor he'd last seen her in. Perhaps in New York, she had no need for her spear and shield. Piers couldn't help staring in awe. He didn't blame anyone but himself for his exile from Thalyria, and he almost wanted to thank Athena for bringing him to Sophie.

A small smile curved her lips, and her golden-brown eyes softened, as if she'd read his thoughts. The radiance around her disappeared, leaving only the electric lights. Athena outshined them all. "Piers of Sinta. You summon an Olympian again. Are you foolhardy or brave?"

Piers bowed his head. "Neither, I think. But I saw no other way."

"Call a god, lose a soul. Is that not what you learned?"

"It is." He lifted his hand, palm up, and presented the Shard of Olympus. Sophie had been able to wear it, though it burned his hand with cold. "But this was in danger of falling into the wrong hands, and it was putting an innocent woman and her family at risk."

Athena hummed in the back of her throat. "Indeed, it was." She reached out, and the shard floated from his hand to hers. Piers watched in wonder as she tucked it inside her chest, passing it through her skin and bones. The glacial-blue glow illuminated her from the inside out before disappearing, swallowed whole.

Piers let out an unsteady breath. A knock sounded at the door.

"In terms of losing a soul, I have an option to present." He moved toward the door. "I know it's not my choice, but please consider who caused the trouble here."

Piers opened the door. Novalight stood there, looking ready to take what he believed was his. He'd come alone, as requested. Maybe his ruffians were down the hall. Piers didn't care. He pulled him inside and shut the door.

"You're not Sophronia Iraklidis." Novalight glared beyond Piers's shoulder.

Piers turned, and his jaw slid ajar. Athena now wore an outfit much like Sophie's—slim-fitting jeans and a loose sweater that hung off one shoulder, something strappy underneath, and bright Christmas socks on her feet. She'd shrunk, though she remained tall. Her tight, upswept curls had given way to long, loose waves that tumbled to her waist. She could sit in a New York restaurant and fit in just like anyone else. Piers snapped his mouth shut. Maybe she did sometimes.

"I hear you've been terrorizing a young woman," Athena said. Even her voice had changed, losing power and resonance.

She sounded human and reminded him so much of Sophie, it hurt. The two females could be friends. Family. In a way, they were.

"I've been trying to get back what's mine from a *thief*. Are you a thief, too?" Novalight demanded.

"What's *yours*?" Athena laughed, the sound like shattered glass falling from a skyscraper. Her human veneer cracked, hinting at the deity beneath. "You speak awfully boldly for a man who doesn't know what he's talking about."

Color mottled Novalight's cheeks. "And who are you?"

Athena's smile turned blade sharp. Maybe she couldn't fit into the city that easily after all. "I'm the one who knows who that...crystal...really belongs to. It belongs to my father. I'm taking it to him."

Novalight barked a laugh.

Athena looked far from amused, and Piers drew his sword, flanking her in the now-crowded room. Novalight looked at Piers's weapon with disdain, maybe thinking it was a fake. Then his breathing changed.

Piers smiled. *That's right. Not a toy.* Novalight had scared Sophie. He deserved to know fear in return.

Piers didn't want him dead, though. Novalight was his alternate solution in this game of bargaining souls.

"If someone must be taken, then why not take him? Maybe you could give him to Ares," Piers cautiously suggested. "See how well he fares?" That would've been Kaia's fate if Piers hadn't offered to take her place. Ares had accepted, but then Athena swooped in and snatched Piers for this. Ares was down one soul he should've commanded, and Novalight could be it.

Athena pursed her lips. "Unfortunately, that's not possible. The Moirai have decreed his bloodline too important to future events. He must go on to produce children here on Earth."

Piers's heart sank. Not even Zeus could overrule the will of the Fates. So, this was it. It would be him.

Or gods forbid, Sophie.

"Here on Earth? What are you two lunatics talking about?" Novalight's wary gaze darted over them both, then to Piers's sword again.

"We're talking about life and death, the fate of men in the cosmos, and the role of destiny," Athena said blithely. "And really, this world considers him a genius?" She rolled her eyes.

Piers barely registered her scorn. His gut had turned to stone the moment his bargaining chip got swept off the table. His only concern now was Sophie and *her* life—making sure she lived it in peace.

Novalight chose that moment to lunge at him. Piers brought the hilt of his sword up whip-fast and cracked him in the face. This journey had begun with a broken nose. It might as well end with one.

Novalight reeled back with a gasp. Piers's mouth twisted in disgust. He didn't even hit him that hard. And if Athena couldn't take the bastard to another world or let Piers kill him, how would Sophie ever be safe?

Desperation filled him. Piers prided himself on solving problems, but he didn't know how to solve this. All the book learning and battle experience of his life couldn't free Sophie from a man protected by the Fates.

Nevertheless, he took a menacing step toward Novalight.

"How do *you* like being faced with someone bigger and scarier?" he ground out. "Think about how Sophie felt when you sent your men after her again and again."

Novalight hyperventilated, sucking in blood and half choking on it as he backed toward the door.

Glaring at Piers, Athena cocked out a jean-clad hip and flicked her hand toward the scientist. "Now I have to fix that."

Fury and confusion clashed like cymbals in Piers's head. Who *was* this goddess? Not the Athena he…really didn't know. He stopped in his tracks.

A noise clicked behind Novalight, the door flew open, and Sophie burst into the room.

"No!" Piers shouted.

"Yes!" Athena clapped.

"You!" Novalight grabbed her and dragged her against his chest.

Piers reacted on pure instinct. He freed Sophie from Novalight's hold with a sharp downward strike, spun her out of the way, and threw the man against the wall so hard the son of a Cyclops shattered the plaster and dropped.

"Ugh. Now I have to fix *that*." Athena scowled at him again. "And the bathroom. You're in Attica now, so you need to get something through your thick, Thalyrian, he-man-warrior head. Destruction and maiming: *bad*. Piers and Sophie live happily ever after: *good*."

"But…" Piers's heart pounded. He kept an eye on the unconscious Novalight as he reached for Sophie. "Call a god, lose a soul. One of us…" He gripped Sophie tighter, whispering to her, "You shouldn't have come back."

"I had to." She wrapped her arms around him. "I couldn't just leave you."

"You should've." Athena wasn't the only danger here. There was Novalight—not that Sophie had known that.

Athena fluffed her hair. "The Fates say I can't have Novalight—although I think he'd make a fun tool for Hephaestus or good target practice for Artemis. Lucky for you both: different place, different rules." Her mouth quirked up. "I'm not *technically* bound to take a soul from Attica. Thalyria is the only place where that rule is set in stone. People there wanted Olympians to intervene entirely too much. It was getting out of hand and had to be controlled."

Shock and cautious hope tightened every muscle in Piers's body. Summoning had definitely been controlled. Those scrolls had been *buried*. And the information half lost and misunderstood.

"Are you saying...we're free?" He hesitated to understand—in case he *didn't*. He feared a trick that would leave him devastated.

Athena's head swiveled toward Novalight, sliding in a way that reminded him she wasn't at all human. "Oh, I can do better than that."

A stick appeared in her hand. She waved it. "Bibbidi-bobbidi-boo." Athena winked at Sophie. "I've always wanted to say that. Or at least, for the last seventy years or so."

Novalight rose to his feet like a ragdoll. Athena spun him around several times with glittering, swirling magic, bringing him back to consciousness and fixing his nose. She hit him over the head with her stick, and he disappeared.

Piers blinked hard, making sure the man was really gone. Sophie's relieved laughter unraveled the knots in his chest.

"That was all for show." Athena grinned, especially at Sophie. "I couldn't resist."

"What happened to him?" Sophie asked, smiling back.

"He's back in his house on Christmas eve, contemplating calling the woman he'll eventually make those fated babies with, and not remembering a single thing about either of you or the Shard of Olympus. The whole thing never happened. His hired guns have no idea why they were out and about and getting pummeled in New York. His archeological site in the Mediterranean turned out to be a complete dud, and he'll sell the entire island tomorrow to a professional soccer player from England who's about to retire."

Piers understood only parts of that, but Sophie nodded, appearing to like the plan.

"That's brilliant. Thank you." Sophie blushed. Athena might seem less intimidating masquerading as a thirty-something New Yorker, but she was still an Olympian and radiated power.

Athena looked at Sophie almost with affection. "You won't have your magic without the Shard of Olympus. The shard was dormant, like all magic here, until it encountered *Heracleidae*. Aaron first, although his blood was very diluted. The shard spoke to him just enough to spark some research into his ancient lineage—and yours. The magic is far stronger in your blood."

"I don't want magic." Sophie shuddered. "It terrifies me."

"As it should." Athena sighed. "The people of Earth have

invented terrible enough weapons as it is. Magic has no place here."

Sophie murmured her agreement as she tucked herself into Piers's side.

"What happens next?" Piers asked, still fearing a trick in the end. He wouldn't put it past Athena to let the other shoe drop now and kick him in the head.

The goddess tsked at him, chuckling under her breath. Then she waved her magic stick again. Several things appeared on the bed. "Well, you're still exiled—sorry. Can't change that."

Piers wasn't sorry. Not with Sophie by his side. Not with the life he could imagine for them.

"So, here's a birth certificate, passport, driver's license, and university diploma—three in fact, including one from Oxford." She handed him several papers, a hard little rectangle with his image on it, and a small blue book. "You own a highly successful auction house in Connecticut that restores, appraises, and sells ancient artifacts from around the world, particularly the Mediterranean basin. Here's the deed to the warehouse and showroom." She handed him something else. "You're well-known in your field and regularly asked to consult on anything pertaining to antiquities. However, you read nothing but academic works and really need to branch out. I suggest Nora Roberts." Athena handed him a paperback.

Sophie gasped. "I have the rest of that series!"

"I know." Athena smirked. "That's the brand-new release."

Overwhelmed by gratitude and relief, Piers could only smile and shake his head while the women talked about something called Netflix. He only partially listened, his mind already focused ahead and happiness welling in his chest. Sophie and he had served their goddess well, and she'd rewarded them. He was still half lost, but he knew he'd catch on fast, especially with Sophie guiding him through every day of this new life.

~ EPILOGUE ~

Four years later, Pinebury, Connecticut

PIERS RUBBED HIS hands together, smiling at a job well done. The Christmas tree was up, the girls were sticky with candy-cane sugar—including Sophie—and he'd finally gotten that stubborn cord of colored lights to work. Met and Moma, their two Golden Retrievers, had only broken one ornament this year so far with their excitedly thumping tails, which seemed a vast improvement over last year's carnage when they'd still been puppies.

Met licked sugar off Athena's face while she giggled, and Moma was doing the same to little Zoe's fingers. In the grand tradition of the Iraklidis of Connecticut, they'd given their children Greek names. Athena, after the goddess, and Zoe, meaning life. It had seemed only fitting to both him and Sophie, since Athena had given them this life they were living.

"Who wants to put the star on?" Piers held up the sparkly golden topping for their Christmas tree.

Both girls jumped up. "Me! Me! Daddy, me!"

Piers's heart grew so big in his chest that it pushed against his ribs. He sometimes still wished his Thalyrian family could see who he'd become and what he'd accomplished, but what he had here in Pinebury—including the extended family that would be arriving soon to "bake the boosh" for Sophie's last week of school before Christmas—made any loss and heartbreak he'd suffered worth it. Regrets were real, especially concerning Griffin and Cat, but he wouldn't change anything. His choices brought him here. To Sophie. To Athena and Zoe.

Clearing the rising thickness from his throat, he smiled at his girls. "Well, I guess it's both of you, then." He hoisted a daughter onto each shoulder.

"Piers..." Sophie gave him a *Be careful* look, but he just grinned at her. There was no way in the Underworld he would drop his children.

"Hold on." Sophie popped up from patting the dogs and getting her own sticky fingers licked. "I'll get the camera."

She came back with her phone and started snapping pictures. Piers got Athena and Zoe to both hold the star and leaned in, helping Zoe with her shorter arms and more questionable balance.

"It's on!" Athena squealed in delight.

"On! On!" Zoe chanted. Her wet little fingers smacked Piers in the eye, and he blinked, grinning.

"Get ready for landing," he announced, pretending to be an airplane until he reached the living room couch and gently tumbled them onto it.

The dogs immediately joined the girls. Where the girls went, the dogs followed. Athena buried her face in Moma's neck and started kissing.

Sophie watched them play, taking more pictures, before turning her smiling gaze on the Christmas tree again. Piers joined her, giving the tall, full tree a satisfied onceover.

"I think it's our prettiest tree yet," Sophie said, resting her head on his shoulder.

Piers looped his arm around her. "Maybe we should get two next year. Really spruce up the living room." He waited for it.

Sophie let out a groan. She laughed, too, though. "That is *such* a dad joke."

"I'll take that as a compliment." He chuckled.

She rolled her eyes, teasing, "You're lucky I love you."

"I know I'm lucky." He kissed her. "I love you, too." So much his heart burned with it.

She sighed happily, snuggling against him. "The star looks nice."

Piers nodded. It did. It was also crooked and had candy-cane fingerprints on it. "This will be our fifth Christmas together." It was amazing how time flew, even without realms to conquer and bloodbath battles to get into. He was glad they'd maintained Sophie's holiday traditions. She now knew the gods of Olympus were more than myth, but they didn't reign here and hadn't for millennia. She'd maintained her faith while recognizing that other powerful forces existed in the universe. But when they told stories from Greek mythology to their children, they treated them as a bit more than fiction. Piers scattered in tales about his family as though they came from ancient times, too, and were long-lost ancestors, just like Heracles. It was the only way for his girls to know their other aunts and uncles and grandparents.

The doorbell rang. The dogs started barking.

"Auntie Xanthe's here with Ya-Ya!" Athena cried.

"Ya-Ya!" Zoe echoed.

The girls ran to the door—well, one toddled—along with Met and Moma. Piers could've sworn Met held back to help Zoe along and let the little girl, whose fist curled into her coat, use her sturdy frame for balance.

"You're helping us bake the *Bûches de Noël* this year!" Sophie called after their daughters. "You, too." She squeezed Piers's waist, gazing up at the bright Christmas star one last time before the door flew open and all hell broke loose for the entire weekend.

Piers smiled. He couldn't wait. The cozy red house would smell like mulled cider, cake, and chocolate, the family would laugh and tease and gossip, especially when Pappou and Sophie's brothers—some with wives and children now— showed up "unexpectedly" for dinner, and Piers would know he'd ended up exactly where he was meant to be when the Fates decided on *his* future.

Dear Reader,

I hope you enjoyed *Of Fate and Fire*. If you'd like to find out more about Cat and Griffin and their epic adventures in Thalyria, I hope you'll check out The Kingmaker Chronicles. You can also find out more about Piers's family and friends in a brand-new novel, *A Curse of Queens*, coming next in that exciting fantasy world.

Curious about what happens with Novalight's family? You can find out just how terrifying one of his descendants becomes as rebel captain Tess Bailey and her crew of Robin Hood-like thieves fight him and his oppressive regime for all they're worth in the steamy and action-packed Nightchaser series.

Thank you for reading!

About Amanda Bouchet

USA Today bestselling author Amanda Bouchet grew up in New England where she spent much of her time tromping around in the woods and making up grand adventures in her head. It was inevitable that one day she would start writing them down. Amanda writes fantasy romance and space opera romance and was a Goodreads Choice Awards top ten finalist for Best Debut in 2016 with her first novel, *A Promise of Fire*.

For more about Amanda and her writing, please visit her website at amandabouchet.com.

Other Titles by Amanda Bouchet

The Kingmaker Chronicles
A Promise of Fire (Book 1)
Breath of Fire (Book 2)
Heart on Fire (Book 3)
A Curse of Queens (Book 4, coming soon)

Nightchaser
Nightchaser (Book 1)
Starbreaker (Book 2)
Dawnmaker (Book 3, coming soon)

A Curse for Spring

For more information about Amanda and her books, please visit amandabouchet.com. You can also connect with her on Facebook, Twitter, Instagram, Goodreads, TikTok, and BookBub.

Thank you for reading!

The King of Hel

by

Grace Draven

Castil il Veras, daughter of lesser boyars, attends the gatherings that celebrate her best friend's upcoming marriage to the cursed king of a sorcerous kingdom. She soon learns that even marked by the magic of the Wastelands, Doranis of Helenrisia is everything she's ever desired in a mate—and absolutely forbidden to her. Bound by duty to crown and country, Doranis has traveled to the Caskadan empire to marry a woman who loathes the sight of him. During the prenuptial celebrations, he meets a scribe who finds him fascinating instead of repellent, but Castil is beyond his reach. Fate, however, would have it otherwise, and a beseeching letter from a dying queen will bring them together again in a land gripped by endless winter and old magic.

Dedicated in loving memory to:

Lori Snow Stevenson

Christopher Downer

Lora Gasway

Whereof the man, that with me trod
This planet, was a noble type
Appearing 'ere the times were ripe,
That friend of mine who lives in God...

Alfred, Lord Tennyson
In Memoriam, A.H.H.

Dear Reader,

THE KING OF HEL saw its first incarnation as a short story entry into a contest with a small digital-only publisher in 2005. To my amazement, it won. The prize was a contract with the publishing house running the contest, and THE KING OF HEL became my first foray into professional publishing. After several years, I decided to extend the short story to a novella for the FIRE OF THE FROST anthology.

The couple of the story is based on real historical figures – Louis XIV of France and his second wife, Francoise d'Aubigné, marquise de Maintenon. I've been fascinated by de Maintenon for decades. Hers is a rags-to-riches story in the truest sense—a woman who was born in a prison, married a disabled playwright who made her a widow, became the governess of several of Louis' illegitimate children, and captured the heart of one of the most famous kings in history. She was three years older than him and married him via a secret ceremony when she was nearly fifty. She was known as the uncrowned queen of France. Louis often referred to her as "Her Steadfastness."

This story is also inspired by Tennyson's poem *In Memoriam, A.H.H.*.It's about friendship, the devastation of losing it, and how it survives beyond death and grief.

Best regards – Grace

~ Prologue ~

A FLARE OF spectral brightness across her closed eyelids and a warning hiss yanked Castil il Veras out of sleep. She opened her eyes in time to see a neatly folded letter take shape in the green-tinged flames of the witch torch on the table near her bed. It dropped to the table's surface with a soft plop before a draft from the adjacent window whisked it over the edge and under her bed.

She sat up, squinting against the torch's fading light until the bedchamber once more lay shrouded in darkness. Not bothering with finding candle and tinder, she flung the blankets off and swung out of bed to crouch down and feel for the letter. It had slid farther under the bed than she anticipated, and the floor was cold on her knees and feet as she crawled partway under the frame to reach it.

Messages sent to her in this fashion came from only one source, and Castil's stomach knotted at the knowledge of its source and the question of why it had arrived now, in the small hours of the night when the dark was deep-set and the dawn still hours away.

Finally capturing the elusive note, she lit the single candle kept at her bedside with an ember from her small brazier and perched on the mattress's edge to view the message.

Written on the finest parchment she could never afford herself, it was sealed shut with a royal seal stamped in black wax still warm under her fingertips.

"Why are you awake at this hour writing letters, Kareena?" Only the thin squeak of a mouse in one corner of the room answered her.

Castil frowned, half afraid of the contents hidden within the parchment's sharp creases. In the months following Kareena's marriage and departure to the far kingdom of Helenrisia as its new queen, her letters to Castil had turned increasingly melancholy. Even the impending birth of her first child hadn't raised her spirits, nor had Castil's replies despite their relentless cheerfulness.

The seal broke with a soft snap, and the parchment crackled as Castil carefully unfolded it to read. Kareena's elegant handwriting was less so in this letter and marred by a few ink blots and stains that looked suspiciously like splattered tear drops. Worry blossomed into fully bloomed alarm as Castil read the contents.

My dearest friend,

It's been long months since I've felt the warmth of the sun. Many would envy my position—a queen, and one who will soon bear the heir to a throne. But this place...it's desolate. The baby drains the strength from me. My consolation is I no longer have to suffer the king's touch. You know my heart. I want to go home but cannot. I implore you, Castil, travel north. You're the sister of my heart, and now, more than ever, I need you and your laughter. Don't wait to reply. The last ships leave for Helenrisia at autumn's waning. I've sent monies to speed your journey. I await you with hope.

Kareena

Heart racing, Castil tossed the letter to the side and strode to the table where the witch torch shared space with numerous ink wells, quills, books, and stacks of poorer quality parchment than Kareena's note. The chair's seat was cold on her buttocks when she sat, her thin shift no protection from the chill. At least summer hadn't completely abandoned them yet. The nights had grown colder, but she didn't yet have to thaw frozen ink before she could write.

This time she wouldn't refuse Kareena's offer to travel north and willingly trap herself in the frozen depths of an isolated, northern kingdom for several months. She'd had her reasons for refusing the first time, some sound and logical, others born of guilt and emotions best left buried. They didn't matter now. Her best friend needed her.

Her own scrawl wasn't much neater than Kareena's and her reply much shorter but hopefully reassuring. The wax seal she used to close the letter bore the arms of the Veras family—a lowly house and one, some would say, not fit to correspond with royalty in any way. Castil had never paid attention to such prejudice.

She turned her attention to the witch torch, a rare and valuable gift bequeathed to her by the king of Helenrisia. Its twin stood somewhere in Kareena's chambers, and the two women had learned to use the artifact's magic to communicate with each other across long distances in a matter of moments. While Castil considered the torch her most treasured possession, in her mind its greatest worth lay not only in its purpose but in the thoughtfulness of the gift-giver.

Guilt snapped its jaws in warning, and she shoved that particular thought away before reciting the spell that reignited the witch torch. Emerald flame flared to life a second time, and Castil held her reply to Kareena in its center, watching as the sorcerous fire consumed the parchment until it was nothing more than sparkles that soon vanished with the dying flame. Once again only the candle's ordinary light cast an anemic pool of luminescence on the table.

Castil rubbed her arms, staring at the now extinguished witch torch and repeated aloud the words she'd written. "I'll be there soon, love. Don't despair. I'm coming."

~ 1 ~

Summer of the previous year

"I CAN THINK of a thousand places I'd rather be right now instead of here. But at least you're with me." Kareena offered Castil a weak smile that went no farther than her mouth. Fear lurked as a shadow in her eyes. "This would be so much harder if you weren't."

Castil clasped her friend's hand, icy despite the heat generated by the crowd in the emperor's receiving chamber. "Of course I'd be with you." The invitation for all boyars, greater and lesser, to attend the welcoming ceremonies for the King of Helenrisia and his delegation had been more mandatory summons than invitation, but she would have gone regardless to support Kareena. "Who else is going to tell you that if you don't stop worrying that hair ornament you're wearing, it's going to fall out, and you'll get an ear-blistering for it from your mother?"

The threat of such an outcome made Kareena drop her other hand from one of the many glittering jewels woven into a braid at her temple. "She's probably hunting for me right now, nose in the air like a she-wolf trying to catch the scent of her prey."

A short laugh burst past Castil's lips, and the sound made Kareena's anemic smile widen to a grin. It was an accurate description of the haughty Dame Marcam, and Castil didn't find it difficult to imagine the formidable matriarch of House Marcam doing exactly that, teeth bared to anyone who got in her way while she searched for her errant daughter among the crush of people crammed into the usually spacious chamber like fish in a barrel. Her snarling visage would only worsen when she discovered her only daughter in the company of "that Veras beggar." Castil looked forward to the chance of tweaking the dame's ire even more when she saw her.

Kareena lost her grin, and her tone turned mournful. "I wish I could stay back here forever, unnoticed and forgotten."

They stood wedged into a corner at the very back of the room. Had such a wish been Castil's, it might well come true, but not for Kareena. Castil sighed, sorry she couldn't grant such a thing, but she was only a powerless scribe with no influence, no real connections, and certainly no magic to change time or circumstance. She squeezed Kareena's hand. "We can stay back here until the guards open the doors to the ballroom. And if you want, I'll accompany you inside to find your parents."

"If they don't track me down here first."

"I'm sure your father is too busy negotiating some pact with another boyar, and I doubt even your mother can overcome this mob to reach you."

The words had barely escaped Castil's lips when the pair of colossal doors separating the ballroom from the receiving chamber slowly creaked open, and the sea of greater and lesser boyars surged forward in a single wave.

Humanity swept inside like an endless tide. Where before there had only been a wall of silk and velvet-clad shoulders in front of them, Castil and Kareena now stared at the empty room's opulence—and Dame Marcam's scowling features when she spotted them in their corner.

She ignored the man standing nearby, curled her upper lip at Castil, and jabbed a finger at Kareena before stabbing it toward her feet in an obvious command for her daughter to attend her immediately.

Kareena spoke under her breath, though they were too far across the room for her mother to hear. "As much as I despise her, I'd live with her the rest of my days if it meant I didn't have to go through with this awful marriage." She didn't let go of Castil's hand as she reluctantly obeyed the command.

If Castil had been cursed with such a mother, she'd marry the neighbor's sheepdog to get away from her. She kept that thought behind her teeth and waved to her father who waited at the entrance as well. She'd lost him to the crush when they'd first arrived but didn't worry. He had many friends here among the lesser boyars, and she'd heard their shared war stories so many times before, she could recite them word for word in her sleep. No need to hear them yet again, and her time with Kareena was very much borrowed.

His weathered features creased into an answering smile. He ignored Dame Marcam as studiously as she ignored him but offered Kareena a quick bow when she approached. "Our best wishes for you today, Lady il Marcam." When she visited their house, he called her Kareena, but here, in the royal palace, all observed formalities.

Kareena paused and returned the bow with a deep curtsy despite her mother's hissing outrage. "Thank you, Lord Veras. I'm so happy to have Castil here with me."

Happy for Castil's company, not for this particular occasion no matter how grand. Castil wanted to hug her forlorn friend but didn't dare with her harpy of a mother waiting to pounce.

And pounce she did, reaching out with a clawed hand to snatch her daughter away. "Stop wasting time with these nobodies and find your spine," she snapped. "Your groom will arrive soon, and you will NOT embarrass me." With that, she yanked Kareena across the threshold.

Kareena cast a desperate look over her shoulder as if begging Castil to rescue her. Castil mouthed "I'll see you in there," hoping she understood the silent message.

"Foul woman," Devilos Veras said, offering his arm to Castil. "And always has been. At least Kareena can escape her clutches with this marriage."

The marriage between Kareena il Marcam and Doranis of the royal House Alisdane had been arranged since before Kareena was released from her nurse's lead strings.

Sons and daughters of the greater boyars were regularly married off to royalty and aristocracy of other countries. Kareena was no exception. Marital ties to the Helenese royal family promised profitable returns in trade as well as political influence in two courts. Kareena, raised to understand her duty as the only child of a powerful nobleman, had been stoic regarding her fate. Only as the time neared for the wedding and her first meeting with her future husband did she grow visibly worried, then frightened.

Castil settled her hand in the crook of Devilos's elbow and the two followed the mother and daughter pair as the great doors closed behind them. "She dreads the marriage more than she fears her mother."

She recalled a recent conversation she'd had with Kareena when the other woman had visited for an afternoon. Castil had put aside her latest commission to spend the day with her and calm her nerves.

Grim and pale, Kareena sipped the tea Castil had brewed with a shaking hand, sloshing some of the liquid over her cup's rim onto the saucer. "They say the king of Helenrisia is cursed. Marked by the Wastelands and their magic." She shuddered. "What if he is a hideous, misshapen creature? And I will have to bed him."

Castil patted her arm, offering whatever comfort she could. "No one has seen him, Kareena. You know how rumor starts. And if he is unhandsome but kind, will it be so bad?" The words sounded patronizing to her ears, for it wasn't she who would soon be sold into the marriage. Yet her words soothed Kareena who smiled weakly and nodded.

"No, not so bad. And I can always close my eyes and imagine that it's Farnoush Salbata who beds me."

"Kareena!" Castil laughed and soon they'd both forgotten the upcoming nuptials and the impending arrival of the mysterious Helenese king.

Months of uneasy speculation had finally culminated in this

mass gathering of every boyar family in the Caskadanian empire, most vying for space and a view of the raised dais at the far end of the ballroom where a trio of portable thrones had been placed—two for the Caskadan emperor and empress, one for the Helenese king.

While there was more space to breathe than in the smaller receiving chamber, the crowd had gathered into another tightly packed knot for the closest spot to the dais. Castil, standing in the back with her father, and lacking both height and a tall stool on which to stand, could see nothing of the thrones or Kareena.

"You'd think by the way they're all practically trampling each other for the opportunity to parade their daughters before him, that the king isn't already betrothed." She exhaled a frustrated sigh. "I can't see anything. Can you?"

Devilos nodded. "Some." He nudged her to step back. "We'll be able to see better if we aren't so close."

She did as he suggested and found that while the thrones were now farther away, she had an easier time seeing them. Kareena remained hidden, no doubt flattened at the front of the crush and shackled to her parents just in case she decided to bolt.

Shy, bookish, easily intimidated Kareena. What a horror this must be for her. Castil's heart broke for the woman she considered a younger sister as much as a close friend.

"Better?" Devilos asked her. She nodded, and he turned his gaze back to the cluster of aristocrats. "The Helenese king may have already chosen his bride, but he might still choose a Caskadanian concubine or two, and there are plenty of families more than willing to offer up their daughters as mistresses to a king, even one rumored to be cursed. Any offspring he sires on them won't be outcasts. A royal bastard is always more royal than they are bastard."

Her gut clenched at such a possibility. Gods forbid Kareena would have to deal with a royal mistress or worse, a pack of them, while navigating the difficult terrain of a new marriage to an unfamiliar man, a new country, and a foreign court. "Pray this king isn't such an insensitive wretch," she replied.

Suddenly, to the right of the dais, a narrow door, decorated to blend in with the wall behind the thrones, opened wider under an unseen hand. Guards instantly ushered the crowd back from the dais, herding the curious boyars until they parted to either side of the ballroom as if waiting for a parade to march down its center. Wedged between her father and the sour-smelling Dame Nibs, Castil leaned as far forward as she could without falling for a better view of the door and cleaner air.

She spotted Kareena with her parents, all three still close to the dais in a position of privilege and separate from the others. Boyars whispered to each other, placing bets as to whether or not the future bride would faint, how generous the dowry Lord Marcam had settled on his only child, and what would a king cursed look like?

Kareena swayed on her feet, her features gray as she clutched her father's arm and ignored whatever furious rant her mother poured into her ear. Her gaze remained riveted to the open door as if she expected Death to stride through instead of her future husband. Castil knew in that moment her terrified friend made no distinction between the two.

An expectant hush settled on the Caskadanian court when a herald emerged from the doorway. He banged the butt of his staff on the floor three times before announcing in a booming voice, "Their exalted Majesties, Emperor Besamor and Empress Pilana."

As one, the crowd bent the knee and bowed their heads before their rulers. Still, not a gaze dropped to the floor as curiosity overrode etiquette and protocol. No one wanted to miss that first look at the cursed king of Helenrisia when he finally entered the ballroom.

The Caskadanian rulers came to stand in front of their thrones but waited to sit, and the court remained kneeling. A few behind Castil muttered their disapproval.

"If it takes this long to walk through a door, we'll be here all night for the rest of this infernal gathering."

"Any longer on this floor, and I won't be able to stand."

Relief came in the form of six men who entered the ballroom in pairs and fanned out behind the remaining empty throne in a half moon barrier. Dressed in unadorned black except for the scabbards at their belts and the cloak pins that secured their cloaks to their shoulders, they reminded Castil of tall crows. All were dark-haired, some swarthy and others pale, and they surveyed the room with expressionless gazes.

Castil thought them a handsome, dignified group, but they lacked a certain stamp of sovereignty on both their somber clothing and their faces. The Helenese delegation, no doubt. Or at minimum, the king's personal guard.

While their arrival had raised the court's curiosity to a

fever pitch, it was the king's appearance that sent a shock through the waiting crowd. Gasps loud enough to be heard outside the palace walls rippled throughout the ballroom. Even Castil, practiced at hiding her thoughts and emotions when forced to swim these shark-infested waters, inhaled sharply.

None of the conjectures she and Kareena had swapped about Kareena's bridegroom did justice to the reality of King Doranis of Helenrisia as he crossed the thresholds from the doorway's shadows to the lamplit ballroom. The herald banged his staff three more times on the floor, announcing the king's presence. A wasted effort. There was no mistaking that a monarch had entered the chamber to take his place next to the emperor and empress who seemed diminished by his presence.

His garb alone was the stuff of wonder. Or nightmares. Like his personal guard, he wore black and was cloaked, but there the similarity ended. A bleached crow skull perched on both of his shoulders, sewn into his cloak and surrounded by a flourish of black feathers that shimmered blue in the lamplight. A double silver chain of office draped across his wide chest, and beneath the shifting folds of the cloak Castil glimpsed intricate embroidery of silver thread stitched onto either velvet or silk.

His headpiece was a monstrous thing, a marriage of black crown embedded with onyx splinters and a pair of spiraled dark horns. Sheer black veils hung from their tips to cascade down the king's back and added to his already impressive height so that he seemed a giant. It served as a kind of wimple as well, framing his jaw and hiding his neck and hair. Doing so only emphasized a face thin and haughty. And vaguely unhuman. Castil, like everyone around her, was riveted.

He's handsome, she thought, though not in the way of any accepted form of beauty. White eyebrows slanted above a pair of deep-set eyes whose irises were so light a blue, they seemed almost colorless, his pupils like black diamonds at their centers. His was a thin face carved of alabaster, with hollow cheeks and a long blade of a nose that he stared down as he returned the stunned court's gawking with disdainful regard. A generous mouth with its lush bottom lip barely blunted the sharpness of his features. Here indeed was the cursed magus king of the northern Wastelands.

Castil managed to drag her gaze away long enough to search out Kareena, still near the thrones. Her pallor matched her bridegroom's, only hers was the result of horror instead of birthright or curse. She looked ready to faint or retch, and Castil chafed at the knowledge that for now there was nothing she could do to save her friend from a marriage she never wanted. At the moment, trapped among the other boyars by watchful guards, she couldn't even offer a comforting embrace. The memory of Kareena's words about imagining another lover in her nuptial bed didn't make her laugh now. Surely, no fantasy of the handsome Farnoush, regardless of how vivid, could possibly blot out the powerful presence of Kareena's soon-to-be husband.

The emperor gave a wordless gesture with one hand and finally sat. His empress and their guest did the same. The crowd of boyars breathed a collective sigh of relief as they were allowed to rise from bent knee.

Castil flinched in sympathy at the creaks and pops of old bones, not to mention a few muttered curses. Even her jovial father, strong and fit, grumbled close to her ear. "Glad to see no one's in a rush to get things moving along." His mild sarcasm made her smile. "This will prove to be a long night for all of us."

He wasn't wrong. At the first notes of music played by the court musicians, the boyars spilled past the barriers no longer enforced by palace guards and into the ballroom's center. Introductions were about to begin, and while Doranis of Helenrisia had already chosen his bride, there were still connections to be made, favors to curry, and diplomacy to be exercised. Every boyar family here tonight, greater and lesser, would present themselves to the northern king. If they were lucky, they'd be done with it all before Castil was an old woman.

The crowd's morbid curiosity about the king of Helenrisia rose to a fever pitch when his bride's family were the first to make their formal introduction. By chance, a sliver of space opened up where Castil could see Kareena's profile as she offered her betrothed her hand. While Lord and Lady Marcam practically beamed with triumph, their daughter wore the look of the condemned. She stared down at the floor as if praying it might open up and swallow her whole.

Castil couldn't hear what the king said, but his face had lost its haughty expression. Still stoic but no longer cold, and she swore a line of sympathy bisected his pale brow for a moment as he held Kareena's hand.

That first meeting was quick and, in Castil's opinion, anything but reassuring. She knew it futile to try and reach Kareena in the milling crowd. She managed to catch her eye briefly, offering what encouragement she could with a smile. Kareena gave a grim nod before turning away to nod at something her mother said.

The evening passed in an endless line of introductions. As lesser boyars, Castil and her father were nearly the last of the families to be presented. She tried to still the butterflies that fluttered madly in her belly. Like everyone else, she had been unable to take her eyes off the king. Unlike them, she didn't find him ugly or strange. He was, in all ways, a striking individual, the air of leadership resting heavily on his broad shoulders.

When they finally reached the dais where the king sat, the herald announced their names in a voice growing hoarser. "Devilos Veras and his daughter, Castil il Veras."

Doranis's bored expression shifted when he noticed Castil staring at the embroidered insignia on his tunic.

"Blood of fey kings," she translated and immediately clapped a hand over her mouth, mortified at speaking out of turn. The king's pale blue gaze sharpened.

Devilos's fingers dug into his daughter's arm as Doranis straightened in his seat, then leaned forward, renewed interest glittering in his eyes. "You read *doa Enrai?*"

She tried to answer, but stopped at the increasing tightness of her father's grip. He spoke for her. "Yes, Your Majesty."

Castil was having none of it. "My father and I are scribes. We're familiar with the old languages such as *doa Enrai.*"

Her lips thinned at the scornful mutters around them. Aristocracy engaged in trade was a thing viewed with contempt. Judging by Doranis's intrigued regard, he didn't hold the same opinion. She found herself admiring the flawless alabaster face with its long thin nose and prominent cheekbones.

"Fascinating," he said. "I have in my possession a set of scrolls written in *doa Enrai*. They are accounts of the last days of the Elder cities before the advent of the Wastelands. I've translated some of the writing. Perhaps I'll send copies to you." His gaze slid over Castil, curious and measuring. "My compliments, Madam il Veras."

Castil blushed, surprised by his remark. She heard the restless murmurings of the boyars waiting behind them and bowed with her father before leaving the king and merging with the crowd.

"Sometimes, daughter," Devilos said. "You can benefit from greater discretion and control of your tongue."

She couldn't argue with him. He was right. "Forgive me, Papa. Sometimes my words run away from me." A thought made her brighten. "He seems pleasant enough and that was a generous offer he made." What a treasure it would be to receive copies of *doa Enrai* scrolls from the king of Helenrisia himself. Not that she held any expectation of such a thing happening. Polite conversation was merely that—polite. Rarely did anything come of it.

Devilos was obviously of the same opinion. "I wouldn't put down any wagers on seeing a leaf of parchment much less an entire scroll. Kings don't make time for the likes of us, Castil."

It wasn't a disparagement, merely a recognition of reality. Castil nodded. "I never gamble anyway, Papa." That short meeting, however, had been fruitful in her opinion. She could use it to offer some small reassurance to Kareena if she ever managed to find her again in the ever-shifting mob of gossiping boyars.

A few cast her disapproving looks as she split from her father so that he might visit with old comrades-in-arms and she could find her friend. Whispers followed, some that made her snort with pent-up laughter, others that made her blood boil and bite her lip to keep from snarling back.

"She's always been a bold one. An embarrassment to her father I'm sure."

"An excellent scribe so I'm told but too eager to speak her mind."

"There's a one in need of a muzzle."

"She's a good example for why lesser boyars belong only in ale houses and brothels instead of palaces. Battle fodder is all they're good for."

Comments like the last two set Castil's teeth on edge. She was much more mindful of the impact on her father's reputation than they gave her credit for. Were she not, she'd respond to those snide whispers with a very personal, very physical response.

Instead, she reminded herself none of these people or their opinions about her meant anything. She hadn't given one care about attending this sheep herding except for how she might help Kareena, and until she found her again, she was no help at all.

Her persistence paid off when she found Kareena hiding behind a colossal vase of flowers adjacent to an equally massive tapestry covering one wall from ceiling to floor. She looked ready to dart behind the covering if anyone approached. Her delicate shoulders slumped when she caught Castil's gaze, and her wide eyes welled with tears. She didn't move from her hiding spot, and Castil shouldered her way through the crowd, keeping an eye out for Dame Marcam who, no doubt, patrolled the ballroom, looking for her escapee offspring.

She took up guard beside Kareena, nudging her a little more behind the tapestry so at first glance it looked as if only Castil hovered by the vase. "Stay right here. People will only see me chatting to myself." A peculiar sight to be sure and one to raise a few eyebrows but that was it. No one here would take the time to seek out the nobody daughter of a lesser boyar for conversation. Within the tapestry's concealing shadows, Kareena wiped tears from her cheeks. "Dry your tears, love," she warned the girl. "Or your mother will be on a rampage for you reddening your nose."

Kareena sniffled. "I know, I know. But I couldn't help it." She made a last swipe across her face with her sleeve. "Did you see him? My gods, he's grotesque."

Castil opened her mouth to argue. The Helenese king's choice of clothing certainly didn't appeal to most, but the man himself was anything but grotesque in her opinion. An unusual beauty brought on by a curse of the Wastelands, or so it was rumored, as if whatever arcane malice laid upon him had leached the color from him. "We all saw him," she said. "Try to look past the crown and garb. Without those, he's simply a tall, soft-spoken man in need of a little sun."

Kareena's watery chuckle broke through her sniffles. "You

make him sound so mundane when you put it like that."

From what Castil could tell after her brief introduction to the king, there was nothing mundane about him. He fascinated her. Utterly. But if mundanity elevated him in Kareena's eyes and made him less frightening, then mundane he would be.

"You have the rest of the evening to discover more about him," she said. "Now that introductions are finished, there will be dancing and conversation. And as his betrothed, you'll claim the majority of his time." Even the tapestry's shadows didn't hide Kareena's blanch. Castil took her hand, frowning at its coldness. "I only had seconds to talk to him, but I found him to be very pleasant and engaging, Kareena. You will too."

"But that's because you have a talent for conversation. You can talk to anyone. I can't. I have no idea what to say."

Were she not trying to soothe her friend's nerves, Castil might have laughed at the irony of her comment. The trait her father felt got her in trouble was the same one Kareena praised and saw as a strength. She squeezed the other woman's fingers. "Ask him to tell you about his country. What his favorite thing about it is. Did he witness anything interesting during his journey to Caskadan? Those topics will guarantee you won't have to say much at all, and he'll do all the talking. You'll learn a great deal about him just by listening."

A brightness lit Kareena's pinched features. "That's a good idea. Hopefully the dancing won't outlast the conversation."

The marriage would last much longer than a dance. Kareena would have to learn a great many things fast, including the art of conversation, if she wanted to successfully navigate a relationship with her new husband. And his court. Castil embraced her father's advice and chose not to mention those things. Kareena had finally achieved a small bit of calm and no longer looked ready to burst into sobs. No need to undo good work.

"Are you ready to go back out there?" She tucked a stray strand of hair back into Kareena's complicated coif. "I'll stay with you until your mother chases me off or the king comes to ask for a dance."

Kareena frowned. "I dread both of those things."

Dame Marcam found them first, the thundercloud darkening her brow warning of an inevitable tongue-lashing. She snatched the glass of wine Kareena was drinking from her hand. "You'll not embarrass me by sinking into your cups and saying or doing something stupid." Her glare encompassed both her daughter and Castil. "The king has left the assembly for a moment but will return soon. You'll take the time to straighten your hair and gown." Her eyes narrowed even more. "Have you been crying?"

"No, Mother." A spark of rebellion lit her eyes. "I've only felt like it."

The Dame's eyebrows arched high. Castil was sure it was the first—and likely the last—time she'd find herself matching Dame Marcam in any way as her own eyebrows rose as well.

Well done, Kareena, she thought, wishing she could applaud that slight resistance to the tyrannical woman.

The dame didn't share in the admiration. She leveled a hostile stare on Castil. "Go away," she spat between her teeth.

Kareena gasped. "Mother!"

Dame Marcam ignored her. "I don't want you around my

daughter for the remainder of the assembly. You're nothing but trouble. A nuisance."

Had this been another boyar woman, Castil might have bristled and fired back an equally insulting reply. Instead, she only offered a snide smile and shallow bow. "I yield to your wishes, Madam." She nodded to Kareena. "Good luck," she mouthed and winked.

Kareena's mother huffed, grasped her daughter's elbow and marched her into the thick of the crowd, no doubt blistering her ears the entire way for associating with the likes of poor scribes who had no business being here in the first place.

Alone once more, Castil looked for her father. She stopped on occasion to chat with other lesser boyar families. The conversations were predictably focused on the king of Helenrisia and Kareena's fate as his future queen. Most knew that Castil was good friends with the bride. Some asked how Kareena fared, their expressions sympathetic. Others displayed a more avaricious curiosity—the kind that fueled gossip. A few were even envious.

"He could be a toad," one young woman declared. "And I'd be thrilled to marry him. Who wouldn't want to become a queen?"

"But he's so strange looking. 'Tis said the curse has altered him in ways that he's no longer truly human. Who knows how Wasteland magic affects a person?"

Castil kept her replies general. Kareena's feelings and thoughts were no business of theirs. Fortunately, those who would pry didn't have time to do so. The king returned with the emperor and empress, along with his personal guard who again took up places behind their sovereign. Once more the crowd gasped as one at the sight of him.

He no longer wore the voluminous cloak with its macabre bone decorations or the frightful headpiece that easily made him the tallest person in the room. He still wore all black—layers of brocade velvet and silk cut and sewn to enhance the lines of his body. The wide shoulders were still wide and emphasized a narrow waist. He was long-legged as well, the close cut of his trousers revealing muscular thighs.

He'd replaced the splinter crown and horns with a simple diadem of carved onyx. It gleamed darkly against his pale brow and a waterfall of silvery white hair that cascaded down his back and over his shoulders.

My gods, she thought. *What a beautiful man.*

How unfortunate Kareena so adamantly didn't feel the same way. Once more standing near the dais, she looked ready to bolt, and her throat flexed convulsively as she swallowed and took the hand Doranis offered her. He led her to the middle of the ballroom floor where they stood together and waited, majestic raven and delicate songbird, for the musicians to play. Doranis bent his head to say something. Kareena nodded but kept her gaze firmly on her feet.

When the music started, the two moved together with easy grace, as if they'd danced together for a lifetime. It was a testament to the years of dance lessons Kareena had taken as a greater boyar woman destined to be queen. Terrified and tongue-tied she might be, but she moved like water in her partner's arms.

They danced three dances in a row, with the watchful boyars joining them at the start of the third dance. The previously empty space filled up quickly, and Castil lost her unhampered view of them among the swirling, flashing mosaic of colorful gowns as couples moved to the rhythm of the music.

Except for a few lesser boyars with whom she danced, including her father and one of his friends, Castil watched from the sidelines. A neighbor partnered with her for a reel, and she even danced with the handsome Farnoush whom Kareena so admired. Castil found him vain and dull, though he was a capable dancer and didn't abuse her toes during the set.

The one person she would have loved to dance with was as far beyond her reach as the moon, his coveted time reserved for Kareena and other boyar woman of much greater rank. So it was to her amazement, and everyone else's as well, when Doranis suddenly stood in front of her, offering an elegant hand to her. "May we, Madam il Veras?"

Castil, who rarely suffered from speechlessness, only gaped at him for a moment before looking frantically for Kareena. She spotted her not far away giving Castil an enthusiastic nod and energetic hand gestures for her to accept the king's offer. With that blessing, Castil placed her hand in his grasp. "It would be a pleasure, Your Majesty."

A quick glance askance and a half smile told her he'd caught the silent exchange between her and Kareena. "It's obvious to all that you and Madam il Marcam are friends," he said as he swept her into the latest dance.

She nodded, quickly losing her nervousness at the possibility of stepping on his feet. Thanks to Kareena's teaching, Castil could dance passably well. Doranis was graceful and guided her with a sure hand through the intricate steps and the narrow spaces between other dancing couples. "We are," she replied. "The best of friends since I was ten and she was six. My father's estate shares a border with the much larger Marcam estate. We're neighbors." She and Kareena had been more than that for a long time. Better than friends, closer than siblings.

"Ah, I wondered if you were older. It seemed so." The corner of his mouth turned up at her questioning look.

Castil's heartbeat stuttered for a moment. Had her behavior been so inappropriate here that she'd caught the king's notice beyond that first clumsy introduction? Panic closed her throat for a moment before she beat it down. "May I ask what made you wonder such a thing?"

"You hold yourself more confidently. It's there in the way you speak and move." He tipped his chin toward Kareena who watched them. "She seems younger, less sure. I'm surprised there are only four years between you."

His observation was accurate, and his tone suggested there was no insult in the comparison, simply something to note. Still, Castil felt the urge to come to Kareena's defense. "She's shy with those she doesn't know but witty and endearing once a person earns her affection. I adore her. She reminds me there's wisdom in thinking before speaking." She offered Doranis a wry grin. "Something I'm not very good at."

"You speak well of my betrothed. I look forward to learning about this part of her character." A tiny frown marred his brow. "Once I can finally coax her into looking me in the face."

"Getting rid of that gods-awful headpiece is an excellent start." Castil closed her eyes and groaned softly the moment the words left her lips.

The flex of his fingers on her back made her open her eyes again. The king wore a wide grin, his nearly colorless eyes glittering with amusement. "How often do you take your cautious friend's advice?"

She winced. "Not often enough." His palm was hot on her back, and she wished they could dance forever. Unfortunately, the familiar song would soon end. She had no more time to waste. "Your patience with Kareena will be greatly rewarded, Your Majesty. She's a lovely person. Intelligent and kind. She will make a worthy queen for you. Her shyness is but a shield. One she lowers it, you'll understand why I love her as I do."

An enigmatic expression settled on his sharp features. "Madam il Veras, it has..." He didn't finish the sentence. The piece to which they danced had ended, and Castil felt the expectant weight of every stare in the room on her and the king. It was time for him to find another partner, certainly one more suitable than her.

Again her heartbeat stumbled in its rhythm at the shadow of disappointment that flitted across his face. Surely she imagined it?

He led her back to where she'd stood earlier, lifted her hand, and inclined his head toward her knuckles. Lamplight shimmered in silvery bands over his white hair. "Another time perhaps, madam. When we might speak of other things such as books and old scrolls."

"Of course, Your Majesty." Castil bowed, fighting to keep her expression pleasant but neutral instead of grinning like an idiot.

He was an amiable man. Certainly her blunt remarks about his garb might well have been taken as insult, but he'd only grinned. And he'd danced with her despite her lowly status, one she was certain he'd been made aware of by many in this assembly. Their exchanges amounted to less time than it took her to don a frock and stockings, but Castil felt it in her gut that Doranis would make a fine, thoughtful husband for Kareena. She just had to convince Kareena it was so before Kareena left Caskadan for the far north.

She turned away from watching him lead another woman onto the dance floor. Gawking would only invite ridicule from the greater boyars. The lesser ones too. She had no business anyway mooning over the man to whom her best friend was betrothed.

"Another time perhaps, Madam il Veras."

Not likely. The dance itself had been a surprise not to be repeated. A lovely surprise, nonetheless, and one she'd hold close in her memory. She'd danced with a fey king.

She didn't speak with Doranis for the rest of the evening, though she did meet his gaze twice and return his nod with a quick one of her own. Even Kareena was beyond her reach, guarded either by her parents or in the king's company, still looking as terrified as the first time she'd beheld him.

The hired cart she and her father took home once the assembly had ended was a spartan contraption of rough boards, creaking wheels and pulled by a horse with all the time in the world to reach its destination. The moon skated the edge of the horizon by the time they reached the Veras estate and the ramshackle house that squatted in the center of the grounds.

"Well, daughter, this was an unexpected evening," Devilos said as he helped Castil out of the cart and paid the driver his fee. "You can brag that you caught the eye of a king tonight."

They made their way up the walkway toward the dark house. No doubt the three servants who lived with them had long since found their beds.

Castil snorted softly. "I'd be laughed at were I to brag of such a thing, Father. The king learned that Kareena and I were friends. I think he hoped I might offer some insight into what she's like."

It was too dark for her to see Devilos's expression but she heard something in his voice—disagreement, caution, a wariness that hadn't been there earlier. "That may well be, but be careful nonetheless, and guard your heart."

His comment puzzled her. "Careful of what?"

He shrugged and said no more, leaving Castil to stare at his back while he unlocked the front door and motioned her inside. Only later did she begin to understand what he meant.

In the days following the grand assembly, the emperor hosted several more events in honor of the marriage between Doranis and Kareena. Some of those gatherings were for greater boyars only and to those, House Veras didn't receive an invitation. But there were other celebrations and the wedding itself to which all boyars were summoned to attend. Those were where she crossed paths with the king of Helenrisia and ignited gossip among the Caskadan court. Doranis sought her out numerous times, causing raised eyebrows and speculation among the boyars and warning glares from the Marcam family.

And there was a chance meeting in a temple ruin, an ephemeral moment in time in which Castil had almost cast aside friendship in the face of temptation. No one knew of that meeting, and no one ever would. Nor would she dwell on it and allow the guilt of a sin almost committed eat her alive.

In the end, the gossip was baseless. Castil posed no threat to Kareena or her family, despite the fact she'd heeded her father's warning too late and forgot to guard her heart. When she spoke with the king, it was of scholarly things: ancient scrolls, and books they both read. Dowerless and low-ranking, she should have been far beneath the notice of a monarch, and most treated Doranis's interest in her as an amusing foible— one odd creature's fascination for another.

The union between the Marcams and House Alisdane commenced without incident, though Kareena looked pale and ill as she held Doranis's hand and spoke her vows before emperor and country. Castil watched the exchange with a mixture of pity and envy—pity for her friend who had been sold into marriage to a man she found repulsive, envy because Castil would have gladly traded places with her.

Kareena refused to look beyond the white mark of the Wastelands, seeing only a man disfigured by the old magic. She didn't know of the remarkable mind and dry wit that lay behind that severe visage. But Castil did, had watched, enthralled, as the days passed in celebration and Doranis revealed aspects of himself that would have surprised his new wife.

On the day the king and his new queen were to return to Helenrisia, Castil made her way to the docks and waited amid a crowd of onlookers as the Helenese royal couple and its retainers gathered at the pier. Tears clogged her throat. She and Kareena had said their goodbyes the previous night, crying as they hugged each other a final time.

"I want to die," Kareena had declared as she wiped the rivulets of tears from her cheeks.

The two women stood together in Castil's bedchamber, hugging intermittently as they wished each other farewell.

"No you don't," Castil admonished in a firm voice. "You want to live and prove to your mother that not only can you be a superior wife but a brilliant queen as well." She stroked the other woman's blonde locks. "You're married, true, but you've finally escaped the dame's tyranny as you've always wanted."

"Only to exchange it for another tyranny." Kareena hiccuped, the picture of despair.

Alarm had coursed through Castil's veins then. She'd chosen not to question Kareena about her wedding night. There were private things even best friends didn't share, and she didn't want to violate Kareena's or the king's privacy. The other woman's remark made her toss that discretion aside. "Has he been unkind to you, love?" Dread made her stomach knot. Surely she couldn't have been so wrong in her judgment of his character?

"No. He's kind and patient." Kareena shuddered. "I just...he's repulsive to me, Castil. I can't bear his touch, no matter how gentle."

Sympathy warred with puzzlement for Castil. Despite being betrothed to Doranis nearly her entire life, Kareena had never expressed either interest or excitement in the union. Even the idea of becoming queen held little appeal. That disinterest had turned into fear as she grew older and more comprehending of what the arrangement meant for her, how it would alter her life forever, and how she was powerless to change it. Those were the times when Castil pitied her friend the most and thanked the gods that, unlike Kareena, she was from a low-ranking house where such matches rarely occurred because they weren't worth the trouble.

For the moment there was nothing she could say in reply that wouldn't sound patronizing or insensitive. She didn't understand or share Kareena's revulsion for Doranis as a person, but that didn't invalidate Kareena's feelings. She pulled the girl into her arms and hugged her close. "I wish I had the power to change your circumstances. You know I would if I could."

Kareena stepped back and gave her a watery smile. "I know. I wish I had that power too. I wish you could come with me. Be part of my retinue."

She had asked, but Castil had declined. Her father's household ran on the monies they brought in from a modest annual harvest and commissions both she and Devilos took in as scribes. They scraped by—barely. Losing one scribe presented a hardship.

Even were the Veras estate less strained, they weren't greater boyars. Greater boyar families paid the Marcams for the privilege of sending their female relatives with Kareena as part of the queen's court, and the cost put significant dents in those coffers.

"I'll write to you often," Castil promised her. "A deluge of letters to tide you over the winter when the ships can no longer travel north until spring."

The other woman's expression fell even more before suddenly brightening. Her renewed smile was almost cheery. "I nearly forgot!" She gestured to a parcel she'd brought with her earlier and placed on Castil's writing table. It was a tall, slender wooden box decorated in tiny jewels and bright paint. The lid was held closed by a latch secured by a small lock. Kareena handed Castil an even smaller key. "A gift for you. This opens the box."

Curious, Castil took the key and opened the lock. The lid was heavy in her hand as she tipped it back to look inside the box at the contents. She glanced at Kareena. "What is it?"

"Take it out and see, silly."

Castil lifted the item, grunting at the unexpected weight. She set it on the table and whistled. An ornate silver candlestick with ornate scrollwork forged into its base. Three feet shaped like a cat's paws stabilized the candlestick, and more of the scrollwork climbed up the tapered stem and shoulders to wrap around an empty sconce. She ran a fingertip down the stem. "How beautiful!"

"A gift for you from the king," Kareena said.

Castil snatched her hand back, her heart slamming hard against her breastbone. "What?"

Kareena chuckled. "I knew you'd be surprised. He gave me

one just like it. It's a witch torch. They're forged as a pair and infused with shared magic." She did as Castil earlier and caressed a delicate scroll with her finger. "They work as messengers. When you invoke a certain spell, a flame lights in the sconce, though it doesn't burn like fire. If you put a letter to the flame, it's consumed, or so it seems. It reappears whole within the flame of its mate." For the first time since this entire marriage celebration had begun, a spark of joy lit her gaze. "We can exchange letters as often as we want and not worry about winter or ships stuck in port or long waits to hear from each other. I just need to teach you the spell as the king taught it to me."

For long moments Castil could only stare at the witch torch and then at Kareena, going back and forth between the two. "What an extraordinary gift," she murmured. "Not just in its magic but in its thoughtfulness."

And its compassion. The sharp edge of envy slid along her soul. *Oh, my friend,* she thought. *One day you'll realize how fortunate you are.*

Kareena's expression turned guarded. "He is thoughtful. I might like him a little were I not married to him."

Castil took her hand. "Maybe in time you'll be able to call him 'friend' as well as 'husband.'" At Kareena's indifferent shrug, she changed the topic. "I'm both thrilled and grateful for so lovely a present and can't wait to use it! Teach me the spell, then we'll practice using it. You can send me your first letter when you return home...to your father's house."

It was a lighthearted interlude, too brief but much treasured and soon over. The two women hugged long and hard outside the front door before Kareena stepped into the Marcam family carriage and waved to Castil from its back window as it rolled away. Castil waved in return, swallowing her tears until the carriage reached the main road and disappeared from view.

Her first letter from Kareena arrived via the witch torch shortly thereafter, a flaring, sparking affair that made Castil's father gape in wonder at the sight. The note itself was short but no less poignant for its brevity.

I am unfortunately alone and yet not alone. Until we meet again, my dearest sister-friend.

"A very short note then," her father said as he dipped a quill into the ink pot in front of him and continued transcribing the work in front of him.

Castil folded and tucked the letter in her apron pocket. She'd respond on the same parchment later when she could find the words that might cheer them both up. "They leave for Helenrisia tomorrow," she replied. "I shall miss her sorely, Papa."

The quill's scratching paused, and Devilos reached across the table to squeeze her hand. "Of course you will. Knowing this day was coming doesn't make the parting any easier." He nodded at the witch torch. "What you have there is worth more than this entire estate three times over. Make use of it."

She fell asleep that night with an aching heart and a throat closed tight with tears. Her plan not to go to the docks and see the Helenese ship sail away went by the wayside. She couldn't not see Kareena off, even if it was just to wave at fluttering sails as the ship turned toward open waters.

Kareena and her retinue had already boarded the ship and disappeared from view by the time Castil arrived at the docks, but not all the Helenese entourage had yet made their way on board.

Doranis was unmistakable among his escort. Mounted on a big bay horse, he rode robed and hooded against the summer sun's bright light and sat tall in the saddle.

As if sensing her eyes upon him, he slowly pivoted the animal in her direction, scanning the crowded docks until he spotted her.

Castil's eyes widened as the bay suddenly trotted toward her, sending bystanders scattering out of the way. She froze in place, squinting as she peered up into the shadows of the king's hood. The light eyes, ringed in heavy smears of protective black kohl, shone with pleasure at her presence. King and scribe eyed each other.

She committed his face to memory. He was, in her eyes, the most beautiful creature she'd ever beheld. Distracted by her fascination with him, she almost forgot to bow, and he laughed gently as she blushed and bent at the waist.

"There's no need for ceremony here, scribe woman." That low, silky voice slid over her skin like scented oil, deep and rich with the promise of decadence.

Her skin tightened across her entire body. Propriety be damned in favor of heartfelt gratitude and forbidden affection. She held out her hand to him. "I owe you a debt I can never repay, Your Majesty. The witch torch...it's a gift of far more than magic and silver, the giver as great a treasure as the gift," she said, just loud enough for him to hear.

He seemed to still for a moment before bending down close enough that she became ensnared in the glitter of his eyes. His long fingers wrapped around hers and tightened. "All men wish to be gods, madam, even fey kings. Were I granted such power, this would not be farewell." He slowly released her hand and straightened, his sharp face drawn with an emotion that made her stomach flip. "You would have made a worthy queen, Castil il Veras." She gaped at him as he wheeled the bay around and trotted back toward the ship. He dismounted and boarded the ship. The retainers filed onto the deck behind him. The horses were loaded soon after and the call to raise anchor carried on the salt-heavy breeze. The sun dipped low on the horizon as the ship took sail, easing out of the harbor toward the open sea. Castil stood at the docks, watching until it was nothing more than a speck, taking with it an unattainable wish and an enduring friendship.

Present day

THE WIND SPUN hard off the sea as the ship neared the jagged coastline, buffeting Castil as she huddled within her cloak's meager warmth. In the distance, a small village clung like lichen to the sloping face of the cliffs. Beyond the quays lay the white lands and the fabled fortress of the northern kings. And there Kareena resided, a melancholy queen.

Sails flapped hard above Castil's head, giant wings beating restlessly from the wind gusting off the water. It was much more comfortable in her tiny cabin, but at the first sighting of Helenrisia's far shores, she tossed her cloak around her shoulders and ran up to the deck. Weeks of endless sailing, its monotony broken only by periodic bouts of sea sickness, had finally come to an end.

Kareena's letter, tattered at the corners from multiple readings, lay safely within the depths of Castil's satchel. A letter of credit to her father had arrived via the witch torch. As much as Castil wanted to take the magical item with her so she could correspond with Kareena during the month-long sea voyage to Helenrisia, she'd decided against it. The torch was too valuable to risk hauling about, and if she taught her father the spell for igniting the flame, he'd have a way to stay connected with her on a daily basis while she was gone if he wished. She had no doubt Kareena would be happy to share her own torch with her.

Devilos had been less than enthusiastic at the idea of months separated from his only child, even with the generous letter of credit to cover all expenses and make up for any loss of income to their household once she left. "If you go now, you'll be trapped there for months, and they say Helenrisia is an inhospitable place in winter."

She shrugged. "I would stay that long regardless, Father. It's a long trip, and Kareena will want me with her for more than a few days, especially with new motherhood upon her and a baby to care for." Even a woman far more resilient than Kareena might find it overwhelming to face so many huge changes in her life over such a short period of time. Who wouldn't want a friend to lean on in the more difficult moments?

He said no more about it, only made arrangements with the captain of the *Estarta* to transport Castil safely north.

After weeks on the water and a few storms that broke the monotony with hours of terror, the *Estarta* had arrived in the kingdom of Helenrisia. It sailed ever closer, and it seemed to Castil as if the lay of the land remained obscured. Shore met sky in an endless expanse of snow-laden gray, the icy water reflecting the color of a dulled sword blade. No wonder Kareena, always a lover of the long Caskadanian summers, called her new home desolate.

"They'll be lowering the dinghy soon, madam. You'd best get your gear together."

Castil was startled out of her musings by the rough, friendly voice of the ship's captain. She smiled, hoping he hadn't been standing there long waiting for her to acknowledge him. "Will there be an escort to take me into the interior?"

Captain Lizera claimed a spot beside her and leaned against the railing to stare at the closing shore. "Aye. You'll travel with us to the trading houses. From there, we'll set up an escort for you to the Frozen Maiden." She raised an eyebrow in inquiry and he smiled. "The fortress of the kings."

The cold of the northern sea faded as memories of a morning in a ruined temple surfaced, and she pushed them down again. Therein lay a dangerous path tangled in yearning and the jagged edges of guilt. She turned to watch as the gray mist blanketing the shore thinned, allowing a view of ramshackle huts and nets hung on poles for mending.

The captain's voice, hard with a black humor, sent shivers down her arms. "Madam il Veras, welcome to Hel."

~ 2 ~

"SHE HAS ARRIVED, Sire," the royal steward announced. "I've instructed the servants to take her to the queen's solar."

Doranis nodded once and placed his son into the arms of the waiting nursemaid. The baby squirmed for a moment before nestling contentedly against the woman's breast. Tiny and fragile, he looked much like his father, save for his coloring. The king still gave thanks to whatever deities listened that the curse of his blood didn't pass to his offspring. He looked to his steward, finding the other man regarding him with hooded eyes. Marcilun always had more to say.

He didn't disappoint. "The news of your wife's death will come as a blow, Your Majesty. What do you wish me to tell Madam il Veras?"

Doranis thought for a moment, wondering if such tidings would be more merciful coming from a stranger or from him. In the end, it mattered little. Kareena was dead, and Castil il Veras didn't know it. The pain would be no less, no matter who delivered the message.

"I'll tell her. Kareena would have wished it, I think. She

adored her friend. And if Madam il Veras was willing to travel so far, the sentiment was reciprocated." He kept silent regarding his wish, his need, to once again speak with the woman who had haunted his dreams these long, bleak months.

"She will fear you, as the queen did."

Doranis's eyes narrowed. "Mayhap, but something tells me otherwise."

Marcilun's tone became diffident. "Forgive me, Sire. I meant no disrespect. I only wished to warn you that your meeting with this Caskadanian may not be pleasant. Like the queen, she may also consider us barbaric."

Marcilun didn't know Castil il Veras, but Doranis did, after a fashion. The idea that she might react to his people in the way Kareena had seemed ludicrous. He contemplated his son, content in his nursemaid's arms. Kareena had despised most everything about her new home. Had she been a more forceful personality, her displeasure would have manifested itself in endless harping and screaming tirades. As it was, she was a stoic, withdrawn woman, one who'd shut herself away in her chambers as the weeks and months passed, and neither Helenrisia nor her son grew dearer to her.

Doranis didn't mourn her, at least not in the way a husband might mourn a beloved wife. He and Kareena had remained distant strangers to each other, coming together only in the darkest hours of the night to beget an heir. Such couplings had been brittle and awkward from the first, no matter how gentle or coaxing he tried to be. His wife simply lay beneath him, colder and more rigid than a corpse, until he finished. Her disgust was palpable in the bedchamber's heavy

silence, though she accepted his touch without argument.
Despite the parody of lovemaking in which they engaged, she
quickened with child, and he left her to her solitary bed, as
relieved as she that neither of them had to suffer the forced
intimacy they both hated.

It was during those dismal moments, when he would rise
from the bed, shivering with cold and a dull emptiness, that he
thought of the fascinating Castil. Had the irony not been so
harsh, he might have laughed at the turnings of Fate. But for
her dowerless state and low ranking, she was a better match
for him. She had lured him to her with her scholarly ways and
ready laughter. There was about her a vibrancy, as if the heat
of a Caskadanian sun burned in her blood. In contrast to
Kareena's exquisite blonde beauty, Castil was nondescript in
appearance—small and dark haired, with a smattering of
freckles across her nose. He had barely given her a second
glance at their first meeting. Until she recited the *do Enrai* verse
stitched on his tunic.

From that moment, she grew progressively more beautiful
in his eyes as he came to admire her intellect and easy humor.
During the numerous prenuptial revels, he sought her out
several times, uncaring that such attention drew conjecture.
Castil fascinated him as no other woman had before, and as she
swayed in his arms during a dance, chatted with him about old
scrolls and ancient civilizations, and laughed with him over the
oddities of court life, he became even more enchanted.

He recalled the morning of his wedding day, when he'd
slipped past the ever-constant vigilance of his retainers and
explored the city's streets as the sun plated the buildings'

façades in gold. Servants already ran errands, preparing for the day's work ahead. He moved among them, cloaked and hooded, gazing at the sights with casual interest. Doranis had pulled the hood forward, protecting his sensitive eyes from the sunlight and obscuring his face from passersby. None paid him any heed as he'd strolled by, nothing more than a tall man in a good cloak. Even the pickpockets left him alone.

A side street caught his attention, and he'd turned onto the narrow path that ultimately led to a small grotto partially hidden by vines and untended hedge. Its cool, dappled shade drew him in, and he discovered the ruins of a temple dressed in trailing veils of ivy.

He ascended the roofless rotunda's steps on soundless feet and paused, stunned to find another had found her way here before him. Castil il Veras had sat cross-legged on the floor, weaving a small garland of pink flowers with nimble fingers. Doranis watched her for a quiet moment, admiring the play of early light on her face, the way she chewed her lower lip in concentration while she worked.

She sucked in a startled breath, stumbling to her feet, when he made his presence known. He'd raised a silencing finger to his lips to halt any cry, and she blinked at him in bewilderment before tilting her head in question.

"Your Majesty?" The disbelief in her inquiry made him smile, as if it was far too strange a thing to find a king wandering among the city without a procession of servants and guards in tow.

Doranis pulled back his hood, and Castil dropped her garland and bowed. "Be at peace, madam. We aren't at court."

His smile widened to a grin when she straightened and looked past him as if searching for an army of retainers lurking in the hedges. "Tell no one," he said in a conspiratorial voice. "I have run away." She'd laughed at his teasing, shaking a finger at him in a gesture of disapproval. He bent to retrieve the garland she'd dropped, handing it to her with a curious look.

Castil thanked him, threading the partially finished piece through her hands. "A garland of sea roses for Kareena. They're her favorite and represent good fortune. People cultivate them in their gardens, but they grow wild here at this temple and have the best scent."

Her gray eyes were thoughtful, and he'd wondered what words were forming behind her lips. He didn't have long to wait for the answer. Her shoulders stiffened with an internal resolve, her features becoming set and determined. "You will be kind to her, Your Majesty?" Her fingers plucked nervously at the garland, but she plunged onward. "Kareena knows her duties, but she's frightened, as any new bride would be in such circumstances."

Anxious she might be, but fearless as well, especially where Kareena was concerned. Doranis admired her fortitude and devotion to her friend. She spoke in support of someone she cared for, knowing she risked offending him with an impertinence.

He'd stepped closer. She refused to give ground, though he didn't miss the slight shiver that shook her frame. "Madam il Marcam doesn't fear becoming a bride. She fears becoming *my* bride." He raised her chin with one finger. A stray beam of sunshine passed across her eyes, making her blink. "And you,

Madam il Veras, keeper of dead languages and old tales, would you fear me were you mine?"

Images flashed in his mind, the result of his concentration and touch upon her. A bright, full moon, blankets of snow on the Laybet Mountains. Things cold, beautiful, bound in winter. It was how she saw him in her mind, and his breathing slowed even as he felt hers speed up.

"Would you fear me, Castil?" he repeated.

She closed her eyes, dark lashes like fans on her cheeks. "No," she whispered against his descending mouth. "I would welcome you."

He'd kissed her then, swallowing her sigh. She tasted of tea sweetened with honey, and her lips were soft under his. His spirit had despaired at the knowledge that the wife chosen for him would never respond to him the way the wife he would have chosen for himself did in that moment.

His hands settled on her hips to pull her closer when the sound of familiar voices calling his name brought him to his senses.

Castil also heard the calls and wrenched herself out of his arms. Doranis's frustrated groan at the unwelcome interruption and her sudden withdrawal carried through the small temple. She'd stared at him, her gaze anguished. Bright flags of color raced across her cheekbones, and her lips were damp from his kiss.

The voices grew louder, closer, sharp and alarmed as they searched the streets for the missing king. Doranis resisted the temptation to pull Castil back to him.

"This is wrong," she whispered, her voice and face stricken

with remorse. "You're marrying Kareena."

And how unfortunate was that for both him and his future bride? "She and I would have it otherwise."

She clasped the small garland to her chest and backed away from him. "It cannot be otherwise. Today is your wedding day, and my closest friend will be your wife."

His gaze strayed to the token of good luck. "I won't apologize for something I don't regret, Castil. Doing so rings false, and this is no love match. Why do you suffer such guilt?"

Tears had edged her lower lids, and she blinked them back. "Because I would rage over this moment were I Kareena." He reached for her, but she held up a hand to ward him off. "Your people call for you, Your Majesty. May the gods bless your union."

She peeked around him a second time before scampering down the steps of the temple to disappear among the overgrown hedgerows. Her scent—of sunshine and salt air—remained, teasing his nostrils and lingering in his memory even as he returned to the palace, played the role of dutiful sovereign and bound himself to a woman who despised him. Even as he sailed homeward the following day.

Doranis had played those moments in the temple ruin over and over in his mind's eye for months, even when his reason admonished him for the futility of it. Some might say he mooned over a woman's lips like a green lad. They'd never know that what he dwelt on was not a kiss but the glimpse into the might-have-been of a happier future than the one set for him and Kareena.

He stretched out a hand to gently stroke his child's dark

hair. The baby lay against the wet nurse's breast, nearly asleep. Marcilun shifted impatiently behind him, awaiting his next command. "See to it that her possessions are placed in one of the south-facing chambers. There's more light in those rooms."

He glided his fingers through Joris's wispy hair once more before leaving the nursery for the icy corridors. His steps barely whispered on the flagstone floor. Cold wall torches ignited with green witchfire as he passed, lighting his path to the solar.

Kareena's sanctuary still held all her possessions. He'd sent her bevy of ladies in waiting back to Caskadan within a day of her death but had left her chamber as it was before she died. Castil didn't yet know of the queen's passing, and it seemed harsh to remove all signs of Kareena from the palace before she learned such bleak news.

Servants had arrived earlier to light the fire in the hearth and deliver a pot of tea and cups. The solitary occupant in the room had her back to him, and Doranis paused to enjoy the peaceful tableau of her warming her hands at the hearth fire. By custom, it fell to a lowly minister to greet guests and see to their initial comfort. But he wanted to see her again, gaze upon her smiling face and discern whether or not the longing he had for her was returned.

He closed the door behind him, the snick of wood on wood alerting her to his presence. She was even lovelier than he remembered, with the firelight playing across her flushed features and her dark hair tamed in a bun at her neck. Hot blood rushed into his groin at her wide, welcoming smile. Her eyes revealed a hunger quickly smothered behind a more guarded gaze, but he had seen it, felt its caress before she bowed and greeted him in a deceptively cool voice.

"I am honored, Your Majesty."

He closed the distance between them and clasped her warm hand in his. Her fingers twitched in his grasp when he brushed a delicate kiss across the back of her knuckles. She gently pulled her hand free, but not before he felt its tremble.

"Welcome to Helenrisia, Madam il Veras," he said. "You please us with your presence."

She laughed. "I'm so glad to hear it, Sire." Her next words, uttered with such heartfelt eagerness, yielded a grim reminder for why she had traveled so far, and why they stood in this particular room. "I'm looking forward to this visit. When may I see Kareena?"

~ 3 ~

E VEN BURIED DEEP into the mountain, away from the hard
biting wind and squalls of snow, the burial vault of the
kings was frigid. As if pulled by an invisible lodestone, Castil
walked past the line of marble effigies. Ancient Helenese kings
and queens, immortalized in stone, lined the walls, their
features captured in timeless repose. Among them, a delicate
woman of the south rested in eternal sleep.

Castil halted at the line's end, and a sob caught in her
throat. Were it not for the size and color of the statue, she
could almost believe she faced a living Kareena. The sculptor
had performed magic with his chisel—the stone woman who
faced her was the perfect avatar for the queen. Like the other
statues, Kareena's had been sculpted wearing the ceremonial
burial robes. She stood with her arms crooked, elbows against
her chest. Her hands faced outward, cupped to hold a gold urn
containing the cremated remains of a once beautiful, shy girl
who faced the monster called despair and lost the battle.

Doranis had delivered the awful news of Kareena's death
weeks earlier, yet it sometimes seemed like only days or even
hours, when the grief cut deep and the finer memories cut

deeper. She'd managed to keep her composure in front of the king, allowing only a few silent tears to escape her closed lids. She'd nearly bitten her lips bloody holding in the sobs as he'd held her hand, sympathy drawing down his mouth and darkening his eyes. "It isn't the news I wanted to deliver to anyone, especially her best friend, but I think the queen would have wanted me, instead of an unfamiliar servant, to tell you. I am so very sorry, Madam il Veras. Truly."

She'd nodded, unable to reply around the knot of tears lodged in her throat. She believed him. He grieved as well. If not for himself, then certainly for her and for his son who'd never know his mother. Since that awful afternoon, she'd succumbed to sobbing in the privacy of her bedchamber more than a few times. Among the Helenese court, she was stoic and pleasant. Most thought her a solemn woman observing a period of mourning. Only the king knew how great the anguish was. The anger too. He saw into her soul in a way no one else ever had—not even Kareena—and his mere presence offered a comfort she so badly needed.

Still, she'd come here to this silent, icy vault many times after he'd shown her the queen's burial place and the sepulchral monument sculpted in her honor. Castil traced the hard edges of the effigy's robes with a fingertip. "My friend," she whispered. "How I miss you." A small draft, cold and sweetened with sea rose blossom, gently buffeted her cheeks, blowing strands of her hair across her face in a light caress.

Castil wasn't a superstitious sort, though she did believe in spirits who lingered among the living for a short while until some task was completed or a grieving loved one comforted enough to resume the task of living. If asked, Castil would swear the companion of her youth hovered near her, glad for her company.

"Again you find me here, pestering your sleep with the dull details of my day." A faint faraway laughter chimed like bells. "I visited your son moments ago. Joris is a beautiful child, Kareena. I see you and Doranis in his small features." A mournful sigh replaced the laughter, and Castil grew ever more certain she was not alone among the statues of the voiceless dead.

Such knowledge didn't frighten her. She found comfort in knowing something of her friend lingered here, not yet beyond the reach of the living. That comfort was mixed with no small guilt, and Castil drew back from Kareena's stone likeness.

"I've been here three months now. The ships return in three more, bringing their goods to trade as well as ambassadors from other lands to present their candidates for the role of queen of Helenrisia." This time the ache in her breast had nothing to do with missing her friend. "It will be inappropriate for me to remain here any longer. I'll return home on one of those ships." Again, that ethereal sigh drifted to her ear, and Castil shivered. "'Tis a good thing that I leave, for I must confess my failure to you." Remorse made it difficult to speak. "I have fallen in love with the king, Kareena."

Somehow she expected a bitter howling, an angry blast of frigid air that would spin her off her feet. But her statement was met with silence, a deepening quiet that waited for her next words. "He is a..." She spread her hands, palms up. "A man like no other." She sensed amusement at her words and smiled in return. "Beyond the obvious, of course." Her smile faded. "He consoled me when the news of your death nearly brought me to my knees, opened his library to me as a way to distract me from my grief, allowed me to hold your sweet son and visit you here, kept me company when the weight of your absence crushed me."

Castil began to pace, the brush of her gown and heavy cloak against the floor sounded loud in the vault. "I confessed to you my indiscretion at the temple. I did our friendship a disservice. But this is worse, far worse." She faced the statue again. "I think of him constantly, look forward to his company when he joins me in the library. He's a hard man, but kind beneath that cold exterior. I've seen him with Joris, and he's a proud, loving father. I truly believe he would have been a good husband to you as well."

The scent of sea rose teased her nostrils once more. "I'll miss you when I return to Caskadan, but it's been hard to resist his allure, and I long for the peace of my dull existence at home. You're gone, Joris is in good hands, and Doranis will take another wife. I'm not needed here."

Silence gathered around her and Castil swiped at the tears trickling down her cheeks. "I am so sorry, Kareena. I haven't been much of a friend to you lately, dear one. He was yours." She turned away from the effigy, her steps dragging as she made her way to the stairs, pausing on the steps for a moment at the faintest sound, an ethereal whisper that her spirit, more than her ears, heard.

"And now he is yours, my dearest friend."

"Kareena?"

Only her voice echoed back to her.

Castil returned to the fortress's upper levels, both relieved and troubled by her confession. It felt right to say aloud what had weighed heavily in her thoughts—an acknowledgment of her feelings for Doranis. Such feelings changed little. Not long from now she would board a trading vessel bound for Caskadan and forget her time here with the pale magus king.

She'd mentioned nothing of her upcoming departure to him, nor had he brought it up during any of their numerous conversations. They were much alike in their interests and passions, often discussing the history of Helenrisia and the creation of the Wastelands while they scoured his library late into the night or debated translations. But they didn't speak of the future. For Castil, that was decided before she even set foot on the *Estarta* and sailed to Helenrisia, before Kareena's death. This was a visit to a friend turned into a twilight that simply waited for spring and seas no longer frozen so that she might sail home. She assumed the king understood this as well. There was no reason to discuss it. When the day came, she'd thank him for his hospitality, wish him well, and leave her heart behind in the frozen north.

The corridors leading to her room were almost temperate compared to the temperatures of the vault. Her cheeks were numb with cold, and she hurried to her chambers, eager to bundle in a blanket and linger by a roaring fire. She passed one of the many closed doors lining the cloister and paused at the sound of familiar voices and the ring of metal on metal.

"Come, old man. I could match you in my sleep." Doranis's deep tones reverberated through the wood, causing

Castil's hands to curl in reaction. Again the sound of steel striking steel echoed, and she could picture the scene, having once stumbled upon it when she first arrived in Helenrisia.

The king engaged in swordplay with his weapons master. Her mouth had fallen open the first time she witnessed Doranis sparring with Etane. Both were stripped to the waist, skin glistening with sweat as they circled each other like wary cats, the curving blades of their swords flashing in the torchlight as they came together in a mock dance of death.

Castil had paid no attention to Etane, her eyes riveted to the arresting sight of a shirtless Doranis. Though tall and slim, he was a study in hard muscle and sinew, his chest and abdomen flexing as he dodged the swinging arc of his opponent's blade or attacked with his own. Silvery lines of perspiration streamed off his skin, and his white hair lay tangled on his shoulders.

She knew if she opened the door this time, a similar sight would again greet her, and Doranis would smile in that smug way when he caught her ogling him. An abrupt hiss of pain, followed by Etane's gloating response of, "Old man, am I?" made her lips twitch in amusement, and she continued on her way.

Her maid awaited her, clucking her disapproval as she helped Castil remove her cloak and dress. "Down in the vaults again, I see. If you insist on lingering there, you should at least wear a hat, gloves, and a heavier cloak."

Castil chuckled at the admonishment. "I didn't think I would be so long."

The maid, a young girl named Thesla, tossed her dress in a

basket for laundering. "That is the coldest place within the fortress. You would be warmer standing out in the courtyard in your shift." She stripped Castil down to a thin chemise and handed her a fur pelt to wrap around herself. Castil huddled within it, standing as close to the hearth fire as was safe to stay warm.

A mischievous glitter entered Thesla's eyes. "Do you know the way to the mineral baths?"

She did. Numerous natural hot springs dotted the landscape, most of them dangerous because of the water's boiling temperatures. There were a few, however, that were no hotter than bath water. Two lay just outside the fortress and the Helenese were fond of frolicking in them on days when the weather was clear. This wasn't one of those days. "That holds no temptation for me today, Thesla. The wind outside would freeze armor."

The maid shook her head. "No, not the common baths." She raised the lid of the chest at the end of Castil's bed to pull out a thick cloth and a heavy frock trimmed in fur. "There's a small spring here, in the depths of the fortress, like the vaults. But it's warmer there and reserved for the royal family."

The idea of relaxing in a pool of heated water not exposed to the outside elements had its appeal, especially now as she continued to shiver beneath the fur pelt. Still, Thesla said it belonged to the royal family, and she was not one of its members.

"I think not. I don't wish to cause offense by intruding where I don't belong." She gestured for the frock. "It would be best if I just dressed."

Thesla held the garment out of her reach. "You're a guest of the king, madam. The springs are open to you." Her voice turned coaxing. "Try them. You've been here several weeks now and never experienced the baths. Trust me. It's something not to be missed."

A little more cajoling from the maid and Castil soon found herself back out in the corridors, her dry cloth and frock in hand. Following Thesla's directions, she found the chamber housing the spring.

The cloister wound downward and back, cutting deep into the heart of the mountain. Green witchfire flickering in the torches lining the walls lit her way, giving the hall a ghostly, iridescent glow. This was the product of magic, and the light gave off no heat as she paused, passing her hand over one of the emerald flames.

She had seen such things in her time here in Helenrisia. The country bordered the Wastelands, its warped magic an awesome, living thing felt by all the denizens of the north. Nearly everyone she met could perform some small enchantment as the residual effects of ancient forces bled across the forbidden borders, touching upon anyone living nearby. Hel's king was the most obvious recipient of its power.

Unlike her own people, the Helenese didn't find his appearance so strange or frightening. Castil had wondered about it until a few conversations enlightened her. It was Thesla who, one evening, revealed the cause of Doranis's coloration, or lack thereof, and his skill with the many enchantments he could perform.

"His mother was abducted, you know." She worked with

Castil to fold back the bed linens and run the warming pan across the cold sheets.

"Abducted? By whom?"

"The Bahauran, when she carried His Majesty in her belly. My mother says the old king went nearly mad with rage."

Bahauran. Legendary denizens of the Wastelands. Descendants of the vanished Elders, they lived in the frozen, ruined cities, surrounded by the magic that twisted their bodies over eons of time. But where it took, it also gave back. There were tales told in scrolls and around campfires as far south as the Sedbar Islands, of the great sorcerers who lived in the ancient and forbidden Wastelands.

"Why would they abduct the queen?"

The girl shrugged. "No one knows. She was returned four days later, her memory of her time among them gone. But you see what that sojourn did?"

Castil nodded, her brow knitted. The prince had been marked before his birth by his mother's capture. He was a magus king now, like and yet unlike the Bahauran. Leached of all color as they were, with the power of the Wastelands coming easily to him, he was neither misshapen nor mad. His people, who lived within the shadow of the forbidden territory, accepted him easily enough. It was only outside their borders that the fear abided, the uneasiness at gazing upon a man so obviously graced with an ancient and mysterious force.

The green light brightened when Castil neared a door surrounded by numerous small torches. The hinges squeaked in protest as she opened it and stepped inside. Her delighted inhalation echoed in the chamber at the sight of a large bubbling spring, nearly hidden within swathing veils of steam drifting off the water. Narrow steps cut into the floor marked a path to the pool and ended under the water.

The chamber housing the spring was vast, with sloping tunnels that disappeared farther into the belly of the mountain. A skilled painter had depicted scenes of Helenese life on some of the smoother walls, and heavy tapestries covered portions of the floor to cushion one's feet. It was a sumptuous place, especially among the more austere surroundings of the Frozen Maiden.

Castil placed her dry cloth, tunic and shoes in a neat pile on one of the rugs before shrugging out of her robe and chemise. Without the protection of the garments, she shuddered from the damp chill. The water looked inviting, and she dipped her toe in to test its warmth. It was hot, but not so hot as to scald, and the effervescent bubbling tickled her feet. She descended the steps and sank into the water with a happy sigh.

An amused, throaty voice shattered her assumption that she was alone. "That certainly took you long enough."

Castil yelped, startled by the unexpected company. Her heart pounded in her chest. She sank lower into the water and discovered Doranis swimming lazily toward her, his white skin flushed a pale rose from the heat. His light eyes were narrowed with laughter and something else that made her heart beat faster.

"Your Majesty," she said between gasps, "you scared me. I thought I was alone."

He circled her in a lazy lap around the pool, the motion emphasizing his muscled back and arms as he slid through the water. "Forgive me, Castil. It wasn't my intention to frighten you."

She tracked his movements, pivoting so she always faced him. The water was cloudy from the steam but hid little from view. And he certainly got an eyeful when she undressed, unaware that he lurked in the pool, watching. His eyes, lit with a faint, mocking humor, assured her of that particular truth.

"You should have spoken sooner," she scolded him, her tone severe. "Sire," she added in grudging tones.

Doranis laughed softly, swimming ever closer to her in diminishing circles. "Indeed? And why is that? I was treated to the most beautiful sight. A lovely woman entering the baths is a blessing of the gods, Castil il Veras." Waves lapped gently against her back as he glided behind her.

A hard ache settled beneath her ribs at his words. She knew her strengths. Intelligent, practical and friendly; these were all the things given to her at birth, traits of which she was proud. But beauty was not among them. "Plain as an unfinished door," some of her less sensitive relatives had said, and she had come to accept that a lack of beauty combined with a lack of wealth would leave her locked from the marriage market. For who among the boyars would want a homely, dowerless scribe? Such a future had never bothered her. Until now.

She looked beyond him to the ripple and slope of a rock wall at the chamber's far end, her voice tense. "Why do you say these things?"

The water stilled. Goose flesh striped the center of her back at the whisper of his presence, so close she could almost feel his heartbeat on her skin. He leaned down to caress her throat with his fingertips, tendrils of his white hair ghosting over her shoulder to leave rivulets of water trickling past her collarbone. A roiling flutter of heat erupted in her belly, spreading to her thighs when his hands settled on either side of her neck.

"I say them because they're true. You are the grace of all women. I have wanted you since you first translated my insignia." His hands dripped water into her hair, and she felt the wetness of his cheek as he bent to kiss the soft skin at her temple. "I watch you, dream of you. Shall I tell you of my dreams? How I awake in the night, covered in sweat, my thighs wet with my own seed because I imagine thrusting between your sweet thighs? Tasting your skin?"

The slide of his tongue along the curve of her ear sent heat sizzling through her blood, and Castil jerked forward, an involuntary response to the sensual caress. Doranis snaked an arm around her waist, splaying long fingers across her belly to steady her. She stared downward, hypnotized by the sight of the narrow white hand resting against her skin.

"You have beautiful hair," he whispered. His fingers fluttered against her abdomen while his other hand wrapped tendrils of her hair around his wrist, bringing it gently to his nose to inhale its fragrance.

Castil didn't move, transfixed by the softly spoken words and the knowledge that he was slowly making love to her through the husky vibrations of his voice and the deep sounds of his breathing against her flesh. His free hand released her hair, only to skim along her hip and down her leg, making her shiver.

The weight of his scrutiny rested heavy on her, measuring, assessing the shape of her body, partially submerged in the hazy water. His lovely words made her reel, yet she wondered if he compared her plainness to memories of Kareena's beauty or to other lovers who once shared his bed.

He put her silent musings to rest when he traced a finger down her spine, making her arch away from him. "My dreams were as nothing to this reality. You are more beautiful than I could have imagined," he murmured.

Castil's eyelids slid shut, her ability to reason, to think, even to talk, obliterated by the touch of his hands on her body, the whisper of his voice in her ear.

So aroused by his seduction, she jumped when his hands gripped her hips, pulling her hard against him. Whatever doubts she had regarding his desire for her evaporated. His erection nudged the cleft of her buttocks, unmistakable proof that he wanted her with the same desperation she craved him. She responded by parting her legs and rubbing against him. He rewarded her with a drawn-out groan, his fingers pressing into her flesh.

Her breathing shortened to pants as one of those graceful hands slid upward, across her ribs, to stroke one of her breasts. She gasped, arching her back as he lightly abraded her nipple. Oh sweet Mother, she wouldn't survive this!

He soothed her with slow caresses, all the while running his tongue along the outer curve of her ear. "Shh, fair Castil. This is only the beginning."

Whether threat or promise, he followed through, teasing her until she danced on the edge of an orgasm and begged him for mercy. He scooped her into his arms and waded up the steps and out of the pool. The rug under her back was rough, but she didn't care. Doranis loomed over her, big, aroused, desire written in every line of his body and every sharp angle of his face. The lines bracketing either side of his mouth deepened, and his pale eyes gleamed like banked coals. Her lips parted instinctively as his head tipped towards her, giving silent welcome as his tongue slid into her mouth, invading and plunging, even as he ground his hips against hers.

She felt more than heard the heavy groan emanating from his chest as she slid her hands around his back and down to his buttocks, curving her hands over the tight muscles. He continued to ravage her mouth and she was lost in wet, suctioning heat as he sucked on her tongue and nibbled lightly on her lower lip.

Doranis broke the breath-stealing kiss to lower his face to her breasts. Castil moaned and rocked against him as he teased her nipples with his tongue, making her arch upward in a silent appeal for more. His voice painted spells on her skin. "You like this?"

She buried her hands in his wet hair, cupping his head to hold him closer. "Yes," she murmured, the word becoming a rhythmic chant as he suckled her with rapacious greed. He dragged her into a whirlpool of frenetic desire and sexual frenzy where nothing existed save the feel of lean muscle, the wetness of a ravening mouth and the swell of his erection riding between her thighs.

Doranis slowly pulled away from her, breathing in slow, deep gasps. He wrapped an arm around her hips, tightening the embrace between them that melded her pelvis to his. "Gods," he breathed. "You cradle me well."

She whispered his name when he slid inside her, implored gods when he set a rhythm that had her clutching his shoulders. His sounds of pleasure mimicked hers, gaining in volume until his back arched and his eyes rolled back, and he held still against her as his climax rolled through him. The sensual rub of his pelvis on just the right spot insured she followed him soon after, her legs squeezing his hips so tight, he grunted in protest.

Wet with water and sweat and gasping for breath, he eased his full weight onto her before rolling them both to their sides. Castil scraped away the hair stuck to his forehead while trying to calm her own breathing. She explored the planes of his face with one finger, noticing for the first time the way his pupils dominated his irises, turning his eyes almost black.

"I think my maid suspected this might happen when she sent me here," she said after a few moments of contented silence.

Doranis grinned and tilted his head so he could kiss her fingertip. "Who is this maid so that I may reward her wisdom and elevate her to grand lady?"

Castil chortled and pressed herself against him, luxuriating in such an indulgence. "That would set the tongues wagging in your court."

One muscular shoulder lifted in a shrug. "I am king. Whom I choose to raise in status is my prerogative."

"Being monarch certainly has its rewards," she teased.

"And its punishments." He cupped her buttocks to nestle

her even closer, and his features sobered. "You'll come to my bed, and there will be no sleep for either of us this night."

She traced the thin bridge of his nose. "Are you asking or commanding, Sire?"

Doranis's eyes narrowed. "Which will bring you most readily to my chambers?"

"What do you think?" Castil was confident in his answer. He was neither tyrannical nor stupid.

His eyes drifted shut for a moment. When he opened them again, she swore she saw eternity in their depths. "Will you share my bed, Castil il Veras?"

Three months. Three glorious months to make memories to last her a lifetime and comfort her in the long years to come when he inevitably forgot her face and maybe her name.

"Yes," she said and captured his mouth in a brief kiss. "I will. This night and all the nights that you'll welcome me there."

~ 4 ~

EARLY MORNING DARKNESS still blanketed his bedroom when Doranis woke the first time from a deep sleep. He rolled onto his side, reaching for the sleek, warm body of his lover. It had become habit for him since the first time he'd taken Castil to his bed. She'd spent every night with him since then. Were he not a king and a servant to council meetings and court assemblies, he'd spend the days there with her as well. The court might snicker behind their hands at their sovereign's infatuation, but he didn't care. Their opinions didn't matter, nor were they privy to his thoughts or emotions. His attachment to this particular Caskadan woman went far beyond infatuation.

He jealously guarded the brief, private hours he reserved for her during the day in the library, and all soon learned that to disturb him during those moments incited an icy, formidable anger. She was good company, lighthearted and quick to laugh when he told her a humorous tale or offered some caustic, witty comment that sometimes made her gasp or choke on a giggle. She handled herself with confidence among the nobility of his own court, as much at home there as she had been among the Caskadanian boyars. She was a fire in his soul as well as in his blood, and he craved her no less when she was with him than when she wasn't.

At the moment, she wasn't. His eyes snapped open when his hands found empty space, and he peered into the shadows of his room, trying to locate her. Shuffling noises from his bathing room reassured him that she had left his bed only to answer nature's call. He dragged her pillow close and pressed his face into its softness, content simply to inhale her scent while he waited for her return.

Some might accuse him of blind obsession, unfathomably distracted by a plain, unremarkable woman who didn't compare with the stunning beauties of the Helenese court, or even the foreign infantas who now vied for the position of second wife and royal consort. Doranis dreaded having to face this first wave of ambassadors who'd arrived two days earlier with treaties, contracts, and portraits of women barely off their nurses' lead strings. Relief blunted the dread. At least now his obligations toward the crown weren't so heavy when it came to marriage and heirs. He had choices available to him, all he'd set aside except one.

After the heated interlude by the hot spring, his and Castil's relationship took a decided turn. There was no returning to the guarded, simmering longing that always lurked beneath the surface when they dealt with each other. Doranis knew of her continued visits to the burial vault, the shadow of guilt that sometimes lurked in her gray eyes, but it didn't stop her from embracing him with the same insatiable hunger he felt for her.

In the weeks that followed their first coupling, he took her numerous times, introducing her to the many joys of lovemaking. Long days of wanting her were punctuated by even longer nights of loving her. As the winter days lengthened with the approach of spring, his need for her remained sharp, lingering. It went beyond the realm of the physical, for he thrived in her presence, was cheered by the simple pleasure of her sitting next to him in the library, reading through a scroll. And there was no doubting that she loved Joris, as much for the fact that he was a sweet child as that he was Kareena's son. He'd known during their first few conversations in Caskadan that Castil had been the perfect match for him, the woman to whom he'd happily bind himself to the remainder of his days. She completed him, and he desired no other.

Doranis drifted off to sleep again, waiting for her to return, and it was much later that he awakened, the sun having risen at least two hours earlier. Castil was not beside him, but he shrugged off the uneasy feeling that began to blossom. It was likely that she'd returned to her rooms.

His disquiet only increased as the hours passed and he caught no glimpse of her in his daily routine. And when she didn't appear for their usual meeting in the library, his disquiet became full-blown alarm. He strode out of the room and headed for the burial vaults, praying he'd find her there. It was silent as always, no living soul to keep the dead monarchs company on that day. He raced from the vaults to the nursery. The two nursemaids jumped in unison when he burst into the room.

"Have you seen Madam il Veras?" he snapped and they stared at him in confusion and no little fear.

One of the women placed Joris gently in his bed and turned back to the king, her expression bewildered. "I thought you knew, Sire. She stopped here this morning to say goodbye to the babe before joining the caravan leaving for the docks."

Doranis turned abruptly on his heel, closing the door quietly behind him so as not to startle his son.

The servants weren't spared. They flattened themselves against the walls as he passed them. Several witch torches flared so bright, their sconces caught true fire.

The caravans! He wanted to bellow his rage, slam his fist into the nearest door or better yet, blister the ears of the woman who suddenly decided this morning to rip his heart out of his chest and carry it off with her.

A servant, suffering from unfortunate timing, crossed his path as he strode to his chambers.

"You," Doranis snarled, and the man blanched in terror. "Get to the stables and have them ready Peresil." The man sprint down the corridor as if demons snapped at his heels.

Minutes later the king slammed into the stables, cloaked and hooded, his eyes outlined in the customary kohl to protect them from snow blindness. "Where is Peresil?" he roared, growing more furious and panicked as time slipped through his fingers, and the trade caravans rolled ever closer to the docks.

A groom rushed out from the safety of one of the stalls, the big bay trotting behind him. He barely had time to leap out of the way before Doranis vaulted into the saddle and urged the horse into a hard gallop through the open stable doors.

Peresil flew across the snow-covered terrain, sure-footed and quick. Soon, the tail end of the caravan came into view, a straggling, haphazard line of wagons and shaggy mountain ponies dusted in a light snowfall.

Surprised exclamations and welcoming cries greeted Doranis when many of the Helenese recognized their monarch racing toward them. Wagons slowed to a creaking stop, ponies brought up short on their reins as the tradesmen halted to bow their respects. Doranis gave a quick nod, his gaze sweeping the line of carts in search of a small, dark-haired woman.

"Castil il Veras!" he shouted. "Show yourself!"

A short, uneasy silence reigned before Castil, wrapped in her thin southern cloak and scarves, jumped down from the back of one of the enclosed wagons and walked slowly toward him. Her eyes were both sad and questioning. She bowed briefly.

"To what do I owe this honor, Your Majesty?"

He guided Peresil closer, leaned down and lifted her, unresistant, into the saddle to sit in front of him. The caravan leader gawked at them for a moment, then shrugged and set the wagons to moving once more. Whatever went on between the king and his foreign consort was no concern of his. He had goods to deliver.

Doranis rode a short distance away before stopping. He dismounted and reached up to help Castil off Peresil. She stood before him, clutching her shawl tightly around her, unwilling to meet his eyes. He huffed out an impatient exhalation and whipped his cloak off to shroud her in its warmth. "You have no business wearing that useless scrap of wool in weather like this. We aren't in Caskadan. You would have frozen before you reached the docks."

She snuggled into the heavy garment. A tiny smiled touched her lips before fading. "So you're rescuing me then."

"From your own wrong assumptions? Yes." His fury swelled once more. "How dare you," he said, the words bitter and pained.

She paled, and tears made her gray eyes glossy, but her back stiffened. "Spring has arrived, Sire. Along with the merchant ships and the delegations sent to negotiate new treaties with Helenrisia. That includes choosing a new queen." She wilted a little then. "I shouldn't have sneaked off. It was wrong, and I am weak. It was never my intention to hurt you." Her gaze begged for his understanding. "I don't belong here, Doranis. My home is in Caskadan; my place is in my father's house at a scribe's table." Her gaze slid away. "And there is Kareena."

His frustrated growl made Peresil shy away from him. "Your home is here; your place is with me." He flung out a hand toward the distant fortress. "Why won't you make your peace with Kareena? She's dead, Castil," he snapped. "Why do you persist in this unwarranted guilt? In thinking you betrayed her? I meant nothing to her. You, on the other hand, meant a great deal to her. Do you not think she'd wish you happiness?"

"You're her husband!"

"I'm her widower!"

They stared at each other, halted at an impasse until Castil blew out a resigned breath. "This isn't just about Kareena," she said in much gentler tones. "This is about you." His eyebrows shot up. "You are a king, widowed, yes, but still bound. To your country and your station. As I am to mine. My nobility is scant. I'm one step up from a peasant. You must marry again, a woman of high status like Kareena, even a princess." Her mouth thinned for a moment, and her chin wobbled. "I can't bear to see that. I refuse to." Her lips tightened, resolve stiffening her shoulders. "Let me go."

Doranis gaped at her, the relief surging through him so euphoric, it almost made his knees buckle. So that was it. Foolish, foolish woman; one he loved more than life itself. He grasped her shoulders, torn between the need to embrace her and the desire to shake her. He cupped her face instead, her cheeks warm under his cold hands, her expression anguished.

"You're partially right. I am bound to Helenrisia, but as king I've fulfilled my duty to the line. I married for my country, gave it another heir. The woman I next take to wife will be of my choosing, and she's an untrusting sort. Lovely but quick to judge and find me wanting." He offered her a wry smile. "Still, I find myself loving her despite her doubts that impugn my character."

The tears welling on her lower lids spilled over to drip down her cheeks. Doranis gathered her into his arms where she sobbed against his chest. He stroked her back, talking to her while she sniffled into his shirt. "We're going to freeze out here in no time. You'll return home with me to the Maiden," he said in his most imperious tones.

That did exactly what he hoped. The crying stopped and the tears dried. She stepped back, sniffled some more and raised her chin in a defiant gesture.

"Are you asking or commanding?"

His lips twitched. Her eyes were red and puffy from crying,

the tip of her nose equally crimson. He had never known a more beautiful woman. "Which will most readily bring you home with me?"

This time it was she who drew him into a fierce embrace and pressed an equally fierce kiss to his mouth. "Either one," she said when they came up for air. "Home is where you are."

~ EPILOGUE ~

TODAY WAS CASTIL'S wedding day, and only a few would know of it, which was perfectly fine with her. She had no need for a great crowd of courtiers to witness her marrying Doranis. And there would be enough grand affairs she'd have to suffer through in her future. One less was a blessing. The handful of people attending this ceremony had been sworn to secrecy until the ceremony was over. The royal steward, two council members, and Castil's maid Thesla. Castil would have liked her father with her, but he was still en route from Caskadan to Helenrisia, unaware that his only child was about to become an uncrowned queen. He'd learn soon enough and no doubt request something stronger than ale to recover from the shock of such news. It was a sure thing the entire Helenese court would join him when they too found out.

She leaned against one of the window frames in the king's bedchamber and stared at the mysterious no-man's land called the Wastelands. Summer had blessed Helenrisia with swaths of green lichen and gray sedge that swept over the tussock tundra and stopped at the towering barrier of ancient fir trees that marked the border of the Wastelands. Part of a history Doranis didn't remember lay behind the dark, evergreen wall. One day she hoped they both might learn more about the place that had left its mark on him physically and gifted him with magic.

"Wishing for a crown, Madam il Veras?"

She turned to discover Doranis behind her and grinned. "Thank the gods, you didn't wear that hideous headpiece or the cloak with bird skulls."

He bowed. "But I'm still in all black."

"And you look very handsome in that color." She left the window to meet him in the center of the room. He drew her into a clove-scented embrace. "I've always liked this crown best," she said, reaching up to touch the thin circlet of faceted onyx. "No need for wimples and veils and horns that smash into lintels whenever you move from room to room."

Doranis laughed and kissed her. His expression turned solemn. "In all things you will be my wife. In all but title you will be queen. I would give you more if I could."

The great disparity in their statuses barred Castil from ever officially claiming the title of queen of Helenrisia. She cared not at all. That which mattered most to her in the world stood in front of her at the moment. An empty title couldn't compare.

She stared at him for several moments, admiring the majestic figure he cut in his dark wedding garb. "You can keep your sparkling hair ornament," she teased. "I've no need of one of my own. I'm happy to claim that most coveted of all titles: wife to Doranis of House Alisdane." She winked. "He happens to be a king, but that's really of no consequence."

Her surprised gasp changed to a soft moan as Doranis gathered her close and kissed her hard. When they paused to breathe, he cupped her face in his hands. "The finest words I'll ever say before anyone, I will say first today before a few and tomorrow before all of Helenrisia."

Her heart beat slow and heavy, and she pressed her cheek into his palm. "And what are they?"

"This is my wife."

A zephyr wind smelling of sea rose swept through the open window, fluttering the hem of Castil's dress and the ends of Doranis's hair. It carried with it the warmth of the sun, the faint chimes of laughter, and the whisper of a blessing to Castil's ears.

"And this is your husband, my beloved friend."

ALSO BY GRACE DRAVEN

World of the Wraith Kings
https://gracedraven.com/world/4

World of Master of Crows
https://gracedraven.com/world/3

The Bonekeeper Chronicles
https://gracedraven.com/world/2

The Fallen Empire
https://gracedraven.com/world/5

Other Works
https://gracedraven.com/world/1

About Grace Draven

Grace Draven is a Louisiana native living in Texas with her husband, kids and two doofus dogs. She has loved storytelling since forever and is a fan of the fictional bad boy. She is a two-time winner of the Romantic Times Reviewers Choice for Best Fantasy Romance and a USA Today Bestselling author.

gracedraven.com
facebook.com/GraceDravenAuthor
instagram.com/grace_draven

FAMILIAR WINTER MAGIC

by

Jeffe Kennedy

It's holiday time at Convocation Academy, but best friends Han and Iliana are finding it hard to celebrate. As a familiar, Iliana is facing her assignment to a life of servitude to a wizard, very soon. And Han... despite being tested by the oracle daily, he is still uncategorized. As Iliana and Han face being separated forever, they at last find the courage—or desperation—to break the rules and acknowledge their deeper feelings for each other. But it will take more than true love to save them from the laws of the Convocation...

Many thanks to Jacqueline Nielson, Colleen Champagne, Kimberly Ladd, and Kristi Teague Goodwin for beta reads and cheerleading. You gals rock!

Also, huge gratitude to the listeners of First Cup of Coffee for all the input on what this novella should be. You were an amazing help.

Thank you for reading!

~ 1 ~

CONVOCATION ACADEMY IN winter tended to be grim. The nights were long and the persistent overcast made them exceptionally dark. That was one reason almost all the students, from the wide-eyed five-year-old kids to the jaded almost graduates of twenty, looked forward to Academy Founders Day.

Normally, Han would be one of those excited for the sleigh races, demonstrations of magical acumen, and the grand feast with all its many, once-a-year treats, but not this time. Though the decorations had begun to go up, with Founders Day just a few days away, and even though the twinkling elemental lights entwined around the evergreen boughs draping the long hallway should have lifted his spirits, his mood was as gloomy as the blizzard-dark sky outside.

"Han!" Iliana called his name, and just the sound of her voice brightened the hallway more than any brace of elemental lights could. He stopped so she could catch up with him, stepping out of the flow of students in the busy corridor and into an alcove where a big, stone-framed window looked out on the heavy snowfall. Technically it was early spring, but in

Convocation Center, winter lasted a good half of the year. They had a couple of months to go before the frigid temperatures would relent and the snow give up in favor of rain.

Sometimes, though, it seemed winter would never end. Just like it seemed Han was doomed never to manifest as either a wizard or a familiar, forever an uncategorized student, despite his looming twenty-first birthday.

Deliberately, he turned his back on the window and edged a hip onto the padded seat, waiting for Iliana to wend through the last of the press. She was breathless, her cheeks flushed, warm brown eyes sparkling. Her waist-length hair bounced in fire-colored curls around her slender throat, highlighting her pale, freckled skin. "I was in my morning meditation class and didn't get your note until I got out. What's going on?" She took a longer look at him and her naturally sunny nature dimmed. "Oh no. You've been summoned to the Testing Tower again?"

"I think they're triangulating," he replied lightly, trying to make it a joke. He was sorry to be such a gloomy influence on her. "If the oracle head determines that I'm uncategorized enough days in a row, then they can just decide I'll never be a wizard and finally boot me from general studies into the classes for familiars."

"Maybe it's the opposite," she argued. "It could be the oracle heads are detecting that your brain is maturing into a wizard's and they want to be sure to catch that transition. You know how they're always gathering data on why that happens for some of us and not others."

He smiled at her, despite himself, her vibrant nature warm

with the House Ariel magical potential that made her so attractive to humans and animals alike. "And they worry about wizards spontaneously manifesting and burning down the dining hall before they remember their lessons in magic discipline."

"That, too," she replied impishly. "Though technically only the tables burned."

"No doubt why Convocation Academy is built out of stone."

"True." She sobered, then took his hand in a rare gesture of physical affection. They were friends, and friends only, but the feel of her skin against his—along with her rich earth magic—sent a pang of longing through him. "Han, try not to worry so much. I—"

"No consorting," the hall proctor instructed, pausing to study them with her wizard-black eyes. Han hastily buried any warmer emotions than friendship, in case the thought-seeker detected his prohibited desire for a fellow student.

"I'm comforting a friend," Iliana explained, but she slipped her hand from his. The proctors could make life miserable even for wizards.

"Comfort him verbally, Familiar Iliana," she replied wryly, giving Han a stern look. "No exceptions, even for uncats, M. Haniel."

Han had long since objecting to the proctors' insistence on using his full name. It was a grandiose name, one that reflected his parents' ambitions that he become a High House wizard. Apparently, they hadn't thought it through, that if their ambition was realized with a contract with House Hanneil as his mother hoped, that he'd become Haniel Hanneil and how awful would that be?

So, mostly he went by Han and only official, and officious types used his given name, which helped him keep in mind their power over him. "Yes, proctor," he replied, trying to sound meek.

The proctor gave them one last penetrating look. "I believe you have somewhere to be, M. Haniel."

"I'll walk with you," Iliana slid off the window seat and waited for him to join her. They entered the flow of students, some in chattering groups, others stalking along in silent aloneness. The latter were mostly older students, many of them newly minted wizards, showing off their distinctive short haircuts, thoughtfully eyeing their fellows, a predatory gleam in their eyes.

He and Iliana threaded through the crush in companionable silence. He'd always liked that about Iliana, that she didn't feel the need to spill words into every quiet moment. He also really liked Iliana, in a way neither of them could afford, or were allowed. Even if he managed to manifest as a wizard, he wouldn't necessarily be allowed to take Iliana as his familiar. The Convocation matched familiars to wizards based on the compatibility of their magical potential scores—and, often, on their likelihood of producing magically gifted progeny. That's why romantic relationships were prohibited at Convocation Academy. The Houses sponsoring the students didn't much like for them to develop relationships that might someday affect valuable contracts and business.

And Han manifesting as a wizard, after all this time as an

uncat, was the best-case scenario. Most likely, however, he'd be a familiar, too. He and Iliana, both with zero control over their lives. So Han had never acted on his feelings for Iliana, and she'd never done more than her naturally affectionate nature dictated, warm hugs and fleeting touches. Of course, it could be she wasn't attracted to him as more than a friend. They'd never discussed it. He liked to think they'd tacitly agreed to wait until their status had been confirmed by the oracle heads.

Some of the older students slept around—pregnancy wasn't a concern as fertility had to be unlocked by an oracle head and disease wasn't a problem as all students received free House Refoel healing while enrolled—and it was allowed so long as their emotions weren't involved. Or weren't detected by the thought-seekers. Most kept to themselves. Which was too bad, really, as this was the one time in their lives that having sex wouldn't be connected to magic exchange.

Iliana, however, would never be the kind of person to have sex without her emotions fully involved. And Han didn't want anyone but her.

They turned out of the stream of students going to classes and into the corridor leading to the Tower of Testing. It was set apart and heavily guarded, by spells and by actual guards. As they approached the guards standing at attention at the base of the stairs leading up into the Testing Tower, Iliana took Han's hand again, slowing their steps. Surprised that she took that risk again so soon after the proctor's warning, Han drew her to the side, out of the guards' line of sight. "What is it?" he asked, noting her uncharacteristically sober expression.

"Han…" She didn't finish, biting down on her next words.

He itched to touch more than her hand. If he could, he'd comb his fingers through her fiery curls, trace her freckled cheekbones with his thumbs. A sweet ache billowed in his heart, billowing like his native magic and pressing on the inside of his skin. "It's just another test," he told her, summoning a smile and putting all the confidence he could muster into it. "They've been testing me monthly anyway; this is just a bit sooner. Otherwise, today is no different from any other."

She reflected the smile, though the worry didn't leave her eyes. "Meet me for dinner?" she asked, instead of saying whatever she clearly wanted to say.

He nodded, squeezed her hand. "I'll see you there at the usual time." Impulsively, he kissed her cheek, almost too shocked at his own temerity to truly savor the velvety feel of her skin, the freckles not palpable and yet he fancied they were like tiny sparks against his lips. He drew away again as fast as he'd darted in, finding her warm brown eyes wide, startled, and… sparkling with pleasure.

She held onto his hand when he would've let her go, just a moment longer. "Good luck," she whispered.

He left her there, not looking back, happiness simmering through his body in place of the dread. Even the guards eyeing him speculatively as he entered the tower doorway didn't bother him. Rumor had it that the guards had an ongoing betting pool, playing armchair oracle head, trying to guess which students would manifest as wizards, which would be relegated to life as a familiar, and when they'd finally be categorized. The guards were careful about it, and meticulously polite in how they treated the uncats, as were all the faculty and other staff at Convocation Academy. An uncategorized student might turn out to be a powerful wizard someday, possibly even the head of a High House, and no one wanted to be on their bad side.

For confirmed familiars, however, no one concerned themselves with treating them well.

Han climbed the steps with heavy feet, dread weighing them down. Sometimes, on this endless trudge spiraling upward through the stairwell that always managed to feel gloomy, despite the liberal distribution of fire elementals lighting the way, he contemplated what would happen if he refused to report.

There were stories—Convocation Academy lived and breathed stories—of students who'd run away. In the wildest tales, some had supposedly escaped the Convocation entirely, and were off living in other realms, magical and not. Han highly doubted the veracity of these stories, especially of familiars escaping to live outside the Convocation. Everyone knew that familiars would go mad if their magic wasn't regularly tapped by a wizard. Unable to release magic of their own will, familiars needed a wizard in order to survive with sanity intact.

And wizards had no reason to escape the Convocation, a world created to enable their least desire.

"Come in, M. Haniel," the testing proctor said with a bit of impatience. "You're very nearly late." Only in the Convocation was almost late as bad as actually late. Han bit back the observation that "very nearly late" also meant "on time."

The proctors had no influence over the findings of the oracle heads—although Iliana sometimes speculated otherwise—but no sense antagonizing those who held so much power over his future. So he only inclined his head politely, murmuring, "Yes, proctor."

The man flicked him an irritated glare, then pointed at the wooden chair placed before a table bare of anything but the tabernacle containing the oracle head. "Sit facing the tabernacle," the proctor instructed, as if Han hadn't done this more times than he could count.

But Han obediently sat, resisting the urge to scoot the chair back from the literally hair-raising magic the tabernacle emitted. Nobody knew exactly how the oracle heads were created, except that they were a result of an ancient collaboration between three High Houses. In a peaceful joint effort, that would be unlikely to occur today, given the intense competition between all the houses, let alone the high ones, Houses Hanneil, Ariel, and El-Adrel had come together to make an enchanted artifact—House El-Adrel's aegis—from a human head, as metamorphosized by House Ariel wizards, and gifted with immense psychic powers from the best of House Hanneil.

Some people claimed they were once actual Hanneil wizards, chosen for their abilities, their disembodied heads preserved for eternity with magic intact. Han always countered with the obvious flaw that the mummified wizard head had no access to a familiar and no way to generate magic of its own, being lifeless, and that it required a wizard proctor to operate. Of course, that left the conclusion that the thing had been a familiar, which was even worse.

Either way, it was unsavory and downright creepy.

Once Han was seated, the proctor moved to open the tabernacle doors. Whoever had thought to prettify the monstrous things by sealing them in the decorated cabinets had missed the mark. Despite the ornate carvings and the delicate inlay that glittered in the exquisitely crafted arched doors of the box, nothing could disguise the ugliness of what lay within. Iliana, as a lover of life and living animals, particularly loathed the oracle heads. Though she'd been disappointed to be finally categorized as a familiar, her relief at never having to confront an oracle head again had been almost enough to balance it out.

Han braced himself as the proctor turned the miniature handles crafted to look like doorknobs and pulled the doors open to expose the head within. It looked like it was sleeping, eyes closed so the colorful scales of gemstones decorating the eyelids showed in artistic detail. Its brows and lips had been recreated from powdered gems as well, which did nothing to make the skin and features look anything but what it was: thoroughly dead.

Painted up corpses in short coffins Iliana called them with devastating accuracy, because that's exactly what it looked like. Until it opened its eyes.

Those were not dead. They looked like normal, living eyes—as normal as living eyes could look in a mummified head—and, wizard black, they stared at him with disconcerting intelligence.

Han tried to think of nothing while the thing took his measure for the umpteenth time. Some students claimed they felt *something* during the testing, but Iliana said she didn't sense anything either. Han cynically suspected that the ones who said they experienced this or that were simply trying to make themselves sound more talented than they were. In a society entirely predicated on one's magical talents, exaggeration and hyperbole were common skills.

When he was younger—and considerably more idealistic—Han had tried to push the oracle head into declaring him a wizard, as if he could will it to be true. Now he just waited while the oracle took his measure, the proctor calling the traditional question in reverential tones. "What is your determination of the candidate?"

The head stared at him, unblinking, a moment longer and Han had a sudden and unsettling glimpse of what it might have looked like in life. A woman, with dark skin and long brown hair. The vision evaporated as quickly as it had flashed into his mind, and he almost fancied that the thing smiled, its thin, desiccated lips cracking the garnet gem dust into a sickle curve.

"The candidate," it intoned in a voiceless whisper that nevertheless resonated in every corner of the room, "cannot be categorized."

Han hadn't been holding his breath, so there was nothing to let out, and yet he sagged slightly. Not in relief, not in sorrow. Just... whatever.

The proctor was far from sanguine, glaring at Han as if he'd somehow deliberately foiled the testing. The oracle head closed its eyes, returning to its slumber or death or stasis, or wherever they went when not activated. The proctor closed the tabernacle doors with deliberate care, activating the magical lock.

"You are twenty years old, M. Haniel," the proctor declared, making that sound like Han's fault, too, as he marked down notes in Han's file. "Very nearly twenty-one. You will report for daily testing until your status can be determined."

Oh joy. "Yes, Proctor." What happened if he remained uncategorized forever—had there ever been a case like that? Only with someone with very low MP scores, he'd bet. Low scores made all sorts of categorization difficult because there was so little to measure. And, in truth, the Convocation hardly bothered themselves. A person with low MP scores was hardly better than a commoner. Anyone that mingily gifted could go find a life among the common folk, perhaps using their scant talents—if they manifested as wizards, no matter how minor— to do what they could to improve their situations.

But Han had high MP scores. Not off the charts like the star students, but enough to guarantee a nice contract with a High House if he manifested as a wizard, or for a bonding to a high-level wizard if he turned out to be only a familiar. Either way, though, he had to be one or the other. He couldn't remain neither fish nor fowl for the remainder of his life, could he?

"Begone already, M. Haniel," the proctor said on a weary sigh.

He stood to go, glad to be released, anxious to find Iliana.

"M. Haniel," the proctor said just as Han reached the relative safety of the door. "I strongly advise you to settle your mind in the very near future. Fence-sitters never do well."

"How am I supposed to do that?" he blurted before he

thought better of it.

The proctor raised disdainful brows. "I suggest you figure that out."

~ 2 ~

ILIANA WATCHED HAN saunter down the hallway toward the Tower of Testing, hands tucked nonchalantly in his pockets. His long, perfectly straight blond hair was tied back in a gleaming tail, giving him an innocent glow that was entirely deceptive. He moved with a dancer's grace, even upset as he was.

And Han was upset. Oh, he tried to brush it off and pretend that he was unconcerned, but Iliana knew him better than she knew herself. If only he'd manifested as a wizard years ago when most of his cohort had, he'd be much easier in his skin.

And Iliana would know where she stood with him.

Surely he'd manifest as a wizard soon. It wasn't *unheard of* for a student, especially the males, to remain uncategorized into their early twenties, but it was highly unusual. And Han was not the kind of person who liked standing out, at least not because he was odd.

Han disappeared into the tower and she sent a last wish for good luck that he'd get an answer. The waiting was so hard on him. Her cheek burned where he'd kissed it and her heart swelled with a keen longing that should've numbed over time and yet grew only sharper. There was a time, up until a year ago, when she'd nurtured the possibility that Han could be one day truly hers. Until she'd received the news that she'd been certified as a familiar.

Since then it had been a daily struggle—against her family, the academy faculty, and against her own weakening resolve—to remain at Convocation Academy. Had her younger self realized what her nineteen-year-old self now knew, she'd have been less diligent in her studies. As it was, she'd completed almost all of the required coursework, including most of the courses in Advanced Training for Familiars. In fact, she'd been second only to Lady Veronica Elal, who'd been a year ahead of Iliana, and the star of Convocation Academy before her crashing fall from grace.

Everyone had been certain Lady Veronica—Nic, to her friends, and Iliana had become sort of a friend—would manifest as a wizard, including Nic. Rumor had it that a number of faculty and staff had lost a considerable amount on losing bets that day, one that Iliana remembered more vividly than her own certification as a familiar. She'd never aspired to being wizard. Well, she'd *wanted* to be a wizard—everyone did—but she never felt like she would be. The final verdict came as no surprise, not like it had with Nic.

Iliana had seen Nic that day, her dusky skin blanched with shock, her striking green eyes glassy as cheap wine bottles, her head nevertheless held high as she moved through the crowded corridors, apparently oblivious to the smirks and whispers. So many students had been viciously pleased with Veronica Elal's abrupt demotion from Convocation Academy golden girl and heir apparent at powerful House Elal to lowly familiar.

Not Iliana. She'd always admired Nic. Some of the wizards and the wizard-presumptives treated familiars as beneath notice—until they needed to use them. Not Nic. She had always been friendly and generous to Iliana, even after Iliana was certified as a familiar. Iliana didn't think that was only because she'd been close friends with Alise, Nic's little sister.

So, when Nic had joined the classes in Advanced Training for Familiars to finish out her education, Iliana had tried to return the favor of being human to her. A lot of the other students hadn't been. The wizards had cut Nic from their social circles with breathtaking ruthlessness, behaving with exceptional cruelty to the former star, as if Nic had somehow deceived them. And the other familiars... well, they hadn't been any kinder.

Nic had remained politely removed from it all, her focus leagues away. She'd also graduated as soon as possible afterward, commencing her Betrothal Trials just a few months ago.

Iliana shuddered at the thought. She couldn't bear the prospect of the Betrothal Trials for herself. She didn't have Nic's spine, her sheer determination to triumph despite being relegated to the life of a familiar. Iliana didn't think she could bear to be sequestered for as long as a year, visited by a different wizard suitor each month until one impregnated her and won the right to make her his bonded familiar. Iliana wasn't exactly surprised Nic had chosen that route. Her MP scores were brilliantly high, so she'd have an exceptional field of High House wizards vying for her. No one so impressive would try for Iliana.

And that was if she could bear for anyone to touch her but Han. She couldn't even imagine it, since her heart had belonged to him for years.

Naturally she'd never told Han how she felt. He didn't need more pressure. Given everything he was dealing with, Han didn't need his best friend pining after him in hopeless and unrequited love. It wasn't as if he could force himself to unlocking the mysterious faculty that allowed a wizard to access the magic a familiar could only accumulate. The Convocation had a long history of experimentation on familiars, attempting to force that ability. It had resulted in a lot of dead or insane familiars. Fortunately, Convocation law protected them now. It would be lovely to think the Convocation protected familiars out of recognition of their basic rights as human beings, but the Convocation set policies for one reason only: profit. Familiars were far too valuable to be squandered.

Regardless, even as a moderately talented familiar, Iliana was destined for a life of service—to an individual wizard or to the Convocation in some capacity. While it was a lovely fantasy to imagine Han as a wizard, who would then choose her for his familiar, it was only that, a fantasy. Han wouldn't have much more say in choosing his familiar than Iliana would in choosing her wizard. And, even if his family did let him choose, and if the Convocation approved Iliana as a match, Han might not choose her at all, an even more potentially heartbreaking outcome.

So she'd never acted on her feelings for him, had never asked him if he thought of her as more than a friend. That kiss on her cheek... it still tingled, but her skin couldn't determine if that had been a kiss of friendly affection or more.

And it didn't bear contemplating, especially since she had class to attend.

ILIANA MADE IT through Wizard–Familiar Dynamics without thinking about Han too much. She actually liked the class, which focused on ways that familiars could support their wizard masters. The topics of study ranged from the finer points of how magic wielding affected a wizard's health and wellbeing—and what a familiar should do to assist—to general education in household management. The familiars jokingly referred to it as The Care and Feeding of Wizards 101, though sometimes that was so accurate that it wasn't funny.

Today's lesson had focused on types of massage that would both relax a wizard stressed from spellcasting and also restore their native magical reserves. Of course, a wizard could always access their bonded familiar's magic to restore their reserves or work any enchantments they wish, provided the wizard didn't carelessly drain their familiar.

The subtext, however, caught Iliana's interest. The professor teaching the class was himself a familiar, once bonded to a wizard who'd died. None of the late wizard's heirs had been interested in taking on the orphaned familiar, so he'd ended up teaching at Convocation Academy. A rather enviable improvement in fortune—and relative freedom—but also a path dependent on several strokes of good luck, so not one anyone could reasonably aspire to. Iliana liked Professor Tracy quite well and absorbed what he carefully didn't say in so many words: that a wise familiar used other methods to rejuvenate their wizard, thus avoiding the painful and exhausting prospect of being drained.

It gave her food for thought and she thanked Professor Tracy on the way out. As she did, he asked her to stay a moment. Once the classroom had cleared out of other students, Professor Tracy leaned a hip against his desk. "I heard Han was summoned to the Testing Tower—any news yet?"

Iliana shook her head, unsurprised that Tracy would ask her, but a bit taken aback at his interest. "No, but I won't see him until later."

Her professor nodded thoughtfully. "I feel I should warn you that even if Han manifests as a wizard, he might not be able to choose you as his familiar."

Face heating, she ducked her head. "I know that. I'm not an idiot."

Professor Tracy clucked his tongue. "I didn't mean to imply you are. What I meant to say is... Your friendship with Han has been noted."

"That's what we are." Forgetting to be embarrassed in her indignation, she lifted her head. "We are friends. We've never crossed any lines."

"We know that," Professor Tracy said gently. "I'm sure you realize the thought-seekers have monitored the situation. I'm asking that you take care of yourself, Iliana. We familiars have very little power. Don't do anything to increase your vulnerability, that's all I'm saying."

She nodded mutely, not trusting herself to reply.

He nodded back. "I believe you should be heading toward your next class."

"Yes, Professor," she said meekly, tamping down the urge to point out that he'd been the one to keep her in the first place. Once again she turned to go and, once again, he called after her.

"The Convocation ways and laws are very old, Iliana," he said, waving a hand at the ancient stone building of the academy around them. "Going against those foundational beliefs will only lead to sorrow."

"Yes, Professor," she said again, and hurried to her next class, which was a joint advanced training course for both wizards and familiars.

Whether or not Iliana enjoyed the class depended entirely on who she was partnered with. If she was lucky, she was partnered with Alise Elal, who'd manifested as a wizard about the same time as Iliana was certified as a familiar. Their formerly close friendship had eroded some since then— wizards and familiars ran in different social circles, and not only because they were housed and schooled in separate wings of the academy—but Alise hadn't dropped Iliana entirely. When given the option, they worked together in the practicum and even had fun on occasion.

Iliana slipped into the class only slightly late, but enough to be a nuisance. The professor, Wizard Angela, paused in her lecture mid-sentence to slice Iliana with a disapproving glare, then marking a note in her attendance book. Likely a demerit.

This was turning out to be a banner day. Worse, when Iliana looked for her assigned seat, she saw her nameplate next to Sabrina Hanneil. The cool blonde wizard shook her head so her sharp bob swung around her jawline, smirked at Iliana, patting the stool beside her. *Oh joy.*

Wizard Angela cleared her throat, pointedly waiting for Iliana to sit. Iliana had to make her way through the maze of work tables and gauntlet of gazes that ranged from sympathetic—Alise sent her a regretful smile—to gleefully malicious to outright malevolent. Sabrina fell in the last category and Iliana sat as far away from her as the short workbench allowed, which wasn't much.

After waiting another beat to make Iliana's disruption brutally clear, Wizard Angela continued her lecture. "As I was *saying*, in today's practicum, we'll concentrate on the familiars learning to release resistance to yielding their magic. All of you familiars need extensive practice in this critical skill. Now, it's human nature to be selfish and attempt to keep what's in us to ourselves, but a familiar, once certified as such by the oracles, becomes a new being. A fully magical one. And the familiar nature finds its greatest satisfaction in giving fully to their wizard. Iliana, please remind the class what we say about waste?"

Sabrina poked Iliana painfully in the ribs. "Answer," she hissed, even though Iliana had already opened her mouth to do so.

Ignoring Sabrina to the best of her ability, Iliana quoted, "A familiar's magic is useless until given to a wizard; it otherwise goes to waste, which is a crime against the Convocation's sacred laws."

Wizard Angela, somewhat mollified by the correct answer, paused significantly, looking around the room with a somber mien, as if already mourning all that wasted magic. "Magic is the most valuable commodity in the Convocation. Does anyone want to see it *wasted*?"

A murmured chorus that no, no one would want that.

Satisfied, the professor continued her lecture. "Naturally a familiar finds their greatest fulfillment in sharing their magic when fully bonded to their eventual wizard master. In the advanced courses for familiars, you all will have been learning about the bonding experience, how it will feel, and how you can best participate in that wholly unique relationship."

Because Wizard Angela looked expectantly at the familiars in the room, Iliana nodded obediently along with the rest of them.

"*Care and Feeding of Wizards, Advanced Study,*" a familiar whispered from across the aisle with an irreverent grin, subsiding with a guilty wriggle when Wizard Angela fixed them with a stern glare.

"Bonding, however, as you all should understand at this point in your schooling, is unnecessary for tapping a familiar's magic. Which is a good thing, or we'd be neck deep in crazy familiars!" Wizard Angela grinned, inviting them to share in the joke. The wizard students laughed and some familiars did, too, though weakly.

"Maybe *that's* your problem," Sabrina hissed in her ear under cover of the laughter. "You're certainly crazy if you think Han will have anything to do with you once he manifests."

"The point," Wizard Angela said over the noise, invoking their quiet attention again, "is that, while the wizards must refine their skills at extracting magic from a familiar—and don't mistake me: every wizard in this room needs considerable practice—that familiars would be making a grievous mistake if they believe they can take the lazy route and simply not fight that extraction. This is not passive on the familiar's part, no matter how accustomed you familiars may have become to thinking of yourselves as unable to affect magic."

Another familiar put up his hand. "Respectfully, Wizard Angela, we familiars *can't* wield magic. Isn't that what makes us familiars, not wizards?"

The professor nodded approvingly. "That is absolutely true. You are vessels in which magic collects and resides. But it *is* within your power—and is your sacred onus—to support and serve your wizard or wizards. Think of yourself as a bottle." She tapped the wallboard, causing one of the diagrams she'd stored there to emerge. "The neck of the bottle can be narrow, as you see here. Or..." She tapped the board again, showing a wide-necked jar instead. "You can open yourselves fully to release all you have to give."

"Beeee the wide-necked jar," Sabrina intoned, snickering.

"So," Wizard Angela said briskly, vanishing the images and dusting her hands together, "this is your exercise for the day. Wizards, you concentrate on your control. Start with small sips and gradually increase. Familiars, I challenge you to open yourselves fully. You may have noticed that I've made an effort to pair you with wizards that I've noted you don't already harmonize with, perhaps even actively dislike."

"Gee, I'm wounded, Iliana," Sabrina cooed.

"These pairings present you with an opportunity," Wizard Angela continued over quietly discontented groans, "a challenge to overcome to improve your skills and banish reticence that will only make you a difficult familiar to work with. Remember, while some wizard–familiar bondings may involve marriage, children, and possibly deep emotions, some of you familiars may end up bonded to a wizard you don't like. Or you may end up in a work-for-hire position where you serve a variety of wizards on call. You must be ready to yield all your magic upon request, willingly and with perfect surrender."

"Wizard Angela?" Another familiar put up her hand. "What about Fascination?"

Everyone stilled, attention caught. Fascination was a topic much speculated upon by students, but rarely discussed by the faculty. Wizard Angela hesitated, pressing her lips together. "Fascination is neither here nor there."

Iliana's classmate persisted. "But wouldn't Fascination remove all resistance and enable us to give utterly to our wizard masters?"

"If Fascination exists," Wizard Angela replied sharply, "and there is no scientific evidence that it does, then perhaps that could be the case. However, no student of mine will graduate relying on a fairytale to help them do their job. The technique I'm teaching you is real and you will all master it. Wizards, for today only, there are no restrictions on how much magic you pull from your familiar. We are working explicitly on draining them as much as possible, so there will be no demerits for excessive tapping."

The wizards clapped and exclaimed in delight while the familiars groaned in dismay. Iliana was circumspect enough to keep her unhappiness to herself, but this promised to make a bad day even worse. She'd never been completely drained, but Iliana had given up enough magic in the past to remember the feeling of sick exhaustion from losing just that much.

"House Refoel healers will be available to any familiar who needs it," Wizard Angela said over the noise. "But, familiars, we encourage you to take this opportunity to practice your other learned skills in replenishing your magic reserves. Being able to recover quickly is also key to being the best at your job that you can be. Now, familiars, take a moment to meditate, calm your mind, and picture yourself as totally open. We'll begin running drills and I'll come around the room and coach each pairing individually."

Dutifully, Iliana closed her eyes and centered herself. Much as she dreaded this exercise, it wasn't in her to do a half-assed job on anything. She would master this skill just as she had all the others. Her hero Nic would have learned this and if the proud Elal scion could do it, so could Iliana.

"Maybe you're Fascinated by me," Sabrina whispered in her ear, "and that's why you hate me so much. You're fighting your own Fascination."

"Maybe I hate you because you're a horrible bitch," Iliana muttered back.

Sabrina gasped. "You are not allowed to talk to me that way, familiar!"

Iliana cracked on eye open to find Sabrina's beautiful face looming so close she looked like a monster. "I'm not allowed to refuse you magic, Wizard Sabrina. But you are not my bonded wizard, so you can't run my life."

"I wouldn't have you anyway," Sabrina shot back. "Han is going to be *my* familiar. I heard he was summoned to the Testing Tower and that the oracle will designate him a familiar today."

Iliana used her self-discipline techniques to still her emotions. Sabrina was baiting her. There wasn't any way the wizard girl could know that yet. "Be quiet. I'm supposed to meditate."

"Wizard Angela!" Sabrina called out indignantly. "Familiar Iliana just told me to shut up."

Iliana didn't open her eyes, but she clearly heard the glares shot in Sabrina's direction as she interrupted everyone else's meditation, too.

"That's because Familiar Iliana is supposed to be meditating, Wizard Sabrina," Wizard Angela replied coolly. "It would behoove you to learn to treat your familiar with more care, or they will not last long in your service."

Nobody outright laughed, but the sifting magic in the atmosphere took on a cast of gleeful amusement at Sabrina's set down.

Under cover of the workbench, Sabrina pinched Iliana's thigh painfully. "I'll get you for this."

Iliana did her best to sublimate the pain and frustration at the injustice into her magic. This afternoon was going to be torture.

~ 3 ~

B Y THE TIME Iliana dragged herself back to her room, her bones felt like one breath might send them crumbling into a puff of dust. One of the Refoel healers had checked her out at the end of the practicum, but said Iliana wasn't in need of healing, that she wasn't suffering anything a good meal and a full night of sleep wouldn't cure—and added an injunction to practice her magic replenishment techniques.

Of course, Sabrina had to saunter past at that exact moment and snidely comment that no doubt Iliana was fine because she hadn't completed the assignment, that Iliana had *failed* to yield up all of her magic without resistance.

The remark still made Iliana bristle, in no small part because it was true. Normally Iliana was very good at her lessons, but today had been an abysmal performance. She simply hadn't been able to get over her intense dislike of Sabrina Hanneil. Iliana didn't want that bitch to have any of her magic, let alone all of it. Infuriated by Iliana's recalcitrance, Sabrina had gotten heavy-handed, yanking on Iliana's magic with wrenching force that felt like her intestines were being extracted from her body through a straw.

Fortunately, their pairing hadn't been the only utter disaster and Wizard Angela had finally cut the practicum off early, saying that she'd clearly expected too much of them and that they'd repeat the exercise with more harmonious pairings the following day, and then work up to the difficult pairings from there. While Iliana was relieved to be able to try again with a wizard she got along with better—she really hated that she'd performed so poorly—she also dreaded having to open herself up again like that, even with someone like Alise. Worse, if she did learn the skill, she'd still have to face the blade of Sabrina's wizardry scraping out her insides again.

Inside the quiet sanctum of her little room, instead of sitting in a meditation pose as she was supposed to, she flopped facedown onto the bed, feeling as if she could dissolve into it and sleep for days. But she couldn't let herself do that. She was under strict orders to eat heartily, too, so she'd get up and head to the dining hall in just a moment...

A knock on her door woke her from such a deep sleep she nearly jumped out of her skin, disoriented and groggy. Getting her bearings, she checked the El-Adrel timepiece on her bedside table and found she'd only been asleep a short time, but wow—she'd really passed out.

"Iliana!" Han called through the door. "Are you in there?"

Oh, right! She jumped up, ran her hands through her hair and saw in the mirror that one half of her face was red and smushed with the pattern from her coverlet. Fantastic. And no way she could make Han wait outside while she got a grooming imp to fix her up.

"Iliana?" Han sounded concerned, knocking again, more

urgently.

"Coming." She tripped the magical lock on the door and opened it for Han, who was glaring at her, hands on hips.

"You didn't show for dinner," he said accusingly, slipping past her and into the room. "I was worried."

Wincing, she closed the door and engaged the lock again. She was a terrible friend. "I'm so sorry. I fell asleep. What did the oracle head say?"

He sat on her bed and flopped back, arms akimbo. "Uncategorized. Still."

"Oh, Han." She sat beside him and stroked his pale hair back from his brow. Fascination might be a myth, and even if it wasn't, she couldn't feel it for someone not a wizard, but she'd gladly give Han all the magic in her to make him feel better. If she had any left, that was. "I'm so sorry," she said again, unable to think of anything better, even though this was another order of magnitude of regret.

He opened his eyes and rolled them. They were an extraordinary shade of blue, with a deep ring like the ocean in summer at the outer edge, shades of crystalline blue inside that, and a sunburst of grass green radiating from his pupil. Finer rays of green shot through the other blues. From a distance, his eyes looked very bright blue, standing out against his dusky skin. Up close... Well, Iliana sometimes found herself staring at the rays of green, and how the concentric rings of varying blues seemed to shimmer from one to the next.

If Han became a wizard, his eyes would eventually turn black from magic wielding. As much as she wanted that status for him, she secretly hated that those lovely colors would disappear from the world. Though that was silly: there was a high probability, nearly a certainty, that Han would disappear from her life completely, let alone his fascinating eyes. Maybe she fastened her proactive grief on that color vanishing because it was easier to imagine never seeing him again.

"It's not a big deal," Han was saying as she gazed into his eyes, memorizing how they looked. "Just frustrating. And, as a special bonus, I get to go for testing *every day* now."

"Oh wow." She'd never heard of anyone getting tested daily. "But maybe this is a good sign. After all, why would they want you to come in every day unless they're worried about you suddenly manifesting as a wizard and blowing up the dining hall?"

His annoyed scowl softened and he sat up, taking her hand and tangling her fingers with his. "You are the best friend there is, you know that?"

"Of course, I know," she replied breezily, covering the twin pangs of emotion—pleasure at his praise and sorrow at being forever only a friend. "But I'm not spinning pretty illusions. You know how high your MP scores are. You're going to be a powerful wizard and everyone knows it." Feeling momentarily dizzy, she rubbed her forehead, willing herself to wake up.

Han narrowed those jewellike eyes. "I, however, am a terrible friend. Here I am, wallowing in my petty concerns, when you're clearly upset." He touched her cheek, tracing an arc beneath her eye. "And exhausted. I can't even feel your magic and you have shadows under your eyes so deep you look like someone punched you."

She jerked away. "Wow, thanks. I'm fine."

"What's wrong?" he persisted. "Something happened to drain your magic."

Restless despite her weariness, she got up and went to her vanity mirror. Han wasn't wrong, which was all the more annoying. Uncorking the bottle with the Elal grooming imp, she set it loose to improve her appearance. As a familiar, she couldn't control the imp, but they came prepackaged with basic instructions. In general, the imps did well with cleaning and smoothing hair, and they did fine with clearing skin and removing blemishes and unsightly shadows, stimulating skin to create a healthy glow that was as close to beauty as Iliana would ever get.

"I didn't mean it like that," Han said softly. "You don't have to fix yourself up. You look beautiful. I just meant I could see..." He trailed off, and Iliana glanced at him in the mirror as the glowing sprite moved through her wayward curls.

Han had shifted to lie on his side, head propped on one elbow and long legs kicked out to drape over the end of her untidy bed. He looked like a lover might, if they'd rumpled her covers with more interesting activities, those blue eyes catching the light and focusing on her. Except he wasn't gazing on her with sensual adoration, like she imagined in her fantasies. No, he was making a face, clearly uncertain how to extricate himself from the hole he'd dug.

"I did need to fix myself up," she replied with a smile, so he wouldn't worry. "Not because you said anything. I was going to anyway, before heading to the dining hall. Can't have a daughter of House Ariel showing up for dinner unkempt."

"Oh, you didn't eat yet?" He glanced at the clock. "It's late. If we want any food, we'd better go soon."

"I fell asleep," she admitted. "What have you been doing that you haven't eaten either?"

He flopped onto his back with a groan and a grimace, drawing up one knee. Because he was no longer looking at her, Iliana indulged in running her eyes over his long, lean body as she wished she could do with her hands. Or lips. Better put that craving down deep where the thought-seekers couldn't get to it.

"A Ratsiel courier ambushed me on my way out of the Testing Tower," he said to the ceiling. "My mother. Apparently there was a rumor I'd been certified a wizard. I ended up having to exchange half-a-dozen messages convincing her I wasn't engaged in a prank by denying it, and then another eight or nine in which I promised to do better in making myself into a wizard by tomorrow."

She winced for him, the grooming imp tickling when she interrupted its work. "I'm sorry, Han."

"Don't be. And somehow I ended up talking about myself again. Why did you fall asleep before dinner? That's not like you. Tell me what happened today."

"Just be glad you don't have to attend the advanced studies classes yet." She tried for sophisticated and world-weary, but sounded a little pitiful.

"The lab practicum?" he asked, sitting up and holding her gaze in the mirror. His pale hair had come loose from his flopping about, a few strands escaping the tie and hanging around his high cheekbones. "What was today's exercise?"

"You know I'm not supposed to tell you," she replied.

"Like I'd tell anyone you spilled Convocation secrets," he snapped, pushing to his feet and coming to stand behind her, resting his hands on her shoulders and squeezing lightly. "You can trust me, Iliana. You should know that by now."

"I know." She sighed. She did trust him, with everything in her. She just couldn't have him. The thought of vile Sabrina taking Han as her familiar made Iliana want to commit bloodshed. *It won't happen,* she consoled herself. Han would be a wizard. He just had to be. "We worked on magic transference is all. The familiars had to practice yielding up every drop of magic and the wizards learned to take as much as possible."

Han glared at her in the mirror, as if it had been her idea. "That sounds dangerous."

"They had Refoel healers standing by and I was pronounced just fine—like I told you—and was told to eat and rest."

He held her gaze a beat longer. "Then we'll feed you. Cork up the imp."

"It's almost done. Rushing me won't help." And she didn't want Sabrina and that crew seeing her looking ragged. Han had done her a favor pointing it out.

"This is more than magic drain," Han decided, scrutinizing her face. "Something upset you. It better not have been Sabrina Hanneil."

"If it was, neither of us can do anything about it." The imp had thankfully finished and Iliana decided she looked marginally better. She coaxed it back into its bottle home and corked it again, turning and smiling brightly into Han's scowl. He stood much too close, so she popped him on the upper chest with the heels of her hands. "Out of my way, you hulk," she said teasingly.

But he wrapped his hands around her wrists, not budging, searching her face. His hands on the sensitive skin of her wrists and the headiness of his full, focused attention made her heart skip a few beats. "You don't have to take Sabrina's abuse," he said in a low voice, looking dangerous in a way he rarely did. That took her breath away, too.

"I *do* have to take however Sabrina decides to treat me," she reminded him. "As she is a wizard and I'm a familiar."

"You're not *her* familiar."

No, and she hoped she never would be. But she'd still trade places with Han if he turned out to be a familiar and Sabrina was serious about bonding him. "You and I both know I have no recourse. *Besides,*" she said with stern emphasis when he opened his mouth to argue, "the professor supervised the exercise and there was nothing that crossed the line."

"Iliana," he began with exasperation, fingers tightening on her wrists in his frustration, though the contact made her wish he was holding her that way for other reasons, perhaps pinning her wrists to the bed so he could... *Don't imagine it.* "We both know that Sabrina is—"

"Irrelevant to this conversation," she interrupted, wriggling out of his grip and slipping to the side, deftly evading him. At least she could breathe now, though her skin felt lonely where he'd touched her. "It was simply a difficult exercise, Han. The point was to know how full magic draining works and how it feels. We all learned something, which is why we're here at

Convocation Academy."

"But, Sabrina—"

"But, Sabrina nothing!" Iliana threw up her hands. "I'm not fragile, Han. I'm a dedicated student of my profession and I *want* to learn these skills."

A muscle in his clean-shaven jaw ticced as he set his teeth. "No one is a more dedicated student than you are," he ground out. "And I know you're not fragile, but magic drain alone wouldn't put that look in your eyes. You don't have to put up with abuse from the likes of—"

"It *does* mean that, Han." She took his hand again, a bit startled when he held on with sudden fervor, his lovely eyes a bit more green than usual with anger. "What if I'm bonded to a wizard that I don't like? I have to be able to work with anyone. That's part of what today's lesson taught us. Also, I don't want to be unkind, but you are an uncat and you have no idea what full magic drain feels like!"

He was quiet a moment, interlacing his fingers with hers. "That bad?"

"If feeling like you've had your guts pulled out and all the blood drained from your body is bad, then yes," she said, trying for a joke, but it came out kind of wobbly and pitiful.

He lifted his other hand to her cheek, caressing it with something like tenderness, sending her heart thumping again. "I'm sorry I was being obtuse. Did you meditate to replenish?"

"I fell asleep first." She rolled her eyes, trying to pretend she wasn't trembling under the feather-light caress of his fingers. "Besides, meditation only does so much when I'm this drained."

"I can only imagine," he replied softly. His fingers drifted down to her throat, where surely he must feel her frantic pulse, then behind her neck under her hair. "There's something else we could try."

She tried to shake her head, but she couldn't seem to move, held rapt by those beautiful eyes and the devastating caress of his clever fingers. "You know the erotic techniques are for bonded wizard–familiar pairings."

"Only because they don't want us getting attached without permission," he retorted, still tracing the skin at her nape, the sensation more dizzying than any magic drain. Except that her magic was rebounding, rising in response to his sweet caresses.

"Which is why we can't do this," she cautioned breathlessly, hoping he'd stop because she didn't think she could.

His gaze dropped to her lips and her heart thumped in anguished anticipation. Surely he wasn't going to kiss her. "Can't we?" he murmured. "One kiss, just to make you feel better."

Oh. Was that his only reason? "Han..." She couldn't think of what to say.

He lowered his head, releasing her hand so he could wrap his arm around her waist, pulling her closer. "Let me kiss you, Iliana, please."

What could she say? "Yes," she breathed, the inevitable answer.

A shudder went through him, a mirror to her own trembling, his keen-edged magic palpable in the narrowing space between their lips. His brushed hers, a tantalizing caress, magic sparking between them. He groaned her name, a tremor of sound against her mouth, and she wound her fingers into his tunic, as if preventing him from escaping. She kissed him fiercely, drinking from his lips, as if she could pull his magic into her. She couldn't, but it felt that way, her magic billowing up to fill the parched lacunae in her deepest being.

Their tongues tangled together, both of them holding tight to each other, like castaways adrift on a stormy sea. She'd wanted this forever, dreamed about it, and it was better than any of her fantasies. If only they had done this long ago... *No.*

With crashing panic, she remembered why they hadn't ever done this. Why they still couldn't.

Wrenching away from him, she nearly staggered, pressing her hands to her racing heart, her breathing ragged. Han stared back at her, blue eyes brilliant and filled with wild desire. For her.

It was everything she'd ever wanted—and everything she could never have.

"Iliana..." Han reached for her and she backed away.

"We cannot do this," she told him, trying to sound firm, instead sounding like she was pleading with him.

"We already did." His gaze traveled over her, leaving fire and lightning in its wake, and returned to face. "It was everything."

"It can't be!" she shot back at him. "This isn't allowed. You know that."

"It only isn't allowed if there's no future for us. But there will be."

Words failed her. He edged closer, tentatively setting his hands on her hips. "I'm going to be a wizard," he said firmly.

"I know you are." She lifted a hand to his cheek, cupping it with a breath of a touch, not trusting herself to do more than that. "You're going to be amazing."

He didn't reply immediately, a fine tension running through him. "If—*when*, I am. Iliana, would you be my familiar?"

Her heart thudded to a full stop, her ears ringing. "Han, I..."

"I don't want anyone else," he said in a rush. "I'm in love with you. Please say yes."

Oh, she wanted to. She'd dreamed of this moment, of hearing these words. And yet... somehow in her daydreams all the other obstacles didn't exist. There'd been a fairytale aspect to the fantasy in which Han loved her and carried her off to some paradisical land where they lived on love.

Which was not the Convocation, with its sharply defined roles and rigid expectations. Besides, Han *wasn't* a wizard yet. He might think he wanted her now, but that could change. And that was before his family got involved in the matter.

"What is it?" Han whispered, stricken. "You can't tell me you don't feel the same. Not after that spectacular kiss."

"Han..." Her throat was too dry and she had to swallow. "We've been friends for a long time and this is very sudden."

He glared at her, eyes full of fire. "It's *not* sudden. Yes, we've been friends for years, the best of friends. I can love you as a friend and as a familiar. Unless..." He hesitated, searching her face. "Unless you don't want me?"

There was no world in which she didn't want him. But this was a crazy conversation to be having. Deliberately, she disentangled herself from him. "First of all, while I absolutely believe in you, you are not yet certified as a wizard, so any decisions like this are premature."

When he opened his mouth to argue, she laid her fingers over his lips. Which was a mistake because they burned her skin, tempting her to replace her fingers with her own lips again. She yanked her hand away again. "Second, we both know the decision won't be up to us. The Convocation will want to determine our compatibility. And your family will want to have a say."

"I can handle my family," he bit out, eyes a blue as hot as the magical fires in the laboratory.

She knew better than to argue with that, as it would only tempt Han to entrench more. "And can you handle the Convocation, too?"

"I'm willing to fight for you," he retorted. "They're not the final say. Unless you're telling me you don't *want* to be my familiar."

And there it was, the scary truth of it all. Maybe it was her classmate raising the specter of Fascination in class today, but it hit Iliana with knee-weakening realization that if Fascination was real, and if she became Han's familiar, then she'd risk losing herself. She was already unhealthily attached to him, even obsessed, as Alise had once gently suggested. As much as Iliana loathed the thought of being bonded to a wizard she hated, like vile Sabrina, or someone equally awful, there would be a certain amount of emotional freedom in disliking them. Her hatred would give her space inside to be entirely herself. If she loved her wizard like she already loved Han, and that was without the bonding or the Fascination...

"Iliana?" Han spoke her name tentatively, rare uncertainty crossing his face that nearly broke her heart.

She put her fingertips to her temples, not an act as her head swam dizzily. "I just can't think right now. I'm so tired, and I'm starving."

"Of course." He smiled, relief and his usual sweetness in it. "Again I'm being thoughtless. Let's get you fed." He tripped the lock on her door, opened it, and gestured her through with a courtly bow that made her laugh.

Han could always make her laugh. But he couldn't be hers. Better to get her head straight about that.

~ 4 ~

A T LEAST HAN could make Iliana laugh, even when he was
dying inside. Fortunately long training with his rank-
obsessed family allowed him to keep a cheerful smile pasted to
his face as he and Iliana walked through the long gallery
leading to the dining hall. They walked without speaking, both
of them concentrating on the mental disciplines that would
disguise their recent activities from the thought-seekers.

Han established a running mental contemplation of dinner
options—easy, as he was ravenously hungry—then let himself
think about his next steps. He wasn't going to let Iliana's
summary rejection slow him down. She'd kissed him back,
with fervor that still had his entire body throbbing with
longing. She might've kicked away the heart he'd laid at her
feet with distressing vigor, but he also knew she was afraid.
And exhausted.

He always did have terrible timing. Fortunately he had
persistence. If he kept trying, eventually he'd hit the right
timing through sheer repetition. The thought cheered him, as
did the gaily decorated gallery they walked through. That was
the power of an excellent kiss with the person you loved. His

gloominess from earlier in the day, the frustration he'd felt in the Tower of Testing, the sullen fury at his mother's lectures— all of that had evaporated in the heat of kissing Iliana at last, leaving giddiness behind. The twinkling lights and sparkling decorations seemed to echo the bubbling joy in his heart.

House Elal had developed the new line of festival lights in recent years. Created in conjunction with House El-Adrel, the cunning magical artifacts radiated bright light from the tiny fire elementals powering them, available in all sorts of colors. Naturally, the Convocation Academy had selected crimson and silver, academy colors, and those lights predominated, brightening the otherwise shadowy arcade.

Banners of the twelve High Houses lined the hall, too, and at each a cluster of lights twinkled in those house colors. Iliana's House Ariel glittered with the deeper tones of earth, sea, and sky, their banner showing the house crest, a similar triad reflecting animals of the ground, water, and air. The House Hanneil banner glittered with red and black lights, the crest of a stylized human head radiating rays in the same colors. If Han did manifest as a wizard, he'd fight taking a contract with House Hanneil, no matter what his parents wanted. He'd had enough of thought-seeking and oracle heads. Surely some other house could make use of his magical potential in psychic magic.

After the High Houses came the second tier houses, then the lower-ranking houses, their banners clustering thick on the walls. Han turned his face away from his own house banner, being thoroughly unhappy with the lot of them at the moment, and his gaze snagged on a new banner. Silver on deep blue, a full moon rose over an argent sea, and the lights clustered at the top, all in white and palest silver-blue.

"Look." He nudged Iliana. "A new house banner. I don't recognize the crest though."

She followed his gaze. "House Phel," she murmured in surprise.

"Aha!" He studied the crest with greater interest. House Phel had been defunct for so long that he'd never seen their symbol before.

"If you studied your house crests," she noted primly, "you'd have known that."

"I memorized all the active houses," he protested. "Why waste brain space on all the defunct ones?"

"For instances like this," she retorted.

"Still, I'm surprised they hung the House Phel banner. Isn't their reinstatement probationary?"

"Yes, but they were a powerful High House for centuries before demotion."

"You mean before House Phel *fell*?"

She slid him a small smile. "Yes, I've heard the joke. Probationary or not, House Phel *is* once again a house, even if whether they'll ascend to being a High House again is in question. Their banner should be hung."

"For however long that lasts. Aren't they a house of one wizard?"

"One is all it takes, especially if that wizard is as powerful as Gabriel Phel."

"Off the charts MP scores are all well and good," Han scoffed, well aware he was repeating his mother's words, though in this case, he agreed with the arrogant wizard, "but without academy training, he can't do much with his magic. He doesn't have a familiar either, so his workings will be limited."

"I wonder," Iliana murmured, but before he could ask what she meant, they passed under the sparkling and ber-ibboned garlands outlining the big archway and entered the dining hall. Sabrina Hanneil and her cohort of wizard friends from the best families lingered at the best table near the huge fireplace. Their avid gazes immediately landed on Han, their voices rising in excited speculation. He didn't at all like that Iliana, for all her denials and bravado, palpably shrunk beside him, slowing her steps so she was partially concealed by his frame, her warm and friendly magic taking on a brittle edge.

He steered Iliana to a table farther away from that venomous group, and also conveniently close to the kitchens. Flagging down one of the younger students who worked as a server, he held up two fingers to summon their dinners, and the boy ran off to comply. They were late, with most of the dining hall empty except for a few groups lingering over wine and conversation like Sabrina's.

Except he felt sure Sabrina had been lying in wait for them. The wizard girl would know of the instructions for the drained familiars to eat heartily. She'd probably been watching for Iliana all evening, with the bonus of counting on Han being with her. Sabrina would want to be the first to welcome him into the wizard circles—or taunt him for being relegated to being a familiar.

Sure enough, the boy had barely brought their wine,

mulled with spices tonight for the beginning days of the celebration, when Sabrina swanned up to the table. Iliana stared stonily into her wine, clearly not in any mood to fake pleasantries, so Han stepped into the social gap, producing his brightest, most insincere smile. "Wizard Hanneil," he said formally, "did you require something? Perhaps your table ran out of wine and they sent you to fetch it."

Sabrina's otherwise pretty mouth thinned with ugly anger at his insult, especially since she couldn't retort that she'd never fetch her own wine (true) without sounding like the insufferable elitist she was. "What did the oracle say, Han—is a celebrational hair-cutting in order? Everyone is agog to hear your news."

"There is no news, Sabrina darling," he replied silkily. "I surely hope you didn't lose your bet by limiting the outcome to today."

By the furious set of her jaw, she had indeed done exactly that. For the first time that day, Han was delighted that the oracle had been unable to categorize him. It was worth it just to see Sabrina stew.

"How can you be *still* uncategorized?" she demanded. "This is getting ridiculous."

"Funny, my mother said the same thing. Have you two been chatting?"

"You are so immature," she spat. "No wonder your brain is lagging back with the little kids."

He raised his brows, making an astonished face. "Also what my mother said!" Squinting at her, he poked her arm. "Are you my mother wearing an illusion?"

Sabrina yanked her arm out of reach, composing herself. "Best speak to me with more care. You know what they say— being a familiar is the default. If you don't manifest as a wizard, and soon, they'll declare you a familiar just to get you through the advanced classes and out of here. It just doesn't look good to have thirty-year old students hanging around."

"And yet they tolerate you," he drawled.

If Sabrina's magic manifested as fire, smoke would be pouring out of her nose at that moment. "*I am only seventeen,*" she declared. "I don't blame you for being jealous, since I'm also about to graduate as a full wizard, the youngest wizard in House Hanneil."

"Tomorrow?" he asked with chipper hopefulness. "Please say it's tomorrow. Buh-bye."

"You think you're so funny and charming." She lifted her nose haughtily. "But it's all a cover for what you are: terrified. And when they finally give up hope on the golden son and declare you a pitiful, impotent familiar, I'm going to bond you. You will be my docile little pet, serving my every whim. I've already got the collar picked out."

"There's no shame in being a familiar," he returned evenly, "but you're wrong if you think I'll ever be yours. My family would never bond me to a Hanneil."

"Not unless you begged them," she replied thoughtfully, tapping a finger against her chin.

"Which I would never do."

"Wouldn't you?" Her gaze and her hand dropped to Iliana's fiery curls, and Sabrina combed her fingers through, as if she were petting a cat, and Iliana shuddered. Her magic, which had been rebounding nicely, grew thin as she withdrew into herself. "What if it came down to a choice? Sweet Iliana here is already available, an unbonded familiar who is undoubtedly compatible. Her family would happily give her to me for a connection to House Hanneil."

"Take your hands off her."

"So protective." Sabrina smiled triumphantly, Han bitterly regretting that he chomped so eagerly on her obvious bait. "I'm betting you'd do anything to protect little Iliana here, even to the point of offering yourself to be my familiar if it would save her."

Iliana moved, ducking out of Sabrina's grip with athletic grace. "You're overstepping, Wizard Hanneil," Iliana said with steely calm. "Unless the Convocation has appointed you consultant to the Advisory Council for Wizard-Familiar Relations?"

Sabrina glared with cool hauteur. "I realize you don't understand these things, silly Illy, else I'd be offended. But I know you can't help being ignorant, coming from a distant branch of House Ariel. It's no surprise that you think the council operates free of influence from the people who really matter." She tutted mockingly down at Iliana. "Unless you plan to subject yourself to the Betrothal Trials—and let's face it, who's going to sign up to try for you?—then you give up any chance of random assignment."

"Which is it?" Iliana lifted her chin. "Am I undesirable as a familiar or am I so desirable that you want me?"

"Your magic is tasty, it's true," Sabrina mused, then slid her gaze to Han. "But I think I've been clear about who I truly want, in my arcanium and in my bed. And my point is that the council does as my father tells them to do."

"I'm sure the other Lords and Ladies of the High Houses would be interested to hear that tidbit," Han snapped.

Sabrina waved that off as a matter of no concern, which spoke to her self-involvement that she didn't give appropriate consideration to the position she just put her father in. Lord Hanneil wasn't a popular figure for many reasons, but he was also far from the most powerful wizard in the Convocation. Other High House heads—notably Lord Elal, Lady El-Adrel, and Lady Hanneil—would absolutely take umbrage at the kind of influence Sabrina was implying.

"As Iliana pointed out already," he said, seating himself again and turning his back on Sabrina, "this entire conversation is moot, as none of this is within our control, and besides which, we don't know yet how I'll be categorized."

Sabrina leaned down on his side away from Iliana, her perfume a bit much at that proximity. "If you were going to manifest as a wizard, it would've happened a long time ago. You're already a familiar and you're already mine. The sooner you get used to the idea, the easier it will be on you." She wrapped her hand around the long queue of his hair. "I look forward to cutting this myself, while you kneel at my feet," she whispered in his ear.

Their dinners arrived and Sabrina straightened. "Happy Founders Day, you two. Prosperity through magic!" she chirped and sashayed off.

Iliana made a low, grinding sound, which hopefully wasn't her teeth grinding together. "I hate her so much," she spat out, stabbing at a piece of meat as if she wished it were Sabrina Hanneil's liver.

"What happened to being able to work with anyone?" Unsettled by the encounter himself, he asked the sarcastic question without thinking it through—immediately regretting it when Iliana shot him a betrayed look, her big brown eyes wounded.

"I *did* work with her," she replied with dignity, "despite my hatred. And I will again, if directed to. That's precisely my point." She went back to methodically eating her food.

"Iliana... I'm sorry." He didn't seem to be able to say anything right today. "It just makes me crazy to think of you being bonded to her. I won't let it happen."

Iliana lifted her head slowly and pinned him with the hardest look he'd ever seen in her eyes. "Don't you dare," she said softly. "Han, if you end up as a familiar and try to sacrifice yourself for me, I'll never forgive you or myself. And if this is what drove you to make that offer from earlier, if this is why you're thinking that you'd bond me as your familiar if you become a wizard, then I don't want that either."

"I thought we were at least friends," he whispered, stricken. "If nothing else, don't you care about me as a friend?"

She shook her head, then grimaced at whatever she saw in his face. "I mean, yes, I care about you. As a friend. You're my best friend. And that can't matter."

"You're wrong. Nothing matters more than friendship," he returned hotly. "And what I feel for you is—"

"Irrelevant!" She cast a look over her shoulder at Sabrina's cadre of wizards, who were laughing at some inside joke. "Our lives our not our own. That is, *my* life is not my own and I've known that from the moment the oracle head confirmed what I'd always suspected—that I'm a familiar. My decisions stopped being my own at that moment, regardless of the illusion of freedom that being a student here, of being still unbonded, has given me." When she met his gaze, her eyes glistened with unshed tears. "It's hard enough reconciling myself to a life of service, Han, without you tempting me with choices I don't have."

He was an ass. An utter and completely self-absorbed ass. Iliana always was the serene pillar of strength in his world and he'd cavalierly let her be that, never giving any thought to her struggles. She'd always seemed happy with her lot as a familiar. She never complained. She was... *reconciled.* "Iliana..." he said, searching for something to say.

She smiled, sadly, knotting her fingers in her lap. "It's all right. You don't have to say anything. I do lo—"

The student server plunked down two plates of ginger cake with brandy sauce. "You're the lucky ones tonight," he informed them with a grin. "Early batch of Convocation cake. Prosperity through magic!"

Iliana ignored the cake. "I do wish you the best," she said, and Han was so sure she'd been about to say something else he wanted to smash that kid's face in the cake. "I hope with all my heart that you'll be a wizard and that you'll never know this kind of powerlessness."

"That's why I'd want you to be my familiar," he urged, "so I could give you a better life."

She pushed away from the table. Away from him. "That's

just it, Han. I don't want you to give me anything. It would be better for me if..." Shaking her head again, she rubbed her temples. "I'm too tired for this conversation. I'm going to bed."

"You haven't eaten your cake."

"I'm stuffed. You have it." Drumming up an obviously fake smile, she put a hand on his shoulder. "Extra cake for you, to sweeten an otherwise difficult day. I'll see you tomorrow."

Though it heartened him that she at least planned to see him the following day, there was a finality to her expression that worried him. "Breakfast at the usual time?"

She'd already turned to go and glanced back. "Probably. But don't wait for me if I'm not here. You can't be late for Magic Theory again. Don't make that face." This time her smile was real. "You'll be glad for that knowledge someday."

Even though he was in the most advanced magic theory class there was for uncats, he still felt he'd learned everything there was to know until they could move him into the wizard or familiar advanced study tracks. Everyone in the class was at least two years younger than him, a lot of them much more. His father had even suggested Han come home until he manifested, then return to Convocation Academy for the final coursework. He wouldn't be the first to do that, but it felt like giving up.

And he didn't want to leave Iliana.

"Meet me for breakfast and I promise to be on time for class," he ruthlessly bribed her, adding his most charming smile.

"Maybe." She gave him a fierce frown, but her eyes spar-kled with amusement and he felt better that they were at least back on their usual terms.

"The sleighing races tomorrow evening, for sure." He pointed a finger at her. "It's Founders Eve and you promised to be my partner."

She rolled her eyes. "Yes, yes, yes. Goodnight, Han."

"Good night, Iliana." He watched her go, her bright curls catching colors from the elemental lights glittering above. Once she was gone, he slid her cake onto his plate and forked up a mouthful. Unfortunately, it didn't taste as sweet as he'd remembered.

~ 5 ~

Iliana overslept—and missed breakfast—but she felt hugely better, rested and restored as the Refoel healer had promised. And as Han had helped with, illicit as that had been. It felt good, though, to have her magic filling her again, the shimmering vitality of it streaming through her body. As she hurried through the decorated halls, it seemed the glittering lights and silver-frosted roses sifted into her magic, making her feel brighter than ever.

Everything would work out fine. She'd just been tired the night before. Physically, mentally, and emotionally exhausted—all combining to make her lose her usual poise and behave badly. Hopefully Han would forgive her. The kiss had been a fluke, born of him trying to help her, and he'd gotten carried away in his concern for her. That was all it had been.

The hallway to her first class of the morning, Familiar Senior Praxis, was nearly empty, she was that late. Ironic after she'd chided Han about getting to his first class on time. Hopefully he had, as... *But no.* Her steps slowed as she spotted the devil himself, slouched against the wall just down from the door to her class.

She had to take a deep breath and let it out again, not because she was breathless from being late, but because her heart thumped so hard at the sight of him. Why did he have to be so beautiful? Hearing her steps, he lifted his head. He'd left his hair unbound this morning and a wave of it shifted to fall half over his face, his full mouth brooding and eyes a startlingly bright blue.

"You should be in class," she hissed at him. "What are you doing here?"

"I was worried about you." He studied her intently. "You didn't come to breakfast."

"I overslept," she admitted. "But I feel much better."

"You look much better." He held up a hand before she could say something tart. "You look beautiful, Iliana. But it's really good to feel your magic back up to snuff."

"For me, too." It didn't surprise her that Han could sense her magic. His always felt dark and delicious to her, like melted chocolate.

"I also wanted to make sure you weren't mad at me," he said quietly, with sober intensity. "I behaved like an ass."

"No!" she burst out, then lowered her voice. "You didn't and of course I'm not mad at you. I should apologize. I was out of sorts and having Sabrina poking at us didn't help."

"You have *nothing* to apologize for," he replied fervently, taking her hand. "But, Iliana, I want you to think about what I said."

Oh, no. She blushed hard, longing warring with rationality. "Han, please..."

He let her tug her hand away, but leaned against the wall

between her and the classroom, not budging. "Just think about it," he insisted. "That's all I ask."

"Fine." She dodged around him and he caught her arm, his grip gentle, but relentless.

"I'm in love with you, Iliana," he said, his gaze fulminous. He was much too close, those gorgeous lips within kissing distance, the taste of cinnamon and dark chocolate caressing her tongue. "I said it badly last night, but I'm going to convince you of the truth of that."

"Even if you are—"

"I am."

"*If* you are," she repeated, "it doesn't make any difference."

"It makes all the difference," he insisted, "unless you don't feel the same."

"Han, I have to go." But she couldn't quite pull away, fighting her own urge to move into him, to snuggle under that strong arm and at last discover how it felt to touch him.

As if reading her mind, he tugged her just a bit closer. "Iliana," he breathed. "Just give me a chance." His lips lowered toward hers. He was going to kiss her. She froze, knowing she should stop him, unable to resist the temptation he posed, especially now that she knew how it would be. *Just one more kiss...*

The classroom door popped open and Professor Tracy leveled a stern glare on both of them as they sprang apart. "Familiar Iliana, you are exceptionally tardy, and M. Haniel, you are an unclassified student and not allowed in this wing. I believe you are aware of those rules?"

"Yes, professor," Han replied, looking cheeky and not at all chastened. "Tonight, Iliana. The sleighing party."

"Yes," she promised, ducking her head so her teacher wouldn't see her blush. "Good luck at the testing tower today."

A shadow passed over his face and she was sorry she'd reminded him. Professor Tracy pointed. "Go, M. Haniel. Don't make me write you up." As Iliana passed her professor into the classroom, he stopped her. "Tread carefully," he said in a voice too low for anyone to overhear. "I thought you understood my warning yesterday. You have very few rights in a situation like this."

"Han is my friend," she replied just as quietly, keeping her expression and tone as neutral as possible. "I'm just trying to be supportive."

"Mm hmm. Take your seat."

As Iliana did, exchanging quick smiles with a few friends, Professor Tracy took his place at the front of the room. "I think today we should review the Rights of Familiars as enumerated by Convocation law," he declared.

"That won't take long," someone quipped, and they all laughed, except Iliana.

Professor Tracy's gaze rested meaningfully on her. "It's no laughing matter," he said, dipping his chin at Iliana. "The rights of familiars are indeed few, so it's important that you all know what they are." He held up a hand at the general eyerolling. "Yes, I know you all have the admittedly short list memorized, but how many of you have had a meaningful discussion about their boundaries and implications?"

He scanned the room and nodded to himself. "I thought as

much. All of you are about to graduate, or you wouldn't be in Familiar Senior Praxis. The intent of this course is to bridge the gap between theory and the reality of practical application. You've spent the last however many years learning how to be a familiar and you stand on the brink of actually living your lives as one. This may be your last opportunity to ask questions of other familiars, without wizards interfering."

He lapsed meaningfully. The implications were clear, as they all knew wizards tended to be self-absorbed, at best, and primarily concerned with furthering their own goals. The laws that protected familiars constrained how wizards could use—and abuse—their familiars, which was a restraint they observed, but grudgingly. And not many familiars were granted the freedom to consort with other familiars, especially unsupervised.

"That's right," he said, as if someone had commented. "You *must* be aware of your rights and how they work in the real world, as you may be the only one advocating for yourself. First, you have the right not to be killed or injured so substantially that you cannot perform your work."

"Lucky us," someone muttered, and Professor Tracy pinned them with a look full of empathy, not reproving at all, despite the interruption.

"Let's speak frankly," he agreed. "We all know that this right, your first and most basic right, only goes so far. A wizard is not allowed to kill, maim, or neglect you so badly that you cannot perform as a familiar. Please note that no one else is allowed to harm you, either. You are a valuable resource, and therein lies your greatest safety. If anyone besides your bonded wizard—or agency if you end up working in that capacity—threatens you in any way, appeal to your wizard or agency. They will be strongly invested in protecting you."

"And if it's your own wizard threatening you?" someone asked drily.

Professor Tracy nodded in acknowledgment. "It's a problem. I won't sugar coat things here. You all live in the Convocation and you've heard the stories. It's against the law for your wizard to kill or injure you beyond repair, but wizards are also not accustomed to being told they can't do something. Particularly in the rush of a major incantation, or a pitched fight, they can forget themselves. I understand in Professor Angela's practicum yesterday, you all practiced with being drained nearly dry. How was that experience?"

Nauseating. Exhausting. Horrifyingly awful. But Iliana didn't say any of that aloud.

"It sucked," someone in the back bit out, and they all laughed, though more with nerves than humor.

"Succinct and accurate," Professor Tracy agreed with a rueful grimace. "Now imagine being magic-drained to the point of death. A familiar's magic arises from their inherent life force. Your personal vitality is intrinsically tied to your magic. If you are drained too far, your body can't recover, and you *will* die." He waited, letting them consider the implications. "The wizard would be held accountable by the Convocation—"

"As much as they ever are," someone muttered bitterly.

"As much as they ever are," Professor Tracy agreed, "though I advise you not to express those sentiments outside of this room. The point being, if that happens, the familiar is still dead. They can note in your obituary that you were wrongfully killed, your family might receive compensation, but you won't be around to enjoy the vindication."

"So what are we supposed to do?" Iliana burst out before she thought better of it. "We can't tell a wizard no."

"You *can*," Professor Tracy replied with emphasis. "And you should. That's what you all need to remember. Invoke your rights. Remind them. The law exists for a reason and you are all citizens of the Convocation—"

"Second-class citizens," another student inserted.

Professor Tracy ignored that one, plowing on. "And as citizens of the Convocation, you are protected by the law. Stand up to your wizard where the law stands behind you."

He caught and held Iliana's gaze, raising his brows as if checking that he'd answered her question. She nodded glumly, not bothering to voice her greatest fear. *What if you're in love with your wizard and don't have it in you to tell him no?* Han's beautiful face swam before her eyes, the earnest plea in their melting blue affecting her even now.

I'm in love with you, Iliana...I'm going to convince you of the truth of that. Though Han would never hurt her... would he?

The understanding hit her with a sharp pang, of why Nic Elal had chosen the Betrothal Trials. It was the perfect way to ensure you'd hate the wizard who bonded you. As always, Nic was way ahead of the rest of them. *Let's face it, who's going to sign up to try for you?* Sabrina's words echoed in her mind. It was true: Iliana didn't have high enough MP scores to recommend her. Even if she could bear to subject herself to the barbarity of the trials, she be rejected as a bad candidate.

A familiar at a neighboring desk put up her hand, a tentative halfway into the air. When the professor called on her, she glanced guiltily around the room, before asking her question in a lowered voice. "Is it true that some familiars have... emigrated from the Convocation to escape service?"

"You mean 'escaped,'" a familiar in the back corrected.

Professor Tracy made a cutting motion with his hand. "I'll address this once, because I did invite you to ask questions, but once only. And I strongly advise you don't discuss this with anyone, ever. It's a good point that 'emigrated' is a poor word because there is no legal recourse for a familiar to leave Convocation lands. That is *not* one of your rights. If any of you attempt to leave, I promise you will be stopped. Don't try it." He sounded grimmer than ever, with a bitter grief that made Iliana wonder if he had personal experience.

"But there are rumors that—" someone else began to say.

"Rumors only," Professor Tracy interrupted. "I know Convocation Academy runs on rumor like a sleigh runs on air elemental power." He essayed a smile, though it came across a bit sick and weak. "Believe me, I've heard all the same stories. They are heavily fictionalized tales born of wishful thinking. Don't stake your life on them, because that's exactly what you'd be doing."

"I thought we're too valuable to kill," someone quipped with quiet anger.

"You are, but there are worse things than death," Professor Tracy replied darkly. "The Convocation has ways of dealing with recalcitrant familiars and they are not pleasant. You all have relatively good lives. Your families can afford your education here, or your MP scores are high enough that the Convocation has given you a scholarship to attend. You are the most privileged of familiars. Appreciate what you *do* have and don't jeopardize your relatively comfortable lives for something considerably harsher."

Everyone absorbed his words, the silence lasting an uncomfortable beat too long. Professor Tracy cleared his throat and continued. "Any other questions, specifically on the first right of familiars?"

Though Iliana tried to pay attention to the discussion of their—sadly few—rights as familiars, the rest of the class passed in a blur. Even her next class, her animal husbandry elective, which was her favorite and chosen on the off-chance that she'd be bonded to a House Ariel wizard, didn't brighten her spirits.

She worried about Han's testing the whole time. She worried that he might be a familiar like her. And she worried about what would happen if Han finally manifested as a wizard. She hadn't been saying that to reassure him, or not only for that reason. The simple fact that they were calling him in for daily testing indicated the proctors suspected he'd manifest at any moment. Late-blooming wizards had a tendency to manifest their suddenly active magic in dramatic fashion. For the safety of the academy, they wanted to catch that early and contain it. Han had all the theory of wizardry, but as the praxis and practicum courses emphasized, there was a considerable leap from knowing to doing. Han would have to practice intensively to get his wizardry under control.

No matter what happened, though, Iliana couldn't see any

happy outcome for herself. All the sparkling lights and cake in the world couldn't change that.

HER AFTERNOON PRACTICUM ran long, though thankfully Professor Angela gave the familiars a light assignment of practicing meditation as a technique to replenish magic, while the wizards were tasked to perform workings using only their native magic. It had the wizards in such a cranky mood, Sabrina throwing vicious looks Iliana's way at every opportunity, as if Iliana had somehow orchestrated the lesson, that Professor Angela dismissed the wizards early. Before they left, she reminded them that it might be considerable time before they earned the right to a bonded familiar, if they ever did, so it behooved them to learn to maximize their skills with only their own magic to draw on.

The caution fell on deaf ears, however. Wizards, by nature, were an ambitious lot, and no wizard could truly rise in power without a familiar to augment their magic. They all planned to secure a familiar for themselves, one way or another.

Once the wizard students left, Professor Angela kept the familiars for another hour, coaching them on tricks to replenish their native magic quickly. Meditation helped, but couldn't be counted on during stressful situations.

She didn't mention the erotic methods of replenishing magic, though she alluded to their future wizard masters having some tricks up their sleeves that would help. But it was incumbent on the familiars, she stressed, to be ready at all times to provide their wizard with the magic they required. A good familiar wouldn't want to leave their wizard powerless during a major working or, worse, a pitched fight.

It made Iliana wonder if her two professors had been discussing her. Coming on the heels of Professor Tracy's warnings, this lesson only distressed Iliana more. She wasn't the only unhappy one, however, the familiars all a decidedly glum group as they shuffled out of the lab. If she hadn't promised Han to meet him at the sleighing tournament, Iliana would've been tempted to grab a plate from the dining hall and eat in her room. Besides, it was Founders Eve and people would notice if she wasn't celebrating.

She did *not* need a proctor checking on her emotional state.

Gamely, she pasted on a smile and, after grabbing her fur cloak and muff from her room, she joined the stream of students, staff, and faculty heading for the frozen lake at the center of campus. No sign of Han, yet, and no one had news of the results of that day's testing. She didn't have to ask—the fact that every other person she encountered stopped to ask *her* about it confirmed that much. If Han had gotten a result, he hadn't told anyone.

Well, whatever he'd found out, she'd do her best to be cheerful and a good friend to him. She owed him that, due to their long friendship. But she also had to make it clear that they could only ever be friends.

And that was that.

~ 6 ~

HAN SPOTTED ILIANA before she saw him. She wore her blue velvet cloak with the hood up against the chill, the white fur contrasting with her bright hair, freckles sprinkled like stars against her pale cheeks. She looked tired, her eyes shadowed with unhappiness, a patently fake smile pasted on her pretty mouth.

"Bad day, again?" he asked, stepping up beside her.

She smiled—still fake, but brighter—and shook her head. "It was fine. What about you—any results?" Her magic had an odd feel to it, kind of fragile, brittle still, not shining with her usual good-natured cheer.

"The candidate cannot be categorized," he creaked out, mimicking the oracle head's awful whisper. Iliana laughed, a hint of her usual humor in it, which was at least something. He'd been looking forward to seeing her again all day and something in himself settled at the sound of her laughter. Now if only he could do the same for her. He could make her happy, he just knew he could. "For you," he said, adding a gallant bow, and presenting her with a cone of piping hot sugared nuts, her favorite.

"Han, you didn't have to." But she immediately plucked one out and popped it in her mouth. "Ooh, they're hot!"

Didn't he know it. It was the fifth cone of them he'd bought, since she'd arrived so late and the previous four had gone stone cold while he waited and watched for her. "You always say they're not nearly as good when they're not piping hot."

"It's true. Thank you, that was thoughtful." She smiled, something of her usual sparkle in her eyes, and he congratulated himself for finding his way back into her regard. The way she'd begun to watch him warily, like he might turn into a Sabrina... well, he couldn't take much more of that.

"I got us a sleigh," he told her. "We're in the fifth race. For familiars and uncats."

"You do it," she said, the cloud of unhappiness settling over her again. "The sleigh will be faster with one person. I only came because I promised, but I'm going to head back to my room, now that I've made an appearance."

"Founding only comes once a year," he protested. "Tomorrow's a rest day."

"Yes, and I plan to *rest*," she retorted.

"It's a holiday, Iliana! Come on—we always do the sleigh race together, and this will be our last one at the academy."

"True," she acknowledged, gazing around at the vast outdoor party.

The second race had lined up on the ice, sleighs of laughing newly minted wizards calling taunts to each other. Alise Elal was in one sleigh, good naturedly waving off the attempts to derail her concentration. Since Elal-trained air elementals powered the sleighs, she was favored to win this race with her natural affinity for the little spirits, despite her raw skills.

Music played, courtesy of House Euterpe, colored elemental lights danced in the air, the scents of delicious food warmed the chill, while a few lacy snowflakes drifted down. It was a perfect evening and Iliana looked like she was attending an execution. "I'm just... tired. It was kind of a shitty day, but for no particular reason. And, no, I don't want to talk about it. I just want to go back to my room."

"All right." He offered her his arm. "I'll go with you."

"No, you shouldn't miss the party," she protested.

"It wouldn't be any fun without you," he told her with perfect honesty, and playing on her good nature ruthlessly. "What will you do in your room alone—mope? Stay and do the race with me," he wheedled.

She rolled her eyes and huffed out a breath. "Fine."

Cheers went up as the race finished—with Alise Elal the winner as predicted—but it sounded like they were cheering on Han's accomplishment. He'd take it.

"While we're waiting, let's dance!" Pushing his luck, he seized her hand and dragged her to the dance floor laid out on the snow, elemental lights clustered thickly above and pulsing in time with the lively reel playing. Iliana had protested some, but Han knew she loved to dance. And soon enough she was smiling in earnest, brown eyes sparkling with laughter as they whirled through the breathlessly fast dance.

They had to run to make it to their sleigh when the fifth race was called, climbing in and settling into line with the others. Since this race was for familiar and uncats, there weren't any clear favorites to win, as no one could actively use magic to influence the elementals. The crowd was also smaller, the wizards uninterested in these later races, which was fine by everyone. More fun that way.

"You talk to the elemental," he told Iliana. "They like you better."

"I really don't think that's true," she countered. "With your House Hanneil blood and MP scores in psychic magic, you should be able to communicate with them." But she didn't press him further. They had this argument every year and the one time she'd convinced him to talk to the elemental, they'd come in last. The little creatures had it in for him, for some reason.

She leaned forward, cupping her hands around the case holding the elemental, whispering something to it. Staying there, she listened for the starting chime. The moment it rang out, the sleigh leapt into motion, streaking ahead of the others. With a startled shriek, Iliana fell back against the padded seat, bursting into laughter, and Han put a quick arm around her to ensure she didn't fall out. Her hood had fallen back and her fiery curls whipped in the wind of their passage, lashing his cheek with silky tendrils.

"What did you tell it?" he shouted over his own laughter, risking a glance at their competition, finding the nearest two lengths behind.

"I promised to bring it a fire elemental to play with if we won. Nic Elal taught me that trick before she left."

"Clever!" Elementals weren't intelligent, per se, not as much as a dog or a horse, but they did understand simple commands—they had to, so even common folk could direct the magical conveyances—and were apparently susceptible to bribes. Usually the air elementals were kept far away from the fire ones, for obvious reasons. That was a fine treat to offer, indeed.

They rounded the far end of the frozen lake, the sleigh going up on one runner as it banked tightly around the marker, making Iliana squeal in excitement. Han's heart thrilled to the sound. For at least this moment, she wasn't worrying about their future. Shouting behind them heralded their fast-encroaching competitor.

"We need more speed!" he shouted, leaning forward as if he could somehow make the sleigh go faster. Iliana leaned forward, too, egging on the little elemental. Slowly they pulled ahead, the finish line with its colorful banners flapping enticingly close.

And they were across! A clear two lengths ahead of their closest competitor. The sleigh slowed to a stop, Iliana leaning to whisper to the air elemental. Amid the congratulations of their cohort, Han and Iliana accepted their trophy, a cup etched with the Convocation crest and marked with the date. Most importantly, it was filled with warmed whiskey of an exceptional quality from House Iacomus.

Iliana glowed with victory, her cheeks flushed, and they watched the next two races together, passing the whiskey back and forth, cheering for their friends. It was almost like old times, when they were both uncats and the world held so much potential, when their futures were only bright.

Well, no matter how things turned out for Han, he would

make sure Iliana would be happy. Not just tonight, but all the days and nights ahead.

ONCE THE RACES finished, Iliana let Han talk her into more dancing. With the excellent whiskey warming her blood, not to mention the heady glow of Han's undivided attention, she could hardly resist. She loved him so much and he was right: this was their last Founding Festival together. Rather than try to hold him at arm's length, in anticipation of their imminent parting, she decided to enjoy his company while she could.

Han at his most charming was impossible to refuse. Which would be a major problem when he manifested as a wizard, but she wouldn't think about that tonight. Since it was a holiday, the thought-seekers gave everyone a break—and were celebrating themselves. The festival was a rare excuse for everyone to loosen up.

A little bit tipsy, the lights and dancing making her feel giddy, she danced with Han until she was so warm she had to shed her cloak. Among his many skills, Han was also an excellent dancer—far better than she, but he was so skilled that he made his partner look good—and they found themselves more than once in a circle of cheering spectators as he whirled her through the vigorous dances.

Then the music slowed, and she fanned herself, blowing out a breath, and headed off the dance floor. Han caught her hand. "Hey, where are you going?" Expertly he twirled her under his arm, then snugged her close, a hand on the small of her back as he led her through the dreamy rhythm.

Iliana braced one hand on Han's chest, his heart thumping rapidly beneath her fingertips, his blue eyes lambent in the starry light. "We never dance the slow dances," she breathed.

"A grievous lapse of judgment on my part," he murmured, gaze traveling over her face. "You feel perfect in my arms, lovely Iliana. I want you here forever."

She tore her gaze from his heartbreakingly beautiful face, focusing on his throat instead. That wasn't much help, as his skin begged to be kissed and nibbled. "I don't understand what's changed between us, why you're being so..."

"Seductive?" he suggested in a warm purr. "Devastatingly handsome and charming?"

Snorting, she made a face at him. "Aggressive. And annoyingly persistent."

"Nothing's changed," he replied, raw honesty in his expression. "I've loved you for years. The only difference is that I realized I have to act on my feelings now or risk losing you forever."

"We're going to lose each other regardless," she told him, hating that she had to say it. "Even if you manifest as a wizard, you'll have to complete your education here while I'm going to graduate very soon. I'll be assigned to a wizard and it won't be you." She swallowed the temptation to explain all the reasons she couldn't bear for it to be him. He'd only argue. "The timing is wrong and we have to accept that."

He growled, low in his chest, the sound rumbling through her. It shouldn't be arousing, but it was. She couldn't help thinking about his mouth on hers, how she'd felt in his arms, just like this, but...

"I refuse to accept defeat," Han told her in a harsh whisper.

"That will only lead to future unhappiness," she predicted glumly.

"We have now," he countered. "I'm happy tonight. And you were happier for a while. I'm sorry I ruined it."

"You didn't ruin it," she told him softly. He'd been right to talk her into staying. The party, the races, the dancing, the treats—it had all been the perfect antidote to her crushing mood. "You made tonight perfect."

"It could be more perfect," he suggested, gaze focusing on her lips. He was only a whisper away, his mouth tantalizingly close, warm with whiskey and sugared nuts. The music swept low and long around them, the elemental lights coloring his pale hair in a rainbow and, oh, how she wanted him. He lowered his lips and—

"We can't!" she blurted, jerking back.

"No one is watching," he coaxed. "The proctors are all drunk by now. Just a kiss."

"Someone is *always* watching," she corrected. "And we've already attracted attention with our relationship."

"Have we?" he asked warmly, snugging her closer, his hips moving in time with hers. "Then we can hardly attract more."

There was a flaw to that logic, but her thoughts refused to align into any sense.

As if sensing her weakening resolve, Han leaned closer. "Come to my room with me."

"Han..." Her heart thrummed, warm desire overwhelming her at the idea. "We can't." But her protest sounded weak even to her own ears. She wanted him, she realized, with reckless desperation. And this might be her last opportunity. As soon as tomorrow, he could manifest and be swept into the wizard-exclusive courses, hanging with the wizard crowd, perhaps barely acknowledging her existence. The prospect made her heart ache. But would it hurt any less if she didn't have him now, while she could?

"If you're right," he whispered against her cheek, brushing her temple with his lips, the caress making her shiver, "and we're soon separated, we won't have another chance to be together. Iliana, I want you to be my first. If we can't be each other's forever, let us at least have this."

Yes. Yes, she wanted him to be her first. If she ended up in the Betrothal Trials or was simply assigned to a wizard, she'd be expected to breed. Han would be gentle and caring as possibly no one else would. "I'm not sure two virgins fumbling their way through this is a good idea," she replied with a smile.

His face went tight, intent. "If that kiss was any measure, we'll figure it out just fine. If that's a yes."

"Yes," she whispered, her heart feeling raw and sensitive, as if she'd opened her breast to the cold night air.

Abruptly, he grinned. Taking her by the hand, he pulled her through the dwindling crowd of dancers, so fast she had to trot to keep up, laughing giddily. He stopped to retrieve her cloak, settling it over her shoulders and tripping the magical clasp to fasten it at her throat, then pulling her furred hood up to frame her face. Gazing intently at her, he smiled softly. "I love you, Iliana. And very soon I'm going to take this off of you. And everything else too."

The fierce desire in his gaze took her breath away. "Then

why are we standing here?"

"An excellent point." He tipped his head back and laughed, full of music, carefree in a way he rarely ever was anymore, especially in these last months. Grabbing his coat, he pulled her along again, breaking into a run this time. "Hurry," he urged, grinning like a madman, and she ran, too, her hood falling back as it had in the sleigh, and she felt as if they were racing still.

Racing, yes—against time, against their looming futures, and against the weight of the Convocation and all it expected of them. They couldn't win this race, but they could snatch a bit of sweet for themselves.

~ 7 ~

HAN'S ROOM WAS bigger and much nicer than hers, partly because he'd been an uncat for so long, which let him move into the better rooms in the uncat wing as they were vacated by newly minted wizards and familiars, and partly because of his wealthy merchant parents. They were a second-tier house aspiring to more and they indulged their high potential son. Though Han often bitterly observed that if he proved to be a familiar, he'd no doubt end up with a single bed in the cellar, until they sold him to the highest bidder.

With a wave of very real fear for him, Iliana realized that highest bidder could be Sabrina Hanneil.

"Let me light a fire," he said as they entered the room. "The fire elemental hates me."

"I don't know what you do to them." He'd had the elemental heating his room replaced a number of times, and they always sullenly faded over time.

"I only kicked it a few times."

"Han!"

"Kidding!" He held up his hands, smiling innocently.

"You should see if Alise Elal would come talk to it for

you."

Han sobered, coming to her and parting her cloak, settling warm hands on her waist. "I don't want Alise Elal in my room. I only want you. Now where was I?" He lifted his hands to the clasp at her throat. "Ah, I remember. You weren't wearing this." He flicked the magic toggle and her cloak whooshed to the floor, leaving her feeling oddly naked, though she was still fully clothed. Were they really going to do this?

"And we were dancing," Han continued, taking her hand in his and settling the other at the small of her back, easing her close to brush against his long, lean body. He began humming the same, slow song, swirling her a few steps closer to the fire as he danced her back into that sweet dreamy space. Firelight flickered over his gorgeous face and lit the inner, crystal blue rings in his eyes so the green spires flared gold. "And then," he murmured, expression rapt, "I kissed you."

His lips brushed against hers, whiskey warm, sugar sweet, and a moan escaped her. Velvet soft and fiery spice. He nibbled, tested, tasted, gradually deepening the kiss as she wound her arms around his neck, leaning into him, into the incredible sensuality of the kiss. They swayed still, turning in slow circles as they rocked against each other, though he'd long since stopped humming the tune.

Still, the music played in her mind, winding with Han's taste and scent, the feel of his arms around her, the beauty of his lips which felt even better than they looked. She swam in a honeyed sea of desire, where only this existed. Bolder this time, she untied his hair from the ribbon he'd used to tie it back, combing her fingers through the luxurious silk of it.

Finally, he raised his head, searching her face. "What are you thinking?" he whispered.

"Same as last night—that I should've kissed you a long time ago."

A half smile quirked his gorgeous lips. "See?"

"Han..." She wound her fingers into the silky tendrils at the nape of his neck. "I don't want to think anymore."

"Let me see what I can do about that."

He kissed her again, this time with increasing hunger that stoked her own, his hands stroking down her back, then tangling in her hair as he tugged her head back so he could kiss her even more deeply. She let herself go, giving herself over the utter delight of his caresses, even as a small part of her stood back in astonishment at the good little citizen being so very bad, and as another, larger part of her jumped up and down in glee that she was here, with Han, at long last.

He traced a finger down her spine, parting the magical back seam of her gown so the bodice sagged around her shoulders. Raining kisses on her upturned face, along her jaw, on her closed eyelids, he eased the gown down and over her arms, letting it fall in a puddle around her, so she stood only in her undergarments. "So beautiful," he whispered between kisses. "I want to kiss every freckle."

"That would take forever," she said on a giggle. She was covered in freckles.

"I want forever." Han paused and she opened her eyes to his ferocious glare.

She laid her fingers over his lips. "Less talking."

"As my lady commands," he murmured, then drew her

fingertips into his mouth and sucking lightly on them, flicking his clever tongue against their sensitive tips so she gasped, trembling with the passion he evoked.

"How do you even know what you're doing?" she breathed.

"I read a lot, instead of memorizing antiquated house crests," he teased, releasing her hand and nuzzling under her ear, sending delicious shivers through her. "I wanted this to be good for you," he said against the hollow there, before licking it.

"What about for you?" she managed to ask, barely managing to stay on her feet, and even then it was mostly because she was hanging on to him as his mouth feasted down her throat.

"It's you," he replied simply. "This is already beyond perfect." He hooked his thumbs in the straps of her camisole, meeting her gaze seriously. "Yes?"

She took a breath, her nipples taut against the silky material. "I think it's your turn, first."

He smiled, delighted mischief in it. "Fair enough."

Stepping away, he pulled his shirt off over his head, tossing it aside. His lean chest gleamed in the firelight, muscles rippling as he leaned one hand against the bed post to toe off his boots.

"You are so beautiful," she whispered, and he flashed a wicked grin at her.

"I think that's my line." He paused, hands at the magic toggle of his pants. "Everything?"

"I may not have read all the books you have, but I'm pretty

sure we have to be naked."

"Not necessarily, but naked gets my vote." He released the waist band and shoved his pants down, kicking them away and standing naked before her. His hips narrowed above his long, shaped thighs. In a nest of pale hair, his cock, as long as the rest of him, stood straight out. Alien and enticing. Begging to be touched.

With a shy grin, he gestured to himself, "And... here I am." He blew out a breath. "Wow, I didn't expect to be nervous."

She laughed, her own nerves dissipating a little, and she stepped to him, holding up her hands. "May I?"

He closed his eyes, a shiver passing over him. "I've been fantasizing for years about you doing so. Yes."

She set her hands lightly on his shoulders, starting there with her exploration, stroking along the lean lines of his muscles. Since he couldn't take any of the advanced courses, he'd been doing a lot of weapons training electives. Sword, staff, and archery, and it showed in his exquisite physique. He shuddered lightly under her caresses, his lips pressed together, hands in fists at his side as if he fought to stay still for her.

"How many years?" she asked, curious.

He cracked open his eyes. "I thought you wanted less talking."

"About anything except this moment," she amended.

"Years ago isn't this moment."

She swirled her fingers over his nipples, so different from her own. "Yes, it is. Stop ducking the question. How many?"

He looked at her, long and thoughtfully. "Since I first met you."

She paused, surprised. "That long ago."

"Yes." His jaw tightened. "If you're not going to touch, I want my turn."

"All right." Emboldened by this startling knowledge that Han had fantasized about her all this time, had wanted her maybe as much as she'd always wanted him, she stepped back. She pulled off her camisole—tossing it aside as he had with his shirt—then skimmed off her panties before she lost her courage. And suddenly understood exactly why Han had blushed in baring himself for her, especially if her expression had looked anything like his.

His mouth had fallen open slightly, his face slack in a way that would've made him look daft but for the piercing blue of his eyes as he raked her with his gaze. "Iliana," he breathed. "As many times as I've dreamed of seeing you this way, my fantasies never came close to the sheer perfection of you." Moving slowly, he took her hand, raised it above her head, encouraging her to twirl in a leisurely circle. "You take my breath away."

"Not so much that you haven't stopped talking," she teased, but she was breathless too.

He narrowed his eyes. "*You* keep talking."

She couldn't resist, she popped onto her tiptoes and kissed that beautiful mouth, gasping when his hands vised on her waist, pulling her against him so her breasts crushed against his hot skin, his cock pressing hard against her belly, as he deepened the kiss, drinking her in like a man dying of thirst. His magic shimmered potent under his skin, just as her own boiled inside, swelling to bursting.

She clung to him, aware of his hands traveling over her, then—dimly—of him easing them to fall onto the bed. This was good as it let her touch him everywhere and feel him against her at the same time, their legs tangling together, his mouth hot on her taut nipples, fanning the flames that threatened to consume her and leave nothing left. "Han," she moaned, pleaded.

"Iliana," he replied in a reverent whisper, making a poem of her name.

She rolled onto her back, parting her thighs. "I want you inside of me."

"So soon?" He stroked a hand down her ribs and over her hip. "We've barely done any foreplay."

"Later for that," she urged, cupping his perfectly muscled ass in her hand and digging in her nails. "I want this, now."

His lips curved in a wicked smile. "I have to check that you're ready."

"I'm ready."

"I have to be sure," he explained, so seriously that she knew he was tormenting her. "Let me see you."

With a groan, she let go of him, staring at the ornate ceiling and blushing furiously as he slid down her body, then parted her thighs further, opening her to his gaze. "Han..."

"Trust me. I want this to be good for you." He caressed her thighs, combing light fingers through her nether hair. "I love that this hair is red, too." He kissed her inner thigh, making her tremble. "And that you have freckles even here."

"Han, please." She squirmed, forgetting to be embarrassed, and he chuckled.

"All right." Carefully he parted the lips of her sex, touching her with exquisite care. "I want to do this right," he muttered, almost to himself, then touched her with a light finger, the sensation so extraordinary she squealed. "Did that hurt?" he asked anxiously, snatching his finger back.

"No," she said on a laugh. "It felt amazing. Why is it better than when I do it?"

"Because we're together," he replied fervently. "Show me where to touch."

So, she did, guiding his hand, sighing at the utter bliss of his caress, moving her hips with increasing urgency.

"You're so wet," he murmured in awe. "So sexy."

"Told you I was ready." She urged him up her body, but he stilled, holding himself away from her. "Did you change your mind?"

He huffed out a chagrined laugh. "I don't want to hurt you. You're so small and delicate down there."

"Babies come out of there," she reminded him. "It's made to stretch." Sliding her hand down his hip, she wrapped her hand around his rigid cock, delighting in how he stiffened, eyes going wide.

"Iliana!"

"Han." She guided him toward her entrance, fitting his head against her and lifting her hips to help with the angle. Tantalizing, teasing her need. Not nearly enough. "Push," she urged him.

His breathing ragged, fulminous blue gaze locked on hers, he eased into her, going torturously slow until she grabbed his ass with both hands and pulled him into her. Their groans intertwined, bodies shivering together. Iliana had never felt so close to anyone, so rawly vulnerable and so complete at the same time.

"Are you all right?" Han asked in a shaky voice.

"Yes." She moved under him. "More, please."

He laughed, huskily, then levered up on his elbows, finding her hands and lacing their fingers together. She wrapped her legs tighter around his waist as he moved in her, their gazes locked. Finding the answering rhythm as he pressed deeper and deeper into her, she felt as if she flowered, opening to him, her heart overflowing. She saw the climax in his face, the wave overtaking him, his thrusts increasing, the rhythm falling apart in his extremity.

To her surprise, the fist of orgasm grabbed her, too, and she followed after him, throwing her head back to cry out in the keen knife-edge of pleasure. He fastened his mouth to her throat, biting down so an arc of fire ran from there to her groin, making her spasm again. "Han!" she gasped, loosing the last of her reserves, spilling herself open in a gush. "Oh, Han, how I love you."

~ 8 ~

I N THE DARK, erotic clasp of Iliana's sweet body, Han nearly
missed the words. His head swam dizzily, his body still
shuddering from that release, beyond anything he'd imagined.
Her scent filled his senses, her skin like softest silk against him,
her perfect curves arousing even as he crested down from the
impossible heights.

He lay over her, boneless, still buried to the hilt in her, his
mouth against her swanlike throat, her fiery curls under his
cheek. Dimly aware that he should move so he didn't crush
her, instead he whispered, "Say it again."

For a long moment, she didn't say anything. Then she
kissed his brow, tightening her embrace around him. "I love
you, Han. I always have."

Closing his eyes, he absorbed the sweetness of hearing
those words from her at last. "You're right—we should've
done this a long time ago."

"This was perfect. I wouldn't change anything."

He lifted his head, managing to make his sluggish muscles
obey enough for him to lever up onto his elbows. She took a
deep, grateful breath and smiled at him, more radiantly lovely

in this moment than he'd ever seen her.

"I'm glad you were my first," she said quietly, her lips rosy from his kisses.

"Me, too." He opened his mouth to say he wanted more than that, but she shook her head sharply.

"No talk of the future," she warned. "Don't ruin this."

He nearly argued, wanted to protest that ignoring the future wouldn't make it go away, but he also didn't want to ruin this magical night. "Will you stay?"

She hesitated, eyes going to his El-Adrel clock, much fancier than hers.

"I have a lot of freckles still to kiss," he coaxed. "Stay the night with me."

"Not all night," she responded firmly. "I want to be back in my room before everyone wakes up."

"People are going to be up and about all night," he argued.

"They'll be going to bed around dawn so they can be awake for the feast tonight. I'll go then." She wriggled out from under him. "Lie back. It's my turn to explore and kiss the secret places."

He heaved out a heavy sigh, pretending to be long-suffering, privately delighted that she wanted to enjoy him, too. Stretching out, he savored the rapt expression on her face, the love she let show at last. Her fiery hair tumbled around her pale, freckled shoulders, outlining her exquisite figure, hips flaring from her narrow waist, and petite round breasts tipped with charming fawn-colored nipples. He could spend a lifetime exploring her lovely body.

"Now *this* is a feast," she murmured, sliding her hands over him, echoing his own thoughts, and set to tasting.

ILIANA MADE IT back to her room in the dark, pre-dawn hours without being observed. That was, without being observed by human eyes. Still, it was Founder's Day and typically there was latitude for everyone to be out celebrating at unusual hours.

Grateful the rest day let her go back to bed, she slept a few hours—much needed, as she and Han hadn't slept at all, making up for lost time with such hunger that she ached all over—and woke midmorning with a sense of being still in a dream. Had last night really happened? In the cold light of the winter morning, it seemed far more likely that she'd fantasized it all. But her body felt the truth of it, both deliciously sated and sore in new places.

Whoa, and her hair was alarmingly snarled, she saw when she went to the mirror. It stood out around her head in a wild tangle, prompting her to uncork her grooming imp and setting it loose even before she liberated the water elemental to bathe her body. She'd love to have a full bath, but the academy had limited facilities for that—students didn't rate—and they were on a strict schedule. But water elementals left a lovely, dewy clean feeling, so she didn't mind too much. As they worked, she took stock of the marks of her night with Han. In particular, he'd left a vivid love bite on her throat, and the memory of his mouth there as they writhed together warmed her all over again.

Unfortunately her Founder's Day gown had a low neckline, something she'd initially loved about it, but not when she'd rather conceal the evidence of her illicit activities. Fortunately, she did have a festive lace scarf that she draped around her neck that looked like part of the outfit.

She made it to the dining hall just before they stopped serving breakfast. A good thing, too, as she was starving, having consumed only sugared nuts, wine, and whiskey the night before. Iliana helped herself to the Founder's Day pastries and a bowl of tea with milk and honey, happily loading her tray. The odd timing also meant the place was almost empty, with no cadre of wizards to alleviate their boredom by annoying her.

In fact, the only wizard in sight was Alise Elal, sitting by herself and looking glum. Iliana hesitated, not wanting to violate the unwritten social rules, but then decided screw all of them. Apparently she'd become a rebel with the loss of her virginity. And Alise had been a good friend.

"Happy Founder's Day, Alise," she said, pausing beside her, ready to move on if Alise scorned her.

But Alise looked up and smiled, crookedly. "Prosperity through magic," she replied, making it sound like a curse.

Tentative still, Iliana asked, "Is everything all right?"

"No." Alise's strained smile crumpled. "Everything is terrible."

"Want to talk about it?"

Alise glanced around the empty dining hall, then patted the bench beside her. "Please. I'd love that."

Iliana set down her tray and stepped over the bench to settle beside her old friend. Alise's plate looked like she'd barely touched it. "What's wrong?"

Alise sighed, glanced around again. "Promise you won't tell anyone? Papa made me swear to keep it secret."

Alise was defying her powerful father, Lord Elal? This *was* serious. "I swear," Iliana said solemnly.

Alise stared at her plate as if it contained mud instead of chocolate pastries. "Nic ran away."

Iliana choked on a pastry crumb, gulped some tea, and ended up burning her tongue. "What?"

Alise shrugged. "She's missing, anyway. Vanished without a trace."

"How can she vanish during her Betrothal Trials?" Iliana asked. Nic would've been confined in House Elal. And, besides, familiars couldn't escape. Or could they? If anyone could do something so bold, it was Nic Elal.

"Papa didn't say," Alise replied, shaking her head. "He is, of course, beyond furious. Apparently she disappeared during the night more than a week ago. They've been searching for her with no luck."

"Do you think she was abducted?" Iliana asked in a hush. The threat of abduction by rogue or landless wizards loomed over the heads of every unbonded familiar.

Alise snorted in disdain. "From House Elal? Not likely. No, Papa clearly thinks she ran away. He sent a Ratsiel courier to me this morning, interrogating *me*, in case I'd helped her or she'd come here."

"But you haven't heard from her?"

Alise shot her a dark look, her sleekly short wizard's haircut making her green eyes stand out in her face. "Of course I haven't. Would Nic trust me? No. She acts like she barely knows me since I manifested as a wizard. Like I somehow plotted to take her place as Papa's heir. I never wanted this, Iliana!" Alise's voice rose, her eyes brightening with tears. "I know I'm supposed to be thrilled to be a wizard, but now I've lost my sister's love, you avoid me, I have no real friends..." She dashed away the tears. "I know I sound like poor little rich girl but now I wonder if wizards become such power-mad assholes because no one loves them anymore."

"Oh, Alise..." Iliana breathed, then took her friend's hand under the table, just in case anyone came in. "I still love you. I haven't been avoiding you. I just thought that you'd moved on, you know. Hanging with the wizards."

Alise hiccupped a little and nodded. "Yeah. Though... you wouldn't believe what jerks those people can be."

"Well," Iliana replied judiciously, "I actually *would*."

Alise burst out laughing, Iliana joining in the infectious giggles, just as they'd been when they were younger. Squeezing Iliana's hand, Alise gave her a sad smile. "I've missed you, so much."

"I've missed you, too," Iliana said. "Now, eat your pastry, because the chocolate will make you feel better, and tell me everything you know. Maybe there are clues you missed."

Alise obediently took a bite of her pastry. "All I know is that Nic's last suitor was that rogue wizard from the swamps of Meresin, the one trying to reinstate House Phel."

"Lord Gabriel Phel."

"That's the one. From what Papa carefully didn't say, I gather that he successfully impregnated Nic. Because he came back to House Elal two weeks later—and why else would he return?—but when he arrived, she was gone."

"But where could she go?" Excitement thudded through Iliana, but she carefully hid her especial interest in the answer from her friend. Alise might need a friend right now, but she was also a wizard.

"That's the question, isn't it? But she's not anywhere Papa's spies can find her, which probably means she crossed salt water. Nander doesn't know anything either," Alise added, a bitter twist to her mouth. "He just went back to sleep."

Hmm. "What did Lord Phel do?"

Alise shrugged. "Papa didn't say. He probably slunk back to Meresin. Humiliating, I'm sure, but what else would he do? Maybe that's why Nic ran, because she didn't want to be bonded to a rogue like Phel."

"He's a powerful wizard, though." Gabriel Phel's MP scorecard had made the rounds, everyone gawking at the numbers.

"Completely untrained," Alise countered. "He never attended the academy at all."

"How could he?" Iliana replied with some irritation. It wasn't Gabriel Phel's fault that he grew up outside Convocation society. Would Nic have rejected him for that reason? Iliana had never pegged her for that much of a snob. "He was a late bloomer. By the time he manifested, it was too late for him to attend academy."

"A late bloomer like Han. Speaking of which, what's going on with you two?" Alise leaned her head in her hand, craning to get a good luck at Iliana's face. "I saw you dancing all night with him."

"Mmm." Iliana acknowledged noncommittally, sipping her tea. "Han is a good friend still." At one time the three of them had been the best of friends.

"You're blushing," Alise pointed out. "Tell me everything."

"There's nothing to tell."

"Uh huh. Then why this thing?" Alise snaked out quick fingers to twitch the lace away, her eyes rounding. "Whoa. I'm aroused just looking at that love bite. How did it feel getting it?"

"Eyew!" But Iliana couldn't help laughing as she scooted away. "I didn't need to know that and I'm not telling you anything."

"That's all right, I can just imagine." She sighed dreamily. "You two are so romantic. Like Sylus and Lyndella, a real wizard-familiar love match."

"Han isn't a wizard."

"Yet."

"We don't know that," she argued. "It could go either way."

"Oh, come on. With his MP scores? Everyone knows Han will be a powerful wizard, and you'll be his beautiful familiar, the new epic romance."

"Everyone thought Nic would be a wizard, too," Iliana reminded her.

"True." Alise deflated. "Life is so unfair." She perked up again. "But you *are* in love?" she asked wistfully.

She was. And, with all the hindsight of the morning after, Iliana recalled all the excellent reasons why being in love with Han was a terrible idea. Living in the moment sounded great during the moment; it was afterward that one had to deal with the repercussions. Nothing had changed—whether Han manifested as a wizard or a familiar, whether they were in love or not, it all spelled doom for Iliana's heart. Losing her appetite, Iliana stared at her plate.

"I don't want to talk about this here," she said in a lowered voice. "I've already been warned."

"Yes." Alise lowered her voice, too. "You should be careful. Besides, here he comes now."

"Good morning, ladies," Han said smoothly. He had his long, pale hair neatly tied back, and he looked unbearably handsome as he sat across from them. He raised his brows at Alise. "Is this a Founder's Day miracle, wizards lying down with familiars?"

"Han, don't—"

"No, it's all right," Alise interrupted. "It's been weird between us and I've hated it. So, yes, I'm having a shitty day and would appreciate a truce." She glanced at Iliana. "You can tell him, but later. Swear him to secrecy."

Iliana nodded, Han looking curious, but he let it go when Iliana gave him a look. He smiled at her innocently, but his eyes glinted with sensual mischief. "And how are you this morning?" he asked in a low, intimate voice.

Iliana's face flushed hot—sometimes she really hated about her translucent complexion—as the previous night flashed through her mind in an erotic kaleidoscope.

"She is glowing," Alise answered for her. "Well done, my friend."

"It wasn't all him," Iliana noted acerbically, stung by the

implication that she'd somehow just lain there while Han worked his magic. Though that wasn't far from the truth.

"It's true," Han murmured. "I feel quite... ravished this morning."

Alise cupped her chin in her hands. "Realllly. Do tell."

"Don't tell." Iliana cut in with a meaningful glare.

Han closed his mouth and shrugged at Alise. "The lady has spoken."

Alise groaned. "She won't tell me anything. I hate you both." They all laughed and, for just that space of time, it was as if nothing had changed between them. But it had, and soon they'd all be going their separate ways. Han and Alise seemed to be struck with the same thought, sobering along with her.

"How are you spending your festival day?" Iliana asked Han, hoping to break the mood. The big celebration didn't begin until evening. "There's ice skating, and then the magic exhibition."

"Sign me up for both," Han replied with a warm smile that quickly faded. "Once I'm done in the Tower of Testing." He dropped his voice into sepulchral tones for that last, but neither Alise nor Iliana laughed.

"You have to go *today*?" Alise asked, aghast. "No one is working today."

"Just proves what we've always suspected," Han replied with an easy grin. "The proctors aren't actually human, but are automatons puppeted by the oracle heads."

"Yuck," Iliana said, scowling at him.

He continued to grin unrepentant. "You just don't have a good counterargument."

"I have better things to do with my brain that think up counterarguments to frivolous theories."

"Oh yes?" he purred, gaze traveling over her. "What are you thinking up, lovely Iliana? I hope you'll try it on me later."

"Stop that," she hissed.

"You two are so good together. I'm happy for you. I'd be jealous if I didn't love you both so much." Alise sighed. "I wish we were still friends," she added quietly.

"We can be," Iliana promised.

Alise smiled ruefully. "I don't think we can. The proctors *really* don't like us consorting with familiars outside of formal situations. You should see—"

A small Ratsiel courier popped into the air next to Han, chiming the testing tower summons. Han glared at it. "And there's my cue." Standing, he leaned hands on the table, waiting for Iliana to meet his gaze. "I'll meet you for skating in an hour or so."

An odd foreboding filled her, but she nodded cheerfully, pasting on a bright smile. "All right. Good luck."

Han cocked his head. "What?"

"Nothing!"

"That's your fake smile. What's wrong?"

Erf. "I'm just sorry you don't get your full day off." Holding his gaze, she willed him to believe her. Or, if not, to let it go.

After a long moment, he nodded. "I'll see you soon."

He strode off, long queue of pale hair streaming down his back like an icicle of gold. Alise watched Han go, too. "I swear you are insanely lucky, Iliana. I'm going to write an epic romantic novel about you two."

Iliana laughed politely, privately afraid of just how tragic their ending would be.

~ 9 ~

H AN WHISTLED AS he skipped up the testing tower steps, knowing that Iliana was the reason for his lighthearted mood, only belatedly realizing the tune in his mind—and heart—was the song they'd danced to the night before. It would be their melody forever. In the years to come, he'd make sure they danced to it on Founder's Eve, celebrating the night they pledged their love to each other, in words and in sensual intimacy.

He only wished Iliana would stop worrying so much. Behind her fake smile, she'd looked like he was going off to his execution, not to be pronounced uncategorizable yet again. But she'd see, he'd meet in an hour for ice skating, and then he'd tempt her back to his room for a bit of alone time before the big feast. They could skip the magic exhibition. It was pretty much the same thing every year—all the showy magics with no substance. It wasn't as if any of the houses wanted to give away their proprietary information.

"Happy Founder's Day, proctor," he greeted cheerfully.

"Prosperity through magic, M. Haniel," the proctor replied without cracking a smile. Really, there was a case to be made that the proctors weren't living people.

Amused by the thought, Han seated himself and waited while the proctor performed the ritual of opening the tabernacle and activating the magic that animated the oracle head. "What is your determination of the candidate?" the proctor intoned reverentially.

A tingle passed through Han, different than his usual dislike of being near the undead thing. Its dark eyes stared through him. As it opened its lipless mouth and delivered its verdict, Han's head swam with crashing dizziness.

"The candidate," it replied in that voiceless whisper, "is a familiar."

The proctor smiled.

Han sat there in stunned silence as the proctor performed the ritual to close the tabernacle again. If he wanted to credit the proctor with any humanity, he'd think he was giving Han time to process the bad news. Which... he couldn't.

Even though he'd known it could go either way, even though he and Iliana had discussed the possibility at length, and even though he'd been so fucking flip about not minding being a familiar because thwarting his mother's ambitions would be worth it, a huge part of him had never really believed he'd be anything other than a wizard.

And Iliana... what would happen to her now? He'd been so sure he'd be able to protect her. Could Sabrina Hanneil make good on her threats? It had been easy to scoff at her before, but the peril had suddenly become severely and seriously real.

"I'll inform the Convocation Academy administration that you've been duly categorized, Familiar Haniel," the proctor said, not unkindly. "But not until tomorrow morning, when they're back in the office. At that point, you'll receive your final MP scorecard showing your categorization, and your new class roster so you can finish out your specialization. Until then, it's entirely up to you whether or not you choose to share the news."

Han jerked his gaze up to the proctor's knowing black eyes. All those times the newly minted wizards had announced their new status, the joyful hair-cutting and celebrating after... Of course those had been spontaneous announcements. He recalled, too, when Iliana was certified, her quiet grace in the face of her friends' commiseration. There were never announcements for familiars. They simply moved to the residence wing for familiars without fanfare, attending their new roster of classes, and everyone simply *knew*.

Gossip at the academy traveled faster than Hanneil thought-seekers. But he had a reprieve, until morning.

Not quite a full day and night to come up with some way to protect Iliana. Which might mean giving her up. If he agreed to Sabrina Hanneil's bid to make him her familiar, Iliana would be safe. His heart would be broken, but maybe that would numb him to life as Sabrina's pet.

"You may go now," the proctor said pointedly, and Han jerked himself out of his chair, the sense of unreality slowing his movements. He felt ill, unable to think. "Take it easy," the proctor added. "It's a shock for the familiars. Though everyone knows it's possible, even likely that they'll be a familiar, somehow everyone thinks they'll be a wizard." The proctor produced a thin smile, his words losing whatever empathy he'd intended, given that he was a wizard, however minor. Even the least wizard was better off than the most powerful familiar.

"You can take comfort in this," the proctor added as Han forced himself to walk on stiff legs. "With your high MP scores, you'll be a desirable familiar. A handsome familiar like you, with your level of magic, a wizard will snap you up. You'll likely get to bed many, many females as the house that acquires you will want to breed you frequently. It's not such a bad life."

Han stumbled out of the room, hanging onto the curving wall of the testing tower to keep from plummeting headlong down the steep, spiraling stairs. He paused halfway down, aware of the cold sweat dripping down his spine, the black hole in his stomach. Curse it, he *felt* pale. Anyone watching for him to emerge from this last test would take one look at him and know what verdict he'd received. At least this testing session had been earlier in the day, so his mother shouldn't have sent a Ratsiel courier yet.

Regardless, he needed to get a grip on himself. So, he sat on the step and did what Iliana always nagged him to practice more and what he'd never done outside of class: he meditated. He'd always hated meditating, his brain forever wanting to zoom off to more interesting thoughts and activities—and his current state of mind only exacerbated *that* problem—but they'd all been drilled in the practice. It was one of the core academy disciplines that served wizards and familiars equally well. Mastering magic required mental discipline, no matter who you were, and the higher your MP scores, the more you needed.

It was time for Han to apply some self-discipline. Banishing all other thoughts, he focused entirely on the mental discipline until he settled into a calm center, his thoughts clearing. Gradually his heartrate slowed, the slick sweat receding, and he could breathe easily and deeply. Thinking back to the day before, his flip insouciance at being forever uncategorized—to think he'd griped about that as a *problem*—he arranged that emotional state over the surface of his mind, like a mask.

By the time he could stand steadily again, a significant amount of time later, he'd practically convinced himself that he'd heard the oracle head pronounce him *uncategorized*. Holding onto that sound and image, to his own exasperation, he braved the remaining stairs and any Hanneil thought-seekers or astute fellow students.

The tower guards nodded to him as he emerged. "That took a long time," one noted.

"Proctor wasn't in any hurry to see me," Han replied with a careless shrug. "Maybe he's tired of looking at my face every day."

Both guards laughed. "Guess we'll see you tomorrow then."

He waved without looking back, striding off down the hallway. He almost skipped detouring to his room to get his coat and skates, as that would increase the odds of running into someone he couldn't easily dissemble with, but it would also look too odd for him to head out ice-skating without them. Everyone knew he'd been to testing, yet again, so they'd be looking for anything out of the ordinary.

So, he strolled to his room, exchanging greetings here and there with friends, accepting their commiseration on his being forever uncategorized. Finally his eternal state of limbo served him well—everyone just assumed he'd come out uncategorized, as always, so they didn't look any deeper than the usual jokes he flippantly tossed out.

Meditation actually worked. Go figure.

It was a gorgeous day outside, almost annoyingly so. Han would've preferred a raging blizzard to match his mood and reflect the fact that his plans had just come crashing down around him. The clear blue skies and bright sunlight seemed to mock him—as did the music, laughter, and ongoing merriment of the festive afternoon.

He spotted Iliana out on the ice, her velvet cloak a deeper blue than the sky. She was spinning in place, raising and lowering her arms to speed and slow her pirouettes. Her hood had fallen back, as it always seemed to, and her long, bright hair flew around her in a coppery cloud. She was so beautiful, the best person he'd ever known, and he would lose her forever.

He sat on a bench to put on his skates, spotting Iliana's slim, black boots and setting his own next to them.

And Sabrina Hanneil sat down beside him. "Happy Founder's Day, Han," she purred, shaking her head a little so the sharp bob of her short, blond hair swung sassily. "How did the testing go?"

"Uncategorized," he ground out, heaving a sigh. Hopefully she'd read his aggravation at frustration with the news.

"There, there, darling," she replied, combing her fingers

down the long queue of his hair and tugging playfully. "You'll know one of these days. I just hope you're reconciling yourself to the likelihood that you'll be a familiar. *My* familiar. My uncle has already prepared a preemptive offer." She simpered at his shocked expression. "I'm his favorite, you know."

"How nice for you," Han said dully.

"It is," she agreed happily. "And what's good for me is good for my familiar. You'll prosper with me, Han."

"Unless I manifest as a wizard." He almost made it sound like a possibility.

"A big if," she pointed out, her gaze sliding to Iliana, pirouetting on the ice, back arched gracefully as her gloved fingers twined in an aerial dance, fiery hair streaming. "But, even if you do, you'll never have Iliana. My uncle has prepared an offer to buy her, too. Immediately."

He stared at Sabrina, gut struck. "Why?" he managed.

Sabrina narrowed her eyes, not quite wizard black yet, but swiftly darkening. "I like the taste of her magic. Besides, she tried to defy me, and no one gets away with that. She can work for our house as a free agent, I can sip from Iliana any time I like. What?" She pouted. "I thought you'd be happy, being together. Of course, you'd never be able to talk to her, or bed her." Sabrina gave him a knowing look, licking her lips. "I know what you two did last night. The emanations from your room were quite delicious."

He stared at her stonily, neither confirming nor denying.

"House Hanneil has many proprietary tricks for increasing magic yield from our familiars," she explained. "Anguish and longing work quite well. I'd maybe allow you two to catch just a glimpse of each other once in a while, unless you were very, very good and deserved a treat. Or if I needed you two to spin up erotic magic for me."

Han ground his teeth. Maybe he could put a stop to this, here and now. Confide his secret to Sabrina and offer to go with her willingly, to submit to her bonding immediately, if she'd agree to let Iliana go. He opened his mouth to say so... Then shut it again. Sabrina would never abide by any such agreement. She was treacherous to the bottom of her cold, black heart.

"Happy Founder's Day, Sabrina," he said, standing and stepping onto the ice. "Prosperity through magic," he sang out. "I hope you choke on it," he added under his breath, as he skated toward Iliana to tell her the bad news.

ILIANA TOOK IT better than he had. She had practice, he supposed. "At least we'll be in the same classes again," she told him, handing him a cup of hot cocoa. They sat at a table on what had been last night's dance floor, well away from anyone else. Though the elemental lights still glowed overhead, the sunlight dimmed them into nothingness, a good match for Han's own spirits.

He shook his head. "Not for long. You're ready to graduate and—" He couldn't bring himself to mention Sabrina's dire plan for them. He might not be able to escape her net—his family would be thrilled to sell their useless familiar son to House Hanneil—but he could get Iliana out. "You need to go home," he told her with sudden urgency. "Sign up for the

Betrothal Trials or ask your family to bond you to a wizard you can live with, right away."

Iliana didn't comment on that, quietly sipping her own cocoa, watching him over the rim with solemn brown eyes. Her starry freckles stood out against her chilled skin and he recalled with considerable bitterness his vows to kiss them all. "I saw Sabrina talking to you," she finally said. "I'm not letting you sell yourself to her in order to save me."

"That's why I want you to go, now, so she can't do that to you."

Iliana's expression tightened, her usually softly cheerful face as stern as a warrior's. "I'm not abandoning you to her. I refuse."

He found himself gaping at her, not quite grappling this Iliana who seemed so much harder than his eternally cheerful friend. "What happened to our sacred duty and learning to work with even the wizards we hate?"

"That was before you became mine," she replied. "Now I have something worth fighting for and I'm not just meekly giving you up."

"Oh," he replied, sounding like a fool, but also… joyful. Iliana loved him. More she planned to fight for him. "Then what's your plan?"

She then drew up her hood around her face. "Let me tell you what Alise told me this morning."

~ 10 ~

H AN LISTENED QUIETLY, not interrupting, though his pale eyebrows rose in surprise, and lowered again in puzzlement. When Iliana finished, he was silent for several long moments. "I don't understand," he finally said.

Iliana leaned her forearms on the table, speaking with quiet urgency. "She escaped, Han. And if Nic can escape, so can we."

Han gazed back at her as if she'd grown a second head and he wasn't sure if it was entirely human. In truth, a big part of Iliana stood back in shock at her transformation into reckless rebel. True love was a grand motivator, it turned out. "We don't even know that she escaped," he said slowly, "much less how. She could've been abducted for all we know."

"Alise doesn't think so."

"Alise doesn't *know*," he countered. "And, even if it's true that Nic escaped, I feel I should reiterate that we have no idea how she accomplished it, or even if she succeeded."

"It doesn't matter how," Iliana replied, a stubborn set to her pretty mouth. "The fact remains that she did, which means it's possible. That means we can, too."

"What if we fail?" he asked.

"Then we're no worse off than we are now."

"That's not entirely true," he argued. "You've heard the same warnings I have. We'll be labeled recalcitrant familiars. They'll send us for discipline and retraining."

To his surprise, Iliana grinned. "Which means Sabrina Hanneil won't be able to get ahold of either one of us."

Cocking his head, he considered this new, cannily rebellious side to his sweet Iliana. "This a diabolically clever plan."

She sobered. "No, it's a desperate one. But I have an idea. Do you trust me?"

Not caring who saw, he put his hands on the table and grasped hers. "With everything that I am."

"Tonight, during the feast," she whispered. "Have a bag ready. Bring your weapons."

"I love you," he replied, feeling hope rise in his breast for the first time in what felt like forever. They might die in this attempt, but dying together would be better than the living death Sabrina planned for them.

"I love you, too," she replied fiercely, squeezing his hands.

IN THE END, Iliana went to Alise. She wasn't positive she could trust her old friend, but there wasn't much choice. She and Han needed wizard help to pull this off, and Alise was the only wizard Iliana came even close to trusting. Hopefully their Founder's Day reconciliation would extend to a favor.

Besides which, a certain wild recklessness had taken hold of Iliana. Even a day ago, she might not have contemplated this, but what she'd told Han was true: she was in love with him and the astonishing truth that he loved her in return had changed everything. He was *hers* and she wouldn't meekly surrender the one thing that gave her life meaning.

She'd rather die.

Well, she'd rather live, happily ever after with Han, but those were the only two options she'd accept.

When Alise opened her bedroom door to Iliana, the wizard girl looked uneasy enough that Iliana nearly second-guessed herself. But Alise recovered, beckoning Iliana to come in, then activated the lock and put her back to the door. "You heard?" Alise asked.

That gave Iliana pause, and she swallowed her prepared speech. "Heard what?"

Alise shook her head, frowning. "No, I'm being stupid. Of course you couldn't have heard. Papa sent another courier. Nic is in Meresin, with Lord Phel."

"Oh." Iliana's knees went weak, her head swimming to catch up. Though Alise hadn't offered, she sat on Alise's bed. Better than passing out on her floor. "So, she didn't escape?"

"That's just it," Alise sat beside her, running her hands through her sleek black hair in agitation, making it stand up. "Apparently she *did* escape, across the sea, to non-Convocation lands, but Lord Phel brought her back. One of our wizard enforcers found them in a harbor town in Ophiel. Phel had put her in an iron collar," she added in a horrified whisper.

"Oh, Alise. I'm sorry." Iliana put an arm around her friend and Alise sagged against her. She couldn't think of anything to say. "How awful for her."

Alise nodded against Iliana's shoulder. "I don't know what

to do."

"Is there anything you *can* do?" Iliana asked tentatively, pretty sure she knew the answer to that.

"No." Then Alise laughed, a watery sound as she wiped her eyes. "Papa is determined to bring Nic back to House Elal, so maybe I can go home then and see her and..." She straightened herself. "And I don't know. Our wizard said Nic wasn't bonded yet, so maybe Phel doesn't know how."

"If anyone can get her home safely, your Papa can," Iliana said staunchly. Much as she hated to be selfish, time was ticking away. The feast started soon and it would be the best chance for her and Han to get away. By morning, Han's new status would be common knowledge, and the thought-seekers would be on the alert again. It had to be tonight. "Alise, do you know anything more about *how* Nic escaped over the sea?"

No fool, Alise gave her a sharp look. "I don't know much, but apparently there was a sort of system for smuggling people out of the Convocation operating out of one of our distribution centers on the coast."

Iliana's heart thundered with excitement, the same as it had that morning when Alise first mentioned Nic's escape. This had to be it. "Which distribution center?" she asked, trying to sound casual.

No luck there. "I'm not telling you that," Alise replied sternly, looking all wizard again. "Besides, Papa says it's shut down. The people involved have been taking into custody. Papa is *not* happy," she added, darkly and unnecessarily.

Feeling the pieces of her plan shatter around her like shards of ice, Iliana stared at her hands, willing herself to *think*.

"Iliana," Alise said, not without compassion, stroking Iliana's hair. "Why did you come here tonight?"

Deciding to risk it all, Iliana faced her old friend. "Han manifested as a familiar. It will be announced in the morning."

Alise put a hand over her mouth, green eyes wide with shock and sorrow. "Oh no. Oh no, Iliana. I'm so, so sorry."

"Sabrina Hanneil wants him for her familiar," Iliana continued.

"That bitch," Alise hissed. "She's the worst of them."

Alise and Iliana had always understood each other.

"I want to escape with him," Iliana said. "I can't let her have him."

Alise stared at her for a long, astonished moment. "I can't help you. I swear I'm telling the truth. Papa shut and locked that door. No one else will be able to do what Nic did."

"Maybe there's another way," Iliana urged her, fighting the panic. "Maybe... Maybe if we go to Meresin, we can talk to Nic. Maybe she knows of other ways!"

For a long, fraught moment, Alise simply gazed at her. "How would you get there?" she finally asked.

Unable to believe her possible fortune, Iliana told her. "The racing sleighs are still out for the party after the feast. There's one with an air elemental that likes me."

Alise looked dubious. "Even if it likes you, it won't go against its instructions to stay in Convocation Center, not unless..." She trailed off in dawning understanding.

"Not unless an Elal wizard gives it new instructions for me," Iliana finished for her.

"But that's... That's..." Alise gave up, sputtering.

"It's not against the rules," Iliana said.

"Because no wizard would help a familiar escape!" Alise burst out.

"No wizard?" Iliana asked beseechingly. "Not even one who wanted to be part of an epic romance?"

Alise stood up, paced to the other side of the room and back. "I can't believe you're asking me this."

"I'm desperate," Iliana replied simply. "Both of us are. But if you would do this one thing, we'll never tell. Han has been doing weapons training, so he can protect us, and he has plenty of coin saved up. We'll be long gone by sunrise and no one will know how we went. I promise to help Nic for you," she vowed recklessly. "I'll find a way to send you word."

"No." Alise shook her head, crushing Iliana's hopes. "No," she repeated, planting fists on hips. "You won't, because I'm going with you."

~ 11 ~

H AN WAITED IN the silent night by the skating pond. The garlands with their elemental lights bobbed over the empty dance floor. Everyone was inside at the feast, drinking and making merry. He gazed up at the remote stars in the black sky above, wishing his magic could read an omen in them.

A whisper of sound had him drawing his sword. Then he relaxed as Iliana's familiar presence brushed across his senses, sweet as strawberries in summer.

Then he sensed the wizard with her and held onto his sword.

"It's all right," Iliana said. "Alise is coming with us."

"Where are we going?" he asked cautiously, taking the hand Iliana held out and pulling her to his side.

"Meresin," Alise replied from the shadowed interior of her black cloak. "We're going to rescue my sister, and then we'll all run away across the sea."

He didn't quite credit it. "Why would you do this, Alise? You stand to inherit House Elal."

She let out a long breath. "I don't want it. Not like this."

"But—"

"Han," she interrupted with some impatience, "I just want to see my sister. I'll figure out everything else after that, all right?"

He sheathed his sword. "Who am I to argue with a wizard?"

Iliana giggled and Alise narrowed her eyes at him. "Just get in the sleigh, will you? I have an elemental to retrain."

Han handed Iliana into the sleigh, tucking the fur blanket over her lap and snuggling her close against his side. She turned her face up to his, so he kissed her. Her lips were cold and sweet, her magic warmly coiling around them. "Happy Founder's Day," she whispered against his mouth.

"Happy Freedom Day," he corrected.

"Prosperity through … love," she answered.

"My favorite new holiday." He kissed her again as the sleigh sprang into motion and Alise settled into her side of the seat. They sped off into the night until the festive elemental lights faded into nothing and only the stars lit their way. This time he glimpsed the omen in them, of hope, and of true love.

Iliana, Han, and Alise will return in
Grey Magic
Coming February 2022

Want to read Nic and Gabriel's saga?
Check out the Bonds of Magic trilogy, beginning with *Dark Wizard*, continuing in *Bright Familiar*, and finishing in the upcoming *Grey Magic*
OR
turn the page for a peek at Chapter One of *Dark Wizard*

~ 1 ~

GABRIEL PHEL CRESTED the last ridge of the notorious Knifeblade Mountains that guarded Elal lands on nearly three sides, and faced the final barrier. The path through the mountains had been narrow, crooked, with blind endings and unexpected pitfalls.

Not unlike his life, Gabriel thought with grimly sardonic humor.

He halted his gelding, Vale, several lengths short of the border, sensing the repulsion spell that prevented the uninvited from crossing. It was a highly refined enchantment—he'd expect nothing less of the powerful Elal wizards—one that barred only humans, but allowed animals and weather to cross freely. Gabriel dismounted so he and Vale could both rest a moment before the last leg of the journey, while the Elal border guardians confirmed his identity. Lord Elal was famously insular and fanatical about guarding what was his. And, as the most powerful wizard in the Convocation, Lord Elal had a great deal to call his.

Finding a spot with a good perspective of the serene and rolling valley below—level enough to stand on and just shy of the border spell palpable to his wizard senses—Gabriel took a stance and opened the placket of his leather pants to empty his bladder. He would honor his first visit to the hallowed soil of the Convocation's greatest High House appropriately.

With a grim smile, he aimed his stream across the border, marking his territory as he studied the land of his enemy.

House Elal stood at the center of the valley below, a towering edifice amid winter-quiet fields and clusters of farmhouses. Some of the smaller dwellings—those with families not wealthy enough to afford fire elementals for heating—had chimneys with smoke coiling fragrantly against the late afternoon light spreading to the horizon. An enormous river, so large that it remained unfrozen, ran through the valley, and House Elal sat in a crescent bend of it that also served neatly as a moat. The house—more accurately, a castle—sprawled in all directions, wings, courtyards, and towers added over multiple generations. At least three kinds of stone had gone into its building over the centuries, judging by the different colors easily picked out from this distance, probably more.

Between the moat, the high walls, and the edifice's sheer complexity—not to mention the guarded narrow passes through the Knifeblade Mountains—House Elal was virtually unassailable. Except via the weapon he currently held in his hand.

Take that, Gabriel thought, shaking his cock dry and tucking it away again. He did so carefully, as that member had important work to do that night. All he needed was some unlucky accident to render him unable to plant the seeds of desperate ambition.

Lowering, when a man's future depended on that kind of performance. But then, nothing much made rational sense when it came to the Convocation's bizarre and arcane laws regarding their precious familiars and breeding the next generation of power-mad wizards. Gabriel didn't like it, but you can't win the game unless you play the game. If he wanted to restore House Phel and ensure comfort, security, and peace for his own people, like that enjoyed by the people below, then he needed to win.

Once, he would have said that there would never come a day when he'd go crawling to the Convocation for anything. But then, the idealistic certainties of youth had a way of collapsing before the exigencies of the present. To be a wizard powerful enough to challenge the likes of Lord Elal, he needed the magical amplification a familiar would give him. Who better than the most powerful available familiar in the Convocation? It was just a bit of extra satisfaction for him that she was Lord Elal's daughter.

The ancient volume on enchantments that Gabriel had found in a moldering library at what was left of House Phel had seemed to guarantee the moon-magic fertility spell would work—and that it would be undetectable. It wasn't cheating, exactly. The extensive Betrothal Trials rules booklet provided by the Convocation only forbade House Refoel interference with fertility, not other enchantments. Gabriel had read the cursed thing enough times to be sure.

Still, his annoying conscience whispered, *it seems unethical.* He banished the thought with a sharp shake of his head. Lady Veronica Elal was in the Betrothal Trials for the same reason he was. As a familiar, she needed to be paired with a wizard, just as he needed a familiar if he wanted to be more than a rogue wizard from a fallen house. She was a daughter of a High House, with a Convocation education and admirable magical potential scores. He was her fourth suitor, and he imagined she'd be glad to be done with being locked up.

He knew he'd hate it.

But will she be glad to be saddled with a no-tier house like yours? Apparently he hadn't banished his irritating conscience firmly enough. Such considerations had no place in his life. House Phel had an opportunity to rise from the ruins, to escape the cycle of poverty that had them forever scraping for the leftovers of the Convocation's wealthier lands.

Returning to his horse, he checked Vale's hooves, then the gelding's tack for fit and chafing. Another hour or so's ride wouldn't change much, but no sense losing his bid for a kingdom because his horse went lame short of the finish line. Satisfied all was well, he extracted his flask of water, tugged off his glove, and poured some into his palm for Vale, the chill biting bright on his wet hand.

How long would these border guardians make him wait? Probably just long enough to make his role as supplicant to the mighty House Elal very clear.

Upon the heels of that thought, a cloaked and hooded figure stepped out of a cloud of fog, closely followed by a bare-headed young man in House Elal livery.

"Lord Phel," the cloaked woman said, tipping back her hood to reveal a stern face made sharper by ruthlessly scraped-back dark hair—and the depthless black eyes of a wizard. She wore a gold pin on one shoulder, the House Elal crest of spirits intertwined in a braided circle. The young man remained a pace behind her, head bowed. "I am Tyrna, wizard to House Elal. Welcome to Elal."

He offered her a nod of greeting. "Thank you." *I think.* Remaining wary, Gabriel kept one hand near the hilt of his sword. Not that mere metal could defend him from a House Elal wizard, but the blade might offer him time to summon a defensive enchantment.

She smiled mirthlessly. "You need not be concerned, Lord Phel. You are expected and may proceed onto our lands. Do not, however, stray from the main road. It will lead you straight to House Phel. You should have no reason to diverge from that path."

"No reason, indeed," he agreed curtly. At least there was some comfort in discovering Elal hospitality was as forbidding as he'd been warned.

"Good luck in your efforts tonight," Tyrna offered with a smirk, looking him up and down and making it clear she thought no amount of luck could help him win the prize. "We're all so interested in the future of House *Fell.*"

Amazing how people managed to make the alternate meaning clear, even while smiling politely. It hadn't taken him long at Convocation to clue into the insult.

Not dignifying her little joke with a reply, Gabriel waited. Perhaps she hoped he wasn't enough of a wizard that he couldn't detect the barrier. Another fine joke for her to get him to walk face-first into the invisible wall, thinking she'd already opened a crossing. If that was her game, she'd be disappointed.

A moment later, with a hint of an annoyed scowl, the wizard yanked off her glove and held out her hand in an impatient gesture. The young man behind her stepped forward, placing his bare hand in hers.

Gabriel watched with close interest. He'd never seen a wizard work with their familiar before. There wasn't much to see, however. No burst of transferred magic, at least to his unpracticed eye. The young man never moved while the wizard made a complicated gesture with her free hand, and an opening formed across the road, like a curtain drawing back. Taking Vale's reins, Gabriel walked the gelding through the opening, then turned back to the wizard with a nod.

"Come, Feny," the wizard said, turning on her heel—tugging her familiar along by the hand—and stepping into a cloud of fog that vanished again, leaving no sign of them. A nifty parlor trick. A waste of magic, though, just to look impressive.

Though, in Gabriel's limited experience, the Convocation wizards seemed excessively interested in anything that made them look good.

"Come, Vale," Gabriel said aloud in snooty tones to mimic the Elal wizard as he mounted again. Swiveling back his ears, Vale snorted in apparent appreciation of the humor. On this side of the border, the road opened up to a welcoming width— in stark contrast to the difficult trail through the Knifeblades, more suited to mountain goats than horses—and Vale kicked into a sprightly pace. Unsurprisingly, the prickle of unseen eyes still followed them.

Among the numerous skills in their magical arsenal, the

wizards of House Elal commanded air elementals and other spirits mostly invisible to the human eye. There were tricks to making them visible. Gabriel could condense some fog or mist to reveal their movements. But, as much as he disliked being spied on, he wouldn't. He'd do nothing to jeopardize this gambit.

Once the well-maintained road—kept dry and clear of snow and ice by more fire elementals bonded during its construction—finished winding down from the foothills, it ran arrow-straight to the gates of House Elal. Now that they were on a level with its base, the castle loomed with majestic splendor, more fortress than home from this angle.

Gabriel began to encounter other travelers, too. Farmers, merchants, and craftspeople—all bundled in wool and furs against the chilly weather—passed by, some with smaller handcarts, others with wagons propelled by air elementals. The people looked well-fed, well-clothed, and reasonably happy, though they gazed at Gabriel with suspicion, eyeing the house crest on his shoulder in puzzlement. A prosperous people, but not so complacent that they didn't notice an armed stranger in their midst—and a foreign wizard at that.

Gabriel nodded in greeting, otherwise ignoring their scrutiny. He'd like to say he was inured to the stares, but one didn't come to wizardry as he had—relatively late in life and with cataclysmic suddenness—without being keenly aware of how people reacted to the sight of him now.

Needing to distract himself, he pulled out the miniature of Lady Veronica Elal and studied it, for the one-millionth time, probably, since he'd received it in the Convocation packet announcing her Betrothal Trials. Her image captivated him, though she was no great beauty, despite the painter no doubt flattering her as much as possible. She had the high Elal forehead and strongly arched nose. Her brows, black as a raven's wing and flattened with a hint of impatience, framed lushly lashed eyes the artist had no doubt intended to look soft and appealing. The green of them had been perhaps difficult to capture, for they looked far too hard—almost unnatural—with nothing inviting about them. Lady Veronica's lips had been fashioned into a pretty bow shape, shaded a deep red. Not prim, however, her lips were lush—and also seemed to be holding back a slicing remark. Her pointed chin tilted with the arrogance he'd expect of House Elal, but the picture overall evoked something else. She struck him as both sad and angry. Frustrated, perhaps, almost to the point of despair.

That, more than anything else, appealed to him about her. He understood frustrated ambition, and the despair that followed close behind. The other available familiars had been presented as handsome and pretty and sweetly serene— obediently invisible like Tyrna's familiar, Feny—and without any spark that interested him. Nothing that made him want to spend his life bonded to them.

Maybe he imagined what he wanted to see in Lady Veronica. After all, how much could one read into a portrait intended as an advertisement of goods? The painting served primarily to confirm the familiar being offered. As the Convocation packet made clear by highlighting Lady Veronica's magical potential scores, her value as a familiar and for the children she could breed were the grand prizes. The miniature had been clearly labeled as assurance that the chosen wizards would indeed be bedding the woman who accompanied the scorecard. Certified and guaranteed by the Convocation.

Yes, all so very cold-blooded, but Gabriel had been assured that the Betrothal Trials were voluntary, so Lady Veronica must be hoping to find a good wizard partner and husband.

The sense that he and Lady Veronica might at least find some common ground had been the final spur that decided him to try for her. Yes, her magical potential scores were desirable, too much so, because that meant he was reaching high. That she was of House Elal, with an expensive Convocation Academy education, also meant she could help him navigate that legal, professional, and social hierarchy.

When he succeeded in impregnating her—which he would, thanks to the spell he'd found—and they married... Well, it wouldn't be a love match like his own parents had. Perhaps, though, he and Lady Veronica had enough in common that they could find a way to being friends.

Regardless, some wizard would have Lady Veronica for their familiar. And none of them could possibly need her more than Gabriel did. It might as well be him, especially since the future of House Phel depended on it.

Pocketing the miniature, he set his sights on House Elal and firmed his resolve.

He would be the one.

Titles by Jeffe Kennedy

FANTASY ROMANCES

BONDS OF MAGIC
Dark Wizard
Bright Familiar
Grey Magic (February 2022)

HEIRS OF MAGIC
The Long Night of the Crystalline Moon
(also available in *Under a Winter Sky*)
The Golden Gryphon and the Bear Prince
The Sorceress Queen and the Pirate Rogue
The Dragon's Daughter and the Winter Mage
The Storm Princess and the Raven King (April 2022)

THE FORGOTTEN EMPIRES
The Orchid Throne
The Fiery Crown
The Promised Queen

THE TWELVE KINGDOMS
Negotiation
The Mark of the Tala
The Tears of the Rose

CONTEMPORARY ROMANCES

Shooting Star

MISSED CONNECTIONS
Last Dance
With a Prince
Since Last Christmas

CONTEMPORARY EROTIC ROMANCES

Exact Warm Unholy
The Devil's Doorbell

FACETS OF PASSION
Sapphire
Platinum
Ruby
Five Golden Rings

FALLING UNDER
Going Under
Under His Touch
Under Contract

EROTIC PARANORMAL

MASTER OF THE OPERA E-SERIAL
Master of the Opera, Act 1: Passionate Overture
Master of the Opera, Act 2: Ghost Aria
Master of the Opera, Act 3: Phantom Serenade
Master of the Opera, Act 4: Dark Interlude

Master of the Opera, Act 5: A Haunting Duet
Master of the Opera, Act 6: Crescendo
Master of the Opera

BLOOD CURRENCY
Blood Currency

<u>BDSM FAIRYTALE ROMANCE</u>

Petals and Thorns

Thank you for reading!

About Jeffe Kennedy

Jeffe Kennedy is a multi-award-winning and best-selling author of romantic fantasy. She is the current President of the Science Fiction and Fantasy Writers of America (SFWA) and is a member of Novelists, Inc. (NINC). She is best known for her RITA® Award-winning novel, *The Pages of the Mind*, the recent trilogy, *The Forgotten Empires*, and the wildly popular, *Dark Wizard*. Jeffe lives in Santa Fe, New Mexico.

Jeffe can be found online at her website: JeffeKennedy.com, on her podcast First Cup of Coffee, every Sunday at the popular SFF Seven blog, on Facebook, on Goodreads, on BookBub, and pretty much constantly on Twitter @jeffekennedy. She is represented by Sarah Younger of Nancy Yost Literary Agency.

jeffekennedy.com
facebook.com/Author.Jeffe.Kennedy
twitter.com/jeffekennedy
goodreads.com/author/show/1014374.Jeffe_Kennedy
bookbub.com/profile/jeffe-kennedy

Sign up for her newsletter here.
www.jeffekennedy.com/sign-up-for-my-newsletter

Made in the USA
Columbia, SC
29 September 2023

23624792R00257